Praise for the Novels
of S. M. Stirling

Lord of Mountains

"A truly original combination of postapocalyptic sci-fi and military-oriented medieval fantasy. . . . [Stirling] has built up a highly complex fictional universe with loads of characters and political intrigue."   —*Kirkus Reviews*

"As usual, S. M. Stirling delivers a rich world readers want to live in. Fully formed and alive characters you wish you could drink a beer with or follow into battle. Because of the diversity of cultures you experience in the series, there's somewhere for every person to dream about; there's a home for you in the Emberverse."
                                             —PNC–Minnesota Bureau

"Exciting . . . the story line is fast-paced from the onset and never slows down. . . . Fans of the saga will appreciate this strong tale as the overarching theme moves forward while the loss of Rudi's longest running ally will be felt by all."   —Genre Go Round Reviews

"Stirling's historical research is always impeccable, and his ability to use that knowledge and understanding of everything from ancient weapons to regional accents to a foodie's obsession with good eats creates a world you can see, feel, and touch. A wondrous universe in which the magic seems to be returning and Powers and Dominions are contesting for the soul of mankind—and just one man and his Companions stand in the way—vintage Stirling."   —Otherwhere Gazette

The Tears of the Sun

"The emerging kingdom of Montival is a damn cool place to hang out. In this postapocalyptic North America, Stirling has cherry-picked everything a fan might wish for in a high fantasy/apocalypse/alternate history mashup. You've got heroes, horses, swordplay, kings, siege engines, and mystics. And all with (somewhat) less patriarchy, because the postmodern world that spawned Montival—our world—has left a big stamp of twentieth-century social progress on the society rising from its ashes."   —Tor.com

continued . . .

"*Tears of the Sun* engages fans of the saga who will anxiously await the next Change."
—Genre Go Round Reviews

The High King of Montival

"Filled with plenty of action, intrigue, and a touch of romance. . . . S. M. Stirling provides another fabulous postapocalyptic thriller to his Change saga."
—Alternative Worlds

"Stirling's series combines the best of fantasy and postapocalyptic genres but rises above them both with his long vision and skill in creating compelling characters, no matter how large or small their role."   —Fresh Fiction

The Sword of the Lady

"This new novel of the Change is quite probably the finest by an author who has been growing in skill and imagination for more than twenty-five years."
—*Booklist* (starred review)

"Well written. Stirling has the ability to make the commonplace exciting and to dribble out the information needed to complete the tapestry of understanding . . . a good tale."   —SFRevu

The Scourge of God

"Vivid. . . . Stirling eloquently describes a devastated, mystical world that will appeal to fans of traditional fantasy as well as postapocalyptic SF."
—*Publishers Weekly* (starred review)

"Stirling is a perfect master of keep-them-up-all-night pacing, possibly the best in American SF, quite capable of sweeping readers all the way to the end."
—*Booklist* (starred review)

The Sunrise Lands

"Combines vigorous military adventure with cleverly packaged political idealism. . . . Stirling's narrative deftly balances sharply contrasting ideologies. . . . The thought-provoking and engaging storytelling should please Stirling's many fans."   —*Publishers Weekly*

"A master of speculative fiction and alternate history, Stirling delivers another chapter in an epic of survival and rebirth."
—*Library Journal*

A Meeting at Corvallis

"[A] richly realized story of swordplay and intrigue."
—*Entertainment Weekly*

"Stirling concludes his alternative history trilogy in high style. . . . [The story] resembles one of the cavalry charges the novel describes—gorgeous, stirring, and gathering such earth-pounding momentum that it's difficult to resist."
—*Publishers Weekly*

"A fascinating glimpse into a future transformed by the lack of easy solutions to both human and technological dilemmas."
—*Library Journal*

The Protector's War

"Absorbing."
—*The San Diego Union-Tribune*

"[A] vivid portrait of a world gone insane . . . it also has human warmth and courage. . . . It is full of bloody action, exposition that expands character, and telling detail that makes it all seem very real."
—*Statesman Journal* (Salem, OR)

"Reminds me of Poul Anderson at his best."
—David Drake, author of *What Distant Deeps*

"Rousing. . . . Without a doubt [*The Protector's War*] will raise the bar for alternate universe fiction."
—John Ringo, *New York Times* bestselling author of *Citadel*

Dies the Fire

"*Dies the Fire* kept me reading till five in the morning so I could finish at one great gulp. . . . Don't miss it."
—Harry Turtledove

"Gritty, realistic, apocalyptic, yet a grim hopefulness pervades it like a fog of light. The characters are multidimensional, unusual, and so very human. Buy *Dies the Fire*. Sell your house; sell your soul; get the book. You won't be sorry."
—John Ringo

"A stunning speculative vision of a near-future bereft of modern conveniences but filled with human hope and determination. Highly recommended."
—*Library Journal*

ALSO BY S. M. STIRLING

Lord of Mountains

A NOVEL OF THE CHANGE

S. M. STIRLING

A ROC BOOK

ROC
Published by the Penguin Group
Penguin Group (USA), 375 Hudson Street,
New York, New York 10014, USA

USA | Canada | UK | Ireland | Australia | New Zealand | India | South Africa | China

Penguin Books Ltd., Registered Offices: 80 Strand, London WC2R 0RL, England
For more information about the Penguin Group visit penguin.com.

Published by Roc, an imprint of New American Library, a division of Penguin
Group (USA). Previously published in a Roc hardcover edition.

First Roc Mass Market Printing, September 2013

 REGISTERED TRADEMARK—MARCA REGISTRADA

ISBN 978-0-451-41476-2

Printed in the United States of America
10 9 8 7 6 5 4 3 2 1

ALWAYS LEARNING   PEARSON

To Jan, forever

ACKNOWLEDGMENTS

More, but not enough.

Thanks to my friends who are also first readers:

To Steve Brady, for assistance with dialects and British background, and also natural history of all sorts.

Thanks also to Kier Salmon, insufficiently credited collaborator, for once again helping with the beautiful complexities of the Old Religion, and with . . . well, all sorts of stuff! Sometimes I feel guilty about not paying her.

To Diana L. Paxson, for help and advice, and for writing the beautiful Westria books, among many others. If you liked the Change novels, you'll probably enjoy the hell out of the Westria books—I certainly did, and they were one of the inspirations for this series; and her *Essential Ásatrú* and recommendation of *Our Troth* were extremely helpful . . . and fascinating reading.

To Dale Price, help with Catholic organization, theology and praxis.

To Brenda Sutton, for multitudinous advice.

To Melinda Snodgrass, George R. R. Martin, Walter Jon Williams, John Miller, Vic Milan, Jan Stirling, Matt

Reiten and Ian Tregellis of Critical Mass, for constant help and advice as the book was under construction.

Thanks to John Miller, good friend, writer and scholar, for many useful discussions, for loaning me some great books, and for some really, really cool old movies.

Special thanks to Heather Alexander, bard and ballad-eer, for permission to use the lyrics from her beautiful songs, which can be—and should be!—ordered at www.heatherlands.com. Run, do not walk, to do so.

Thanks again to William Pint and Felicia Dale, for permission to use their music, which can be found at www.pintndale.com and should be, for anyone with an ear and salt water in their veins.

And to Three Weird Sisters—Gwen Knighton, Mary Crowell, Brenda Sutton and Teresa Powell—whose alternately funny and beautiful music can be found at www.threeweirdsisters.com.

And to Heather Dale for permission to quote the lyrics of her songs, whose beautiful (and strangely appropriate!) music can be found at www.HeatherDale.com, and is highly recommended. The lyrics are wonderful and the tunes make it even better.

To S. J. Tucker for permission to use the lyrics of her beautiful songs, which can be found at www.skinny whitechick.com, and should be.

Thanks again to Russell Galen, my agent, who has been an invaluable help and friend for a decade now, and never more than in these difficult times.

All mistakes, infelicities and errors are of course my own.

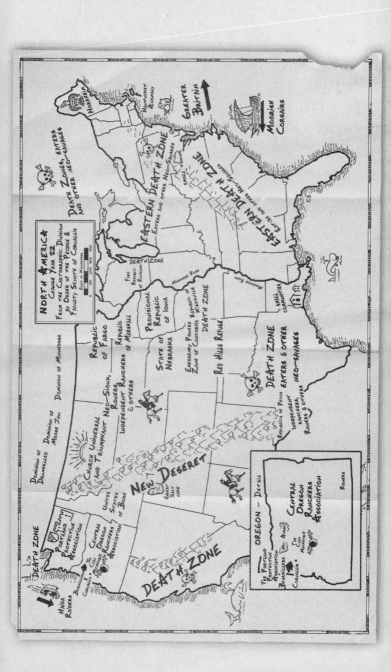

PROLOGUE

The High King's Host
Horse Heaven Hills
(Formerly south-central Washington)
High Kingdom of Montival
(Formerly western North America)
October 28th, Change Year 25/2023 AD

"He is coming!" Rudi whispered again.

Then he shook himself and let his hand fall from the crystal pommel of the Sword. His helmet was already slung from the high pommel of the war-saddle, and the wind cuffed at his long red-blond hair, giving an illusion of coolness as it dried the sweat bred in the rage and heat of battle.

"Where? When?" Mathilda said sharply, her strong-featured face frowning a little under the raised visor of her own sallet.

It was a bright autumn noon, and the rolling hills showed a ghostly tinge of green under their summer's cloak of golden sun-dried grass; the first of the autumn rains had already fallen. It would have been a fair day, except for the thick drifts of dead men and horses on and around the hill where his rearguard had made their stand. Most of them were enemy—horse-archers from the wilds of Montana, men of the Church Universal and

Triumphant. But more than enough were Montivalans; they'd held hard, the Yakima pike and crossbow regiments and the Association cavalry, and he'd arrived at just the right moment with another thousand lancers to be the hammer to their anvil.

"Soon," he said to his High Queen looking eastward. "Not today; not tomorrow. But soon. The Prophet Sethaz will be here and ready."

Above them a glider turned in a greater circle with a glitter of aluminum and Plexiglas; one of his, a pre-Change craft that needed no engine to fly, catapult-launched over the Columbia cliffs and riding the updrafts like a great-winged bird. His eyes turned grimly to the wheeling circle of living carrion-eaters below the human machine, ravens and buzzards tilting lower as the living humans withdrew. Comrade or foe, all the dead waited for them alike.

She nodded, following his thought. They'd been friends—*anamchara*, oath-bound kin of the soul—from the age of ten, though their parents had been at war then; and they'd been from Montival all across the continent to Nantucket and back together. Though they'd only been handfasted a bit more than a month, their minds operated with the sort of smooth unison he'd seen in couples forty years their senior.

Tiphaine d'Ath, Grand Constable of the Association, looked exhausted but grimly satisfied. He'd given her the task of delaying the enemy onset, and she'd managed a fighting retreat all the way from Walla Walla without letting the enemy trap her force.

And as is the usual case, I shall reward her good work with more work.

"Lady d'Ath, your field force is hereby dissolved with accolades for good service; I wanted you to screen us while we massed and you've done just that. The *arrière-ban* of the PPA has mustered and you're in command of that, of course. You'll deploy the Association foot to the right wing of our position and the chivalry will be part of our general reserve."

"Forward base is at Goldendale, Your Majesty?" she said.

"Yes, and our field hospitals and supplies will stage out of there. Mathilda has been overseeing our buildup in the area. Matti, you'd better brief the Grand Constable."

She nodded and d'Ath scrubbed at a spray of blood across her long stark-boned face.

"I'll get there and see about slotting people in, then," the Grand Constable said. "Her Majesty can brief me on the way back."

Rudi nodded. "I'll be there by dawn tomorrow; we'll have everything up within two days except the rear-guard. There's enough forward to hold, but I don't expect the onset until then."

She nodded back. "They'll want to have everything in place; they have the advantage of numbers, after all."

The High King of Montival grinned starkly. "Yes. And we'll see what we can do about that."

CHAPTER ONE

Rudi had been inclined to think the final ball a waste of time and resources, one of the peacocking Associate habits that he had to put up with for the sake of harmony and which the north-realm nobles insisted upon even on the eve of battle. And perhaps there *was* an element of sheer vanity in it.

But on second thought, who should say how a man prepares his innermost self to die? Or a woman, sure. They have to be here, and most of their ladies too, for they're working in the field hospitals or managing the supplies or something of that sort, waiting for their lovers and brothers to be brought back on their shields. The only real burden is that they've brought their party clothes . . . garb, they call it . . . along this far; and we're close to the river. There's a certain mad gallantry to it, a defiance of fate; my foster father says the Duke of Wellington's officers did the same on the eve of Waterloo.

Torches and fires of pinewood in iron cages and strings of softly glowing paper lanterns lit the interior of

Castle Goldendale's bailey-court, the broad paved expanse at the heart of the inner keep. The Great Hall and the Chapel and the quarters of the seneschal and his officers surrounded it in an irregular circuit of roofs and balconies, spires and pointed-arch windows; candles glowed in the church, through the rich colors of stained glass wrought in saints and angels.

Mathilda and some others had had their Mass there, though most of the host had used household chaplains and field priests in the encampments. A lingering scent of incense mingled with burning conifer sap and the cool night air. Sparks drifted heavenward.

The narrower slits of the solars and guard-rooms in the high round towers of the keep were bars of yellow against the half-glimpsed soaring heights, as much sensed as seen where their dark bulk blocked out the stars. Folk more humble crowded some of them; the castle staff, maidservants and men-at-arms, watching the gaudy flower-petal brightness below as a show arranged for their entertainment.

Black-armored spearmen of the Protector's Guard stood at intervals around the enclosure, motionless as statues of gleaming dark metal, with the visors of their sallet helms down and leaving nothing to be seen but an occasional glint of eyes behind the vision-slits, the gleam echoing the yellow and scarlet of the Lidless Eye on shields like four-foot elongated teardrops. Kilted longbowmen of the High King's Archers shared the duty— and honor—with their great yew bows in the crooks of their arms.

The walls enclosed the sound of the players as well, shawm and lute and recorder and viol, the sweet tinkle and buzz and fluting notes of Portlander court music. The tune ended, and the dancers turned and bowed or curtsied to politely applaud the musicians on their dais; several of them had the jeweled dagger that denoted Associate status or even the golden spurs of chivalry on their heels, for a troubadour might be a gentleman by Protectorate standards. The tale of the dance would be woven into that of the battle to come, for they'd be fighting in it too.

"Five minutes," the Mistress of the Revels said; she was Dame Lilianth of Kalama, who did something administrative for the Grand Constable most of the time. "Then *The Knights of Portland*, gentlemen, chevaliers, demoiselles and ladies."

Her shrewd eyes took in the situation, and she made an almost imperceptible gesture; everyone except the two nobles with whom he'd been talking business withdrew enough to give a degree of privacy as Mathilda came up to him.

She was wearing a dark chocolate cotte-hardie with tight sleeves that showed rounds of her pale flesh between each button and a headdress with two low peaks in warm dark gold silk and pearls. It made a striking contrast to the tone of her sleek brown hair where it showed at the sides in elaborate braided coils, and she was laughing as she extended a hand to him.

"I need a partner for this one, darling," Mathilda said as he caught it in his and raised it to his lips. "And if you won't dance with me, it'll have to be Tiph here, and that would be a scandal."

"Delia can make me dance in public, but only at home on our own barony and when she's not nine months pregnant," Tiphaine d'Ath said. "Besides, how did our Lady Regent put it . . ."

She nodded towards the spot where the Lady Regent and a few other dowagers and lords with a good deal of gray in their hair sat, with pages offering tiny crystal glasses of liqueurs or brandy snifters on trays.

". . . ah! *Modern Protectorate culture doesn't handle gender confusion well.* Which reminds me, since it's from her private stash I could use another cognac. Lioncel . . . no, serve His Majesty first."

A tow-haired young squire slid forward noiselessly and poured for them both. Lady Death, as she was commonly known, was dressed to fit her nickname tonight; her tight hose were onyxine black, as was the sleeveless neck-to-thigh jerkin of soft chamois, fastened up the front to the throat with ties of black silk and jet. Her soft Court shoes were chamois as well, and the toes turned up—moderately. The loose black knee-length houppelande over-robe had buttons of some dark mottled tropical wood so hard it seemed metallic carved like black roses, and a collar open at the front and ear-high behind; the lower hem was dagged, and so were the turned-back sleeves that hung almost as low, showing a dark forest-green lining. Only the links of her belt and the buckles at the ankles of her shoes showed brighter colors.

"I wear hose and houppelande fairly often too, Tiph," the High Queen replied.

"Yes, but not at formal dances, Matti . . . Your Majesty," Tiphaine said. "Delia has to arrange it carefully even at Montinore Manor, or people end up turning and bonking heads and knocking each other over when they should be switching line, trying to figure out where I fit."

"Now you're drawing the long bow!" Mathilda laughed. "Young gentlewomen learn who's on the right and left by dancing with each other."

"I wouldn't know." Tiphaine shrugged, deadpan. "I spent my teenage years as your mother's assassin."

Mathilda gave a chuckle that was half a wince; that was a joke, and the more effective for being literally true, which was how Tiphaine's rare excursions into humor usually worked.

"Half the time in a youngster's dancing class it's all girls anyway," Mathilda said.

"Yes, but it would be fun if it all seized up like that, wouldn't it?" Tiphaine said, her face expressionless as she sipped her brandy.

Sure and the prospect of a battle relaxes her, Rudi thought, amused. *I've rarely seen her so whimsical.*

"I would be honored to dance with you if all else fails, Your Majesty," Rigobert de Stafford, Baron Forest Grove, said gallantly with a low bow, sweeping off his round chaperon hat with its rolled brim and dangling liripipe tail.

"Yes, but you'd outshine me totally, my lord Forest Grove," Matti said with a smile and a little mock-curtsy in return.

"Or, since he's wearing a skirt, I could dance with His Majesty . . ."

"In your dreams, Rigobert," Rudi said genially. "And it's a kilt. Calling it a skirt has been known to turn Mackenzies berserk."

De Stafford was a ruggedly handsome man in his forties, with a short-cropped golden beard and bowl-cut hair too fair to show the first gray strands, broad shoulders, thick wrists and large hands that were shapely but scarred where they rested on his belt of golden flowers. His court dress emphasized gold and scarlet down to the parti-colored hose—nothing too gaudy by northern fashion, but still a blaze of color and jewelry, including the chain of office that marked him as Marchwarden of the South.

For height and coloring, he and d'Ath could have been siblings, though he was six or seven years older. His wife, Delia, was Châtelaine of Ath, an arrangement which suited all three of them very well indeed for a multitude of reasons.

Mathilda's teasing manner dropped away. "This one's a little political, Rudi," she said. "The High King has to participate in the last dance of the evening. Sort of a fealty thing."

"I haven't even been crowned yet and already there's protocol!"

Mathilda nodded, entirely serious. "It's a *chant du Brabant* step, but with a new lyric. Or so Mother told me. One of her troubadours came up with it, modifying some old Society piece, I think. She says they hardly need to be prompted anymore."

"Yes," Tiphaine said, in her ice-water voice. "Apparently a genuine monarch blessed by a visitation of the Virgin—"

"That was Father Ignatius . . . Lord Chancellor Ignatius, now," Rudi pointed out. "I'm a pagan and *I* had a vision of the Threefold Goddess."

"Ignatius was one of the Companions of the Quest,"

d'Ath said. "In propaganda terms, the Lady Regent as-
sures me you each bask in the other's reflected glory,
but it shines more strongly upward."

*Is that irony, or is she just copying the way Sandra usu-
ally speaks?* Rudi thought.

The Grand Constable of the Association went on:

"—a High King married to our Princess, accompanied by signs and wonders, with a magic sword gained
on a heroic Quest, gets their artistic juices flowing to
the point where they barely need a subsidy from the
Crown."

"She used the phrase *creaming their hose*, in fact,"
Rigobert said. "Archaic vocabulary, but expressive."

Rudi sighed gently and set his brandy snifter on a low
round table of polished granite. His mother-in-law had
always been shrewd enough to know that song and
story were as much tools of power as hoarded gold or
castles and catapults and men-at-arms. Sometimes he
suspected that she didn't really know quite *how* powerful they were, though. A glance in her direction brought
her up to her feet and then down in a curtsy, spreading
the pearl-gray silk of her skirts and sinking gracefully,
her smooth middle-aged face smiling and revealing
nothing except her usual catlike satisfaction as he bowed
slightly in return.

*Sometimes when she's sitting with a white Persian in
her lap, it's downright eerie how similar they look,* he
thought whimsically. *And I will never know precisely how
much of what's happened hereabouts these last two decades
was by her plan and will, and what wasn't, and what
wasn't but was fitted and shaped to suit her afterwards
behind the screen of her wit, like my blood-father killing*

her husband . . . the end result of which is that her grand-
children, and his, will rule all of Montival. So who was the
victor and who the vanquished, on the Field of the Cloth of
Gold?

"All right, acushla," he said to his wife. "I will be
most honored and pleased to lead the dance."

"And I'll be back in a moment. *Don't* discover an
emergency elsewhere, my love, or I will challenge you
to a joust *à l'outrance* with sharpened lances."

Their eyes met, and for a moment he lost himself in
the warm brown depths of hers.

"Get a room, you two . . . monarchs," de Stafford
said.

Rudi laughed. "The palace isn't built yet, my lord."

The Sword of the Lady was hung in his quarters,
with a score of the High King's Archers as an honor
guard—not that he thought any human agency was
much threat to it. It had been hard enough for *him* to
come to it undamaged. But that absence let him pretend he was simply a man among his own kind tonight,
and such chances were rare enough to relish.

Mathilda moved back into the open, circulating
among the younger noblemen and ladies. A lady-in-
waiting and a squire—

Yseult Liu, Demoiselle de Gervais, he reminded himself.

Seventeen, with tilted blue eyes and a maiden's loose
hair streaming in a yellow mane down from under a pale
blue headdress, just on the verge of turning from pretty
and fresh to spectacular.

And her brother Huon, three years younger. By Brigid's

cauldron and Lugh's spear, he looks more and more like Odard every day, save that his eyes are dark!

—moved among the revelers, collecting little folded pamphlets they'd been studying; those would have the steps and music.

He closed his eyes for a moment in remembered grief, remembering also the look of almost mocking affection in Odard's own as he lay dying so far away in Kalksthorpe on the shores of the cold Atlantic. It had been a long way for a knight of the Association to go to die; and it hadn't been until he died that Rudi had fully realized how real a friend he'd become after years of not-quite-trust. Odard had been a very complex man, but the steel had been there at the core, when the Keeper-of-Laws came to reveal what he really was.

No man outlives his fate, he thought. *He died as well as a man can when it's far from home amid angry strangers; ah, but, Odard, I miss you at my back this day!*

Sandra Arminger raised her glass to him as his glance passed her again; she was talking to a barrel-built nobleman with a shaven head and rich dark clothing with a silver-and-gold linked chain of office around his bull neck, marking him as Conrad Renfrew, Count of Odell and Chancellor of the Portland Protective Association. Rudi snorted slightly, taking up the snifter to return the toast and then sipping at the smooth fire within the balloon shape. The man beside Portland's Lady Regent inclined his massive head, one corner of his mouth turning up in an ironic smile that twisted the hideous white keloid scars that covered much of his face.

"Your Majesty?" Tiphaine asked.

"I was just thinking that the Count of Odell, over there, led the army that tried to conquer the Mackenzie *dùthchas* back in the War of the Eye and nearly did burn Sutterdown to the ground. Some of the roundshot from his catapults are in the wall still. Yet here we are, allies and more or less friends. Forbye his sons most definitely *are* my friends, if not my closest."

Tiphaine turned her snifter between her hands, the long slender wire-strong fingers flexing about the glass. She'd been fourteen or so on that day in 1998 in whose shadow the whole world lived, which made her one of the bridge generation between folk such as Sandra or Conrad, who'd been adults then, and his own generation, the Changelings.

"For that matter, I kidnapped you a bit before that, when I did that clandestine op to get Matti back," she pointed out. "And killed your bodyguards."

"I mourned them," Rudi said sincerely.

For I liked Aoife and Liath well, and keened them as sincerely as a ten-year-old could, he thought. *I make a sacrifice beneath the tree where their ashes lie mingled every year. But . . .*

He tactfully didn't mention the earlier attempt, when the first Baron Gervais, Eddie Liu, and Katrina Georges had tried to get Matti back and failed and both died in the process. Katrina had been Tiphaine's first lover, and he knew she still mourned her even though she'd been happily settled with Delia de Stafford for a decade and a half—Rudi had been a hostage at Castle Ath when the newly ennobled Tiphaine met Delia, who'd been a mere miller's daughter on the estate then.

People in general thought Tiphaine d'Ath's most notable characteristic was a ruthlessness as complete and hard as the honed steel on the edge of a knife, but if Rudi had had to sum up her mind and character it would have been *constancy* he'd have put first.

Though she's ruthless enough, too, and no dispute.

She was also an intensely private person, and he went on instead:

"But that was honest war. We'd raided the Association territories and took Matti, after all, and killed quite a few of *her* entourage in the process. And then you saved my life, you and Sandra between you. The Lord Protector would have killed me sure, in the end, if I'd stayed in Todenangst like a bit of grit under his eye. You taking me off to your new fief . . ."

"That was Lady Sandra's orders; she got me the title and the grant for rescuing Matti and snatching you, after all," Tiphaine said judiciously. "Mind you, I agreed on taking you out of sight and mind, and even then it only delayed matters. Norman was like that. God, how I hated that man. I used to daydream about killing him."

He turned his head sharply for a moment; it was unusual for her to express that much emotion. Her long handsome-regular face was as calm as ever, and her pale gray eyes calmly considering as they flicked over the crowd looking for threats and weaknesses. That appraisal was probably so automatic that she would require an act of will to stop it.

And it's a fair bit I've learned from her, in all the years since. Much of the art of the sword, just for a beginning.

Rigobert snorted. "You weren't the only one, my

lady d'Ath. Even in the Protectorate. Lady Sandra actually loved him, though."

"Aphrodite is a powerful Goddess," Rudi said seriously.

That was both literally and metaphorically true, if there was a difference in the Changed world. He drew the Invoking sign and went on:

"And sea-born Cyprian has Her own purposes when She bestows Her gifts. For that matter, Norman loved Sandra and Mathilda . . . in his way. I think it was his desire to look well in Mathilda's eyes that preserved me when I first fell into his power. We were already close friends, from her time at Dun Juniper."

The two Associate nobles nodded; they were both nominal Catholics, of course, but he knew Tiphaine wasn't one in practice—that owl he'd glimpsed once on a chain under her shirt was a hint at exactly how not— and he strongly suspected Rigobert wasn't either in his heart, though he didn't know what Powers the man did follow. Sandra was that modern rarity, a complete atheist, or had been until recently. Not that she'd ever given any public indication of disbelief, but he suspected that the sheer overwhelming evidence of late had made her slide from joyfully hypocritical and political lip-service to the Protectorate's established Church to something more sincere; she had the unusual sort of mind that used logic and evidence to produce conclusions, rather than the other way around.

Mathilda finished her task and came back to him, curtsying. He bowed in turn, making a leg in the Clan's fashion, his shoulder-length red-gold hair flowing forward. His garb was his own people's festival style; fine pleated tartan kilt to just above the knee with silver-buckled shoes and a little bone-and-silver hilted *sgian dubh* tucked into his right sock-hose, tight green Montrose jacket with a double row of silver buttons, lace at throat and cuffs, badger-skin sporran and tooled-leather belt and dirk, Scots bonnet with a spray of black feathers in the clasp that marked his sept totem as Raven, and a great broach of silver and jet graven in curling knotwork to hold the plaid pinned across his torso. There was a slight sigh from a clump of ladies nearby; his six-two of broad-shouldered, narrow-waisted, long-limbed height took full advantage of clothing designed to show a man off.

"Every woman here is envying me," Mathilda said softly as she laid the tips of her fingers on the back of his left hand to let him lead her out on the dancing floor.

"Except our friend the Grand Constable and a few others," he whispered back. "Some of them envying *me*, perhaps? And then my lord de Stafford might well be envying you, you know . . ."

Then he grinned more widely as she pinched his wrist painfully with a hand strengthened steel-hard by years holding the grip of a fifteen-pound knight's shield.

"You're incorrigible!"

"No, I'm the improbable bearer of an impossible Sword; nevertheless, I exist! Your mother doesn't seem worried, by the way," he murmured to Mathilda.

She kept her head high and step gliding so that she seemed to drift forward in a rustle of silks, as if her feet were motionless, floating a fraction of an inch above the smooth stone paving blocks. It was as much a product of rigorous training as a swordsman's stance, in its way.

"Mother doesn't worry about battles," she said. "Not that way, at least. She picks people to fight them by judging their character and record, she told me once, and gives them everything they need, then sits back and lets them do their work."

Well, the Powers picked me, but from Sandra's point of view there's not much difference, eh?

The chant du Brabant wasn't fundamentally all that different from a lot of Mackenzie dances; rings and lines of men and women, moving in set patterns to the music, changing places with the rhythm. It was a good deal more complex, though, and involved the participants singing at some points as well as the musicians playing. Rudi had spent months every year in the Association territories after the War of the Eye—what the northerners called the Protector's War. That had been part of the peace settlement, and it had involved a good deal of the same schooling Mathilda got just as she'd learned Mackenzie ways in her stays at Dun Juniper, but he hadn't done much Associate-style dancing since reaching his majority, and none since they left on the Quest two years ago.

He closed his eyes for an instant as the ensemble played the first four measures, then opened them and let remembered skills flow back into nerve and muscle as the dance began on the repeat; the lead couple didn't have to sing, at least, though Matti had given him the cues.

The sprightly tune began again and they started the hand-in-hand advance. That opening phase ended with the company around them, men in the inner ring and women in the outer, circling in opposite directions. The strong male chorus began to the sound of the instruments and the scuff of leather on stone:

The squire serves the gentleman,
And the gentleman follows me,
And in so doing learns the ways of skill and courtesy.
I ever serve my lady for the love she gives to me—

The men turned and faced Rudi and Mathilda where the royal couple pivoted beneath the arch of their own joined hands in the center, and as one they stopped and bowed:

And the knights of Portland stand and serve the
*   King,*
For our King!
The knights of Portland ever serve the King.

Rudi blinked; that chorus wasn't in any of the versions of this piece he'd heard before, though the rhythm and scansion were the same. Each man straightened, took three paces backward and extended a hand as the women passed through, so that now the circles were reversed; the whole ensemble skipped in a complete circuit and then the ladies took up the song:

The girl becomes a maiden,
And the maiden follows me,
And in so doing learns the ways of skill and courtesy.
We ever serve the household with our hands and hearts
*   and deeds—*

They stopped and faced inward, and a uniform deep curtsy ran through them as the men circled behind, the wimples and headdresses bowing like wind through a flower-field made of silk and vair and jewels:

And the demoiselles will stand and serve the Queen,
For our Queen!
The demoiselles will ever serve the Queen!

Now the circle broke as it turned inward, into a moving line of male and female dancers linked by their hands. Rudi and Mathilda danced towards them in their turn; as each pair passed, they opened out and spun around the royal couple.

We serve as those before us
And we teach it to our young.
And fair the blooms that face the sky
That from our soil have sprung!

A crashing chord and they all halted and threw up their linked hands:

And our monarchs' deeds are roared aloud
Whenever honor's praise is sung!

This time they were facing Rudi and Mathilda in a spaced line, lord and lady alternating. They bowed and curtsied together as Rudi and Mathilda passed through to the head of the line and turned to face them; all hands were linked in a great chain:

*And the knights of Portland stand and serve the
    King,*
For our King!
The knights of Portland ever serve the King.

The voices wove together again:

*And the knights of Portland stand and serve the
    King,*
For our King!
The knights of Portland stand and serve the King!

The dance ceased, amid a shout of laughter; the dancers turned and did their bow and curtsy to the musicians,
applauding, and then deeper to the royal pair. Rudi
smiled as he and Mathilda inclined their heads in return.

Servants brought around trays of hot spiced wine.
He took one, and Mathilda did too; they interlinked
their arms so that each took a sip from the other's glass
first. Then he turned and raised it to the crowd, the
flame dancing on silk and silver and shining eyes.

*And in a day and a night, how many of these laughing
young lords of the earth will lie stark with their blood
draining into the thirsty soil?* he thought, and fought to
keep his face merry, as they'd expect.

"A fine dance tonight, and the dance of sword and
lance to come," he said, pitching his voice to carry. "So
one more cup, seek your beds and sleep untroubled, my
lords."

*For I have other business tonight, with the Powers of the
land.*

"Artos!" someone cried; he thought he recognized Rigobert's voice. "Artos and Montival!"

"*Artos and Montival!*"

Stonehenge loomed on its knee of land above the steep drop to the river a thousand feet below. Moonlight painted the standing stones, and hoarfrost glittered; the carriages and teams and horses and bicycles were far enough away that their noise and presence were easy to ignore. Beyond the huge spectacle of the cliff-fringed Columbia fell away to where the light made a glimmerpath on the water, seeming to lead beyond the world. Silk banners hung amid the great rough stones tonight; they were written with the names of those who'd fallen in the Prophet's War, for more than one coven held this place sacred. The local— semi-clandestine—High Priest and Priestess were here, granting her and the others leave to make their plea in the sacred place.

Juniper Mackenzie stopped, the hood of her robe flung back, and planted a staff that bore the Triple Moon itself on its top, waxing and full and waning. The celebrants halted behind her, the cold wind making a ripping sound when it fanned the torches. Sparks flowed past her into the darkness, flying on a scent of burning pine resin.

A very slight smile quirked her lips. What she saw was a replica—and one built by a Quaker named Samuel Hill a bit more than a century ago, ludicrous myths about Stonehenge being a site of human sacrifice making him think the shape appropriate as a memorial for the dead of war; before the Change it had been a tourist attraction more than anything else. He'd had a great many plans for the area, very few of which had come to fruition . . . but Stonehenge remained, and was a center of ritual and rite and in all likelihood would be for uncounted generations.

Juniper suspected that somewhere Someone was smiling a little at that, and perhaps Sam Hill himself, beyond the Gate where all things were made plain.

Then she sobered completely and opened herself to the night and the place. Something like a keening touched her inwardly, a thread of lament leavened with pride.

Yes, went through her. *This is the proper ground. Here where the bones of the earth are laid bare and the names of the dead and the minds of mourners have rested for generations.*

Sacredness grew like a pearl, sometimes around the most unlikely bits of grit. That didn't make its power any the less real. They were come to ask aid and guidance of the Powers; near the turning point of Samhain—and to make battle magic. They came to invoke the Dark Mother in Her most wrathful aspect: Scathach, the Devouring Shadow Beneath, She Who Brings Fear. And the God Who was storm and sky and war, the spear from heaven, the bright-maned Stallion who fought for the herd and sanctified the land with his blood in turn. All things were holy in their proper place and season, even the most terrible.

"Let it begin," she said, lifting the staff, until moonlight gleamed on silver.

"Let it begin," said the man beside her.

His face was masked with the fox, and his tone solemnstern. Nigel Loring never did anything unless he did it properly; some corner of her warmed with the settled love of middle age.

Rudi—Artos in the Craft—drew the Sword of the Lady, and a slight gasp ran through the celebrants. He paced deosil, sunwise, around the perimeter of the standing stones, and initiates with torches took up positions at the Quarters. Others followed with salt and water.

"*I conjure you, O Circle of Power, that you may be a meeting-place of love and joy and truth, a shield against all wickedness and evil, a boundary between the world of humankind and the realms of the Mighty Ones . . .*"

The Sword traced patterns against her eyes, or perhaps the eyes of her soul; patterns of light and darkness, veils huger than worlds falling endlessly through memory and time.

"*Hear you the words of the Star Goddess, the dust of whose feet are the hosts of heaven, whose body encircles the Universe . . . And you who seek to know Me, know that your seeking and yearning will avail you not, unless you know the Mystery: for if that which you seek, you find not within yourself, you will never find it without.*"

Her voice rose in somber triumph: "*For behold, I have been with you from the Beginning, and I am that which is attained at the end of desire!*"

She lit the fire made ready before the altar-stone, and it cast shadows stark against the great menhirs. Sparks rose upward to join the starry Belt of the Goddess and the full Moon; the clean hot-sweet smell of the burning applewood joined the strong musk from the thurible and filled the clean emptiness of the desert night.

Then the Calling. She had felt that as a oneness with

all that was. Now it was storm and darkness and lightning and whips of ice.

The robed figures behind her began to pace the circle, and their voices rose in turn, to the light plangent
notes of a harp:

Darksome Night and Shining Moon
Balance of the dark and light,
Hearken ye our Witch's Rune,
As we perform our sacred rite!

Rudi laid the Sword of the Lady on the altar, beside the
censor and the cauldron and the Book of Shadows. A
white flash seemed to consume her, and instead of humankind pacing a circle it was as if the world and the universe
beyond were pivoting on this spot of space and time.

Her son's strong voice called: "I am the Lady's
Sword, guardian of Her sacred wood, and Law. Let the
Powers aid Their people now, as we defend them."

The covens replied, their voices in an eerie unison,
not like a frightened mass of near-strangers that need
had assembled. Some distant part of her knew that they
were an instrument for a greater will to play upon this
night:

Mother of the harvest fields,
Goddess of the silver moon,
Join with us as power builds!
Dance with us our witch's rune!

And it was a dance indeed, faster and faster about
her, widdershins and sunwise they danced, crossing and

braiding the power. She thrust the staff to the sky before the altar.

> *Father of the ripened corn*
> *Hunter of the winter snows*
> *With open arms we welcome you!*
> *Dance with us as power grows!*

When she became herself once more the movement had slowed, as the shuttle of her loom did when she battened the last threads home. The cloth was whole now, the weaving tight and strong, the colors sliding into each other and blending.

> *By all the light of moon and sun,*
> *By all the might of land and sea,*
> *Chant the rune and it is done.*
> *As we will, so mote it be!*

CHAPTER TWO

The High Queen of Montival bent over a map table with the Grand Constable d'Ath and a clutch of lords and officers this morning. Huon Liu could see them, though it wasn't polite to stare. Even if you were heir to a wealthy barony like Gervais, which he was, a squire was a very lowly form of military life. Though you didn't realize it when you were looking at it from the worm's-eye-view of a page, which he'd been until a couple of months ago.

Even a royal squire was out in the cold—literally, since he was about twelve feet from the edge of the pavilion tent's door, along with a gaggle of other squires and couriers and their horses. He could see the heads and hands moving, but nothing of the map. There were a pair of spearmen from the Protector's Guard in black-enameled three-quarter armor standing by the entrance as well, their faces invisible behind the vision-slits of their visors, the butts of their glaives braced against their right boots and their four-foot kite-shaped shields blazoned with the crimson and gold Lidless Eye at the parade position. He didn't envy them, though the guige strap over the shoulder took some of the weight, but they were as motionless as statues.

Huon had been excited to finally make the step from page, and hence child, to squire, which made you a youth if not a man yet. At over fifteen he was past due for it; though he lacked an inch or so of what would probably be a medium final height. He was already broad-shouldered and lithe and active. His high-cheeked face, stubborn lack of beard and slightly tilted dark eyes—legacy of his father's father—made him look a little younger than he was, and he was well-versed in all the weapons he had the size and strength of arm to use.

But there was nearly as much standing and waiting involved in squiring as in page work, even if you didn't serve at table as much.

At least it's a warm sort of cold to be out in.

Dawn had been frosty, but now it was a fine day for the end of October, bright sunlight with a few white clouds, and warm enough that his light outfit of brigantine and mail sleeves was making Huon sweat a bit as he stood at parade rest by his horse's head. Carrying messages was the likeliest duty. The rolling plain around them had mostly emptied of troops now, but there were still a few encamped on the stubblefields; the man-stink of the great temporary city was gone, leaving only the smell of horses and dung, dust and woodsmoke and hay and greenery, the scents that were the common background of life. A group of varlets with a wagon were waiting to take down and pack the pavilion, feeding the mules from nose bags

and currycombing them. There was a troop of the Protector's Guard not far off too, men-at-arms in full armor
and mounted crossbowmen, mostly standing by their
horses; you didn't burden them when it wasn't essential.

Dust smoked from the fields where the fall plowing
was underway, teams of oxen or mules or big platter-
hoofed horses pulling double-furrow riding plows and
disk-harrows and seed-drills through stubble or clover-
ley. It had rained hard yesterday, but there wasn't the
constant gray drizzle he was used to in the Black Months
of his home in the northern Willamette, west of the
Cascades on the wet side of the mountains. The clumps
of elm and oak and beech around the villages and manors were streaks of brighter yellow against the dun-gold
and brown and faded green, with only their size to show
that the landscape was not much older than he. The
straight lines of candle-shaped Lombardy poplars that
outlined the great common fields with their villagers'
strips were bright as well. Vineyards scattered here and
there had just finished yielding their last grapes to the
harvesters, and the leaves drew notes of scarlet and orange.

Huon gave a quiet chuckle as he glanced at the plow-
teams. Next year . . .

"What's funny?" the squire next to him said quietly,
as the horses stamped along the picket line behind them.

"Just thinking that the crops ought to be good
around here next year, with all the crap the army left
getting plowed in. You can follow the path of glory by
the trail of shit it leaves."

The other boy chuckled. He was younger than
Huon, about fourteen, but already slightly taller and

with big hands and feet that promised six feet or better eventually; a little gangly, and you could tell that his white-blond hair had just recently been sheared from the pageboy's bob to a squire's bowl-cut. The surcoat over his light mail shirt had the arms of Barony Ath, a delta Or over a V argent, quartered with a blazon: *Gules a domed Tower Argent surmounted by a Pennon Or in base a Lion passant guardant of the last*. The arms of Forest Grove, the barony just north of Ath.

"You're one of the Grand Constable's household?" Huon said, a polite statement of the obvious as a way to start.

"I'm Lioncel de Stafford, heir to Forest Grove. Squire to the Grand Constable, Baroness d'Ath."

"Huon Liu, heir of Gervais," Huon said quietly, blinking a little against the morning sun. "Squire to Her Majesty."

They fell silent again; it wouldn't do to chatter too openly while they waited for orders. The Queen and the Grand Constable were consulting with men who commanded units assigned to protect the lines of communications, since the eastern enemy had lots of light cavalry for raiding around the flanks. It was essential work, but Huon didn't envy them one bit. The great battle was coming, and they would be missing it.

I'm going to be right in the middle *of it. Right behind the High Queen,* he thought, with a mixture of excitement and longing and a trace of fear. *We'll be moving up tomorrow morning. A day or two, no more, and then the biggest battle since the Change!*

A squire cantered up, one of the Grand Constable's. He dismounted, threw the reins to a groom, and nodded to the two boys since they were formally more or less equals, though the squire in question was at least eighteen and in half-armor like the commanders. Then he passed the sentries with a clank of salutes, bent the knee to Mathilda and handed a dispatch to Tiphaine d'Ath.

That gave them a little cover, and they exchanged a bow. Huon looked warily at the other boy and got the same in reply.

They knew *of* each other, roughly, though with the way his own life had been disturbed the last couple of years with House Liu's political troubles he wasn't sure if they'd ever actually met beyond seeing each other about their duties. But there just *weren't* all that many heirs to baronies south of the Columbia. Lioncel was the eldest son of Rigobert de Stafford, Baron Forest Grove, the Marchwarden of the South, and his wife, Lady Delia. His mother was Châtelaine of Barony Ath for the Grand Constable, too.

According to almost-certainly-true rumor Lady Delia was also Tiphaine d'Ath's girlfriend and had been for fifteen years, which the Baron of Forest Grove didn't mind at all since he liked men himself. The three of them seemed to be the best of friends, too, insofar as the Grand Constable *had* any friends . . . Lady Delia's modest tally of three children (with one on the way) all looked respectably like her husband or her own dark comeliness. Mother and children mostly lived in Barony Ath when the family wasn't at court in Castle Todenangst or Portland, but visited Forest Grove frequently.

They . . . all three of them . . . must have serious pull to keep the clergy from getting on their case, Huon thought.

He supposed he disapproved himself, though it was really between them and God and none of his business; he hoped he was a good son of Holy Mother Church, but didn't pretend to overmuch sanctity and he'd never seriously entertained the thought of a vocation.

And judge not, lest ye be judged *is really sort of scary when you think about it. I'm not that brave, or maybe not that self-confident.*

Lady Delia was beautiful in a lushly feminine way, and much admired as a leader of fashion; Huon had seen her a few times at Court or social events, and felt the same awed, goggle-eyed lust as any boy his age. Baron de Stafford was ruggedly handsome, a noted champion in the lists, victor in two duels, and a respected leader in the field. Lady d'Ath was known as *Lady Death*; she'd been the Regent's hatchetwoman for years before she became a commander, and she was victor in more than a *dozen* duels, about which rumor told equally credible and really, truly hideous details. Not many people liked her and a fair number hated her bitterly, but he'd never heard an Associate nobleman refer to her with anything but wary respect shading into outright fear.

She certainly scares me, he thought. *Of course, if things had gone a little differently, the Regent might have sent her to kill the rest of House Liu; I'm pretty sure she was the one who . . . executed . . . Mom.*

He grimaced slightly at the thought. His mother hadn't really been herself that last year or two before things fell apart; it had been like living with a stranger who just *looked* like the mother he remembered. A dangerous and utterly unpredictable stranger. According to rumor, again, she'd been *possessed*, a thing of evil. He could believe it—though he very much didn't want to—and a lot of his nightly prayers were for her soul. He couldn't even really resent the way the Regent had dealt with her.

On second thought, with the Spider of the Silver Tower behind them, it's no wonder nobody makes trouble for d'Ath and de Stafford, even if they're not scared of ending up in a dueling circle. Which I would be. But the Regent's mind scares me even more than Lady Death's sword, now that I've seen Lady Regent Sandra Arminger in action at close range.

"Were you with the Grand Constable at Walla Walla?" Huon asked Lioncel, a little enviously.

D'Ath had commanded the Montivalan vanguard there, the army screening the gathering of the High King's host and turning to snap and slash at the eastern invaders as they advanced. The war-camp was full of the news of their deeds, and the way the High King had led a charge to rescue them when they were surrounded by the Prophet's cavalry just before they reached safety a few days ago. Huon had been part of that, but you didn't see much even if you were involved; it was all a whirling confusion, not the neat lines and duel-like blow-by-blow encounters of which the troubadours sang.

"Yes," Lioncel said; his face was sober as he replied, as if he were suddenly looking somewhere quite different. "My lord my father was too. It was . . . there were so *many* of them, the enemy, even when they split up to try and trap us. If we'd made *one* big mistake, none of us would have gotten away. It was . . . like dancing backward while someone really big tried to hit you with a war hammer, but my lady d'Ath never let them get a grip on us. And we hurt them, hurt them badly."

Then he smiled. "At first the regiments from the Yakima League didn't like serving under the Grand Constable."

"I suppose the Free Cities remember the old wars," Huon said. "My father fought there, when we took the Tri-Cities; I'm too young to remember it."

"Mine too. And do they *ever* remember the old wars! Not the way we Associates do, either. But by the end, they were cheering her whenever she rode by. And the enemy got a lot more cautious, even with their numbers. I grew up with her, but that was the first time I knew, really knew, why so many people are so frightened of her."

Huon nodded respectfully; they both served warriors of note and of famous deeds, even if they were women.

And running the Grand Constable's messages or carrying her spare lances must have been pretty dangerous too. He's younger than me, but he's already well-blooded.

He glanced through the door of the tent; Lady d'Ath was speaking, referring to a notebook in her left hand and tracing something on the map. Just to add to the puzzle, she looked a lot like Lioncel, enough to have actually been his mother herself; blond and regular-featured and tall. Not ladylike or feminine, but not really mannish, either—very female and very, very dangerous, like a she-tiger.

"You're Baron Odard's younger brother, aren't you?" Lioncel asked. "The late baron, of course. We've all heard about his deeds and how well he died."

Huon nodded. Lioncel was looking at *him* a little oddly, too, because the Barony of Gervais wasn't exactly normal either. House Liu had produced his elder brother, Odard, who had been one of the Companions of the Quest with the High King and Queen, all the way east to Nantucket. He hadn't come back.

So far, so good, he thought. *I miss Odard. He was a good guy and a good brother when he remembered me at all, but a knight has to expect to die by the sword—and he died like a hero from a* chanson. *He brought honor to our House and he saved Yseult and me. Without him, when Mother was arrested for treason . . .*

The problem was that their mother hadn't just been arrested and executed for treason; she had been *guilty* as the proverbial Dragon of Sin itself, in league with the Church Universal and Triumphant, and so had his uncle Sir Guelf been. They'd both died for it, and nearly taken House Liu down with them; he and his sister had spent a lot of time under arrest and parole, not to mention constant suspicion. It hadn't been any fun at all.

That's over by now, thank God and His Mother, but I'm still feeling . . . prickly . . . over it.

The High King and the Queen had been generous to a fault since they got back from the Quest. He was a royal squire now, a post a lot of young noblemen would kill for, and Yseult was a lady-in-waiting to the Queen; she'd been promised a dowry of manors from the Crown demesne, and it had been made known the High King and Queen would stand godparents to any children either had, a priceless *cadeau*. All that made them a lot less of a pair of lepers socially. It still hadn't stopped suspicious glances out of the corners of eyes.

He wondered if anything would, except the passage of more time than he liked to think about.

"Huon!"

The High Queen's voice snapped him out of his reverie. He left his tethered horse and strode briskly into the tent, sweeping off his brimless squire's flowerpot hat and bowing before standing to attention.

"Your Majesty," he said.

Mathilda Arminger had been a kindly mistress to him in the month of his service, but she was all business in the field. Which was just what you wanted, of course. Nobody who'd met her was going to tease him about being a woman's squire.

"You're going here," she said, tucking a lock of her dark-brown hair back into place with one finger, then tracing a path on the map.

He watched closely as she tapped four points in the high country north of the town and Crown castle of Goldendale.

"There are posts here . . . here . . . here and here."

He memorized the locations; map-reading and knowing terrain were skills a nobleman had to master. She handed him four envelopes with the Crown seal.

"You're to take these messages to the commanders at each; they're just signal and scout detachments. Take any reply — written or verbal, they won't be urgent or they would have used their heliographs."

"Your Majesty?"

That was Tiphaine d'Ath, in her cool, inflectionless voice. "Sending him alone is *almost* completely safe. Remember what we have Ogier nosing around up that way for."

The High Queen smiled, her strong, slightly irregular face lighting for a second. She was in her mid-twenties, a decade and a half younger than d'Ath, but tired enough by the labors of the last few days that you could see what she'd look like in middle-age when the freshness of youth was gone. Indomitable, like weathered rock.

"Good point, my lady Grand Constable," she said with a nod. "Which is not the same as *absolutely completely* safe."

D'Ath raised her voice in turn: "Lioncel!"

The blond youngster seemed to appear magically. "My lady?"

"Her Majesty's squire is carrying dispatches to the posts north of the city. Accompany him, under his orders. Both of you keep a sharp lookout. If you see any sign of enemy activity, get out immediately and report it to Castle Goldendale. It's not likely, but the unlikely happens sometimes."

"Yes, my lady!"

Huon inclined his head. "When and where shall we rejoin, Your Majesty?"

Mathilda looked at her watch.

"Nine fifteen. We're moving out to Castle Maryhill down on the Columbia in a couple of hours, once we get this cleared up. Rejoin there by no later than sundown, we'll be moving east at dawn."

"And you have a new sister," d'Ath said to Lioncel, handing over a parcel and a sealed note on lavender-colored paper. "Her name is Yolande. Your lady mother sent this for you with the courier."

"Thank you, my lady! That's wonderful news!"

Huon suppressed a pang of envy; *his* mother probably wouldn't have sent the parcel. Even before she turned strange. Certainly not just before or after an accouchement.

So much for unnatural mothers, he thought a little sourly, seeing Lioncel's unaffected delight.

Both the squires bent their knee and turned about smartly. Both were smiling as they left; a day spent dashing about was a *lot* more exciting than standing and watching the grass grow. And they had all day to do it in, plenty of time. He suspected it was partly a test of his land-navigation skills, too; he hadn't been given a map.

"Congratulations," Huon said. "Sisters can be fun; Yseult and I get along really well."

"Thanks, but she's older than you, isn't she?"

"Two years," Huon said. "It was Odard, then Yseult, then me. Then my father was killed in the Protector's War, so I was the last, that's why it's such a small family."

"You're the youngest, but I'm the oldest in ours. Little Heuradys is still toddling and drooling, and when they're babies they're about as interesting as a lump of dough and not nearly as cute as puppies. Plus a puppy doesn't take years to housebreak, as Lady d'Ath says. I'm happy for my lady my mother, though; she always wanted two sons and two daughters. A matched set, she called it."

"Don't worry now, they'll both be old enough for you to be worrying about their suitors in no time!"

They unhitched their fast coursers from the picket line, vaulted into the saddle and cantered off northward, turning west along a rutted lane bordered with London plane trees to avoid the city wall, riding off onto the verge now and then to dodge the odd cart or wagon and once sweeping off their hats and bowing in the saddle as a lady went by on her palfrey, with maids and guards in attendance. She nodded back at them and smiled regally, teeth white against her brown face.

Lioncel had stuffed the package in a saddlebag after sniffing hopefully at it.

"My lady my mother is always sending me stuff," he said. "Little things, but it's usually stuff I really *need* as well as being cool."

He slit the note open with his dagger, a thin-bladed misericorde, and read it. Huon caught a slight waft of scent, some cool floral fragrance, maybe verbena.

"Oh good, thanks be to the Virgin. The accouchement went easily—*like a watermelon seed*, she says, and they're both doing well. Lady Valentine Renfrew was there at Montinore with her—the Countess of Odell—they're old friends. And the Renfrew daughters were there, all three; they're nice girls. It must have been a lot of comfort to Mom. And them. It's hard on women, waiting, when there's war."

"Bearing children is like battle," Huon said, which was a cliché but had the advantage of being true. "You're lucky to have three brothers and sisters."

The smile ended as Lioncel read the end of the note, and Huon could see a flush spread up to the other boy's ears, along with an audible grinding of teeth.

"Oh, sweet Saints, *Dolores sends her regards!*" he muttered angrily under his breath, and started to crumple the letter before he smoothed it out and tucked it into a pocket in his trews.

"Ah . . . who's Dolores?" Huon asked.

They were thoroughly alone. The only sounds were the creak of saddle leather, the dull hollow clop of hooves on dirt, and the wind in the trees. Yellow-brown leaves fell around them, and a flight of starlings went by. Through town would be the most direct route, but impossibly crowded and slow. The witches-hat tops of the town's towers and the taller ones of the castle on its northern fringe edged by, with the green slopes of the low mountains behind. You could see the peaks of Adams and Ranier from here, and sometimes the cone of Mt. Hood southward and west.

Lioncel's face had relaxed a little. "A girl," he said ruefully. "A really pretty girl. Friendly, too."

Well, at least it is *a girl,* Huon thought. "Your leman?" he said.

Lioncel was distinctly young to have a recognized lady-love and he wasn't wearing a favor-ribbon on his arm, either, just a plain mail shirt and surcoat.

"Ah . . . no," he replied, and his mouth quirked, apparently halfway between humor and embarrassment. "She's a servant girl at Montinore manor house. Part-time, boon-work, you know. Her father's a blacksmith, and her mother's a midwife."

Huon nodded; he did. All peasant families on a manor owed labor-service as part of the rent for their holdings. Usually the skilled upper house-servants were full-time retainers who moved with the nobles they served from manor to castle to court, but the routine scrubbing, potato-peeling and fetch-and-carry was done by young women from the nearest estate village, fulfilling part of their kin's obligations. It wasn't as hard as working in the demesne fields and there were other advantages.

But Lioncel was rather too young to have an acknowledged mistress, either. Even if his parents were *very* indulgent.

"And . . . well, Mom . . . my lady mother . . . caught us in a linen closet," Lioncel went on doggedly.

"Ouch," Huon said sympathetically, trying to imagine *his* mother's reaction . . . even when she'd been herself. "Trouble?"

"Well, no. I mean, Dolores was nice about it. She didn't try to pretend I'd *made* her do it which *could* have gotten me into trouble and her out of it; my lady my mother and Baroness d'Ath are both really strict about good lordship. Mom laughed at first, but . . . then she *teased* me about it. She's still at it, and that was months and months ago."

"Oh, ouch, ouch," Huon said sympathetically. "Totally *ouch*."

And I mean it. It would be bad enough having a brother tease you about something like that. Having your mother do it . . . you'd want to turn into a vole and crawl into a tunnel and never come out.

"And then Lady d'Ath just *looked* at me and said that if Dolores'd gotten pregnant, the compensation money would have come out *my* allowance for the next three million years. And then I had to confess it to Father Lailard and got this *unbelievable* penance. And I didn't even *get* that far! I just had my hand under her outer tunic! And Dad . . . my lord my father . . . he killed himself laughing."

Huon laughed himself, but slapped the younger squire on the shoulder to show it wasn't unkindly meant.

"They probably think embarrassing you is the best way to keep you on the straight and narrow," he said.

Lioncel laughed too after a moment. They fell silent as they turned off the rural lane and through a gap in the row of trees onto a trail that meandered through rocky grassland northward. The mountains were much closer now, and they were leaving the settled zone where people were omnipresent. Which meant . . .

"Time to arm up," Huon said.

They both stuffed their hats in the saddlebags and put on their helmets, coalscuttle sallets with flared neck-guards, but the lighter open-face type without visors. The felt and leather pads closed around his head. He'd adjusted them carefully, but you still got a headache if you wore it all day; though that was better than getting your brains spattered by a mace. The chin-cup and straps had to be just right too, so he swiveled and tossed his head to make sure everything was firm without being too tight. They half-drew their swords and daggers and re-seated them with a slight hiss of steel on wood and leather greased with neatsfoot oil. Lioncel slipped the crossbow off his back, worked the lever set in the forestock to cock it and clipped a quarrel in the firing groove. Huon preferred a saddlebow, and he pulled the horn-and-sinew recurve out of the boiled-leather scabbard at his knee and set an arrow on the string.

They were coming up through meadows to the Little Klickitat River and a thick scattering of trees along it, big cottonwoods and willows, pale-barked white alder, the odd elm or beech someone had planted since the Change and a thick understory of bush and saplings. Their trail led down to the water and up the other side, and from the tracks was made mostly by cattle and sheep. The water was shallow, gravel and riffles showing as often as pools, but the rainy season had started in the Simcoes to the north and it was rising from its summer lows.

"You first," Huon said; it was his mission, so he was in charge. "Cover! Move!"

Lioncel crossed as Huon brought up his bow and covered him, eyes flickering along the edge of the riverside woods for any telltale sign of movement. There wasn't any, save for a badger trundling off with a ground squirrel in its jaws, and the usual birds, including a bald eagle perching on a lightning-killed pine and ignoring them. Once he was across the blond boy turned his horse right and dropped the reins on the mount's neck. The well-trained animal stood stock-still, not even bending its head to crop at the green grass that grew in clumps by the river's side.

"Cover!" Lioncel called, bringing the crossbow up to his shoulder. "Move!"

It was a heavy weapon for someone the young squire's age, but he kept it steady. Huon let his weight shift forward slightly, and Dancer walked into the water, placing his feet carefully and raising his knees high. He wasn't using a knight's saddle, which cut you off from contact with the horse for the sake of locking you into a standing position. This was a light pad type, and of course he'd trained in all the equestrian arts under experts since he was old enough to walk.

The water was still low; at the deepest spot it came up to the bottom of his stirrups, and he could feel cool wet on his woolen trews where splashed drops hit. He smiled as the horse muscled its way up the slope on the other side. This *was* a lot more fun than waiting around the tent.

Beyond was a savannah with scattered lodgepole pine and rather shrubby Garry oaks, probably stinted communal common-pasture for whatever manor held this area. Then they were into the hills with the pines thick around them, steep trails—steep enough to make them dismount and lead the horses at times—and jays scolding, squirrels running up the tall trunks in gray chattering streaks, bright sunlight spearing down. The air smelled a bit damper here and full of the sweet scent of the wood. Once Dancer shied a little; a tree nearby bore long parallel gouges and there was scat on the ground by it.

"Cougar," Huon said, pointing at the gray hairs caught in the bark, and Lioncel nodded.

"Not nearly big enough for tiger and that's the wrong color," he said.

"Lots of deer sign too, and elk, I think."

"And sage hen and grouse. There'd be good hawking here, and some most excellent hunting. But no boar," Lioncel added.

"We get lots of boar near Gervais," Huon said animatedly. "In the marsh along the river, mostly. I'm looking forward to that when I'm older!"

"Me too. Ours are in the Coast Range forests, except that my lady d'Ath says they spend every night in our vineyards and gardens, eating."

They shared a nod at that. Swine were smart; their wild cousins were wickedly intelligent, making nothing of fences in their raids on crops, and they hated men.

Hunting them was part of a lord's obligation to protect his lands and dependents, as well as fine risky sport and a useful source of meat and hides. Lioncel went on enthusiastically:

"My lord my father took one that weighed *five hundred pounds* last year! Lady d'Ath got one nearly as big that afternoon too, I was her spear-bearer. Dad let me have a tusk."

He rummaged in his belt pouch and proudly brought out nearly six inches of polished ivory threat, like a curved dagger. Huon whistled appreciatively and handled it for a moment.

"I'm going to have it worked into a hilt for a hunting knife when I get the time," Lioncel added.

"That *will* be cool."

Neither of them had the years or heft for hunting boar yet; you took the beasts by getting in their way when they charged and letting them spit themselves on a broad-bladed spear. One with a crossguard forged into the base of the socket, so the prey couldn't run up the shaft and rip you open with their tusks. Usually the nobles waited while dogs and beaters flushed them out of thickets, though some preferred a lone stalk. The boars came out on their own fairly frequently too, like huge black projectiles shot from a catapult and armored in bone and gristle. Some thought them nearly as dangerous game as tiger or bear, and every year a few reckless or unlucky men or ones stupid enough to go hunting drunk were killed.

That's how a troubadour gets rid of an inconvenient character if it isn't time for a battle or duel, Huon thought. *'Ripped up by the boar.'*

*   *   *

They swapped hunting stories for a while and discussed
horses and hawks and hounds. Hoofbeats carried farther
than quiet voices, so it didn't make them any more conspicuous. Then they fell silent as Huon held up a hand,
looking around; he could feel eyes on them. It was a
relief when two crossbowmen stepped out from behind
trees and demanded the password; he'd begun to think
he must have missed the trail. The grim graying man-at-
arms in command of the outpost took the sealed enve-
lope with a salute and grunted:

"My thanks, young sir."

Meaning, get lost, kid, Huon thought, returning the
gesture and nodding gravely in reply.

He didn't mind, since he was fully aware of how
young he must look to the scarred veteran. Being a
squire was supposed to teach noblemen humility, among
other things.

"No return message," the man added.

The next two were the same. The last had something
different; only one soldier on guard, to start with. When
they pushed their horses through a screen of brush into
a sloping meadow of ten or fifteen acres Huon's eyebrows went up as he saw why. His bow did for a second
too; there were about twenty men there in the gear that
Boise's light cavalry wore. Just leather breeches and
mail shirts, but unmistakable in detail, along with their
helmets—sort of an understated sallet they called a
Fritz, which together with the stars-and-stripes flag emblem were their inheritance from the ancient world.

But they were disarmed and dismounted, under the
guard of the outpost's complement and a couple of *con-*

roi of men-at-arms led by a knight Huon recognized. None of the enemy were wounded, so they hadn't been captured in the course of ordinary fighting. That probably meant they'd come over of their own wills. Being a royal squire meant you heard things; among others, that a lot of people in the United States of Boise weren't happy with their General-President Martin Thurston, especially now that the story of how he'd murdered his own father to take over the position had gotten around.

Especially now that his own wife and own mother and own sisters escaped with the aid of the Dúnedain and are telling the truth to everyone. Not to mention his brother Frederick is the High King's friend and one of the Companions of the Quest, so there's someone for soldiers to go over to. Boise will be part of the High Kingdom too, and under the High King's peace!

"Sir Ogier!" Huon said, dismounting and saluting; high politics weren't his affair yet, but that didn't stop him thinking.

The young knight looked up; he'd been a royal squire too, until the High Queen gave him the accolade on the field of honor not long ago, and was still a fairly junior household commander of the High Queen's *me-nie*. He was a little over two years older than Huon and around six feet, probably his full height though he was still lanky with late adolescence; his hair was a very dark brown-yellow, like barley, and there was a spray of acne across his cheeks and nose—something Huon had been spared so far. His smile was genuine and warm beneath the raised visor; they'd served together, after all. And though Ogier of House Renfrew was a son of the Count of Odell, one of the great Peers of the Association, he was the *youngest* son, with two elder brothers, not to mention three sisters who'd be needing dowries.

"Good to see you again, Huon," he said, taking the dispatch, looking at the address and handing it over to the signal detachment commander. "And you too, Lioncel."

"I noticed you'd been sent on a mission, Sir Ogier," Huon said.

The knight nodded. "I was out meeting these fellows, they slipped a message across the lines that they wanted to switch sides, and Her Majesty thought a man of rank should meet them, being tactful and so forth."

A snort. "And thirty lancers with me, to make sure they were honest about it."

He turned his head to Lioncel: "Any news from your brother?"

"Not lately, Sir Ogier," the blond youth said. Then he grinned: "But my lady my mother is delivered of a daughter, who'll be christened Yolande. Your lady mother the Countess and the ladies your sisters were there at Montinore manor for the accouchement."

"Excellent!" Ogier said; he seemed to be happy with the world today. To Huon: "Lioncel's little brother Diomede is paging it with Countess Anne in Tillamook off on the Pacific shore."

"Don't let him hear you say *little* brother, Sir Ogier," Lioncel said, grinning.

It was all part of the network of fosterage and service that tied the great houses together. There had also been persistent talk of a marriage between the Countess-regnant of Tillamook, or the County on the Edge of the World, as it was also known, and Count Conrad Renfrew's youngest son. Marriage was another part of the network.

He went on to Huon: "I just got this from Her Grace."

He tapped a knot of ribbons in Tillamook's colors on his shoulder, gray and green and silver around an embroidered rose. Wearing a lady's favor wasn't precisely a pledge of marriage, that depended on circumstances. But it did entitle you to fight for her name and fame, and it was a serious matter, where the honor of each depended on the other.

"I sent a letter by heliograph after the Battle of the Vanguard, telling my lady Anne how I'd been knighted by the High Queen on the field of honor and begging leave to send her my first spurs and dedicate the deeds to her glory. This came in this morning with the couriers, and this."

He pulled out a locket strung on a silver chain, shaped from an oval of walrus-ivory as long as a man's thumb and half as wide, carved in delicate filigree and clasped with granulated gold. When he clicked it open there was a portrait of a striking fair-haired young woman, with his own on the other side.

"It's beautiful, Sir Ogier," Huon said. "She is, I mean, your lady the Countess; most fair and gracious, fitting for a Peer of the Association. She gave my sister Yseult shelter when it was, ah, awkward. We'll always remember that with gratitude."

He spoke quite sincerely; that too was a bond. The locket was fine work, and Anne of Tillamook was lovely . . . though also several years older than the young knight. And Ogier had been a good companion to work with, not stuck-up or birth-proud at all.

So I wish him all good fortune in his marriage, and her too, when and if. His son will be a Count, after all.

Huon stepped back so that Lioncel could take a look as Ogier beamed at the picture. That let him pivot at the first shout of alarm, and his bow was still in his hand with a nocked arrow resting in the cut-out. One of the not-quite-prisoners had ducked under a guard's horse, slashing the girths as he went, and he was throwing himself headlong at Sir Ogier with a long glitter of steel in his hand, dodging the rider's draw-and-cut as the man toppled onto his own sword with a yell.

"*Look out!*" Huon called crisply, into the chaos of rearing horses and men shouting, drawing and loosing as he'd been taught.

He hadn't had time to aim except by raw instinct, or to worry about missing and hitting someone else. The string struck his forearm, hard enough to feel through the stiff leather of his arm-guard. The arrow hit, low and at an angle; he could hear the wet smacking impact. There was a screech, and the body of the attacker struck *him* and he went over backward with a painful thump, too quickly for his training in how to fall to do more than help a little. It gave him a good viewpoint to see the assassin who'd been masquerading as a deserter run into Lioncel. He was a grown man, though wiry and slender as most light cavalry were, a third again as heavy as the young squire. But he stopped rather than overrunning him. The curved dagger in his hand slit the surcoat on Lioncel's shoulder and grated off his mail, then fell to the ground point-first and stood quivering.

The man slumped downward, leaking blood from nose and mouth. When he hit, Huon could see the silver

wire around the hilt of Lioncel's misericorde dancing in
the center of his chest. The narrow blade of the weapon
had slipped easily between the links of the mail shirt,
which was what it was designed for. And equally easily
between two ribs and into the big blood vessels over the
heart, driven by the man's own weight and momentum.
Behind Lioncel, Ogier Renfrew extended a steadying armored arm against the squire's back as he staggered.

When the knight spoke an instant later, it was to his
men, though, in a sharp carrying voice:

"Put up your weapons! I'm all right, by the grace of
God and St. Dismas! No killing! Remember the High
King's order!"

The crossbowmen and men-at-arms raised their
weapons, or lowered the points of their swords. The
prisoners were in a tight clump, hands raised or on their
heads, mostly blank-faced but slightly crouched; they'd
thought themselves about to be massacred . . . which
might have happened, if Ogier hadn't spoken swiftly.

OK, make a note of that, Squire, Huon thought,
struggling to draw a breath and then get back to his
feet. *Focus on the immediate need. Prioritize!*

"Not one of us!" one of the Boise men called. "Bastard wasn't in our platoon! Just turned up and said he
was switching sides too, on his own."

Ogier stepped forward and indicated the curved dagger
with the toe of his steel sabaton. It was fine work, with a
rippling watermarked pattern wrought into the blade, and
the pommel was a ball engraved with the shape of a rayed
sun.

"Hand of the Prophet," he said. "Kill-dagger. Those
sons of whores operate in threes."

The prisoner who'd spoken before did again: "He was alone. We haven't seen any others."

"Then they may turn up. Or you could be lying." He shook his head and went on to the deserters: "I'm afraid we *are* going to have to tie you and search you."

In a harder voice, directed at his own followers, who were shuffling their feet:

"Search you again, only thoroughly this time." Then he went on to the prisoners:

"This is a temporary measure, until we get you to Goldendale and sort out who's who. That's how the enemy operate, trying to destroy honest men's trust in each other."

One of his own men-at-arms bent to retrieve the assassin's knife.

"I wouldn't use my bare flesh on that, if I were you, Teófilo," Ogier said dryly. "It was consecrated to the service of Hell and the death-demons in Corwin, probably by the Prophet's own hand."

"*¡Dios mío!*" the man blurted. "Thank you, my lord!"

He used a stick to push the knife onto a cloth, stuffed the bundle into a leather sack, and put that on a packmule. His comrades attended to binding the prisoners, and the knight turned to the squires.

"Good work, very good work," he said. "Her Majesty will hear of it, and the Grand Constable, too, of course."

"Lioncel did the work . . . killed him," Huon said, suddenly feeling a little weak as he looked down at the dead Cutter, wrinkling his nose at the coppery metallic stink of blood. There was a lot of it in a man. "All I did was shoot him in one butt-cheek."

Ogier laughed, and Lioncel gave a startled chortle. "I . . . just drew and stabbed," he said, his voice wobbling a little.

"And jumped in front of me towards the danger, like Huon," Ogier noted. "It's when he's surprised that a man shows his real instincts, or his training, or both. My lord my father told me that once and I've never forgotten it."

Huon looked down at the dead assassin; the arrow *had* gone in over the hip-bone and then down through one buttock. The red point stood out just where it joined the upper thigh. He didn't pull a very heavy bow, but flesh was so . . .

Tender, Huon thought uneasily.

"And you can truly say that this is now a thoroughly *half-assed* assassin," Lioncel said.

Something unknotted in Huon's gut as he joined in the laughter.

CHAPTER THREE

"Was that your first?" Huon asked an hour later; he thought the younger boy wanted to talk.

Lioncel shook his head. "No . . . they, assassins like that, tried to kill my lady the Grand Constable in Walla Walla a few months ago, the very same day I'd been made squire. And the Count, and my lord my father, all on the same night."

He stiffened with unconscious pride: "But my lady was ready for them! We were waiting!"

Maybe because she used to be an assassin herself, Huon thought; he wasn't sorry that she *had* been ready, though. *That would have been a disaster for our cause, to lose the commanders in the County Palatine just as the invaders came west.*

Lioncel went on: "I shot one of them with my crossbow then, in the apartments my lady was using, and I had to give him the mercy-stroke. And . . . I think since, during the fighting, but I'm not sure. But that's not . . .

so close, mostly. You shoot, or someone comes out of the dust, and you hit or dodge and you don't see him again. Usually I'm behind my lady d'Ath, of course, and the senior squires, well behind."

They were out of the mountains again, well into the settled lands around Goldendale. Huon took off his helmet, relishing the breeze through his sweat-damp hair, a feeling of lightness and release. A swale at the base of a low rise had been closed off by earth banks, and a spring kept it filled with water that lay mirror-still, reflecting the blue sky and puffy white clouds above. Willows surrounded it, and reeds grew in the edges; to the east was a long narrow strip of apple orchard along the irrigation furrow that kept it alive, with some of the fruit still glowing red among the faded green of the leaves.

Apart from that the land around the pool was a long sloping hayfield, the alfalfa recently cut and packed in big round mows all centered around a column made from the trunk of a tall lodgepole pine. Each haystack had a thatched roof on top of its circular height, and they looked as if they were huts taken in two giant hands and stretched like taffy. The smell was as sweet as candy, and it drifted over him like a benison, a reminder of a world where feeding your cattle and horses and sheep through the winter was about the most important thing there was.

Oh, devils and damnation, I'm not cut out to be a cleric!

"Let's stop here for lunch," Huon said. "We've got plenty of time. And nobody can say we haven't been doing a day's work today, man's work!"

"Yeah," Lioncel said, and smiled.

After all, we're noblemen of the Portland Protective Association, Huon thought. *War is our work. We're the guardians of the land.*

Sir Ogier had thoughtfully given each of them a re-mount from among the captured horses. They both rode light in the saddle, and switching off mounts every couple of miles, they could cover the distance down to the river in a few hours without overstraining the horses. Neither of them considered that sort of ride anything of a hardship.

"It's a nice spot," the heir of Forest Grove said.

Huon forced down a slightly queasy recollection of the sound when the arrow struck. The one he'd shot had been a bad man, not just an enemy; an assassin, an agent of the CUT who'd sold his soul to demons. On the other hand, you couldn't help thinking how it must *feel.* Or that once the bad man had been a perfectly or-dinary little kid. He hadn't thought of that before.

You take the good with the bad. I don't think I'm ever going to like *killing men or hurting them. Fighting's ex-citing, but I don't like that part. I can do it when it's necessary, I guess.*

They watered the horses, rubbed them down and poured small mounds of cracked barley for them to lip up off the turf before they hobbled them and left them to graze beneath the willows. He enjoyed the homey, familiar task, the earthy, grassy smell of the horses and the way Dancer turned his neck and lipped at his rider's hair.

The hobbles weren't really necessary with their own mounts, he'd bought Dancer from a first-rate training farm when he was taken into the royal household and worked him since then, and Lioncel's Hardhoof was just as good. The remounts were eastern and of quarter-horse blood, and most of all they didn't know them and their *horses* didn't know them. It was better to have them all hobbled while they sorted out who was boss-horse and got used to each other.

Then they opened their bags and sat under a willow to eat, leaning against their saddles and putting one of the small bucklers they wore on their sword-scabbards down to serve as a plate. Huon had managed to pick up a three-pound ration loaf of maslin bread, a mixture of whole-meal barley and wheat flour that was dense and coarse but fresh that morning, and a length of strong-tasting salty dried pork sausage full of garlic and sage. Lioncel contributed a block of cheese wrapped in dock leaves tied with twisted straw, some honey from the package his mother had sent, and a canteen of watered wine.

Huon sawed and slapped together a set of massive sandwiches, while Lioncel struggled with the top of the honey jar. Then they signed themselves, said grace and tore into the food with the thoughtless voracity of hard-working teenagers who'd gone six hours since the morning's porridge and raisins.

"This is *good* cheese!" Huon said after a moment.

Most of the cheese you got with the army was just . . . cheese, issued in big blocks to groups. Even in the royal household, when they were in the field them-selves; Mathilda was a stickler for not dragging too much in the way of personal comforts in the baggage train, and the Grand Constable was notorious for see-ing that nobody exceeded what was allowed in the

Table of Ranks. Huon didn't mind; enduring hardship was a knightly duty, the cheese was usually not too moldy, and it made dry bread or the rocklike double-baked hardtack the troops called *dog biscuit* go down a lot better, especially if you could toast it over a camp-fire.

This was quite different, firm but not hard or rubbery either, with a rich lingering taste that was just a little sour-sharp, and bits of hot pepper had been worked into the curd and cured with it. He hadn't had better, even as the last course at a banquet.

"My brother Diomede sent it up from Tillamook even though he's absolutely *green* that I'm here and he's stuck there," Lioncel said. "He's not a bad kid, and Anne's a good mistress to serve."

Huon nodded; Tillamook cheese was famous, and had been even before the Change. Nowadays it was traded all over the Association territories and even beyond.

"The wine's from Montinore," Lioncel went on. "Our home manor near Castle Ath."

It was good too, though the water didn't help, but he already knew better than to drink it straight with work to do and half a day ahead of him. The honey was *really* good; mostly clover but with fruit flavors, he thought.

"We live . . . lived in Castle Gervais full time," Huon said; the castle and lands were under a Crown-appointed seneschal right now, while he was underage. "My mother liked it that way."

Better not to think about that, he added to himself, and went on:

"I'm going to build a manor house south of town when I'm Baron. It's a pain keeping the Castle Gervais quarters warm in winter. The wet moat means the concrete weeps during the Black Months; the amount of wood we go through is unbelievable. Why live like you're under siege until you're *really* under siege?"

Lioncel nodded. "My lady my mother says she had to pretty well *drag* Baroness d'Ath out of the castle to the Montinore manor house after I was born . . . it was built a long time before the Change, it's really cool, and it didn't have to be worked over much. It was in the Crown demesne before we were . . . that is, before Lady d'Ath . . . was given the land in fief."

"It's weird, the way they forgot how to build something you could live in just before the Change," Huon agreed. "A lot of them don't even have *fireplaces*. Creepy! No wonder God sent a judgment on them! Gervais town doesn't have much from before the Change. It all burned down. The new town's modern, half-timbered stuff mostly, my parents oversaw that after the castle was built. Yseult can remember some of that, but I can't."

"You're lucky to have it all modern. Refitting is a pain, my lady my mother talks about how much it costs. We're only now getting all the villages up to scratch. Well, we would be except for the war delaying things."

"Hand me some of that honey, will you?" Huon said, then poured it on a heel of the maslin. "Thanks."

"I'm glad you had the bread," Lioncel said, with his own mouth full. "Mom has these special hives in the gardens at the manor, or near the turn-out pasture or the demesne orchards, and it feels sort of funny to put it on dog biscuit. Though it makes it taste a lot better. The dog biscuit, not the honey."

"Boiled turnip without salt would make dog biscuit taste better," Huon said, and they both chuckled. Then: "Let's take a swim. My hands and face are sticky and we're going to be awfully busy the next couple of days. I doubt there'll be baths."

"Have we got time?"

"If we don't take too long," Huon said, with a glance at the sun and a mental estimate of the distance to Castle Maryhill. "It's only twelve miles, maybe fourteen. Steep, but steep downhill and the road's good."

They stripped and ran splashing into the edge of the pond, then struck out; it was big enough to swim comfortably, though only the center was more than waist-deep. There were fish in the water, some sort of small catfish, and after a while they started trying to catch them with their hands, whooping and splashing and falling.

Wait a minute, Huon thought. *That's someone else laughing.*

He stood up dripping, appalled at his own carelessness. Lioncel was an instant behind him. He could lunge for their weapons—

Girls! he thought.

For a moment he simply thought that. Then he realized that the water right here was only up to his thighs and squatted abruptly; Lioncel did too. The girls laughed again, not giggling but outright laughing. They stood side-by-side next to the saddles, but they didn't seem to have touched anything. Huon blinked and started seeing details; one of them was about his own age, he thought, and the other a year or two older. The younger one was taller and buxom and the hair that flowed out from under her kerchief was the color of dark honey with brighter sun-streaks. The older was more slender and dark-haired like him.

They were both brown as berries with the summer sun, dressed in the short-and-long tunic combination of countrywomen, with coarse burlap aprons belted on and their under-tunics drawn up a bit for case of move-ment, which exposed their calves and bare feet. Both of them had baskets woven of osier-withies full of apples, which explained what they were doing here, picking the last fruit to come ripe in the orchard.

Peasants, of course, he thought, and tried to put au-thority into his voice.

"What do you two think you're doing?"

It was hard to project authority when you were squatting on your hams in slightly muddy water and were buck-naked except for your crucifix on its chain. He felt the blush running up his face.

At least it doesn't show as much with me as it does with Lioncel, he thought.

The other boy was very pale except for his face and forearms. Then Huon rated himself for cowardice; he was the elder, he should be dealing with this.

The older girl answered through her laughter: "We're watching the pretty little page boys at play!"

"We're not pages!" Lioncel burst out indignantly; it didn't help that *his* voice broke in a squeak in mid-protest. "And you girls ought to be ashamed of yourselves! We're squires, fighting-men!"

Huon pushed himself back, bobbing in the water until he could stand up, dripping, with the level about at his belly button. Lioncel followed, crossing his arms over his chest and throwing his damp hair out of his eyes.

"Oooh, Oriabelle, they're *fighting-men*," the dark girl said. "I'm so *scared*."

"Let's bombard them, Ava! With *trebuchets!*"

The honey-haired girl named Oriabelle picked an apple out of her basket and took a bite out of it, then threw it at him—fairly hard, and it would have spatted on his forehead if he hadn't caught it. The other girl threw at Lioncel, who was distracted, and it *did* hit him; the peasant girls seemed to think that was extremely funny.

"*We* ought to be ashamed of ourselves?" Oriabelle said. "Ava and I are *working*. You're going around naked as frogs! We ought to run off with your clothes and leave you to ride home that way!"

Dark Ava giggled this time and did a wicked imitation of a man riding naked, clutching himself and wincing as he came into contact with the saddle.

Huon thought for an instant, took a bite out of the crisp sweetness of the apple himself, then spoke with a lofty air:

"You girls should be more respectful and kinder to strangers as the Lord commands. We might come out of the water and chase you!"

Ava threw another apple; Lioncel managed to catch it this time.

"Chase us?" she said. "You couldn't chase us. You have nothing to wear, you're as naked as Adam in the Garden of Eden!"

Huon pointed at the reeds. "We could grab some of those. Then we'd be clothed like Adam *after* the Fall."

"You couldn't *catch* us," Oriabelle said. "Not through the hay-stubble. You have soft, white, tender feet. Gentleman's feet, not like this."

She put her hands on her hips and turned, standing on one foot and waggling the sole of the other at him as she looked over her shoulder. It had the calluses you'd expect on someone who didn't wear shoes for the warmer eight months of the year. The movement also drew her tunics rather tight, and he found himself swallowing with difficulty and glad the water was cold.

"You wouldn't *dare* to chase us," Ava said, standing hipshot.

Her eyes were on Lioncel and her teeth white against her tan as she taunted:

"Why, I bet the young, cute blond one with the sweet blue eyes couldn't chase us even as far as . . . oh, that haystack there."

She pointed at the nearest one, about a hundred yards away. Huon tossed his apple aside and looked at Lioncel. The other squire met his gaze and nodded slightly.

"A nobleman is supposed to show resource and initiative," Lioncel whispered. "Lady d'Ath told me so herself."

"One . . . two . . .

"*Three!*"

They dashed for the bank in a shower of droplets, pausing for a few seconds to rip up reeds in their left hands, holding them strategically as they bounded up the bank. The girls snatched up their baskets and retreated across the hayfield. The hay-stubble *was* painful on soles accustomed to socks and boots, and Huon was

conscious of the way he was prancing and lifting his feet;
fruit bounced off his chest and shoulders as the girls
made a stand near the haystack.

"No catapult can stop a knight's charge!" Huon
roared.

Ava dashed off around the corner of the stack, holding the skirts of her tunic up with both hands and giving
little mock screams, with Lioncel in close pursuit. Huon
caught Oriabelle around the waist and they collapsed
into the prickly-sweet embrace of the hay.

Huon sat bolt upright some time later, as he heard Lioncel's voice shout:

"Oh, sweet Jesu, *look at the sun!* The Grand Constable will *roast* us!"

He looked at the shadows and moaned himself; Her
Majesty wasn't as much of a dragon as Lady Death, but
you didn't want to slack off around her either. He darted
upright and helped Oriabelle as well. They walked hand-
in-hand back to the poolside willows, with Ava and Lioncel following; Huon was aware that he was smiling rather
foolishly, but he hoped it wasn't as simpleminded-looking
as the younger squire's expression.

And we're both walking tiptoe, he thought.

"Poor feet!" Oriabelle said. "Poor gentleman's feet!"

"We're late," Lioncel said tightly, as the two squires
rode the final downhill mile to Maryhill.

The last hot sliver of the sun was just sliding under the
horizon westward, silhouetting the mountain peaks, and
the sky was purpling above where it wasn't clouds tinged
crimson and yellow and cream-white. Huon crossed

himself as they passed Stonehenge and brought out his crucifix to kiss. The circle of standing blocks stood on a bench with a breathtaking view across the gorge and the river. This was supposed to be a duplicate of the first one in far-off fabled Britain, ancestral land of Arthur and so many of the ancient tales, where the King-Emperor of Greater Britain reigned from Winchester these days.

It had been built long ago, more than a lifetime before the Change. There were rumors of unhallowed pagan rites there; such things *did* happen, especially among peasants and Tinerants.

Maybe Oriabelle and Ava are witches! he thought with a pleasant shiver. *Hmmm. For that matter, the High King is a pagan. Of course he's not an Associate, he's a Mackenzie, and they're all witches.*

Lioncel crossed himself absently as he saw the other squire's gesture and the way he was looking. There was a rumor that Lady Delia was a witch on top of her other irregularities, but Huon didn't know whether that was true; she was pious enough in public. He didn't think Lioncel was one, though. He was probably just worried about the reaming they'd get if they were past the time they'd been given.

Rightly worried, Huon thought, drew a deep breath and went on as they rode cautiously onto the steep section of the downward slope:

"I'll accept full responsibility for delaying us," he said. Then, with a grin: "Do you regret it?"

"Ummm . . . no," Lioncel said frankly. "Not now I've found out what all the fuss was about!"

Huon grinned wider and nodded, as if from a vast well of amorous experience.

Absolutely no way am I going to admit I was a virgin too, pretty much. Nearly. I mean, technically you're supposed to be until you're married and my confessor is going to give me a penance that will keep me on my knees a while. But that's really more important for girls, gentlewomen at least.

Lioncel frowned: "But look, Huon, it was my idea as much as yours. I can't let them drop an anvil on you."

Huon shrugged. "Hey, actually it was the *girls'* idea, pretty much. But we can't say *that*, I mean, *sorry, a couple of peasant girls dragged us into a haymow and there was nothing we could do but oblige?*"

"No," Lioncel acknowledged ruefully. "It wouldn't be chivalrous to do that, anyway. Plus nobody would believe us. And it would be even worse if they *did*."

"And you're the one who noticed it was past time."

"Oh, I had to. It was a lot of fun, but by then I'd started thinking Ava was going to eat me alive!"

They both chuckled. Huon went on doggedly:

"I was in charge. I'm not looking forward to telling Her Majesty, damned right . . . we shouldn't *lie*, but maybe we can just sort of . . . fudge it? They'll be busy and it doesn't matter *why* we were late."

Lioncel winced. "Telling my lady the Grand Constable . . . You're right. No details. Though if either of them *asks*—Look, let's get it over with."

Maryhill was a little strip of irrigated gardens and orchards along the Columbia, lost in the immensity of tawny bluffs on either side that were falling into darkness with the onrushing night. A bridge of the ancient world spanned the width of the great river here, and from the very beginning PPA policy had been to secure those. A small but strong castle reared on a terrace just beyond the northern abutment, the banners flying from the peaks of its towers black against the sky-glow eastward. The air was very cool now, and the night would be chilly; it was coming up on All Hallow's Eve, after all, warmth increasingly a fleeting thing of sunny afternoons. The interior was hotter in the summer than the gentle lands west of the Cascades, but it was colder in winter too.

The curving line of the railway followed the river eastward; as they cantered down the steep road they could see the rear lantern of a train disappearing as its team of big mules hauled it west towards the High King's host. There were stone and concrete docks along the river, and more temporary wooden ones with a few sailing barges and two small fast galleys of unfamiliar style still tied up, with the black-and-silver flag of the Rangers flying from their masts, seven stars around a tree and a crow on top. A few days ago the whole area had been swarming with men and horses and piles of supplies. Now it was preparing to return to its usual somnolent existence, or something approaching it.

They turned onto the new-made road that led to the castle gate, the hooves of the four horses crunching on the pounded crushed rock that made up its surface. It was well-engineered, but not as smooth as the ancient world's asphalt; the only way to get that for a new road was to pry it up from an old one and re-melt it. Lantern-light came on in the slit windows of the round towers as they watched. The gates were still open, the drawbridge down and the portcullis up, but a squad of Protector's Guard footmen crossed spears before them as they reined in beneath the deep shadow of the wall.

"Who goes there?" the non-com in charge said, using the top edge of his shield to knock up his visor with a *clack* of metal on metal. "Advance and be recognized!"

"Esquires Huon Liu de Gervais, of the High Queen's household, and Lioncel de Stafford of Forest Grove, of the Grand Constable's *menie*," Huon said, obediently moving Dancer forward at a slow pace so that the lights would fall on his face. "Returning from a mission."

The man-at-arms in charge knew him; Huon blinked as the man raised a bull's-eye lantern and shone it on his face for a moment. You didn't take chances when you were at war with an enemy who liked assassinating leaders. Particularly with the CUT, who'd been known to do things to the minds of men.

"Pass, young masters," he said. "Your lieges arrived an hour ago; I expect they'll be in the Great Hall by now."

Huon and Lioncel looked at each other; it wasn't quite as bad as they'd expected, no dashing in after the tables had been removed and everyone glaring at them. They rode through into the courtyard of the outer bailey in an iron clatter of horseshoes on stone paving-blocks, handed their horses over to the grooms—not without a qualm on Huon's part, since he preferred to see to his mounts himself in a strange place—and then did a hasty wash in a watering trough and helped each other out of their armor. Nobody would expect them to look court-sleek, but Lioncel borrowed his comb.

"I gave mine to Ava for a keepsake," he said a little shyly.

"Chivalrous," Huon said approvingly. "Really marvelous girls, even if they were lowborn."

Then he laughed. When Lioncel looked a question at him, he went on:

"Back before lunch, I remember thinking how I wasn't the type to enter the Church. Now I'm *sure* I don't have a vocation!"

"Clerics sin too, they're human."

"Yes, but they're supposed to feel worse about it when they do!"

They dashed into the inner keep; all the castles they'd grown up with were basically similar, since nearly all were built to a set of standard designs, slightly modified to fit the site. Only a few of the greater ones had been worth more trouble, in the terrible years. The Great Hall here, where the garrison and staff and their families would eat most days, was built along one side of the court across from the chapel and castellan's quarters. Lamplight shone through the high pointed windows, but without the halo of moths that would have been present a few months ago. They slowed down to a quick walk, left hands on the hilts of their swords, trying to look briskly casual and not at all tardy.

"You're lucky we were delayed," Sir Rodard said.

He was a young knight of the Grand Constable's *menie*, standing by the doors in breastplate and tassets and fauds, half-armor. The squad of crossbowmen behind him were calmly alert, not expecting trouble but very ready for it.

"And that we got that message from Ogier. Good work, by the way. Come on in, make your devoir and get something to eat."

They nodded to the brown-haired knight and ducked into the hall. It was fairly well lit by high-placed gaslights, a barnlike structure of plain plastered concrete floored in basalt blocks, and full of the smells of the evening's inevitable stew and not-particularly-well-washed soldiers of the two households and the Protector's Guard. Nothing fancy at all; this was a Crown castle, designed simply for a garrison at a strategic spot rather than a resident lord or as a possible headquarters for the high command like Castle Goldendale. It didn't have any of the plundered artwork the Lady Regent's salvagers and their imitators had used to furnish the greater keeps, or the modern equivalents she'd sponsored. Logs crackled in a big, shallow hearth backed with slanted iron plates that threw the heat out into the room.

The two squires went and made their bows before the Grand Constable and the High Queen at the upper table on the dais, sweeping off their hats and bending a knee. The two leaders were deep in conversation with a cluster of scouts and officers as they ate, folded maps and documents amid the platters and bread-baskets and one propped up against a hunk of cheese with a knife in it.

Mathilda looked up, extending her hand for the kiss of homage.

"That was good work, Huon," she said, smiling. "And you too, Lioncel. Especially for junior squires. A knightly deed. I'd have hated for Ogier to die in a scuffle like that."

Lioncel flushed. "Sir Ogier would probably have handled it himself, Your Majesty," he said. "We just . . . reacted."

"It was the *right* reaction, both of you. That did you credit, and any honorable accomplishment of yours rebounds to the honor of your lieges."

Tiphaine d'Ath nodded. "Though from the time stamp on the heliograph message, you took your own sweet rambling way getting back. What were you two up to all afternoon?"

Lioncel froze, wide-eyed, and made a choking sound. Huon coughed and managed to say:

"Ah . . . this and that, my lady. The High Queen did say *sunset*, my lady, so we didn't push the horses."

D'Ath made a slight throat-clearing sound, looked at him for an instant with an unreadable expression, and then went back to the report and sketch map which had claimed the High Queen's attention. Lioncel mimed wiping his brow as they went over to the trestles where dinner was being handed out, barracks-style. They took big chipped plastic bowls from a stack; the cook ladled them full of the stew that steamed in a cauldron, and her helper stuck a spoon in each and stacked thick slices of bread and butter on top. They took their meal to the juniors' benches, signed themselves, murmured Grace and ate in contemplative silence for a while.

I've got a lot to think about.

The stew was better than usual this evening, with plenty of onion and garlic, dried tomatoes and chunks of potato as well as the inevitable beans and salt meat.

Or maybe it's just relief, Huon thought as he spooned it down. *What a day!*

They went back for seconds, and Huon had another mug of the raw red wine. As they turned in the empty bowls, he paused to extend a hand.

"You're all right, de Stafford," he said seriously. "I'm glad to have you at my back anytime."

The blond youngster flushed as they shook, meeting his eyes with a look as firm as the grip of his hand.

"You too, de Gervais. We're comrades now, brothers-in-arms who've stood side by side in battle!"

Rodard looked up as they passed on their way out, tired as the day caught up with them and eager for their bedrolls.

"Ah, Huon."

"Yes, Sir Rodard?"

The young man grinned, with a slight hint of a wink. "You're quick-witted, Gervais. But while you were *doing* 'this and that,' Mistress This and That bit you on the neck."

Lioncel choked again, and Huon clapped his hand to the sore spot behind his right ear.

"Boys will be men, it seems. There are worse ways to spend what may be the second-to-last day of your life. Go get some sleep. The High King's ordered the general reserve to close up behind the main force. The enemy are coming. It ends now."

CHAPTER FOUR

The High King's Host
Horse Heaven Hills
(Formerly south-central Washington)
High Kingdom of Montival
(Formerly western North America)
October 31st, Change Year 25/2023 AD

The High King of Montival drew rein, turning off the road past the time-wrecked and rust-gnawed length of an irrigation machine of the ancient world, all wheels and pipe at the foot of a low rough rise.

"Sooo, sooo, Dando," he said, stroking a gloved hand down the beast's neck; it was lively with good oats and alfalfa, mouthing the bit and stepping high and showing every sign of wanting to run. "Easy does it, lad. We've a long day before us, and more work tomorrow and the day after that."

The courser turned its head nervously at a harsh whicker from the remount herd following as the headquarters crew badgered them past and took the opportunity to let them roll and graze. Rudi's charger Epona was there, and she was never altogether easy seeing him riding another horse. Even her own get, much less some anonymous gelding she barely acknowledged as one of the horse-tribe at all. Moving this many strange horses together was always tricky, though at least few disputed Epona's claim to be lead mare of any group she was in . . . and she didn't tolerate sass from stallions, either.

One shied a little from her rolled eye and cocked hoof-ready hip even as he watched, probably wisely. He could see Edain Aylward grinning at the pale anxiety on the faces of the horse-handlers as he deployed a platoon of the High King's Archers off their bicycles and into a loose screening formation about Rudi; they all had high-geared mountain bike models and could keep up with horse-soldiers easily on this sort of terrain. Epona would tolerate the master-bowman . . . mostly . . . because he'd been Rudi's friend from earliest boyhood and because he knew better than to take liberties. Strange grooms were fair game, and she had never liked the human-kind in general much.

A platoon of Bearkiller mounted crossbowmen were sharing the guard duty today, grimly silent and business-like as they cantered about to check folds in the land for a couple of hundred yards in every direction. Catapults and aircraft aside, that was as far as bodyguards need worry.

"Epona's getting even more testy in her middle-age," Rudi said.

The jest hid real concern. She'd been all the way to the east coast with him, and he'd been worried for her the way she'd lost condition then; Epona had amazing endurance for a seventeen-hand warmblood, which was what her looks said of her breeding. But even so she wasn't an Arab, or a cow-pony used to living on grass and hard work. Coming back had been easier—big chunks of it through the Dominions where they'd been able to haul her on a horsecar on the rails—but the fact remained that she was nearing the end of her working life.

He remembered the look that had passed between them, all those years ago at Sutterdown Horse Fair; the boy he'd been, and the young mare who'd come to hate the human-kind while she was still a filly. A secret knowledge, a complicity between just the two of them . . .

And she'd never forgive me if I left her behind, he thought, casting a look at the sleek black figure that paced along with arched neck and flying mane. *She's not a horse you can turn out to pasture and bring an apple now and then. There have been times I doubted whether she was not Epona Herself. It wasn't an accident I named her for the Lady of the Horses.*

"I suspect we all will become less tolerant in our age," Father Ignatius, Knight-Brother of the Order of the Shield of St. Benedict said. "If the Lord blesses us with years, which is by no means certain. And being Lord Chancellor of an inchoate kingdom still in the womb . . ."

"Will age you before your time, eh, Father?"

Ignatius chuckled; apparently being away from the offices and documents suited him, and he bore the weight of his armor with casual unconcern.

"Not as much as being your chief of staff in an army also inchoate will age me, Your Majesty," he said dryly. "Bureaucratic tangles are easier to resolve when there isn't a battle going on at the same time, my son."

They both shared a chuckle at that, even more dry. Rudi cast his eyes sideways at the gaggle of staff officers, commanders from seven different realms of the High Kingdom and the allied but separate Dominion of Drumheller, messengers and clerks and map-drawers and everything else down to the people a half-mile back driving the wagons with the tents and supplies for the command party.

It does them good to see the high command cheerful, and no need whatsoever to tell them it's mostly gallows humor. I wish Mathilda were here, he thought. *She* will *be, come the fight. Tomorrow probably, or the day after possibly, depending on how eager the enemy are to strike. But the reserve is mostly Protectorate troops, and those Yakima regiments d'Ath had with her retreating from the Tri-Cities. She'll get them going better than anyone else I could appoint.*

"Tired of improvising, Your Majesty?" Ignatius asked.

The warrior-monk was a few years older than Rudi; a borderline Changeling, born before the Change but not old enough to really remember the ancient world. His knight's armor didn't disguise his slim build, and he was of only medium height—standing flat-footed his eyes were level with the High King's nose, and the tonsure that exposed the scalp in the middle of his bowl-cut black hair made him look older than his years. An expert would notice other things, though. Starting with the thickness of his wrists, and the ring of swordsman's callus all around the thumb and forefinger and web of his right hand.

Rudi had seen him fight often enough, on the Quest. More often than not against much bigger men, and the only time he'd seen the Shield-Brother pushed to his limits at anything like even odds was when they'd both taken on a High Seeker of the Church Universal and Triumphant in Des Moines, one of the magus-warriors the Prophet had set on their track. His mind was even more formidable. The slanted dark eyes were calm as he watched the army of the High Kingdom of Montival pouring past them up the road, the calm of a man who'd done every single thing he could and who was leaving the rest to his God.

"Tired of improvising? Tired of life, you mean?" Rudi replied after a long moment, and this time they *did* laugh, unforced merriment. "Not yet."

The roadway up from the Columbia was not much to start with and hadn't been repaired since the Change, not until he threw five thousand men and a group of Corvallan engineers at it a few days ago. It would hold while the portion of the host's men and supplies that had barged and sailed up the river or used the waterside rail line climbed up to the plateau. He'd picked it for the relatively low grades and for being as far east as he felt comfortable with given what he knew of where the enemy was. Hopefully the warning wasn't enough for them to react in time and catch his forces before they massed and deployed.

A glance upward showed the morning sun glinting off the wings and canopies of gliders, dozens of them turning in the thermals and updrafts along the river like a swarm of eagles as they kept guard. There wasn't much a glider could do to another of its kind; opening the canopy and firing a crossbow at a moving target was usually dangerous only to passersby below. But they could harass each other enough to make reconnaissance difficult, if the pilots had enough nerve to risk one near-collision after another, and his did.

Most of them were wild girls, each picked from dozens of volunteers for nerve and for being lightweight bundles of strong sinew and cat-quick reflex; a lot of them came from Associate families, demoiselles who weren't content to roll bandages or tally hard-tack, or from Mackenzies without the heft for the longbow and their like elsewhere. You didn't need as much weight of bone and muscle to fly a wind-riding machine as you did to carry a twelve-foot lance on a barded destrier in plate armor or pull the string of an eighty-pound yew stave past the ear over and over. Lightness was a positive advantage in a soaring sailplane, where every ounce might make the difference between *safely home* and *crash-landed behind enemy lines.*

A glance back southward showed little white curls on the blue mile-broad surface of the Columbia and a mass of barges and oared tugs around the landing points. Farther out, war-galleys with their masts down and lashed for action waited, most at anchor like sleeping river-pike. A dozen kept station, bows pointed into the current as the great varnished lengths of their sweeps flashed, rowing *a scaloccio* with six men to an oar. Water curled around them, a slow multiple synchronized *splash . . . splash . . . splash . . .* of foam on either side to complement the wave that curled forever around the dull enameled steel of their rams, beneath the brightly painted and carved figureheads. They were beating just fast enough to keep position against the current of the massive river, slowed as it was by the ancient dams that still made it as much a series of lakes as anything.

It all made him a little nostalgic for the campfires of the Quest, when it was simply him and nine friends against a hostile world.

"A pity we could not pick a place for battle where our river flank rested on a castle," Ignatius said a little wistfully. "They have more cavalry, but that would keep our right flank safe at least."

Rudi snorted. "Ah, that would be the comfort and consolation of the world, it would indeed. If only the enemy were such utter and complete fools as to fight at a place so certain to give us the victory."

"A point, Your Majesty. Still, the number of castles on the Columbia limits them in the ground that *isn't* so covered, to our great advantage. If they will fight at all, and not wait and try to force us to come to them."

"They must fight," Rudi said, grimly satisfied for a moment; he'd worked hard to put them on the horns of that dilemma. "It's too late in the year for them to do anything but accept battle or withdraw until spring . . . and half their forces come from deep in the Rockies or farther yet, past passes the snow has closed already, or will within days."

He closed his eyes and laid his hand on the pommel of the Sword of the Lady. Energies swelled and swept across the surface of the world; the Sun kissed Earth, and moisture rose from the Mother Ocean, sweeping in curling patterns that crashed against mountains in a slow violence that would grind stone to meal over aeons as more welled up from the world's warm beating heart . . .

"Yes, the snow will be deep this year. Far to the east, far into the Bitterroots, and blizzards on the High Line as well. Which means . . ."

It was a little like the sensation you had playing a five-pound trout on a light line. Months of time and many lives had gone into the intricate balance. He blinked, for a moment lost in calculations of time and force and space, like a game of chess but one where all the pieces had minds and wills of their own, and more than half were hidden. He went on:

"I *think* they'll accept battle a little east of here."

"With the lower Yakima to their backs? And the water rising with autumn?"

"Ah, but they don't expect to lose, you see, and it's not so very close to their backs, though close enough if things go as I hope . . . No castle, to be sure, but the bank of the Columbia there's much steeper; that will have to be advantage enough. So long as we don't dally and let them get around our left before we're deployed, of course. I need to know where the bulk of their horse-archers went, and soon. Too mobile by half, they are, and with plenty of room to work. I fear the commanders on the other side have heard of Manzikert as well as I."

A rumbling went through the ground. He looked up. Batteries of field-pieces were going past up the slope, twelve-pounders pulled by six big horses each, the crews walking beside and ready to jump in to pull brake levers.

The machines themselves were stubby things on a pair of spoked five-foot steel wheels, a ton-weight each and the heaviest weapons commonly taken along with a marching army. The metal frames showed the ranked coil springs within, taken from the suspensions of heavy trucks and ready to resist when the curved throwing arms were racked back against them. The troughs for the roundshot that were their most common load jutted forward through the angled steel shields that protected the crews in battle; behind them the trails were clamped together, resting on the wheeled limbers that carried the ready ammunition and the pumps and armored cable for the hydraulic bottle-jacks.

Most of this set had the Lidless Eye on the shields, sometimes freshly joined by the Crowned Mountain and Sword of Montival, and the crews tramping along were in half-armor with glaives over their shoulders. They were part of the standing army of the Protectorate, but mostly men from cities and towns rather than the rural manors and fiefs that supplied men-at-arms and infantry to the PPA forces. The officer at the head in three-quarter armor rode competently enough, but not like a knight, and he didn't have the golden spurs on his heels either. Instead a banner beside him hanging from a staff showed a blue-mantled woman crowned with stars, a babe cradled in her arms.

The Virgin Mary, Rudi thought. *The Crown City of Portland's patron. Not a Goddess, no, perish the thought! She's just what you'd expect to see with Jehovah of the Thunders . . .*

The amusement died as he glanced aside at Ignatius; for just an instant the cleric's usual shrewd, reserved gaze was unguarded, and filled with an utter love.

Rudi smiled and thumped his armored shoulder. Christians could be annoying at times, and Ignatius was swordblade-certain in his faith, but it was a large part of what made him a blessing as a comrade in arms, and an unshakeable pillar of a new and still unsteady throne. This was a man you could trust to do any task with all his very considerable talents, and who you could trust at your back without a second's doubt.

As he will be for my children after me, he thought. *Absolutely honest men who are also capable are not so common. Not teasing him is an exceedingly small price to pay.*

"To battle then, Knight of the Immaculata," he said gently. "*Miles* of Christ."

He looked northward. A form was swelling there, another glider, slender wings flexing as it stooped towards the road and the command party. Two of the flock circling the landing-place on the river peeled off to examine it, then wagged their wings to show it had passed their scrutiny.

Edain's head was already pointing in that direction; he raised binoculars, then barked an order and the High King's Archers took stance, readying to shoot, just in case, and despite the sigil of Benny the Beaver that marked the aircraft as one in the city-state of Corvallis' armed forces. Edain reached over his shoulder for an arrow, then drew his great yew longbow and shot nearly directly upward. It was a warning shot, with two bright red ribbons tied behind the arrowhead to say *sheer off*. Even so it soared a hundred yards into the air before it turned and plummeted back, striking a rock and snapping.

"Sure, and it's a waste of a perfectly good arrow," Rudi could hear his follower grumble.

He didn't turn, though, and another shaft was resting through the cutout of the bow long before the first came down; this one a plain businesslike bodkin. A glider was seldom a threat to a single man on the ground; it wasn't as if the fabled explosives of the ancient world were available, after all, and if you were free to run you could generally dodge a single canister of the napalm that was the most deadly alternative natural law allowed in the Changed World. But Edain Aylward Mackenzie was not one to take a chance with his charge when he didn't have to.

The glider waggled its wings in acknowledgment, banked, stooped again. This time it was a hundred yards away when it pulled up. Something shot downward, trailing ribbons of its own, thin ones in a rainbow of colors meant to make the passage through the air obvious and the tube easy to find on the ground. A finned metal dart the length of a small man's forearm went *chunk* into the rocky volcanic soil. The glider dove downslope and started to rise in a widening gyre, building altitude for the return to its launching point farther north.

An archer pulled the message-cylinder free and examined it as Rudi and Ignatius dismounted; only after Edain had checked it over himself and opened it briefly did he reseal it and hand it on to the Lord Chancellor.

The monk's strong hands unscrewed the aluminum tube. He unrolled the paper within.

"Dúnedain Code A7-b," he said. "Do you need a decryption, Your Majesty?"

That was a formality, to the bearer of the Sword of the Lady. Rudi took the thick paper and spread it out.

"That's where most of their horse are, at least," he said with satisfaction as he read the report collated from dozens of scouts. "Good work! To the northeast of Prosser, or what's left of it; they burned the town last year."

"How many?" Ignatius said.

Numbers were the bread and butter of war at the command level. Or at least the hard-tack and beans and jerky.

"Hmmm. Twenty-five thousand at least, plus the re-mount herd—I wish them joy of feeding that many horses in country this dry and at the tail-end of the year, even if they're cow-ponies for the most part. All light cavalry, though, no sign of the Sword of the Prophet that they could see."

"They're using the rancher levies to cloak the point of the spear." Ignatius nodded. "The part of the Sword they brought west is ten thousand men . . . less a few thousand, probably, given their losses in this campaign to date and other needs. Add in twenty-five to thirty thousand light horse and that's the bulk of the CUT's forces in this theatre."

"Plus their foot, another ten thousand or so that they haven't left for sieges or line-of-communications work. Spearmen, but fairly good ones. Now, that leaves the question of where Boise's main thrust will be, their heavy infantry. Logically south, to form the hinge on which the CUT's army pivots fast . . . but I can't just assume it . . ."

Decision firmed. "Couriers and encryption team!" he said, raising his voice a little.

A trio dashed over from the headquarters group, Portlanders in half-armor. Sandra had always loved codes and worked hard on her messenger service, and the Protectorate's espionage and counterespionage were second to none.

"To: Her Majesty; enclosed is Dúnedain scout report north flank our position. I expect to engage the enemy main force in Prosser area within forty-eight hours maximum, probably sooner. Move general reserve forward under Grand Constable; follow yourself when deployed, as per previous."

He bared his teeth for an instant. That committed him . . . but leaving your reserve too far back was as much a mistake as throwing it into the fray at the beginning.

The cryptographer's fingers danced, and the paper was finished, copied and sealed. The message itself was a solid mass of letters and numbers; decoding it by sheer brute-force mathematics wasn't impossible . . . but you needed big calculating machines, and even so it would take *time*, by which time it would be stale news.

For that matter, the Church Universal and Triumphant hated such machinery with a bitter passion; their official theology called the Change the judgment of the Ascended Masters on humankind for using too much of it. Boise had been more liberal in the old General's day, but his son was the Prophet's puppet now. Or the puppet of the force that controlled them both . . .

"Surface courier to the High Queen's field HQ at Goldendale via Maryhill," Rudi said.

No need to risk the heliograph net or a glider that might not make it that far.

"And another: Dúnedain code. To: Lord Alleyne, *hîr Dúnedain*. I direct high-priority reconnaissance for—"

This went a little more slowly; the message was not only to be encoded, but in Sindarin to begin with, which meant he had to spell it rather than speaking. The enemy *probably* had at least a few who could puzzle the language out with a set of the *Histories* to hand, but equally probably didn't have anyone who could really *speak* it, particularly the way the tongue had developed among the Rangers over the past generation. Combining that difficulty with the randomizing code ought to make it unbreakable in any time that mattered.

"Or perhaps Sethaz or his High Seekers could read it," Ignatius murmured, as the team cleared and packed their equipment.

Rudi nodded; if you'd spent two years of travel and battle and sickness and wounds and the death of friends and final triumph with a man, and him keen-witted, it was no great surprise when he followed your thought. The enemy was strong, strong, and they both knew it.

"Or perhaps not," he said. "The raw power is there, yes, but—" he touched the hilt of the Sword "—not the . . . the *affinity*, would you say? The Powers behind the CUT hate the very touch of us, including the ones they use and possess, because they hate the universe of matter itself. Contact with us is like wading in a sewer to them, or cramming yourself into the mind and body of a maggot. You've seen how their touch destroys. Those Ones who gave me the Sword tried very hard indeed not to tear asunder the fabric of things by doing so; *my* fabric in particular, for which I'm grateful. The others don't have that, mmmm, subtlety of touch."

Ignatius nodded. "A point indeed. Diabolism is its own infinite punishment."

The leather-clad couriers on their fast light horses took the messages and sprang into motion. They galloped along the edge of the now crowded road. A battalion from the confederation called Degania Dalet was coming up it now, ranked pikes alternating with recurve bows, singing something in a guttural minor key to flutes and some stringed instrument.

And before the Sword came to me, I'd have just said it had a fine stormy roll for a marching song to make the miles go by, he thought. *Now . . .*

> *. . . as drops of blood in our veins*
> *Flow with heart's beat*
> *Upon the graves of our fathers*
> *Dewdrops still fall . . .*

He could not only understand the words; he could feel the ache of millennial sadness in them and the fierce determination beneath. He bowed his head a little with fist to chest in salute as the blue-and-white banner in the lead dipped to him, and called:

"Am Yisrael Hai!"

They broke off to give a baying cheer of *Artos! Artos!* to the counterpart of the ram's-horn *shofars* in reply, then took up the song again as they passed; that league of villages was tightly organized for war and peace both, but not a large nation, even by today's standards. Then came more supply wagons, big Conestoga-style vehicles loaded with tinned meat and dried beans and hard-tack, and then . . .

"And I recognize that, sure and I do," he said, grinning.

The droning squeal of bagpipes came first, and then the rattling boom of Lambeg drums. Then a chorus of voices, thousands strong, a deep, rhythmic male chorus with women's higher notes weaving a descant through it. The complex measure was carried effortlessly, the mark of a people for whom music was part of who they were and every gathering a choir:

As the sun bleeds through the murk
'tis the last day we shall work
For the Veil is thin and the spirit wild
And the Crone is carrying Harvest's child!

"Your compatriots, Your Majesty," Ignatius said, smiling. "And a song of the season."

He'd spent a good deal of time in the Clan's territories before the Quest, and made friends there despite his faith. And despite not being of the Old Religion . . .

Despite being cowan, as most of us would say, Rudi thought.

. . . Ignatius didn't find their ways alarming. Rudi had rarely met a cowan who didn't find that this particular tune made them uneasy, but the monk was apparently one of them.

Samhain!
Turn away
Run ye back to the light of day
Samhain!
Hope and pray
All ye meet are the gentle fae.

The bagpipers marched with the drones of the instruments bristling over their shoulders. The archers behind were all pushing their bicycles up the slope—modern models, with solid tires of salvaged rubber. Their bows and quivers and knocked-down swine-feathers showed over their backs, fastened to the rings and loops in the green leather surface of the brigantine jacks; most had their bonnets on and the helmets hung from their sword belts as well, and a swinging rattle went by beneath the music. More gear was slung around the cycles, which was part of the reason for using them, that and the fact that you could cover about four times as much ground per day as on foot and keep it up longer than a horse could.

The slope was easy enough to let the Clan's warriors sing, a tune with a haunting dying fall in it:

Burn the fields and dry the corn
Feel the breath of winter born
Stow the grain 'gainst season's flood
Spill the last of the livestock's blood
Samhain!
Turn away
Run ye back to the light of day

Samhain!
Hope and pray
All ye meet are the gentle fae.

Riding at the front of the Mackenzie host was its
First Armsman, Oak Barstow Mackenzie, a big man in
his thirties with his yellow hair in a queue down his
back, wrapped in an old bowstring in the Clan fashion.
He raised a hand in salute, touching the tuft of wolf-fur
in the clasp of his bonnet. Spears jutted up from here
and there in the ranks, bearing the sigils of Duns and
the outlines of the sept totems—wolf and bear, raven
and elk, dragon and fox and more.

Let the feasting now begin
Careful who you welcome in!
The table's set with a stranger's place
Don't stare openly at his face—
Samhain!
Turn away
Run ye back to the light of day
Samhain!
Hope and pray
All ye meet are the gentle fae.

The Mackenzies didn't stop to cheer, though many
flourished their weapons. The Clan wasn't much for
military formality beyond what was necessary to the
task; Bearkiller snap and polish had always struck them
as mildly ridiculous, and the ostentatious chivalric pag-
eant of the Association was something they usually
mocked. But too many of them knew him personally, at

least a man or woman from each Dun, and all of them had too much pride to break stride before the High King who was the son of their Chief.

And Samhain was close; the feast for the dead and the ancestors, when their spirits and the beings of the Otherworld both walked, and were invited in for good or ill:

Stranger, do you have a name?
Tell us all from whence you came!
You seem more like God than man—
Has curse or blessing come to this Clan?

"They wait for you to lead them to battle, Your Majesty," Ignatius said. "It's a heavy burden."

"*There go my people,*" Rudi said, quoting a favorite saying of his mother's. "*I must hurry to get ahead of them, for I am their leader.*"

They mounted their horses, waiting for a break in the road traffic.

"Yet leadership has something else to it," Ignatius said. "To be a true King is to be touched by something beyond the human. By the finger of God, as David was when he danced before the Tabernacle of the Lord."

"Beyond, beneath, and yet always kin to it," Rudi said softly. "For the lord and the land and the folk are *one*. I may lead them to battle, and the chroniclers may record this or that stroke as mine . . . yet how much of that is illusion? Such a mighty thing, a battle like this; so many tens of thousands, such courage and fear, rage and desperate cunning, the wills of so many—each of them with a world within their skull, just as I do. It's not my story any more than it is theirs."

Samhain!
Turn away
Run ye back to the light of day
Samhain!
Hope and pray
All ye meet are the gentle fae.

"Where?" he murmured to himself. "I must know *where*."

CHAPTER FIVE

Mary Vogeler winked at her twin sister as they settled side by side into the steep upward slope, a vastness of moon-washed rock and sage and occasional scrub conifer. There was just enough of the light of stars and full moon to make the gesture visible at arm's length, and to see the way Ritva's answering grin moved her face under the gauze half-mask that covered the front of her hood.

Behind the Ranger scout party the broad slow Columbia was palely luminescent, and deep shadow lay in the gullies that ran south from the hills towards the riverbank. Chill desert air bit as she drew it in slowly through her nose, not as dry as it would be in other seasons and with a little of the creosote scent of sagebrush and the volcanic dirt in which she lay.

And the wool and leather of her clothing and gear, which had the fusty-sweaty-old-socks odor that was unavoidable in the field.

I've been on the move for years now, since the Quest be-

*gan and a lot of the time before. You know, I would really
like to spend a while living in places with baths and roofs
and windows and fresh underwear, and beds with linen
sheets and decent kitchens. Where answering a call doesn't
mean going behind a bush with some leaves in one hand
and a spade in the other and then you itch. Preferably a
place where nobody was trying to kill me, too, but that may
be asking for a little much. I'm not eighteen anymore. I've
got a man of my own, it's time to have a home and some
kids.*

There was time for thought, as long as she didn't lose
focus. They weren't going to be moving for a few minutes. You took this sort of thing slow, slow and steady,
and you tried to *think* yourself inconspicuous as well as
hiding physically. Both the Havel twins were good at
that . . .

*Thêl vell! Since I have to do this, it's good to be on an
operation with Sis again,* she thought. *Though I miss Ingolf something fierce. Granted it's the best use of our skill-
sets to have him with that regiment of his and me here, but
dammit he makes me feel better. The Quest was . . . well,
not easy, all the running and fighting and getting cut up
and scared silly and so forth . . . but at least it was all
personal. This war is too big. I feel like one spindle in a
Corvallis linen mill.*

Since Mary's left eye was missing and covered with a
soft black eyepatch, that wink had left her blind for an
instant. Before she'd lost the eye to a Cutter High
Seeker on the Quest she and Ritva had been so identical
that one of their favorite pranks as children had been
impersonating each other.

I lost the eye. On the other hand, when we threw for

Ingolf a little before that I won and that was a big score. Call us even.

She didn't count the fact that Ritva had saved her life in the fight with the Seeker; they'd been saving each other's lives since their mid-teens, not long after they left Larsdalen and decided to become Rangers rather than Bearkillers.

Because Mom was getting just fucking impossible. I love her and Mike Jr. too, but I'd have ended up hating them both the way she treated him like Dad's reincarnation-in-training. Though it doesn't help that he looks so much like Dad. And he's not High King, Rudi is. Learn to live with it, Mom! The Music-of-Eru Powers chose him! In his cradle, complete with signs, wonders, portents and everything but a certified letter on parchment with a red wax seal! So Mike's not going to be High King, so what? He's going to be Bear Lord of the Outfit, not the third-class cook on a riverboat. If you love Mike that much, you should be glad he's not saddled with the throne; Juniper envies the hell out of you for exactly that reason. Mike may live to see his grandchildren. Poor Rudi, he's not only a fated hero but he has to spend most of his time listening to reports and having meetings since he became High King. It must be Angband on stilts.

She tried to imagine an epic about *being* High King, rather than *becoming* High King.

Ú! she thought. *You'd have to . . . oh, concentrate on his companions or something. And skip a lot of the meetings and reports.*

Waiting stretched. The Dúnedain weren't many, only a troop of thirty and the crews with the boats. There was no doing this by anything but stealth; not by force, and not by the speed that would make them obvious. Wait for the signal, not tense but loose. Tension traveled, it *smelled*.

A very soft chittering sounded. She rose into a low crouch and moved forward, elf-boots silent even on the rough basalt, keeping the edges of her war-cloak gathered up with a tuck of her fingers on either side. If she tripped over it she'd never hear the last of it from the other Rangers.

Well, never until the enemy killed us, she qualified mentally as she sank down behind another rock.

And then for a long, long time in the Halls of Mandos. Aunt Astrid would . . . I can't imagine what she'd do if I came early because of a screwup. Tell me how much better they did things in the old days in Eriador, I suppose. She was my liege-lady and kinswoman and a great leader but . . . a bit obsessive-compulsive sometimes.

It was impossible to think of the *Hiril Dúnedain* as really, truly dead; she'd been a part of Mary's life since she was born, as her mother's younger sister, and she'd been the re-founder of the Rangers here in the Fifth Age, together with her *anamchara* Eilir Mackenzie. Their liege-lady since the twins moved to Mithrilwood.

It was especially hard to believe her gone when all you'd heard was the tale of it and all you'd seen was the urn with the ashes—she'd been mortally wounded in Boise on the clandestine mission that rescued Fred Thurston's mother and sisters and sort of by accident his sister-in-law, who'd been desperate to get herself and her son away from Fred's brother Martin, the parricide and tyrant.

The murder and usurpation hadn't bothered Juliet

Thurston since it made her a ruler's consort and her son the heir, but the way he'd become enslaved to the Church Universal and Triumphant *had*. Mary was almost sympathetic; she remembered the High Seeker's eyes, windows into nothing. Waking up with something like *that* on your pillow . . .

Almost *sympathetic, not* really *sympathetic. But Aunt Astrid is dead and she died saving that worthless bitch's life. Well, the bitch and her son, who's just a little kid. And Ritva was there . . . I'm glad one of us was. They'll be someone can tell the story to* our *children.*

Wryly, with a smile that combined sorrow and humor:

Aunt Astrid will be even more powerful as a legend than she was as Lady of the Rangers. And Uncle Alleyne is taking it . . . well, he's perfectly functional. In wartime, that's all you can really ask. Afterwards he'll have Diorn and Fimalen and Hinluin. Children take you out of yourself.

They completed the next leapfrog maneuver. Everyone's equipment was silenced—no sounds of metal on metal, no creak of leather, no rattle of arrow on arrow in the quivers, swords worn slantwise across the back rather than at the belt, and the dark green and mottled gray of the Ranger garb blended into the late night better than black would have done. The sound of a score of her people settling into their new positions was less than the scuff of a glove on stone.

The cloth mask of the hood left a strip across her eyes bare, with a screen of gauze pinned up for nighttime; she let her eye travel with a slow methodical scan. Watching for movement. Watching for *patterns*, the outlines that would mean a man hiding, that you didn't need to see as much as sense. Not the narrow focus that excluded everything but a target, instead the wide-open acceptance that took in all your surroundings as a network connected each thing to the next. Yourself a part of it, sensitive to the slightest tug on the web.

Nothing. A desert mouse hopped by, squeaking faintly and making a prodigious sideways leap as it realized a human was six inches away; Mary grinned behind her mask at its expression of bulge-eyed terror. It fled even faster as something half-visible ghosted through the air above, the wilderness going on about its own life heedless of the humankind. The night was intensely still but the stars were dimming with high thin cloud coming in from the west, the tail end of fall storms hitting the Cascades and spilling into the interior . . .

She chittered. The faintest of passing shadows as the team behind hers moved forward and upward. Again, and again; not mechanical, but a subtle dance with every slightest fold of the land, each loose rock and clod of earth and miniature gully washed by the recent fall rains, testing each foothold and handhold before committing to it.

The final leapfrog left her, Ritva, and Uncle Alleyne at the head of the sparsely-dotted column that now snaked up from the river to the plateau above. She inclined her head to see faint shadows cast by irregularities in the ground that didn't fit the landscape, then crouched and ran her fingers over the ground to take in details that even an expert couldn't see when it was this dark and in the distorting moonlight.

All shod horses, she battle-signed, when the other two came close enough to see the broad movements. *Some of it very fresh. Enemy cavalry sweeping the area, repeatedly, in the last few hours.* Lots *of enemy cavalry. And all shod . . . Boise regulars.*

They both made gestures that meant: *I spotted that too.*

They settled in, picking blinds that would work as well in daylight if they had to stay that long and tenting their war-cloaks out around them. She dug a rock out of her position and set it carefully where it wouldn't draw notice; even with a Ranger tunic on—light mesh-mail between two layers of thin soft leather—a pointed stone digging into your belly button for hours at a time could get old. The lighter beaten dirt of the road to the north of their position glimmered like a silver ribbon through the heath, with nothing else but the rusted, tattered snags of a pre-Change building of sheet metal half-buried in dust and brush beyond it to say this wasn't somewhere east of Rhûn a couple of Ages of the World ago.

Like the Paths of the Dead, she thought with a slight shiver; it was that season. *Come on, now, Ranger, control your imagination.*

Once they were certain there weren't any enemy observing them, there was a brief clipping of vegetation and rubbing of soil to make the cloaks perfect matches for the locality. She stifled a sneeze at the spicy scent of cut sagebrush. Then they took position and waited; Dúnedain got a lot of practice at that, and the Quest had driven it home. Mary sucked on a hard candy to keep her energy level up, worked her muscles against each other on her bones to keep from stiffening in the cold and at long intervals took tiny sips from a flexible tube that ran to a flat bladder on her back.

Euuuu.

It tasted horrible, flat and rubbery. Also she didn't want to drink too much, because eventually you had to get rid of it. Peeing yourself was an occupational hazard sometimes, you couldn't be fastidious when things were serious, but the smell could give you away to an alert scout close-by.

Speak of Morgoth and He appears, she thought, an hour later.

She controlled her breathing to damp down the spurt of tension. It was still some time to dawn, and dense-dark now that clouds had covered most of the sky. The sound came first, shod hooves thumping dirt; she could feel it through her belly and breasts where they pressed against the soil. From here you could see the dirt road running east and west and then the dark shapes of riders spread out in a long line, with the odd lantern they were using more to keep alignment than for light.

The cavalry patrol were taking their time and picking their way forward slowly. They were Boise cavalry from their gear, horse-archers with sabers at their belts, but a number of them had light lances as well. They were using them to prod at the odd suspicious spot, little gleams of dull silver in the night.

Too professional for comfort, Mary thought.

With a practiced effort of will she pushed aside the visceral knowledge of how much steel slicing your flesh *hurt* when it happened. That was just her body's memory reminding her how she'd acquired so many scars at a still-young age. If they got that close, wounds would be the least of her problems. The Dúnedain were superb fighters at their skulk-and-snap style of war, but they didn't have any disguised Maiar with long beards or shining elf-lords with magic swords to even up impossible odds right now.

Though my big brother does *have a magic sword, genuine article, so maybe someday . . . Hmmm. They're combing their line of march over and over and not just going through the motions either. Old General Lawrence Thurston did his job well.*

One of the horsemen passed within ten yards of her blind; he must nearly be on top of Uncle Alleyne. He stood in his stirrups to look southward, down the slope towards the Columbia; the river would be a glowing ribbon from here, catching what starlight and moonlight there was. This one was in a centurion's cross-crested helmet rather than cavalry gear, some battalion or brigade commander who wanted to check for himself and not just take a report.

"Goddammit, something doesn't feel right," she heard him say. Then, much more quietly: "Goddamn this war."

He shook his head wordlessly and neck-reined his horse aside, then turned and cantered back east with a purposeful air.

Mary let her breath out slowly. Most of the cavalry went on; several platoons' worth stayed and screened the road and the flat land on either side. More time crawled past, and then a different sound came through the earth. A thudding like the world's biggest horse, only each beat was somehow a little blurred. Then she saw glints of light, regularly spaced and moving at about walking pace; someone was using shuttered lanterns as guides. Then starlight glinting on metal to the eastward, and the noise increased, with rhythmic clattering and clunking sounds underneath it and the peculiar rumbling of six-horse teams drawing heavy weights on steel wheels over rutted country roads.

Field artillery and ambulances on the road, she thought. *Light baggage wagons too, spare weapons and medical supplies and maybe some packaged field rations. Enough for a day or two.*

The vehicles were blurs, but she could pick up the outlines; off to either side the spaced-out lights became men with bull's-eye lanterns, each marking march routes through the empty rolling fields.

Infantry to either side in the open country, marching in battalion columns every hundred yards for as far as I can see. Probably the same thing on that road north of this. Valar and Maiar, but they've got good march discipline, to do this in the dark without everything tying up in a mess!

That was dry textbook stuff; the books that Uncle Alleyne and John Hordle had made part of the Dúnedain curriculum said pushing a big army down a single road or a few roads was like trying to pour the Columbia through a straw. It would take forever and the men at the end would still be breaking camp when the ones at the head got where they were going. The books had a lot of complex rock-paper-scissors stuff about how you couldn't fight while you were in column of march, but if you deployed to fight you couldn't march well . . .

Theory. Reality was the dull bronze gleam of the eagle standards, and the blackness below that was the heavy silk banners with the Stars and Stripes stirring slightly in the night as the standard-bearers carried them forward, the tanned masks of wolves on their helms and the hides flowing down their backs. It was rank on rank of pila-points moving in unison behind, the heavy javelins swaying over each man's right shoulder to match the big oval shield on the left as their hoop armor clattered and the apron of metal-bound leather thongs that guarded their groins rattled. It was hobnailed boots hitting the dry soil and thin grass of the arid plain like the feet of so many giant centipedes. It was the massed smell of leather and male sweat and oiled metal and dirt ground open to the air, the scent of war drifting through the cold dampness.

Slowly, slowly she raised the night-glass monocular to her eye and details sprang close; the tight intent face of a centurion, the stolid endurance of the rankers pushing through the darkness and a man's head tossing as he tripped a little on some rock or pocket and recovered without even cursing . . .

Mary felt a furious bubble of anger beneath her breastbone. Lawrence Thurston had created this awesome *thing*, this mighty instrument of human will and effort and devotion, courage and discipline, for a purpose. It had been a thoroughly demented purpose—the United States had perished in the moment when the wave of Change flickered around the planet and trying to restore it was like trying to make rivers flow backward—but that had been a noble madness. A faithfulness and steely honor that had refused to bend its oath-given word even at the death of a world. She had met the man: she knew.

His traitor son Martin was *wasting* it, stealing it for mere ambition; or at least he had planned to do that, before he'd fallen into a trap more subtle and more cruel than anything he could have imagined himself. Which meant he'd put it in the service of the enemies not simply of humankind, but of *existence* itself.

All the while her mind was counting the movement that turned the darkened plain into a rippling carpet, a skill so automatic that it was like the breath in her lungs. The answer it presented made no sense, which was like having your eyes tell you that down was up. Then she counted again, and this time she used the tricks consciously, counting the men in an area, estimating how many multiples . . .

That's twenty or thirty thousand men. That I can see in this fucking cloudy night. There must be nearly as many again out of sight! Dulu! Help! Manwë, Varda, Mother!

The only time she'd seen more human beings in one spot was in Iowa, looking down from the city wall on Des Moines . . . and Des Moines was a monster, the biggest inhabited city left in all the millions of square miles from Panama to Hudson's Bay. Seeing an *army* this size made her swallow, even after watching the host of Montival forming up for the past couple of months. War wasn't particularly complex, but it certainly was *hard*.

The march seemed endless, though she knew from the stars that it lasted hours rather than the days she felt. She spent her time identifying unit banners so that the High King's staff could fit them into their appreciation of the enemy's TOE. At last it was past them; heading towards the west, towards the heart of Montival, towards the host of the High King, towards . . .

My handfasted husband, my family, my friends, and everything I hold dear, she thought. *The forests where my children not yet born will walk. Well, we knew they were coming. Now we know how many of what, where, and when.*

The stars wheeled on through gaps in the clouds. Those closed, and a light rain began to fall, cutting visibility to nearly nothing by the time the infantry had passed and the cavalry followed; trickles of cold wet soaked into the front of her clothes where she lay in the blind, but there didn't seem to be any more patrols. Even *this* enemy didn't have enough men to put them everywhere they might be useful without dispersing effort fatally; war was a matter of prioritizing, and sometimes that rose up and bit you on the ass even if you did everything right.

Another chittering from Alleyne and they rose cautiously, moving together in the drizzle. The war-cloaks had the added merit of being rain-repellant, since the base layer was woven tightly of greased wool. They crouched in a triangle, close enough together that the brims of the hoods met.

"Compare figures," Alleyne said. "Ritva first."

His voice was dry, but not as numb as it had been a while ago. Work helped grief.

"*Nelc-a-meneg, hîr nín,*" she said crisply.

"Thirty thousand, my lord," Mary agreed. "But perhaps as many as forty thousand or more, if the road north of this is being used on the same scale. Catapults in proportion to infantry, according to the Boise scales. That would be the full reserve the US of Boise has in this theatre, though they'd have to strip their lines of communication to do it."

"Good analysis," he said, and wrote quickly on a pad. "They're not trying to hedge their bets, which is precisely the right thing to do from their point of view."

Another figure loomed out of the mist-like rain at his low-voiced call.

"Hírvegil. Relay this. The Folk of the West need this information. Tell Lord Hordle and Lady Eilir that they're to send the first boat on with it. Maximum priority. They're to follow with the second if we don't rejoin within an hour. The third to wait for us until the morrow."

He handed over the message. Hírvegil disappeared, quiet as a ghost, and the paper went with him.

Ritva's right about Uncle Alleyne, Mary thought. *About what she sensed at Aunt Astrid's funeral pyre.*

They were speaking Edhellen, of course, but there had been a subtle shift in the way the Lord of the Rangers used it; not as those raised to it as a cradle-speech did, but also less like a running translation from the English he'd used for his first twenty-odd years. More in the manner of the Histories, or the way his wife had taken the Noble Tongue.

He's going to live her dream for her and do it perfectly. That's his grave-offering.

Uncle Alleyne was very much Sir Nigel Loring's son, so reserved and self-controlled that if you didn't know him well you could think he wasn't a man of strong passions at all. But Mary knew him very well indeed.

The rain built from a drizzle to pouring for a few moments, a hiss that cut hearing in a burr of white noise. The horse was almost on them before they heard it.

"One up," Alleyne said calmly. "Two down and then in."

The two young women took a dozen rapid paces away, fanning out on either side of the approaching rider, and sank down as they gathered in their warcloaks. It was amazing how much like a rock you could look in the dark. A man on horseback appeared out of the wet blackness, muffled in his own cloak against the rain and swearing under his breath.

"Goddammit, it just doesn't *feel* right," she could hear him say in the peculiar tone you used talking to yourself when you were all alone and the rather harsh accent of the far interior. "We're missing something and I don't know what."

Not a cavalryman, though he rode with a careless ease peculiar to those raised on horseback; there was a traverse red crest on his helmet, and in his free hand was a swagger stick, a vinestock about three feet long, gnarled and twisted. A big oval shield was slung over his back, and she could just make out the brass thunderbolts-and-eagle on it.

US of Boise officer, she knew. *Maybe the one I saw earlier. Some conscientious type working a hunch. Too bad for him.*

Alleyne stood and reached over his shoulder to draw his longsword, the steel a bright streak in the rainy dimness; if someone was going to see you anyway, you controlled how they did it. That way you held their eyes. To an experienced man, the way he set himself and held the

blade and the way his left hand stripped his round buckler off its clip on his belt *would* hold the attention. They
all marked someone you didn't turn your back on if you
wanted to live.

The Boisean flipped the vinestock to his left hand and
drew his own short gladius with smooth speed; he
didn't shout for help, which meant he really *had* come
alone. Alleyne was probably smiling behind the cloth
mask as the Boisean raised his sword for a moment in
salute and then prepared to charge. He and his father
had both been soldiers before they came to Montival-
to-be, but of a particular sort—SAS, it had been called
before the Change and still was, over there in the Em-
pire of Greater Britain. So had Sam Aylward been.
They'd taught the Clan and the Rangers still more.

"*Take him down,*" he said in a conversational tone.

Mary and Ritva moved in like the chucks of a drill-bit
tightening, Ritva moving a fractional second first to
draw the man's eye. The Boisean shouted and cut to his
right, leaning over to reach with the short sword.

Mary leapt, her long legs taking her to the horse's
side in six bounding strides. Her hands clamped on the
man's foot at heel and toe, and she ducked, heaved and
twisted with all the strength in her five-foot-nine of lean
muscle. Steel split the air a fraction above her head as he
cut left and backhand frantically at the last instant; the
man was *fast*. But the point of the sword just tugged at
the tip of her hood rather than striking the steel cap
beneath.

And the shove shot him out of the saddle and off to
the right like something launched from a catapult. The
horse started to bolt forward with a whinny of alarm,

and Mary dove through the space where it had been. That was just in time to see Ritva landing on the man's back in a cat-jump, something flashing in her hand—a length of linen bandana, doubled and with a gold coin in one end to give it weight. The wet cloth whined through the air as she flicked it forward in the same instant as her feet left the ground.

The man had lost his sword as he fell, possibly deliberately; it was all too easy to come down on the edge when you pitched over like that. The strap holding his shield broke, and it went away end-over-end like a flipped coin. Both his hands flashed up to grab for the bandana as it struck his neck and whipped around snake-swift, the coin slapping into Ritva's gloved right hand and the cloth making a complete overlapping circuit of his throat. He was too late; she already had her wrists crossed and wrenched them apart, driving the fabric into the flesh under his chin with terrible leverage as she grappled him around the waist with her legs.

The twin assaults of the *rumal*-noose and a hundred and fifty pounds of Dúnadan on his back toppled him forward onto the muddy ground. Half a second later Mary landed on his kicking legs, wrapping her limbs around them, snatching the dagger out of his belt and tossing it aside before he thought to draw it.

"Quiet!" Ritva hissed in English. "Or else!"

He went limp in acknowledgment of defeat, wheezing in a breath as she slacked off a very little. Mary's fingers did a light flickering search for holdout weapons. If there had been anyone close, they could have cast their cloaks over him and done a fair imitation of a lump in the ground within moments. Instead Ritva came up

as Alleyne approached, with one leg out and a knee
planted between the man's shoulder-blades.

"*Hîr*?" she said. "*Boe?*"

That meant *Is it necessary, lord*? It was probably fortunate that the man they'd defeated didn't understand
either that or the unspoken codicil: *to kill him?*

"It's a *girl?*" the man under her knee choked out in
surprise. "I got dry-gulched by a *girl?*"

"No, it's a woman Ranger," Ritva snapped in English.

"Two, actually," Mary added.

"So *no dhínen*! Which means *shut up*," Ritva finished.

He made a gagging noise as her hands poised for the
second twist that would snap the neck. Mary could feel
the tension in the man's body through his legs and hips
as he strained up with his neck creaking.

The *Hîr Dúnedain* swept his hood and face-mask
back with the same motion. His handsome face and
trimmed blond mustache were blurs in the rainy night.

"Do you yield yourself?" he asked the man softly, going down on one knee as he sheathed his sword without
looking back.

"I yield," the man grunted, slapping one palm on the
ground in a wrestler's gesture of concession. "Obviously!"

"Let him live," Alleyne said softly, with the very
slightest hint of a smile, and in English.

Shifting back to the Noble Tongue: "We'd have to
carry the body out anyway. Better not to kill without
need and he might be useful one way or another. Make
him safe, though."

Ritva nodded, and muttered:

"*Oltho vae*," to the prisoner, which meant *sweet dreams*, or close enough.

She let the *rumal* drop. The man went on his face, choking and gasping for a moment. Before he could recover Ritva had a sealed container opened, and another cloth in her hand; that she clapped across his nose and mouth, holding them firmly and planting her other hand on the back of his head. There was a moment's sweet smell, and she removed it as soon as he went limp. It was rather too easy to overdose someone on chloroform, given that the stuff had to be made out of seaweed by a complex chemical process and that you never really knew for sure how strong any batch was.

No point in sparing someone and then having him die of heart failure, Mary thought as she helped bind and gag the unfortunate Boisean.

Or extremely lucky Boisean, she thought.

Her snicker and Ritva's came at the same instant, and Mary knew they were sharing a thought:

He's obviously brave and that means he leads from the front. Thousands are going to die before the next sundown, but now he probably won't end up on the receiving end of a lance or an arrow or a roundshot. As opposed to say, the blameless and far more deserving personal me, *who'll have to go through the whole ghastly damned thing from beginning to end doing Rangerishly dangerous damned stuff to live up to our doubly-damned reputations.*

That sort of mental communion had been happening between the Havel twins all their lives.

CHAPTER SIX

Half a dozen more Rangers were there around Mary and Ritva and the Lord of the Dúnedain by now, kneeling silently in a half-circle about them with arrows on the string, bows hidden by their cloaks to keep the rain off the sensitive recurves until the instant they had to draw. Wax and varnish did a good deal, but it wasn't wise to count on them.

Another had caught the Boisean's horse, gentling it and offering it an apple while two more quickly went through the saddlebags and the bedroll strapped behind the saddle for anything that might be documents or maps. It shifted and laid back its ears, backing its stern in a half-circle, then consented to take the fruit, though its eyes still rolled nervously. Horses were conservatives who thought a strangeness probably meant something wanted to eat them.

"*Rochiril, novaer,*" the Ranger crooned softly, stroking the mare's nose. "Be good, horse-lady."

"Imlos," Alleyne said to him. "Mount. Ride east;

abandon the horse where you can make your way to the riverside about ten miles east of here without leaving a trail. Take his sword, shield and helmet and drop them somewhere along the way where there are plenty of tracks. You know the Ranger shelter."

"I know it, lord," the young man said; it hadn't been a question. "I helped build it."

Well, alae, duh, Mary thought. *Why do you think he picked you?*

They'd all memorized the hideouts and blinds the Dúnedain had established along the river before and during the war; most were merely small camouflaged dugouts with supplies . . . often including an inflatable boat. Still, there was knowing and *knowing.*

"Rejoin when you can, Imlos, but don't take unnecessary chances," Allcyne said. "Go!"

The man nodded, bowed slightly with right hand to heart and vaulted into the saddle amid murmurs of *galu*—good luck—from the rest. Even as the hoofbeats died away in the hiss of rain, the others were examining the surroundings, blurring footprints with careful speed. One flipped the Boisean's broad-bladed dagger to Mary, and she tucked it into her boot-top. The captured officer was stripped of his sword belt, tied into his cloak and slung between two rangers. One of them flashed Ritva a thumbs-up sign as he helped carry the prisoner downslope.

That was *not* a Ranger gesture, but Ian Kovalevsky was from the Dominion of Drumheller. Originally the slim, fair young man had been a liaison between the Questers as they passed through on the last stage of their journey back to Montival and the Force, a red-coated equivalent of the Rangers which helped keep the peace in the Dominions. He'd ended up as Ritva's new boyfriend, and might well drift into the Rangers as well—it wouldn't be the first time something like that had happened when an outsider fell for a member, and Mary thought Ritva was serious about him. He'd been along on the rescue mission in Boise, too, for which Mary rather envied him.

Though getting snatched off a roof in the middle of a hostile city by an airship that *almost* missed, with the usurper's troops closing in all around in a shower of crossbow bolts, then getting tossed hundreds of miles in a thunderstorm with lightning crackling around the highly-inflammable gasbag . . . that sort of thing was a lot more fun in retrospect. On a cold winter afternoon in Stardell Hall back at Mithrilwood, say, lying back in one of the big leather chairs in front of the fireplace and roasting chestnuts, with the carved timber of the walls all dim up by the banner-hung rafters, a mug of mulled cider in your hand, a cat in your lap and a bunch of kids and noobs gathered around, sitting on the floor and listening with *that is just* so *cool* expressions on their faces.

They went down the slope faster than they'd climbed it, doing their best to leave minimal tracks; as they cleared each party of two or three the little groups would cover trail as they fell back. Two light galleys were still waiting in the little cove, but they'd been pushed back into the water and the camouflage netting removed, their oars waiting ready in the locks like the legs of a water-spider. Both were fragile-looking things like racing shells, with aluminum masts folded down and stored in the well between the oar-benches.

John Hordle and his wife, Eilir Mackenzie, were there; this was a *very* important mission, enough that all three of the remaining founder-leaders of the Rangers were on it. Uncle John was six-foot-six and broad enough to seem squat, built like a hobbit crossed with a troll, with a face like a good-natured ham. He leaned on the hilt of his sheathed greatsword and chewed a grass stem with his graying reddish-brown hair gleaming with raindrops as the rest came up, his shrewd little russet eyes missing nothing. After a few mugs of shandy at festivals and feasts, one of his party tricks was to bend horseshoes straight and then toss them to the unsuspecting, who then howled and danced after they'd gripped the torsion-heated metal.

Aunt Eilir was Juniper Mackenzie's eldest child, black-haired, pale-eyed and slender-strong and just short of forty. She had a clipboard and was checking people off as they arrived, soundlessly . . . which was appropriate, given that she'd been deaf from birth and was one of the reasons Rangers used Sign so much. No matter how well-trained and experienced troops were, it was always shockingly easy to lose someone in the dark if you weren't *very* careful. Eilir and Astrid had refounded the Rangers a few years after the Change, and a few years before John and Alleyne and Sir Nigel had arrived from Greater Britain fleeing Mad King Charles.

Mary had always thought it was all madly romantic, especially the part where the two young comrades had courted and won the *anamchara*-sworn Ladies of the Dúnedain. Though she knew Uncle John had always quietly considered Aunt Astrid barking mad and wouldn't have had her on a bet. And she suspected that

Uncle Alleyne had thought she was crazy too, but just didn't care, the way Uncle John didn't care that Eilir was deaf. Both of which facts *were* romantic too, when you thought about it, in a more grown-up way.

Imlos? Eilir Signed.

"Sent on with the horse," Alleyne replied. "Going to ground in one of our underground shelters and rejoining later."

"'opefully," John Hordle said, in his inimitable burring Hampshire-yokel version of Sindarin. "Good practice sending 'im, though, Oi think."

Alleyne nodded. "Hopefully they'll find the horse far away and won't have any idea *where* their man was lost. They've been having a serious desertion problem, we know that. Some coming over, some just going home."

There were younger Rangers who thought Alleyne's more plummy Winchester-and-Sandhurst tones were a Quenya high-elven accent and had imitated it. Aunt Astrid had frowned on that and Uncle John had encouraged the rumor to drive her distracted . . .

Mary sighed a little at the memory as the Boisean was slung onto the second galley. *Aunt Astrid would have loved this op like a bowl of blueberries and whipped cream. With toasted walnuts sprinkled on top.*

Everyone clambered aboard with swift care; the narrow hulls rocked anyway.

"Let's get him out of the way," Mary said.

She was smiling at the same time; they were going home. Going home to a giant murdering battle, granted, but the principle was the same. Being isolated among the enemy just *felt* worse than openly confronting them, whatever the odds might be. If a hundred thousand men were going to try and kill her, at least she'd be among Montivalans when they did.

"*Raich*, he's heavy!" Ritva said, as she took him by the loop of rope tied under his arms. "For a sort of cutely slim guy."

"Or his armor is," Mary said, as they navigated the narrow path between the rowing benches.

Mary and Ritva sank into position on either side of the prisoner in the bows. Two of the oarsmen used their shafts to push off, and then both of the boats turned their sharp prows westward. A soft chant of:

"*Leidho . . . bado . . .*" started as the oars swayed backward and forward.

Water hissed by outside the thin metal sheath of the hull. The prisoner's armor was shoulder-protection and a back-and-breast of hoops and bands of plate, fastened with catches at the left shoulder and under the left arm. Ritva pushed him on his side and Mary worked the catches to release the forty pounds of steel. It went overboard with a *plop* as they reached deeper water; the little ship-by-courtesy was crowded enough that the room and weight-loss were welcome, even if it felt a bit wasteful.

The sky was clearing after the rain-shower; she could see more stars now, and the eastern horizon was slowly turning from dark-blue through green to a baleful and somehow ill-omened pink, though she usually liked the pre-dawn hush. The broad expanse of the Columbia revealed itself, with wisps of fog glimmering and vanishing, and the great steep brown bluffs on either bank, with black streaks where the basalt showed through. The air was chilly, on the edge of frost. Her damp clothes warmed only reluctantly, tempting her to take a spell rowing. After a few minutes the rhythmic stroke of the oars and the grunting *huff* of breath settled into a background music. Water purled away from the sharp bows in an endless chuckle.

Someone opened a basket and started handing out cakes made of pressed cracked and toasted grain, honey and nuts and bits of dried fruit, and *cram* sandwiches— flat leathery tortillas wrapped around ham and cheese. The Boisean at her feet was stirring and kicking, so they turned him upright, propped him half-sitting against the inside curve of the bow and bent to look him in the face with theirs side by side and filling his field of view.

"You promise to be sensible?" Ritva asked. "No tussling on the boat?"

"So we don't have to stab you or hack off your head," Mary added.

"Or cut your throat or drown you," Ritva finished cheerfully.

"Which would be sort of silly after all the trouble we took to get you here alive," Mary pointed out. "Which we really didn't have to do."

"It was just our inherent Folk-of-the-West niceness."

"So give us your parole until we reach our dock."

"It isn't far," Ritva clarified.

The prisoner's eyes flicked from one of them to the other, as blue as their own; his brown hair was short on the top and tight at the sides. They'd shed their war-cloaks and steel caps, and the identical blond fighting-braids lay on their shoulders as they beamed at him. Ian leaned around Ritva to add with a slightly alarming smile:

"And they really mean it, you know."

The prisoner nodded, and the twins reached to untie his hands and remove the gag.

"Let's hear your parole," Mary said.

"I won't try to escape or attack you until I'm taken off this boat," the man said, his voice rough from the near-throttling. "Or it sinks. On my honor as an officer."

"That'll do," Mary said. "But we'll get *really cranky* if you don't keep it."

"Even a bit mean and bitchy," Ritva said, pointing a warning finger at his face.

"And they *really mean* that," Ian said. "Have a sandwich."

Mary grinned to herself as he glanced from one to the other, startled by the unison of their movements. It had been even more effective in the old days.

Uh-oh, she thought when he frowned. *He's recognizing us.*

The problem with heroic deeds like the Sword Quest that brought undying fame was that it made you . . .

Sort of famous. Which can be awkward when people just recognize you out of the blue. Sometimes they think they know you just because they've heard the stories, too.

His face changed: "Christ. You're Ritva and Mary Havel, aren't you? The woo—" He visibly reconsidered something that was probably on the order of *woot-woot.* "The Dunydain? That King Artos guy's sisters?"

"Yup. Though that's Mary Vogeler now that I'm married and respectable. Sort of."

"And we're the High King's half sisters; same father, different mothers," Ritva said.

"*Very* different," Mary clarified.

The Boisean was a young man but older than they were, with a lean weathered face. Ian's hand snaked in with a canteen, and as he drank cautiously—chloroform didn't make you feel all that good when it wore off, and being throttled didn't either—the shape of his cheekbones tugged at Mary's memory . . .

"You wouldn't be named Woburn, would you?" she said. "Of the Camas Prairie Woburns? Head of the family is a Rancher and Sheriff there, a big landholder near Grangeville?"

The man nodded. "That would be my father. I'm Centurion Dave Woburn."

She shot a covert glance at her sister; it wouldn't do for her to mention the visit Ritva and the Rangers had paid to Sheriff Woburn's ranch on their way to the rescue mission in Boise. The elder Woburn was willing to give actual help to Martin Thurston's opponents; as far as they knew his oldest son was just dissatisfied. Ritva gave her an annoyed *do-you-think-I'm-stupid* glare in return.

"I met your brother!" Mary said instead to the prisoner.

That had been far east of here, in Barony Tucannon, in one of the opening skirmishes of the campaign. The enemy alliance of Boise and the CUT occupied that area now . . . except for the walled cities and castles, which they didn't have the time or resources to take, and the guerillas who were making their life less than joyful every hour of the night and most of the days. She'd heard someone describe it as the flies conquering the flypaper.

"My brother Jack?" the man said, suddenly eager. "But he was taken prisoner—"

"A couple of months ago. My husband and I were in that fight," she said happily. "We had lunch with your brother afterwards at the Baron of Tucannon's manor house at Grimmond-on-the-Wold. Lovely place, I hope you guys didn't burn it. He's OK, and the left arm healed well, I heard. In fact, he's working for Fred now. You know, Frederick Thurston. The one of your ruler's sons who *didn't* kill his father."

Dave Woburn gave an alarmed glance to either side by pure involuntary reflex, which said something about the United States of Boise under Martin Thurston. Mary raised a brow as he became conscious of what he'd done, and his jaw tightened as he saw it and took the implication.

"Fred's also the one who *didn't* sell his soul to demons," Ritva added helpfully. "Well, pretty much demons. We've met *them*, too and it's close enough."

"Fred's actually sort of a nice guy," Mary put in. "He was on the Quest with us and we got to know him."

"Pretty cute, too," Ritva said. "This lovely cinnamon skin and a nice tight butt . . . Hey, Ian, I'm just recognizing it in a sort of abstract way! I'm at least serially monogamous. Plus Virginia would kill me."

"Literally," Mary said judiciously.

She liked Fred's wife, Virginia, née Kane, who was a Rancher's daughter from the Powder River country in what had been Wyoming.

She'd joined the Quest as a refugee from the CUT's seizure of her family's ranch as they passed through to the Seven Council Fires territory, and she and Fred had fallen for each other. She was smart and loyal and brave, a superb horsewoman and a pretty good fighter, if not up

to Ranger standards, and even well-educated for someone from the back of beyond; she'd read the Histories,
though just as stories. You could forgive her habit of
scalping people who really pissed her off as a local foible;
after all, there were people who were all censorious and
judgmental about Dúnedain customs too. And she always killed them before she scalped them, which showed
a certain basic moral goodness. But . . .

"Virginia *is* sort of possessive about Fred," she concluded. "And anything connected with Fred. And anything she thinks Fred should have."

Like being General-President of Boise, she added
mentally; that was another thing that would be tactless
to say right now.

"She's sort of . . . carnivorous," Ritva said. "But in a
good way."

Dave Woburn shook his head as if trying to clear it
and get his thoughts back on track, then winced.

"You want some willow-bark?" Mary said sympathetically. "I've been choked unconscious before . . . have
you? No? It gives you a *terrible* headache every time,
just really ugly. And a *rumal* totally puts your neck out
of alignment."

Even when it doesn't kill you, she added to herself; it
would be tactless to say that aloud, too. *And even when
you have to kill someone, it doesn't cost anything to be polite.*

"Ah . . . yes. Thanks. But did you have to drug me
too?"

"The chloroform was safer than thumping your
head—"

Knocking someone out meant a concussion, which

was *not* like going to sleep, whatever some people thought or some stories said. She'd been knocked out several times herself, and once the headaches had lasted for weeks. You could just suddenly die from it, too, or end up a drooling idiot. If it happened too often you *did* end up as a drooling idiot.

"—and we couldn't risk you yelling at the wrong moment if we ran into your friends."

She passed him a paper twist of the powdered extract from her field kit pouch. He threw the bitter stuff into his mouth, washed it down with a grimace and a drink of water, then doggedly started in on his honey-and-nut cake and sandwich. He probably wasn't feeling very hungry, but she approved. If you weren't actually nauseous, it was better to eat something after an experience like the one he'd gone through. The body burned up its reserves when it sensed approaching death and got ready to fight or run, and if you didn't eat you risked a sort of shivering feeling and lethargy and weakness.

"So Jack went over to the enemy?" the Boisean said quietly.

He probably believed them; there wasn't much point in a lie that he'd be able to check on so soon.

"Depends on who you think of as *the enemy*," Ian put in. "I'm from the Dominion of Drumheller myself."

The man nodded warily. "The Canucks, right. I'd heard you'd gotten into the war."

"My parents were Canadians. There's really no Canada now, any more than there is a United States. That's why they chose the new names. Our Premier . . . Premier Mah . . . said it was because, mmmm, *Nostalgia isn't a politically productive emotion*."

"That's . . . debatable."

"But either way I don't have a dog in this fight, except that we're at war with the CUT. And hell, I'm from the *Peace River* part of Drumheller, north of that it's trees and Indians all the way to the tundra and then it's Eskimo and polar bears all the way to the Beaufort Sea. The only people my district have really fought since the Change are the PPA, when they took over the old British Columbia part of the district and split it up into fiefs and built castles on it. Would have taken the rest too, if we hadn't punched them out of the idea."

"Why are you here, then?"

"They're part of Montival now, and we believe the new management when they say they don't have big eyes. We've got no problem with Rudi . . . with High King Artos . . . as a neighbor."

"You're a monarchy too," Woburn said a bit sourly.

"Theoretically. *Very* theoretically. We have contact with Greater Britain maybe once every three or four years. Thing is, we didn't have any problem with *you* people in Boise as a neighbor, when Fred's father was running things; he left us alone and we returned the favor. But we sure as shit have a problem with the Church Universal and Triumphant as a neighbor. Or anyone who carries water for them."

"We don't want a King," the prisoner said tightly.

"You'd rather have a Prophet?" Ian said dryly. "A deranged one with *evil incarnate* tattooed on his forehead? Hey, mister, I was in Boise when we took your guy Martin's *wife* out, and *she* said Martin is the Prophet's puppet *and* that he killed his dad. In fact, when she started shouting that, he tried to kill *her*—personally shot a crossbow at her while she was holding his son in her arms."

"That's true?" Woburn whispered, with the gut-punched look of a man who'd been trying to avoid believing something he knew was so.

"Damn *right* it's true; I was there; I saw it."

"The . . . government release . . . said she'd been kidnapped."

"She was *begging* us to get her out. And I was with her all the way back west and she said—"

Mary touched her sister on the shoulder and dropped back into Sindarin:

"I think we should leave him and Ian to talk, Sis. You were there too, but I think he'll listen more to your fellah. Seeing as we're Rudi's sisters and all and might be biased."

"Only my identical could be right as often as you are," Ritva grumbled; neither of them were naturally the keep-quiet-and-wait types.

Woburn gave them a glance.

"*Iston peded i phith i aníron, a nin ú-cheniathog,*" Ritva said sweetly.

I can say what I want, and you can't understand me, Mary thought/translated, and hid her grin again.

Damn, it's good to be back with Sis for a while, she thought happily. *When she settles down and the war's over, we'll really have to set up somewhere close to each other. We can babysit each other's kids and swap cookies and stuff. Maybe we could found a new Ranger station somewhere . . . somewhere* warm. *Somewhere warm with good vineyards.*

That half-giggle turned to a shout of alarm as she

turned. Something was diving out of the sun that had just cleared the horizon, silent and very swift.

"*Yrch!*" someone shouted. "Enemy!"

"Errrk!" Mary called; or it might have been Ritva talking, she couldn't tell. "No shit!"

The glider was like a flying tadpole with long, slender wings, a sleek melted-looking metal shape out of the pre-Change world, gleaming polished metal beneath the plastic bubble of the pilot's canopy. A red-and-white shark's mouth was painted below the nose, and *USAF* and a star on the wings. Something tumbled down from it . . .

Uncle Alleyne was looking over his shoulder while he stood at the tiller, feet braced apart on the tiny plank of decking beneath him.

"*Flank speed!*" he shouted.

The rowers moved up to sprint pace, throwing themselves forward and back with gasping effort. The cylinder came closer and closer, something like a big elongated *pill*, tumbling around its axis and trailing a very faint line of smoke.

Uh-oh, Mary thought. *Napalm*.

She'd had it shot at her from catapults and seen it pumped from flamethrowers, and it was very nasty indeed. Never dropped on her head from the air before, though . . .

"*Now!*" Alleyne snarled, and swung the tiller far over.

The slender form of the little galley heeled. Mary's eyes went wide as a thin sheet of water began to curl over the side. There was a shout as everyone threw themselves the other way, herself included, leaning overboard as far as she could with her boots braced and

LORD OF MOUNTAINS   127

hands locked on the bulwark and the frame that supported one of the oars and the cold water of the Columbia running just under her straining back. The galley fell
back, rocking onto an even keel, and she slid forward
amid a clatter of gear and thud of people hitting people
and things and a clanking rattle as the sweeps tangled
like a heap of jackstraws.

"Row! Row!" Alleyne barked.

His handsome, aquiline face looked wholly alive for
the first time since he'd come back from the mission to
Boise. *Not good, but alive.*

A gout of flame rose far too close on the starboard,
as the napalm spread itself over the still surface of the
river. The oarsmen flung themselves back into their seats
and got going; the glider went by overhead—her mind
automatically estimated that it was at least twice long
bowshot up and moving faster than a galloping horse—
and skimmed over towards the bank of the river. Her
head swiveled to follow it, hoping desperately that it
would drop into the water like a landing goose or crumple in the steep rock that rose from it.

Instead it seemed to strike something invisible in the
air, turning and banking and rising upward as if thrust
by a hand. *It must be updrafts along the cliffs.* She'd
flown gliders herself, but only a few times for sport in a
double-seat model, off a cliff and then gently down.
The pilot attacking them must be an artist at reading the
invisible currents of the air.

"Well, shit," she said, spitting out blood from where
her teeth had cut the inside of her mouth.

For emphasis, she repeated it in English, with embel-
lishments:

"Well, *shit on toast!*"

"Double damn!" Ritva agreed.

"*Bother!*" Mary finished.

"Where the *Utumno* are *our* gliders?" someone shouted.

"Shut up and row, you son-of-a-she-warg!" the man behind him snarled.

The oars were moving in unison again. The other galley was a hundred yards ahead of them, rippling through the water like a centipede. The glider rose until the low sun in the east sparkled on its canopy, breaking out of the relative gloom of the river and its girdling cliffs, then turned like a stooping hawk.

"It will be coming in lower this time," Alleyne said, his voice crisp and steady.

To aim better, Mary thought. *And it was far too close the last time. That one would have landed right on us if Alleyne hadn't turned us out of it.*

Alleyne went on in the same businesslike tone: "And he's coming head-on. Get ready to shoot, it's a no-deflection aiming point. Oarsmen, listen for the word of command."

There were twenty at the oars and six who weren't, not counting Uncle Alleyne with his hands full of tiller or the prisoner. Mary reached over her shoulder and pulled the recurve out from the harp-shaped scabbard that rode between her back and the quiver, then flipped out a bodkin-pointed arrow and set it through the cutout in the curly-maple riser and on the string.

Dave Woburn slumped down a little more into the curve of the bow, giving them a clear shot. Which was strictly in accord with his parole, of course. He'd agreed not to hinder them. Plus, if they burned, so did he. Black smoke was still rising from the patch where the first canister had struck.

"Never did like those air force pukes," he said and unexpectedly smiled at her. "Even when they weren't trying to kill me. Friendly fire isn't."

Mary chuckled. Ritva did too, and then said:

"Ian, you get between us and a little forward, you've got a heavier draw."

She looked over her shoulder; the Rangers who had their hands free were putting arrows to their strings as well.

"Just as heavy as yours, Hírvegil, and he's just as good a shot too, so don't crowd him."

"*Ego, mibo orch*," he muttered; he'd been very stand-offish with Ian.

Which was rude, as was *go kiss an orc*, but then he had had a crush on Ritva even before the Quest. Or Mary. Or both. But he settled back a little into the crowded forepeak of the galley.

The Rangers can be awfully like any other village some-times, she thought, making herself calm. There was the target and there was the bow and nothing else mattered. *Nowhere to get away. I got used to moving on while we were on the Quest.*

She'd talked to people in big cities with tens of thousands of people, and many of them thought life in places like a Dun of the Clan or a Ranger steading or a Bear-killer strategic hamlet or a Portlander manor was like one big, close happy family.

Family, yes, she thought. *Close, yes. Happy, sometimes, but not necessarily. And if you get to quarreling with someone, you are* so *stuck with them anyway. Until I saw cities I never realized you could live any other way.*

The glider had finished its banking turn, graceful and silent and frightening. Now it turned into a dot in the middle of a thread as it came at them nose-on, much clearer this time as it dove out of the fading purple of the western sky instead of the dawn. Aiming the bow was like breathing, since she'd been doing it nearly as long as she'd been walking; all she had to do was decide to do it.

But correct for the speed, she reminded herself. *It's getting faster and faster as it gets closer and closer and it's already faster than anything you've ever shot at.*

She took a long breath and let it out, then pulled in another. The string lifted off the ends of the staves as the recurve bent; the double-curve shape let her bend it into a deep C, the secret of drawing a long arrow from a bow only four feet long. The kiss-ring on the string touched the corner of her lip as the muscles in arms and shoulders and belly levered against the springy power of the laminated stave.

Ritva was calling the shot; she was a little better at estimating distances, now that they had three eyes between them.

"Wait . . . wait . . . *now!*"

Mary's fingers rolled off the string. *Whstp*, and the surge of recoil that was always a surprise when you were doing it right. A little cloud of arrows lifted from the galley; the other one was too far ahead. The glider didn't swerve, though Mary thought some of the arrows at least punched into the thin metal of its hull. The pilot was boring in regardless, determined to plant his last napalm canister where it would do the most harm.

Then a shout from the rear:

"*Back oars!*"

The prow surged down and then up in a burst of spray as every one of the rowers stood and dug in their oars. The galley's speed dropped as if a kraken had caught the keel in its tentacles and yanked hard. The archers dropped as the sudden halt yanked their footing out from beneath them. Two people landed on top of Mary, and the horn nock on the end of a bowstave poked painfully into the sensitive flesh behind her left ear, breaking the skin.

Flame roared at her. She shouted in involuntary alarm as it broke around the bows of the galley, heat that made her face crinkle and a choking chemical stink not like anything else she'd ever smelled. Then someone not far away started screaming, and she smelled something quite different. Cloth burning, and hair.

One of the people who'd landed on her was Ritva. They were used to that—they'd been sparring partners since they were little girls pulling each other's hair over who got the last scoop of blueberries and cream—and they'd developed a routine for it. This time it involved heaving Ian up off their backs with a united buck and twist, but that was all right too. The prisoner, Dave Woburn, had blood running down one side of his head where he'd bashed it against a thwart.

His arm was also on fire where a stray gobbet of clinging liquid flame had come over the gunwale. They reacted with smooth precision; Ritva grabbed the man by the front of his tunic and jerked him up so the limb thrashed free, and Mary pulled it against her and wrapped herself around it, careful to keep her hands and any bare part of her body away from it. You couldn't put napalm out by splashing water on it; you had to smother it completely. The flames died down, enough that she could grab the cloth above it with her left hand and slash at the seam with the dagger she flipped into her right. Linen thread parted, and she pulled the thick linsey-woolsey cloth of the sleeve free and tossed it into the river. An instant later they had the man maneuvered over the bulwark too, and plunged the limb into the cold Columbia. There hadn't been an obvious burn, but the skin looked a little red.

That gave her a good view as the glider banked. *It can't have* more *fire-bombs, can it?* she thought. *Gliders can't lift much weight!*

Whether it did or not, this time it didn't catch an updraft on the edge of the river. Instead it headed straight in towards the bluffs, then slowly heeled to one side. More and more, until the wingtip touched the surface, and then there was a sudden whirling, splashing chaos. When it ended the glider was broken and resting on the rocky shore. She felt a moment's pang; it had been so graceful, and so old and alien.

After an instant, the canopy opened. A man emerged, doll-tiny with distance, slithered out and stood propped against the side of the broken craft, slipped down prone, laboriously stood again and shook a fist at them.

Mary laughed as they manhandled Woburn back into the bow and the oars took up their rhythm; Ian assisted, since it was surprisingly difficult to move a man with his feet bound.

"I'm glad he lived," she said, offering him more of the willow-bark powder. "Hope he keeps on doing it, too."

"Why?" the prisoner asked bluntly, taking it and applying some of the burn ointment Ritva handed him to the red patch on his arm. "Thank you, by the way."

"You're welcome," she replied. "Why? He's a brave man doing what he sees as his duty."

"We'd kill him if we had to, but why shouldn't I be glad we didn't? Have to kill him, that is."

"And he's out of this fight," Ritva put in, handing Mary back her bow.

"Which applies to you too," Mary said.

"You're . . . strange," Woburn said.

Ian grinned at him. "Tell me. But wait until you meet their big brother. The one with the magic sword."

Woburn snorted. "Oh, a *real* magic sword? You expect me to believe that?"

"No, we expect you to *see* it, soon," Mary said.

All three of them looked at him and smiled.

"You're not . . . kidding, are you?" Woburn said, his eyes going a little wider. "You really believe that."

"Oh, you have *no* idea," Ian said helpfully.

CHAPTER SEVEN

The High King's Host
Horse Heaven Hills
(Formerly south-central Washington)
High Kingdom of Montival
(Formerly western North America)
November 1st, Change Year 25/2023 AD

Rudi Mackenzie looked up from the folding map table.

"Ah, most excellent!" he said, as the Lord of the Dúnedain dismounted and approached. "*Hír* Alleyne, *mae govannen. I chyth 'win dregathar o gwen sui fuin drega od Anor.*"

"Well-met, Your Majesty; and indeed our foes shall flee." A pause. "Your command of the Noble Tongue has improved."

Rudi smiled; he hadn't spoken more than a few words or rote phrases until he reached Nantucket and stepped outside the world of common day to return with the Sword of the Lady. He tapped the hilt:

"A benefit of this, I fear, and not my own merit."

It gives me command of tongues . . . including ones that don't exist, or didn't until fairly recently when an Englishman invented them. Including, and here oddness becomes very odd indeed, both words and grammar that weren't *in what poor Astrid called her Histories, or indeed in any of the man's writings, but which fit the rest perfectly. Which is a puzzlement I don't intend to think about; it makes my head hurt.*

There was a Dúnedain bard about, scribbling down the added vocabulary whenever she had a chance. She had a list, and she'd give him paragraphs and ask him to translate them and take notes in shorthand. Given what had happened to Astrid and how it had aided the kingdom's cause, he hadn't had the heart to tell her to take herself off. Among other projects, the Lady of the Rangers had been working on a translation of the Histories . . . into Elvish.

The handsome man with the haunted eyes and the first silver in his blond hair bowed with hand on heart in the Ranger manner, bending the knee as well. So did the others—though his twin half sisters gave him antiphonal winks as they did.

They had a prisoner with them, a Boisean officer in the rough olive-green uniform that host wore under their armor, and he remained proudly standing. One sleeve had been ripped off, and ointment glistened on the skin there; doubtless there was a story behind it. He wasn't bound, but two of the Rangers stood near with their long knives bare in their hands.

Something clicked in his mind, as if working some mathematical magic on the shape of face and eyes and hands. *That's close kin to the prisoner who went over to Fred last month.*

He didn't know if it was his own wit working there or the Sword of the Lady working through him.

Sure, and I should stop wondering that. There's no way to tell, and often enough it just seems to exaggerate *the way I've always thought, like attaching a water-mill to a saw to give it added power. It's obsessive I could become about it, to my own detriment.*

The prisoner's stiff refusal to bend showed courage, particularly if he believed any of the propaganda Martin Thurston was putting about concerning what a feudal tyrant Artos the First was. In what the Lady Regent Sandra considered one of life's little ironies, much of the black tale was lifted from the actual deeds of Norman Arminger . . . who would be Rudi's father-in-law, except that he was long dead.

And good riddance; I wouldn't have liked to be in his skin when he had to make accounting to the Guardians of the Western Gate. Even such a man as he probably deceived himself about his deeds. But there's no lying before Them.

Alleyne stepped up to the portable map table and opened his report, reading and pointing things out at the same time, and one of the attendants put little carved hardwood chip markers on it and moved them around with something like a billiard-cue rake. It was now light enough to see the map well; the smell of the just-extinguished lamps hung in the air with a musky wax for a moment, and someone was cooking porridge not far away. Even a very new kingdom could be well-organized, if you had a competent Chancellor and other helpers.

The scents were soon lost in the wind that blew over the vast rolling landscape of the Horse Heaven Hills, even the stronger stink of the troops not far away. He felt he could see forever from here, and you really could see very far indeed. That air was cold and clean, and birds rode it high above—crows, buzzards, ravens, hawks, even eagles. They'd had time since the Change to learn it meant a feast spread for them when men gathered in such numbers; it wasn't an accident that one of the Dark Mother's names was *Crow Goddess*.

He was in full plate now, save for the helm and gauntlets, the marvelous alloy-steel suit Mathilda's mother had had made as a wedding gift. It felt indecently light and easy compared to some gear he'd worn. Only a monarch could have commissioned it, and not a minor monarch at that, given the difficulty of working those refractory metals under modern conditions; most plate was made from ordinary salvaged sheet-steel. Although his still performed armor's twofold miracle, making you too hot in warm weather and obstinately refusing to protect you from even the slightest chill.

The little markers on the map seemed to glow with significance as he watched, trembling with possibilities as his right palm rested on the moon-crystal pommel of the Sword of the Lady. He was used to the way it affected him now, the way it made him more of the man he had to be to do the job the Powers had handed him.

But I'm still not altogether certain I much like that man, he thought absently. *I'll just have to try not to be him so much I dislike myself, which would be a grievous fate given that I'm stuck in here with . . . me. To be sure.*

Beside him Frederick Thurston grunted thoughtfully, his hard brown young face calm as he nodded.

"I'd have bet anyway that they were winding up to hit us here on our right, close to the river, but it's nice to have confirmation. Well, that removes some of the uncertainty from the next twenty-four hours," he said.

Rudi knew what he meant. Still . . .

"We know what's going to happen in the next day, Fred," he said. "A great many who'd rather be home tending their crops or their workshops are going to die, more still will be crippled, children will keep asking when their parents are coming home until they're old enough to understand an ugly truth, and many a household will know want and hardship for years to come. Everything else is . . . *arra*, how did they put in the old days . . . *damage control*. The only consolation is that this isn't just about which pair of buttocks will be gracing which chair, so to say."

Eric of the Bearkillers traced the huge blunt arrow that was heading westward on the map with his metal left hand. This one was a utilitarian slotted trowel-shaped thing that fitted into the round shield across the big fair man's back and would do as a weapon in a pinch, rather than the dramatic one that gave him his nickname of *Steel-Fist*. The Boiseans were coming in just a little north of the bluffs along the Columbia, the closest ground that would give them room to deploy.

"That's not particularly subtle as an opening move," he said, the plates of his armor clinking a little as he moved to stare meditatively eastward.

Rudi nodded. "They outnumber us five to four and they need a swift victory. Otherwise winter will kill them if they stay and force them to fall back on their bases of supply if they don't; and the League of Des Moines is marching up their backsides, the which is a most uncomfortable sensation. Winter will slow the war over there in the east, too, but not altogether until they hit the mountain passes. If your troops are willing to suffer and you can feed them, you can move on the high plains in winter; it's the one time of year when footmen have the advantage, since there's not much grazing. Come spring the CUT must be able to shift troops east to meet the Midwesterners. Hence they must come to us and break us the now or lose the war over the next year. There's no more time for slow maneuver. And if they can knock us away from the river, they win this round."

He turned his head to the messengers. "Observation balloons up now; this will be the battlefield. Gliders concentrate on denying the enemy air reconnaissance."

They scribbled and dashed away; heliographs began to blink. Rudi went on:

"Chief McClintock!"

The McClintock was a big man, with a two-handed sword slung across his back, a *claidheamh mòr* with a four-foot blade and a cross-and-clamshell guard. He looked rather like John Hordle in seven-eighths scale, save for the bushy brown beard that fell down his chest over the steel and leather nearly to the big dragon-shaped brass buckle of his belt, and the rather baggy look of the Great Kilt he wore.

That garment wasn't much like the neat, tailored pleats of the Mackenzie version; the skirt and plaid were all one five-yard-long stretch of woolen cloth held by waist-belt and shoulder-brooch, in a tartan of dark brown-red, blue and hunter green. He straightened a little when the call came.

"Aye, Yer Majesty?" the clan chief asked.

The McClintocks spoke in what they thought was a

Scottish fashion, one that Rudi's mother's fine ear found even more excruciatingly artificial than the imitation of her Irish brogue which had settled in among Mackenzies back at the beginning. The McClintocks had formed in the forested hills and narrow beautiful valleys between Ashland and Cave Junction, down south of the Willamette, in the post-Change period; partly with Mackenzie assistance, and partly in imitation of them as a model that had worked in the wild and terrible years—the latter something they fiercely denied, of course.

Their Chief's father actually had been named McClintock, at least, and he'd been a man of great strength of will and vision . . . and probably what the old world would have called certifiably insane, either before the Change or driven so by the terrors and horrors he'd seen. There had been many such in those years, and the mentally damaged were still common in the older generation. Rudi had always suspected, and since he first touched the Sword he *knew*, that the more successful of those founders had done more than dream and make dreams real. They'd tapped into patterns more ancient and strong than anything the old world had suspected, a subtle force pushing and shaping through individuals attuned to it.

So the Powers have their jests with us. Did our ancestors create the myths that now walk naked among us in the light of common day? Or do they but return from an age of legends much like this new world of ours, an age whose recollection echoed down many a thousand year? For walk the world again they do, now, most certainly and uncomfortably real whether we believe in them or not. More real

*than the world or we its dwellers, sometimes, you might be
saying. So heavy with reality they threaten to tear through
the gossamer fabric of our lives.*

"I want your clan's warriors to hold this area—" he
pointed south with one hand and traced the scrambled
contour lines on the map with the other "— between the
riverbank and the plateau up here, as we discussed. Now
we know it'll be this stretch in particular and though it's
rough as a cob we can't let them move through it. Sure
as the Lady's love they'll put troops in there; light infantry, at a guess. Dispose your clansfolk as you will, so long
as you don't let them through."

"Aye. We shall be th' strong castle ye dinnae hae."

Rudi nodded; the man was no fool. "The riverboats
will support you with their catapults and flamethrowers,
but they can only control the strip right along the water.
Work east and come in on their flank if you can, but
hold them you must."

The hairy man nodded. "It's gae bare for oor taste,
but steep and rough enough tae suit. We canna complain, and we'll hold it waur there's bluid in oor veins."

Chief Collin wasn't crazed; often uncomfortably
shrewd, in fact, but he had to use what his father's ob-
sessions had left. Things had jelled in the generation
since the Change and become less fluid; back then there
had been plenty of survivors eager to follow *anything*
that looked as if it would keep them alive and their children fed. More than ready to dive headlong into what
they thought was the past, since the present had be-
trayed them, though from what he'd heard and read,
what they made usually had only a passing resemblance
to anything in real history.

Real *being a term much in dispute in these times, of course.*

Mackenzies had been known to refer to the Mc-Clintocks as *the Clan Wannabee*. Epithets in the other direction included *Clan Little Wussy Pleated Skirt* and went downhill from there. There were probably about as many of them as there were Mackenzies, but nobody knew for sure; they didn't go in for census-taking.

But they've certainly sent everyone who could walk and do anything useful in a fight.

A little west the grassy plain was covered in them, in a dense mat of tartan and bonnets and plaids, mail shirts and boiled leather and hide vests sewn with pre-Change washers and crude noseguarded helms, all spread down a long slope. Banners rose above them, and a forest of steel; spears, gruesome-looking hooked Lochaber axes with broad blades two feet long, a fair number of yew bows, two-handed swords worn across the back in rawhide slings as well as the more common basket-hilted broadswords, round nail-studded shields with spikes in the center. The two men walked over to a jutting knee of hillside above them and Chief Collin drew his great blade with a flourish.

"Clan McClintock will hae the honor of holding the right wing! Och aye, there we wa' stand, and there die maun we must—for our homes an' oor bairns and this tall lad here! Hurrah for bonny *Ard Rí* Artos! Artos and Montival!"

"*Artos and Montival!*" Then a rhythmic pulse of: "*Ar-tos! Ar-tos! Ar-tos!*"

Rudi raised a hand, and the roaring cheer sank away. When he spoke it was in the Scots variety of Gaelic; he'd grown up familiar with the closely related Erse dialect, and the Sword made him preternaturally ready with tongues used anywhere in Montival. He shouted:

"Clamar theid na h-uaislean cruinn
Gun Cailean 'bhith san airmh!"

Collin McClintock grinned widely in his burst mattress of a beard. That translated roughly as:

How can there be a gathering of warrior chiefs without Collin?

It was part of an ancient poem about the Mc-Clintocks, too, and before the Change Collin's father had owned or accumulated quite a set of tomes on the subject of the Highland clans. From which he and his followers had afterwards pulled a dreadful muddled mulligatawny of ideas from history, legend, myth and bad romantic fiction all simmered to taste with a curry-sauce of things wholly their own.

They no more spoke the tongue in their daily lives than Mackenzies did Erse, but enough of his followers knew the phrase for an enormous roaring cheer to bellow out amid brandished weapons. McClintocks didn't paint their faces for war like his own clan . . . but a *lot* of them tattooed instead, everything from woad-blue to screaming scarlet. Rudi suspected they'd have frightened the victors of *Cath Raon Ruairidh* into fits, or possibly hoots of slack-jawed laughter.

Chief Collin leapt down among them, and dozens of sub-chiefs crowded around. A brace of his armored gallowglass bodyguards heaved him up on a shield as he harangued his followers with sword flourishes for punctuation. They surged about him, a tossing sea of weapons and contorted faces and banshee shrieks.

"By the Threefold Morrigú and the Dagda's Club, will you look at that lot of prancing monkeys?" the commander of the High King's Archers said under his breath. "They'll be setting up a Wicker Man next. With real *people* in it. Where do they think they're livin', the boothie next the Dá Derga's hostel?"

He nodded at one woman with bars of red and orange across her face and bones through the knot of black hair on the top of her head who was doing an improvised war-dance with a javelin in each hand and more in a hide bucket across her back.

"Poetry in motion, I *don't* think," he concluded.

Rudi grinned to himself as he walked back to the map table.

"I happen to know that their Chief's sire forbade the ancient sacrifices as *gessa* to their whole clan. Admittedly, it's without doubt or question a very good thing that he did just that before they got completely out of hand, so. Forbye they have their uses, *mo bhearthár.*"

"Breaking heads and bottles and windows in a tavern, would that be, Chief?" Edain Aylward Mackenzie muttered, his square, stubborn young face frowning. "Or gettin' more friendly with their sheep than is right altogether or proper?"

"Well, my mother did say once they'd all be fanatical Jacobites if only there were any Stuarts about the place for them to be loyal to, the which there are not. As it is, I'll have to do."

Edain and the archers took stance behind him as he rejoined the party around the map table, their strung longbows in their arms; compared to the southerners, their green brigandines and sallet helms and neatly uni-

LORD OF MOUNTAINS   145

form kilts and plaids looked very disciplined indeed. Eric Larsson was looking dubious himself as the hairy mass of McClintocks went pouring off south at a swinging trot. The massed rumble of their feet made a counterpoint to the keening wail of their pipers, which Rudi had to admit were just as good as any the Mackenzies produced. Or they would have been, if only they'd all been playing the same tune, which they manifestly were *not*.

"They're reliable?" Eric said.

"Down among the rocks and gullies?" Rudi said. "Most certainly. To stand against cavalry in open country, no; to fight in ranks against a pike-hedge of heavy foot, no, not that either unless they carried all before them in the first charge. But for this? They were born for it."

Everyone around the table nodded; a few just looked relieved to get the wild men out of the way and doing something useful where they didn't have to look at them. Feeding the McClintocks and keeping them from starting epidemics with lax hygiene had been a continuous trial. They were battle-hardy enough, experienced from constant skirmishing with the bandits and the remnants of the cannibal bands down towards the old California border and sometimes with each other. And it wasn't that they didn't wash, but they also lived widely scattered in the forests and dells and by the hunt about as much as from their flocks and fields. Gathering together in numbers was something they simply weren't used to, and they'd lost the necessary habits. Things that were tolerable in small doses were lethal when you crammed tens of thousands into a limited space.

"Eric," Rudi went on. "Lady Signe."

They were fraternal twins, tall and fair and in their early forties, and they ran the Bearkillers as war-leader and head of state, more or less—the post of Bear Lord had been vacant since Mike Havel died at the end of the War of the Eye, fifteen years and a bit previously. Signe had never liked Rudi overmuch . . . but they respected each other, and he did like her son and heir, Mike Jr. Right now they were both in browned-steel armor, suits of plate that differed only in detail from Association styles, with the snarling crimson bear's-head of the Outfit on their chests.

Mike was standing in the rear as befitted a junior, and in mail and arm-guards because he was still growing, but he had the mark of the A-List between his yellow brows, the Bearkiller elite, granted for his deeds south of the Columbia when the enemy invaded the lands of the CORA—the Central Oregon Rancher's Association. That land had been overrun, but the dwellers and the Clan and the Bearkillers had charged a stiff entry-fee and guerrillas were still collecting rent. Rudi went on:

"They'll try to push you away from the river. The *other* thing they'll try to do is tie up our reserves here. Take us by the throat with their left hand, so to speak, so they'll be free to punch with their right."

Eric grunted again, looking at the map. "So you'll want us to hold without reinforcements."

Rudi nodded. "It's sorry I am, but that's so. They've more light horse than we do by a wide margin, and out on the north where there's room to move that will be crucial. I must have the men there to deal with that.

Time . . . you have to buy me *time*. Remember, we win if we don't lose. They lose if they don't win."

"Point taken." Thoughtfully: "I'll put Arvid Sarian and his boys in to form our junction with the Mc-Clintocks. His lot are hairy enough too."

"And I'll leave the Degania Dalet contingent behind you. Use them if your hairy men fail, or at need elsewhere; but that's all I can spare."

"Good. They're reliable. And we'll need them before the day's out."

Signe traced the twisting south-to-north line and the blocks marking the patched-together coalition that was the host of the High King of Montival.

"And the Protectorate's knights?" she said, tapping the figures for the reserve behind the line.

"I'm going to shift some of the men-at-arms about and take a few whacks to keep the enemy guessing where the main weight will fall, draw as many of their light horse as I can on to the Clan's archers—they're still not used to foot soldiers who can outshoot them—and then concentrate the Association's lancers for the decisive point. I'll want the most of them fresh for that, too, where the place is right and the time ripened."

"For the *Schwerpunkt*," Eric said.

Rudi nodded; he'd learned that term from Sir Nigel Loring, his stepfather, who'd been a trained officer well before the Change over in Britain, where he'd attended an ancient warrior's school called Sandhurst. It summed the concept up more economically than *point of main effort*, which was the alternative.

"I'd be happier if I knew where the Sword of the

Prophet was, for that would be the target I'd prefer," he said.

That was the elite force of the Church Universal and Triumphant, better than eight thousand men according to the latest estimates, superbly trained from their earliest years and fanatically dedicated. The others glanced at the Sword of the Lady. Rudi shook his head.

"Sethaz is here. He can't see me or know my mind . . . or I him, nor his. Not beyond the usual way of deduction from a man's deeds. So it's mortal minds and eyes and swords that will settle things, and all the better for it."

He turned to Frederick Thurston. "And you, Fred—here."

His finger stabbed down on the map. Fred winced. "I was hoping we wouldn't have to . . ."

"Fight your countrymen, yes. That's precisely the point. I think things have come ripe right now in that regard as well."

Fred rubbed his shaven chin. His crested helmet was under one arm, and he looked quite dashing in the hoop-armor and scarlet cloak, with the loose black curls of his hair moving slightly in the breeze.

"I won't be able to talk anyone into actually switching sides in the middle of a fight," he warned. "We don't think that way in Boise. Those who fight are going to give it everything they can."

Rudi grinned. "I know. But just *not fighting at all* . . . eh, maybe that's possible?"

Fred brightened. "A sit-down strike? Now, *that* might be possible, you're right. As long as all they see in front of them is their own people. We know a lot of them are very, very unhappy about the situation. If they don't get started, they won't have to stop."

He looked at the prisoner the Dúnedain had brought. "Centurion Woburn?"

The man nodded. "Centurion David Woburn, Sixteenth Battalion, AE12774," he rattled off, conspicuously not coming to attention or saluting, and the battalion number was on his gear in any case.

"And you're a man caught between two fires." Frederick Thurston smiled grimly. "Either my brother is lying, or I am. I don't expect you to take my word for it. I've someone here you should meet, though," he said.

Then slightly louder: "Captain Woburn! Front and center!"

Rudi cut in as a man pushed through from the rear where he'd been standing with Fred's staff and subordinates:

"Just to make one thing clear, Centurion Woburn; if you choose, you can sit out this war as a prisoner in safety and comfort. And when we've won, you can go home free as a bird and live just as you please and tend to your crops and cattle; I understand you've a wife and children back home on the Camas Prairie. If we were to *lose*, however . . ."

The prisoner winced; he had to have some notion of what his father had been doing in clandestine opposition to Martin's regime, and it would get back that his brother had openly gone over to Frederick. Martin Thurston had never been the type to tolerate waverers, and since he'd met the Prophet eighteen months ago, he'd become utterly merciless.

Rudi's nod was not without sympathy, but not overflowing with it either; too much rode on this war to be excessively tender of any one man's feelings.

That's the problem with punishing any sign of wavering harshly, he thought. *Once a man or his kin have wavered at all, it's in for a penny, in for a pound and he must see your head nailed over the door of his hall, because neither he nor his can be safe while you live and have power. Those who despise mercy are as much fools as those who can't withhold it at need. More, for mercy can be a weapon as real as a war hammer to the head.*

A man came forward and saluted Frederick, with the same lean, brown-haired, high-cheeked look as the prisoner, tanned and weathered like any outdoorsman but no more than a few years past twenty. He was in Boise light-cavalry gear, mail shirt and Fritz helmet under his arm, a curved saber at his belt and quiver over his back.

"Sir?" he said to Frederick.

Then he saw who was standing near. "Dave! Christ, they caught you too!" he blurted to his elder brother.

"Looks like you landed on your feet, Jack."

"It was a Goddamned stroke of luck, is what it was," Jack said; then he looked over at the Dúnedain party. "I see you met Mary Vogeler. She and her husband . . . now there's a man who knows his cavalry work! . . . and a bunch of wild Indians and Baron Tucannon and his *menie* mouse-trapped my command. Baited it with a flock of sheep, of all things."

The brothers stood awkwardly for a moment, then embraced even more clumsily and stood back, looking at each other more carefully. Dave went on in a more normal tone:

"Dangled sheep in front of you, hey? What's the difference between a cavalryman and an ordinary sheep-stealing rustler?"

His brother grinned as he completed the joke: "Same as the difference between bandits and tax-collectors: *official permission*. Yeah, it was dumb, even if the logistics were shit and we were hungry. But it got us . . . me . . . where we could find out for sure what's really going on."

His face went bleak. "I lost some good men. But not as many as staying in the campaign would have, and . . . We need to talk, Dave. I've talked to Fred's mother and sisters . . . and to Juliet."

"The President's wife?"

"Martin Thurston's wife. After she and the . . . Fred's mother . . . came and gave us a talk, nine-tenths of my men came over in a body. And the rest were mostly just sick of the whole thing and wanted to sit it out somewhere nobody was sending arrows and round-shot their way. We *really* need to talk."

"Ok . . . Jack."

Jack looked at his commander, who nodded and jerked his head slightly aside. They drew off together. Rudi nodded to the younger Thurston himself.

"Sure, and that was well done, Fred. You're learning. Not least when to speak and when to leave it to others."

"Got the basics from Dad and the details from you, Rudi," Frederick Thurston said as he smiled whitely, but it was a slightly grim expression for all that. "It's like a snowball running downhill in winter now. And every one I talk over . . ."

". . . is one we don't have to kill. That's what war is about, sure and it is, for those who don't love it because it's the most rapid and efficient way of producing a great whacking heap of corpses. It's a way of getting people to do what you want, and not the most economical when there's an alternative."

"And every one we talk around is another who can fight the Prophet's men later. We're not going to talk many of *them* around."

"Arra, I fear you have the right of that, not until we've hit them hard enough to break the hold he has on their hearts. Though I have my hopes for the long run."

Dave Woburn must have been thinking hard for some time; the conversation was brief. He clapped his brother on the shoulder and strode briskly over to Fred.

"Sir, Centurion Woburn reporting for duty," he said, coming to attention and saluting.

"Right," Fred said with a nod, returning the gesture. "First thing, let's shed the pseudo-Roman crap; you're a major. My dad drew on that stuff because it was useful, not because he was some obsessive with a man-crush on Julius Caesar."

Unlike Fred's elder brother, Rudi thought, silent.

"Next, I'm operating under the High King's orders here. You do understand that?"

The young officer's face grew a little grimmer. "Yes, sir, General Thurston."

"Good. We're going to have a referendum on joining the High Kingdom after the war . . . *right* after the war, not 'when circumstances permit' which is another way of saying 'Fifth of Never.' "

Woburn's eyes flicked to Rudi. He nodded, his hand on the hilt of the Sword.

"That has my public oath," he said, meeting the blue eyes of the Rancher's son. "I'm confident the result will be yes, which would be best for the peace and prosperity of all Montival; but I'll abide the result, come what may. I've no desire to bring any land or folk into the High Kingdom against their wish and will. Save for the CUT territories, and that's a matter of common sense and necessity. Just for your information, what's left of Deseret wants to join us, as well."

"I've never heard that your word isn't good," Woburn said after a moment. Then, after another pause: "Your Majesty."

Rudi smiled, a little bleakly. "*And* you may have heard that no man can deceive me with effect while I hold the Sword of the Lady. Which, by the Lady and the Hornéd Lord who is Her consort, is nothing less than the truth. If you find that alarming . . . well, so do I. Not that either of our opinions matters a great deal."

Woburn swallowed. "I wasn't planning on lying, Your Majesty."

"No, you weren't. I know."

And for me falsehood now feels like . . . very much like biting down on a piece of metal foil with your back teeth. Or a smell. I was always fairly good at reading men's faces, but no more than that. Now it's like a banner waving in the wind, if I concentrate. Lord and Lady witness, when this war is over I will hang the Sword on the wall and take it down only at direst need, making a sacrifice of Power to Justice, as Jason did of Medusa's head. Too much truth can destroy you, or destroy your capacity to live among men as one of the humankind.

"Good man," Fred said to the elder Woburn brother. "But first we have to *win* the war. Which means you're going to debrief, Major, and do so fully."

"Yes, sir."

He moved over to the map table, put his hand on the markers for the Boisean forces and rearranged several.

"You had it mostly right. Here's the order of battle as far as I know it, and how the brigades are going to deploy—"

Rudi's eyes went north and east. The battle would be starting by now, the fringes of two vast hosts intent on violence meeting and clashing where they met, and battle was chaos where a slipped horseshoe or a man blinking as sunlight struck his eyes could change the fate of kingdoms. But he could feel factors shifting now, shifting a little in his favor.

Favor bought with blood, he thought. *So, Ard Rí, let's be about the work of the day.*

He signed, and the attendants put away the markers and packed up the map table. Before they left he took Alleyne Loring aside for a moment.

"Lord Alleyne," he said in *Edhellen*. "Rescuing Fred's mother and sisters was a worthy deed, and it's a help to us their testimony has been. But rescuing Juliet Thurston, and the manner in which it was done . . . that's helped us more still, even though it was no part of your plan in the beginning."

"Plans don't survive contact with the enemy."

"Call it a lucky chance, then, amid so much ill-luck."

"If chance you call it," Alleyne said with the ghost of a smile.

Rudi nodded. "Not because Juliet's beloved as they are, but because being who and what she is her word carries extra weight about Martin Thurston's doings, and because his trying to kill her to silence her doubles that credibility, the which too many saw to hush up. He—"

He inclined his head to indicate where Dave Woburn was being introduced to his new comrades, then put a hand on the older man's shoulder for a moment.

"—is not the first fighting-man who's been brought to our side from Boise by the tale of it, and I'm thinkin' he won't be the last either, in this war. The battle today *may* turn on that, and with it our homes and families; and for a certainty, there will be many on our side walking the ridge of the world come sundown who'd be lying stark and dead save for what you and your lady did that day. I won't presume to tell you how much comfort to take from that, but for what it's worth, there it is."

Alleyne took a long breath. "Thank you, Your Majesty," he said. "Astrid . . . Astrid knew what she was doing and why. And *I* knew what might happen, every time we went on an operation together."

He hesitated. "When she . . . her last words . . ."

"My sister told me," Rudi said. "*Like silver glass . . . green shores . . . the gulls . . . a white tower . . . home, home, at last . . .*"

The older man swallowed painfully. "I always thought . . . it was a pardonable eccentricity? The, ah, interpretation of the Histories. It gave people comfort and meaning in their lives, and so I went along with it. But . . ."

Then he shook his head. "No. That's being too gentle. I thought it was a functional madness. It didn't interfere with the *rest* of our lives, and it did no harm . . . did good, rather. People need stories to live by, and why

not those? Something *like* the Rangers was essential, Astrid had already set the . . . the process in motion, it was
too late to use a different set of myths. And the Histories were no more fictional than the Bible, allowing for
the difference in age. But . . ."

Rudi looked him in the eye. "Now you're wondering
if there could really be anything to it," he said.

A nod, and Rudi went on: "My friend, after Nantucket, I think there actually may be something to it; to
that, and to many another vision folk have had; to the
Bible of the Christians, for that matter, as well."

"All at once?"

Rudi shrugged ruefully: "Why would you expect to
understand all of a God's mind, save that part of themselves they make apparent to us? Any more than a dog
can understand a man . . . though he understands the
food, and the warm spot by the fire, and the hand of
love upon the head, and the joy of a day's hunt together."

"Not a flattering comparison."

"Now with that I don't agree; there are few men so
good as a good dog, for such will neither lie nor will
they break faith. And I've always believed we pass from
here to a place of rest and beauty where we heal ourselves and then return. What your lady saw . . . I don't
understand it, and I'm not going to pretend I do. But
this I *do* believe; that your lady saw exactly what she
thought she did, and that she is home indeed this very
moment, the home for which she longed all her life.
And that she is waiting for you when you've completed
the tasks duty and love lay on you here."

"I . . . Thank you. Thank you very much."

He took a deep breath. "And now there's a bloody great job of work to do, Your Majesty."

"That there is. I want you and your Rangers on the northern flank now, which will mean some swift riding."

"We'll be there, Your Majesty." More softly: "And someday . . . it would be very interesting to see. Very interesting indeed."

"And now we've a battle to fight," Rudi said. He shook his head. "Are fighting now, the opening steps."

CHAPTER EIGHT

THE HIGH KING'S HOST
HORSE HEAVEN HILLS
(FORMERLY SOUTH-CENTRAL WASHINGTON)
HIGH KINGDOM OF MONTIVAL
(FORMERLY WESTERN NORTH AMERICA)
NOVEMBER 1ST, CHANGE YEAR 25/2023 AD

A n arrow went by overhead with a slight *whppt* sound, arching down at a high angle. It stood quivering in short brown-blond grass still coated with hoarfrost until steel-shod hooves trampled it a second later. The sound of hundreds of horses moving fast filled the air around them, the heavy hollow thuds merging into a continuous stuttering rumble. The dust-plume they kicked up from the fine soil followed close behind, their speed a little greater than the wind that carried it in their wake.

"Uff da!" Mark Vogeler swore as he ducked.

The shaft hadn't been very far from his ear on its way down. One of the many unpleasant things about arrows was that if they were fired on a high arching shot, even at maximum range they hit going about three-quarters as fast as they'd been when they left the string.

"When do I start getting used to that, Unc' Ingolf?" he called plaintively over the noise. "Uh, Unc' Ingolf, sir?"

Ingolf Vogeler grinned at the teenaged nephew riding at his left stirrup. The young man was tall and gangly and with bits of straw-colored hair leaking out from beneath his helmet and near-invisible fuzz on his cheeks. At just short of eighteen he'd nearly reached Ingolf's six-two height, strong and fit for his age though still lacking the full thick-armed bear strength of his kinsman. He wasn't unblooded anymore, but he also lacked the experience that decades of hard living and harder fighting had brought his father's younger brother; the slight crook to Ingolf's nose and the scars that left white lines through his short brown beard and on his hands were simply the most obvious traces. The dark blue eyes told more, if you knew what to look for, and the way he held himself and moved.

"That's *Colonel* Ingolf, sir, to you, kid," he said. Time and travel had worn some of the slightly guttural singsong accent of the Kickapoo Valley out of his voice, but enough remained to be another mark of kinship. "And you *don't* get used to getting shot at. Not really. It just gets less surprising. And everyone ducks."

Which is true. And it's even worse once you've been hit a couple of times. The damned things hurt, and if you end up with a field surgeon who's already used all his morphine grubbing around with an arrow-spoon to get it out, you scream so they can hear you in the next county. Mind you, you don't see the ones that hit you, usually. And never the one that kills you, the saying goes . . . though how would you check that? Ask dead men? I've seen a lot of them, and they never said a word.

The First Richland Volunteer Cavalry were moving westward at a hand gallop in double line, the three-hundred-strong formation writhing like a ripple in a river as it moved over the rolling surface of the Horse Heaven Hills. It was a relief to have the morning sun at their backs as they retreated towards the main force; trying to shoot with it leaving glare-spots in your eyes was a pain.

Like most of his countrymen, Ingolf wore what was called a kettle-hat helmet, mostly because it looked a lot like a kettle, with a central peaked dome and a wide flat brim. It had the added advantage that on a bright day like this it gave your eyes some shade. He looked over his shoulder and the circle of the round shield slung over his back, squinting; the sun was only a handspan over the horizon. The pursuit was gaining, and there were a thousand men or better in the . . .

Clump. Gaggle. Whatever.

. . . that pursued them.

OK, this is going to be tricky.

It always was, when horse-soldiers were moving at speed. At a gallop you could cover a couple of hundred yards awfully fast. As usual, timing was the margin between success and . . .

. . . *and*, oh shit we are so fucked. *Well, I trust the Mackenzies to do what they say they'll do . . . or really, I trust Rudi's judgment of what they can do and he trusts them to do what they say they can do. Getting into position this fast is awfully quick work for infantry, and not full-time soldiers at that. And doing it without being obvious. These levies we're fighting may not be much at field drill, but there's nothing wrong with their field*craft. *Especially in open grassland.*

He'd been a paid soldier kicking around the Mid-western realms for years himself before he went into the closely related salvage trade, and he'd seen that like any-thing else you got better at it the more you practiced.

Though sometimes even that doesn't work, he thought, studying the pursuit.

The nearest of them were a hair under three hundred yards back, just close enough to tempt them to shoot when you added in the wind at their backs but far enough that you'd have to be dead lucky to hit a herd of buffalo, much less a man. Flags flying from the shafts of spears beat the wind among them, spiky brand-symbols of the Ranchers who led their cowboy-retainers to war, the golden-rayed sun on crimson of the CUT. Another arrow arched out, falling ten yards short this time.

Only an exceptionally strong saddlebow combined with great skill and more than a bit of luck could hope to send an arrow this far; actually hitting anything would be sheer dumb luck. In an outfit with more fire discipline some noncom would be roasting the enthusi-ast's ass about now, for wasting an arrow he might need desperately soon. The enemy cavalry were superb riders and very good archers, herdsmen from the mountains and valleys and high bleak plains of what had been Montana and northern Wyoming. They were raised in the saddle and lived by the bow, but he'd seen more organization in brothel-and-bar brawls than in most of the CUT's Rancher levies. The Sword of the Prophet wasn't here right now, thank God . . . or Manwë and Varda. No regular troops of any sort from the CUT-Boise alliance, not yet.

Down into another swale, a spurt of soil and gravel flicking forward under the hooves, the horse and the rider as one. He looked left and right; the landscape here was deceptive, closing in and opening out suddenly into huge vistas that seemed to go on forever. Rudi . . . the High King . . . had picked this battlefield and spent months patiently drawing the enemy onto it for the possibilities, which was a sign of cool nerves and confidence. If you could surprise the enemy they could return the favor, and war was a matter of split-second chances. He'd have been a lot more uneasy personally if he hadn't spent a lot of his youth fighting on the Great Plains west of the Red River, especially the Dakota badlands. That was tricky country too.

And running a fight is like playing four games of chess at once, only you can't see half the pieces. Crap. I used to think this was exciting. Of course, I was young and stupid then, a hard-on with legs.

The air was still cool to chilly and fresh with recent rain; about ideal for fighting, if you had to do it. It kept the dust-pillars of units moving to engage separate too, so far, rather than merging into a single choking pall. He scanned them and judged that nobody traveling with a lot of friends was likely to come uninvited to the dance in the next twenty minutes, so he could carry on with his original plan. Balances of time and distance and numbers moved in his head beneath the surface of conscious thought.

"Signal *at speed*," he snapped.

Mark raised the trumpet to his lips, filled his lungs and blew. Most of the horses were already reacting by the time their riders shifted in the saddle; the First Richland had come a long way since it was a collection of quarrelsome blue bloods from the Farmer and Sheriff families of the Kickapoo Valley back in the Free Republic. They'd known what to do even then, but now they just *did* it. Beneath him Boy rocked up to his best speed, nostrils flaring as his head pumped. Ingolf moved easily with the long swooping rhythm of the big bay gelding's gallop, a lifetime skill.

Up the other side of the swale, and the enemy saw that their prey were escaping. Raw whoops rose, a kiy-yi-yipping sound, and then the harsh eerie *Cut! Cut! Cut!* war-chant of the Church Universal and Triumphant. He looked over his shoulder and judged distances; they were getting a burst of speed out of their horses, but it would leave them winded soon. And they didn't have their remount strings right with them. Trade-offs, everything was trade-offs . . .

Now just watch the stakes, he tried to project at his men mentally.

There was a set of four peeled withes stuck in the low rise ahead, spaced about a hundred yards apart. Totally inconsequential unless you were looking for them.

Come on, you cheeseheads, you were briefed.

"Signal *columns of platoons*," he barked.

The trumpet sounded again, brassy and harsh. The long formation stuttered and changed, as if the sound were playing directly on the nervous systems of men and horses; it turned from a long double line into four columns each, three men across and twenty deep. They did it without even a moment's check to their speed, like a square-dance on horseback, and Ingolf felt an instant's flickering glow of pride under his focus.

Over the low swelling crest, each column trampling a stake as it went. The Cutters were after them fast now, ready to plaster them with arrows and then close in with the shete, the eastern cutting-sword. Being outnumbered was a recipe for a massacre in a swarming melee fight like that, where drill and discipline counted for much less. Down into the shallow draw, up the other side and—

"*Left wheel!*"

The trumpet sounded. Ingolf peeled out of the formation as each snake of horsemen turned in its own length, the whole becoming a thicker column again. Mark was beside him. The others thundered by, and he waved sharply to Major Jaeger as he passed. The second-in-command had been promoted this summer, after his predecessor had stopped an arrow in a skirmish far east of here, but he was shaping nicely.

Then he turned in the saddle to look back where they'd come. The ground itself just on this side of the crest writhed and shook, or so it seemed. That was a thousand Mackenzie archers shedding their war-cloaks, the shaggy surfaces studded with loops holding bits of bunchgrass. They could be hard to spot if you were walking within ten feet of them, much less riding a galloping horse a hundred yards away.

Even Mary, with proper Dúnedain Ranger loftiness, admitted that they did it *fairly well, usually.*

"Get 'em, kilties!" Mark shouted enthusiastically, as the savage wail of bagpipes playing "The Ravens Pibroch" echoed, and beneath the hoarse drone sounded the thudding, booming, rattling hammer of the Lambeg drums.

Ingolf nodded grimly himself. They'd stood with arrows on the strings of their longbows, the great yellow staves of mountain yew coming up as they walked a half-dozen steps to top the crest in their three-deep harrow formation. Nobody was going to miss them now; the morning light on the arrowheads was like sun sparkling on mica in rocks, and their faces were painted for war in a riot of black and scarlet and blue and green.

By then the Cutters had realized what was happening. Some of them shot a patter of arrows, some drew their shetes to try and charge home with cold steel, and more turned to run; none of their choices did much good, except to tie the not-really-formation into an immovable mass of cursing men and rearing, neighing horses for half a hideous minute.

"*Let the grey geese fly!*" he heard the Mackenzie bow-captains shout. "*Wholly together—loose!*"

The Clan's warriors pulled the arrows back with that peculiar-looking half-squatting, half-leaning motion and the right hand ending back behind the angle of the jaw, as if they were standing between two trees and trying to push them down—what they called shooting *inside the bow*. Then a long snapping crackle with a whistling tone beneath it as they shot. The enemy horse were fifty yards from the bow-line, no more, about half trying to wheel and run and the other half still pushing forward. Coming to a dead stop on a single galloping horse was hard enough, doing it *en masse* without warning was a nightmare of bone-breaking collisions waiting to happen unless you'd practiced it over and over.

The heavy cloth yard shafts sleeted out, a thousand together and then two hundred a second, moving in long shallow arcs that were a blurring flicker of deadly speed through the air, tipped with narrow punch-headed bodkin points and twirling as the curved vanes of the flight-feathers spun them. Two hundred feet a second. Half a second to the target.

None of the enemy horsemen wore more than a light mail shirt, and those were usually made of old fence wire with the rings just butted together rather than riveted. Most were in boiled leather vests with a few pieces of metal added, their shields were light round hide circles on bentwood frames, and some didn't even have helmets. That sort of gear was about as effective as a wet wool shirt against what was going to hit them.

The sound as the bodkins struck was halfway between hail on a shake roof and hammers hitting meat in a slaughterhouse. The enemy seemed to stutter in mid-stride, and then their mass burst like a glass jar under a boot. Horses screamed, louder and more piteous than the cries of men; he could see them rearing, bucking at the intolerable pain of steel and cedarwood gouging into their bodies, going over and then more horses hitting them and tripping, bumped into each other's paths by companions on either side, or trying to leap the sudden impassable obstacle thrashing in front of them. Men would be crushed under ton-weights of panicked writhing horseflesh, and when horses fell over at speed they *broke*.

More flights of arrows lashed down into the tangle, and more, and more. Probably half the riders had been hit in the first thirty seconds, over a hundred killed, many more wounded, and more of their mounts. A spray of the lucky or slow or timid exploded from the back of the enemy group, spurring frantically westward and not even bothering to turn and shoot over their horse's rumps.

Ingolf winced slightly. He'd had enough experience of the Cutters, as a prisoner of theirs for starters, that he didn't pity them even slightly. But war was always hard on the horses, who had no choice in the matter.

Some of the running men were on foot, and others were pulled up behind by comrades; once they were out of range, many of the survivors slowed enough to grab the reins of horses running loose. Here and there a banner went up again, and cowhorn trumpets blatted to rally them.

Ingolf turned Boy's head and shifted in the saddle to send him into motion. The reins were knotted together and looped around the horn of his saddle; you were useless as a mounted archer if you couldn't guide your horse by balance and leg-signals alone, just as your horse was useless unless it could read those signals. He reached over his shoulder for an arrow. The Richlanders swung wide around the southern, rightward flank of the Mackenzie archers, shaking out into a double rank line again as they did.

The clansmen stopped shooting well before they'd emptied their quivers. They stood for a moment shaking their bows in the air and yelling a chant like one great voice:

We are the point—
We are the edge—
We are the wolves that Hecate fed!
We are the bow—
We are the shaft—

We are the darts that Hecate cast!

Ingolf shook his head and shivered slightly. He *liked* Mackenzies, the little he'd seen of them apart from Rudi and Edain. They were friendly to strangers—that had saved his life when he first arrived in Sutterdown with the Prophet's assassins on his heels. And fine musicians and craftsmen and farmers and some of the best cooks he'd come across in all his travels, and they partied with childlike enthusiasm. But sometimes they could give you the heebies. It had been about this time of year when he'd gotten to Sutterdown; Samhain Eve, in the Clan's calendar.

He could remember that, too, the eerie music and the dancers whirling through the darkened streets masked as Raven and Bear, Wolf and Elk, and the feeling of another world pressing on a veil stretched tissue-thin. Even Nantucket hadn't been all that much weirder.

Mark was looking over his shoulder. "The Mackenzies are pulling out!" he said.

"Yeah." Ingolf nodded.

One reason he had Mark as his signaler was so he could learn command first-hand, even young as he was. Back . . . not his home, not anymore, but Mark's home, the beloved place they'd both been born and among people he still loved too . . . Mark was in line to be Sheriff someday. The way things had worked out in most of the Midwest, it was the Sheriff who called out and led the Farmers and their Refugees when a district had to fight. It was a *good* idea for the Sheriff to have a real grasp of how to handle men in a fight. You hoped for peace, but in the world as it was after the Change, you couldn't depend on it. He wanted Readstown to keep doing as well as it had under his father and then his elder brother.

"You notice how the Cutters put their dicks on the chopping block when they ran into our Mackenzie friends?"

Mark nodded, and Ingolf went on: "But that arrow-storm thing they do works best when someone's willing to charge into the teeth of it with their fangs out and hair on fire. It's hard for infantry to attack horsemen who refuse to engage. This particular trick wouldn't have worked against really disciplined opposition, either, or not as well. Right, there's the signal."

They were well out east in front of the ridge the Mackenzies had held; the archers were simply trotting to the rear at a wolf-lope that covered ground surprisingly fast, some of them carrying wounded slung between them sitting on a bowstave, a few others carrying bodies. Northward a fierce blink of light showed, a handheld mirror catching the sunlight.

"Now *this* is going to get complicated," he muttered to himself. Louder: "Sound: *Advance to contact with fire and movement!*"

The First Richland was in line east-west now, facing north towards the shattered, retreating Cutters, who still outnumbered them. They moved up to a canter and then back to a controlled hand-gallop. He angled in towards the main guidon of the regiment, a flag of dark brown with a bright orange wedge. He went past grim-held faces under the kettle helms; they were young, but by now they all realized down in the gut you could get killed just as dead in a victorious battle as a lost one and leave your bones a very long way from home. The confused boil ahead was sorting itself out.

Yeah, the Cutters're fighting-men, and experienced, he thought. *They're not drilled troops but they're survivor types. They took a hard punch in the face but they're getting over it.*

Whoever the leaders there were, they'd gotten all the men who could ride onto horses that could run and they were pulling out fast. Arrows began to whine towards the Richlanders, fired over the rump in the way that made chasing about as dangerous as being chased in this style of fighting. They'd be planning on running north until they'd broken contact and then angling east back towards their main body. He brought his own bow up.

"Sound *shoot*!" he shouted.

To himself: *Let's keep their attention well and truly on us.*

With a grunt of effort, he pulled his shaft to the ear, thick biceps swelling as he brought his bow up to a forty-five degree angle and drew against the resistance of horn and wood and sinew and bent the stave into a deep curve. The string rolled off his gloved fingers and recoil slammed him back in the saddle.

His voice wouldn't carry far in the rush of wind and the drumming thunder of hooves. The action did; the trumpet would, and the way the squad and platoon leaders followed suit even better. Three-hundred-odd arrows whipped up in a high arch, twinkled as they turned and plunged downward, then a steady stream as men shot and shot and shot. Not as many shafts were coming back but they were just as dangerous; here and there one banged off armor or went home in meat. Men or horses dropped out or fell, and the line rippled as the others opened out and then closed up.

Ingolf ducked his head from sheer instinct, letting the brim of his kettle helm shield his face before he was consciously aware of a threat. In the same instant something hit, *hard*. His head jerked around, but the broken arrow flicked away before he saw it; there would be an ache in his neck muscles tomorrow and a bright scar across the browned steel of the helmet, but it beat dying. He'd tried the Associate-style knight's sallet with a visor, and it made him feel like his head had been riveted into a bucket.

And head-to-toe plate's just not right for a horse-archer's battle, he thought, as something banged off his chest as well, making him grunt in reflex. *But this breastplate has a mail shirt beat all to hell, even good riveted mail from Richland, I've got to admit.*

It was made of overlapping ripple-edged steel plates in the fashion western knights favored, cunningly curved and fitted and riveted, so that it covered your torso without confining it. Just about as flexible as mail, no heavier, and much stronger—which meant it was a damned sight better at stopping sharp pointy things, particularly arrows and crossbow-bolts. With that and short mail sleeves he felt properly equipped.

And . . .

Up out of the ground to the north came another clot of several hundred horsemen who'd been lying beside their prone horses, springing into the saddle even as the mounts surged to their feet, and at a gallop almost at once. They weren't in neat lines either, but there was a terrifying wolfish vigor in their attack as the feather headdresses or buffalo-hair crests they wore streamed in the wind. Their shrill screams split the air, and they crashed into the Cutters in a shooting, slashing melee.

"*Hokahe, Lakota! Le anpetu kin mat'e kin waste ktelo!*" *Go for it, Lakota! It's a good day to die!* he translated the scream mentally.

He could speak the language of the lords of the high plains, or at least get along in it. As well as a lot of people who belonged to the Seven Council Fires did, at least; most of them spoke English as often or more so. He snapped the bow back into the saddle scabbard at his knee, slid the shield off his back and onto his left arm, and swept out his shete. Shield up under the eyes, sword up and angled back . . .

"*Sound Charge!* And *Blades!*"

The jaws of the trap swung closed; not many of the Cutters escaped, as the greater wear on their horses told. One turned and drove at him with a spear poised. Ingolf judged the distances and angled his round shield. The point hit it hard enough to jar his arm and shoulder, but slid over the sheet steel facing. Before the man could recover, the Richlander's shete lashed down, splitting mail links and driving into the meat and bone of his arm.

Ingolf wrenched the heavy curved shete free, using the momentum of his horse as they sped by each other to drag against the clutch of riven bone and muscle, looking around for another foeman. None were visible, unless you counted the ones who'd gotten a good head start eastward. The Richlanders rode right through what was left of the Cutters, leaving a trail of empty saddles behind them—striking in a mass doubled or tripled the impact.

By then . . . A galloping figure pulled up next to him.

"More coming up from the east, sir," a man from the flanking platoon said. "De were close on dis bunch's ass."

Developing our position, he thought. *Somebody over there is feeding in troops to make sure where we are and what terrain we'll fight for.*

The flanker was panting, and blood cut through the dust on his face along with the sweat, from a slash that reached from his right ear nearly to his pale-blue eye through stubble so fair it was nearly invisible. He had his shete out. There was red clotting on it, and his round shield had score-marks where blows had split the thin metal facing over the bullhide and plywood. Two black-fletched arrows stood in it as well, and he absently broke them off with the blade of his shete as he spoke.

"How many?"

"Can't be sure, sir, dey had more than us out screening, but plenty, you betcha. Yah hey, two, t'ree thousand, maybe more, from the dust. N'less dey're dragging brush."

"Good. Dismissed, and get a bandage on that cut."

"Uff da, I am cut!" the man said, touching his face in mild surprise before he saluted and rode off.

Rick Three Bears cantered up. "We've . . ."

"Got trouble coming, yah," Ingolf said to the Sioux *incantan*, war chief.

Rick grinned, which with the war-paint of black and white on his proud-nosed face and the buffalo-hair and horns on his steel cap gave him a faintly alarming look.

There were eagle feathers woven into the not-quite-black braids that fell past his shoulders and a look of ironic good cheer in his dark hazel eyes; he was a tallish rangy ropy-muscled man, but not quite as thick through the shoulders as Ingolf. There was a ceremonial vest of white bone tubes over his perfectly functional shirt of riveted Iowa-made mail, too, and scalp hair sewn into the outside seam of his leather britches.

"More trouble than this," Rick clarified. "But then again, we won't have to deal with it ourselves. There's something to be said for this white-eyes army shit. Nice to have friends when you already have a lot of enemies."

Behind him his men were finishing the last of the Cutters; there were about as many of them as the Richlanders, a token of the Lakota nation's allegiance to the new kingdom while most of their men fought out east. There was an occasional scream and the guttural shout of *Hoon! Hoon!* as they worked with spear and shete and long knife.

Hoon! was what a Sioux said when he stabbed you to death, sort of a more elegant tribal equivalent of *Die, you cocksucking sonofabitch, die!* They weren't stopping to take scalps. Not very often, at least.

Ingolf had spent the first few years of his adult life fighting the Sioux, or what a nineteen-year-old taking an excuse to go running away from home had thought was adult life and looking back from his middle thirties, he considered a period when he'd been a large, very dangerous child blundering and hacking his way through obstacles and people. He'd been part of a Richlander volunteer force helping the Bossmen of Fargo and Marshall fighting to keep the Red River Valley and

vicinity. Nominally in command of a company of enthu-
siasts just as pig-ignorant as he was, but mostly not as
lucky. It had been a bloody draw, more or less; at least
the border had stayed just where it started out, a little
more than halfway across what had been North and
South Dakota before the Change. With the main difference being a lot of fresh graves and burned-out farms
and lost crops and slaughtered livestock.

Those years had been an education in many senses of
the word. Nobody who'd ridden with Icepick Olson
and come back alive from the freezing red ruin of the
Badlands Raid was ever going to be completely relaxed
when someone screamed *Hoon!* close by.

It produced an almost irresistible impulse to shout
Guard your hair, boys! and dive for cover, shield up and
shcte ready.

*Even if you've been adopted by the Oglalla and called
Iron Bear*, he thought. *And Christ . . . by the Valar, I
mean . . . that was pretty damned scary too.*

Rick held up two fingers split in a V and then pulled
them back towards himself with his palm parallel to the
ground. "Still want to pull 'em after us that way?"

"Yeah, it's working so far and it's what we said we'd
do," he said. "Let's go. It isn't really a very good day
to die."

"Who said anything about *us* dying, cousin? Better to
give than to receive."

The dead and seriously wounded had gone back,
mostly over captured horses with a few of the walking
wounded leading thcm; walking wounded meant men
who could move but not fight. Nobody thought of minor cuts like the slash on the scout's face as real *wounds*.

Everyone else had dismounted, and all the smarter ones had poured their canteens into a helmet and held them for the horses to take a drink. Sergeants encouraged the others to do that too, often with a cuff across the back of the head.

A thirsty man could keep going on willpower much longer than a horse; horses just lay down and gave up when they got sufficiently miserable. Willpower didn't mean squat if a slow horse got you an arrow through the gizzard, though.

"Boots and saddles!" Ingolf said, and Mark raised his trumpet.

CHAPTER NINE

THE HIGH KING'S HOST
HORSE HEAVEN HILLS
(FORMERLY SOUTH-CENTRAL WASHINGTON)
HIGH KINGDOM OF MONTIVAL
(FORMERLY WESTERN NORTH AMERICA)
NOVEMBER 1ST, CHANGE YEAR 25/2023 AD

More plumes of dust were moving half an hour later. They stretched as far as Ingolf could see, north and south for many leagues and east and west as units moved behind the front. The armies were well into the opening steps of their dance, probing and shifting for advantage like all-in fighters at the beginning of a bout. He was far enough west now that he could just see the line of tethered balloons the Montivalan forces had put up behind their position, each of them a finned orca shape with its canoe-sized gondola hanging below and the cable that held it slanting away in a long pure curve.

Ingolf was the son of a Sheriff, lord of broad acres, and hence an educated man who could read and write fluently and use practical mathematics to calculate volumes and heights, all useful skills for a military commander or someone who had to keep track of the food-stores that would take a community through the

winter. He understood the theory; the hydrogen produced when zinc shavings and strong acid met in lead
containers filled the bags of impermeable pre-Change
fabric. The balloons were lighter than an equivalent vol-
ume of air, just as the air in a ship's hull was lighter than
the water it displaced and so floated upward. It still awed
him to see so many of them. He could remember his
own childish delight when there had been a single hot-
air balloon at a county fair in Richland City. His father
had sworn in astonishment, too; that had been . . .

Two thousand eight, in the old style, Ingolf thought;
around here they mostly used the Change Year count.
*He hadn't seen anything fly for ten years. Not since the
Change. That was the last year Dad and I weren't fighting really bad. It got worse from then on.*

The Upper Midwest was as populous and wealthy
and advanced as anywhere in the known world after the
Change, but the Free Republic wasn't exactly at the
center of things back there. More like the frontier boon-
docks.

"And those balloons'll be damned useful," he murmured to himself. "Must be able to see as far as infantry
could march in an hour or more, or twenty minutes'
gallop."

And if you made a horse gallop that far flat-out, it
was done in. The enemy had gliders, but those had far
less endurance, and the prevailing wind was from the
west. A blinking light snapped from the nearest balloon,
plain uncoded Morse:

*Approximately . . . three . . . thousand . . . enemy . . .
horse . . . in . . . pursuit . . . you. Forces . . . moving . . . as . . .
planned.*

"That won't last long," Ingolf said.

"Sir?" Mark said.

"Plans don't last long once the fighting starts," Ingolf amplified. "So we don't want to get too far ahead and give 'em time to think. It's like playing a brown trout back on the Kickapoo. Sound *walk-march, trot*."

The trumpet sounded again. Being a commander's signaler-aide was good education for a young man like Mark; you got to see everything, hear all the plans and consultations, and you acquired a *really* good command of the language a commander used to turn a cavalry regiment into an extension of his will.

"I wish Aunt Mary was with us," Mark said suddenly. Hastily: "She's, ah, a *really good* scout. All those Dúnedain—" he pronounced it Dunny-dan "—are."

"I wish she were too, Mark," Ingolf said. *Though the real reason is you've got a gawd-awful crush on her*, he added tolerantly to himself.

Mark was a good kid, and smart, and wouldn't make a nuisance of himself. Though that sort of thing could really *hurt* when you were his age.

"But we've all got our jobs to do," he finished.

Which is true. Mary makes a pretty fair horse-soldier but she's a goddamned ghost as a sneaker-and-peeker. And I'm a pretty good sneaker-and-peeker . . . for a goddamned good horse-soldier.

The First Richland slowed; so did the Sioux on their right. They came over another low ridge. Ingolf grinned.

"And here's the reception committee for those dumb cowboy fucks chasing us to get revenge for their dumb dead cowboy fuck friends."

Rick laughed loud and long, and Mark smothered his

snort as befitted a very junior officer. The troops waiting there were mostly infantry, and newly arrived, double-timing forward to a brisk squeal and rattle of fifes and drums from the spot where they'd laid their bicycles down.

Ingolf's eye estimated upward of ten thousand, serious numbers even on *this* battlefield. He recognized their banners and the devices on shields and breast-plates, brown with a bright red-white-black bear's-head, snarling and shown face-on. Bearkillers, the Outfit as they called themselves, the people who lived across the Willamette from the Mackenzies. Which made them in-laws of his now that he and Mary—née Havel—were hitched. The Bearkillers had come together in the year after the Change, like the Clan Mackenzie. Montival was a pretty new kingdom; he'd been around while Rudi's friends came up with the idea on the Quest, and folks back here . . . back home, now . . . had taken to it like Polaks to vodka. They'd been desperate because they were facing defeat from the Boise-CUT alliance, desperate enough to clutch at a new-minted myth and shelve their local rivalries.

Sorta shelve the rivalries. Like my sorta in-laws. I'm married to their boss-lady's daughter, Rudi's half sister. Same dad, Mike Havel, the guy who founded the Bearkillers and killed Norman Arminger ten years later. But his widow is the boss-lady of the Bearkillers for all that they've got councils and elections and she really didn't appreciate her hubby getting Rudi's mom, Juniper, knocked up before she got hitched to him. Or Rudi being the big bossman, instead of one of her kids. My mother-in-law, Signe Havel, née Larsson . . . Damn, but there are some scary women-folk in this part of the world!

The troops had left their bicycles farther back, with the ambulances and forward aid stations. They were deploying at a jog-trot from column of march—the denser formation that was quicker for movement—into the longer blocks in which they'd fight. Doing it smoothly, too, only the occasional shout or rat-tat-tat-tat of drums and blare of bugle under the hard many-fold thump of boots. The Bearkiller infantry weren't the A-List, which was what their Outfit called its full-time elite fighters; they were militia, but it was damned *good* militia. The only way you got out of serving in time of war among Bearkillers was to be pregnant, nursing, or a cripple and from what he'd heard they practiced a lot.

As he watched, the heavy infantry stopped and unslung the twin eight-foot poles they were carrying across their backs and then fitted them together. A metal sleeve clipped them into one sixteen-foot pike, topped with a spearhead shaped like a double-edged dagger the length of a forearm; that was an ingenious trick, and gave you a shorter spear as an alternative weapon for close-quarter work like storming a wall. The pikemen wore visored sallets, and jointed steel-plate armor covering their torsos, arms to the hands, and lower bodies to the knees. What they called three-quarter armor here, and in a mass they looked like so many walking beetles, a murderous ordered bulk of steel and muscle and wood.

Their thirty-five companies were eight ranks deep and thirty long; each suddenly bristled like a hedgehog as the command rang out:

"Pikes up . . . Ground pikes! Stand at ease!"

Thousands of the steel-shod butts thumped into the ground, like a single sound. Ingolf nodded in approval as the Richlanders and Sioux threaded their way through the formation, passing between the companies like smoke through a picket fence. The Bearkillers were as immobile as a rattler coiled under a rock; even the pike-points didn't waver as the breeze caught them, and there was a lot of leverage in those things. It needed more than just muscle to hold one steady, though it needed muscle to start with.

I feel better about this now, he thought; appraising troops he had to rely on was a professional reflex ground in by long habit.

Drill *mattered*, and never more so than when men were moving something as awkward as a pike around. He didn't have to imagine the jammed-up mess a pike phalanx could collapse into if it all went into the chamberpot; all he had to do was remember it. And the screaming mass of dead and dying men and hacking riders that had followed when the line broke, and his own blind fear and rage as death came avalanching at him and his.

Christ, the things I do!

Behind each block of pikes were two more files of men armored much the same but carrying glaives instead, six-foot shafts with a heavy pointed chopping-stabbing blade on the end and a cruel hook welded to its back; they would move quickly to contain any threat the pikes couldn't handle. Between each block of pikemen were units of crossbows—less strictly crossbow-*men*, since a substantial proportion seemed to be women. They wore open-face helmets and the sort of articulated breastplate he had on himself, carried sword and buckler, but depended on the lever-cocked bolt throwers they carried at port arms across their chests. Even with the cunning mechanical assist, the weapons were slower to shoot than a bow, but they had plenty of range and they hit damned hard. Plus you didn't have to start at six and train every day to be really good with them.

It's no wonder the Mackenzie idea of a pleasant afternoon is herb tea, crumpets, a sing-along and archery practice. Or archery practice followed by beer and a pig-roast and a sing-along. Or any damned thing combined with archery practice. I swear they take those bows to bed with them and shoot arrows into the ceiling in the intervals between making babies.

The batteries of springalds and scorpions and twelve-pounders that also waited along the line of foot soldiers could throw their four-foot darts and cast-iron round-shot and globes of napalm farther yet. He was glad to see them, but he still didn't like them or the crews who were digging them in, throwing up waist-high earth berms in front and spreading their trail legs behind and working the aiming wheels to make sure the elevation and traverse was smooth, while handlers led the six-horse teams to the rear.

He didn't know any soldier who did like the damned things, artillerists aside. They killed men beyond bow-range like a boot on an ant, and there was nothing you could do but pray and close ranks over the dead and screaming maimed.

With any luck they'll spend most of their time shooting at each other.

That happened sometimes.

The Bearkiller cavalry were farther back, off to the

south in a brown mass topped with the thread-thin lances and the bright reflection from their heads, a standing menace like a poised sword. A command party cantered from there over towards the Richlanders and Sioux in a flutter of banners.

"Your in-laws," Rick Three Bears said. "Better you than me, cousin."

"I've seen worse. Rudi's mother-in-law is *Sandra Arminger*, for God's sake."

Rich shuddered a little theatrically. "Yeah. Met her last year when Dad came out to negotiate the alliance. Real motherly type."

The funny thing was that it was true . . . as far as looks went; she was small and slightly plump and you could imagine her with a tin baking tray of cookies in her hands, or at least pouring afternoon tea in a garden. For that matter, Sandra really did have her daughter Mathilda's interests at heart.

Stone-cold, genius-intelligent manipulative killer-by-proxy heart.

He'd met plenty of men who'd slash you into bloody gobbets in a rage—he'd been that man, now and then. Sandra killed like a housewife picking a chicken for the pot.

The Bearkiller leaders drew rein. Eric Larsson might have been Ingolf Vogeler, a few years older and blonder and a missing left hand replaced with a steel fist and maybe a hair less self-control. He was the Bearkiller military commander, pretty much. Signe Havel was his fraternal twin, a tall blond woman in her forties, tautly fit and dangerous as a wolverine, and ran the civil side of things—though she looked at home in that armor too. Her son Mike Jr. was beside her, and *he* was a pretty good kid, a little older than Mark. He looked a lot like a younger version of Rudi, in fact, except that his hair was wheat-yellow rather than copper-gold. Their faces had the same chiseled handsomeness, which was apparently the way Mike Havel had looked.

Goes to show you can't always judge someone by their parents. Of course, Mathilda's father, Norman, was a complete bastard and all-round evil monster shit, by all accounts, and her mother's a polite *and* smiling *monster, but Matti's* fine.

Right now the twins were both all business. "You've got a couple thousand Cutter cavalry chasing you?" Eric asked.

"You betcha," Ingolf said. "Infantry following them, probably, but we couldn't punch far enough through their shielding screen to be sure. The balloons should confirm one way or another soon."

"Yeah, Rudi thought they'd poke hard here too, and we got intel confirmation," Eric said. "Heavy column of Boise regulars, say thirty thousand foot minimum and as many batteries of artillery. They want to knock us back away from the river here, that's their opening move and pin as much of our reserve as they can. Should be coming into view any time now, but we're ready for them. Well, we and the Corvallans—they're coming in on our left as soon as they get their asses in gear. Hopefully before noon, or sunset, or dawn tomorrow. We'll cover that flank with our cataphracts until they're in place."

"How'd we find out exactly where the Boiseans were going in?" Ingolf said, impressed.

Eric grinned. "Your wife—both my nieces—and the rest of the Legolamb Brigade of the Dúnedain. They got direct observation on the Boisean's line of march and they took a really communicative and useful prisoner. I didn't know elves could have eyepatches too. *Arrrrr, matey*," he added, which for some reason seemed to amuse both him and his sister.

Maybe some family joke, Ingolf thought. *Or maybe some pre-Change thing. Those two were eighteen when it happened—not really Changelings all the way. I am, for all practical purposes. I was six and I can't really remember the old world, and Mary certainly *is*.

"And now we get to take a whack at the people who killed my little sister," Eric added.

"*And* the ones who cost my daughter that eye," Signe said.

His smile turned into something you might expect to see coming out of the woods at night. So did Signe's, and for an instant looked even more gruesome; she and Astrid hadn't gotten on, and she'd quarreled with Mary and Ritva too, but family was family.

*Damn, but I'm glad they're not *my* enemies*, Ingolf thought. *The official line is that only the Boise government *is really an enemy; their troops are just friends who don't know it yet. I don't think Eric's enthusiastic about making fine distinctions, or Signe either—though she'll make sure he follows orders; she's colder-blooded that way.*

It was odd hearing someone referring to Astrid Larsson as a kid sister, too; though of course that was how Eric would remember her.

Another burst of code from the balloon brought Ingolf's head up; that and the familiar massed drumming of hooves. The Cutters surged into view, a massive clot of horsemen. Eric made a signal, raising his hand and chopping it down ninety degrees.

"*Shoot!*" he called.

Trumpets and kettledrums blared and hammered. The artillery along the Bearkiller front all cut loose within a second or two of each other. Ingolf squinted into the sun as the four-foot javelins arched out. Scores of them hit the Prophet's horsemen all at once. He winced, even though it was nearly a thousand yards away. They kept coming, though, at a fast canter.

Nothing wrong with their instincts, he thought.

Running *towards* trouble was the right reflex to have, even if it had to be controlled by second thoughts.

Another gesture by Eric, and drums and trumpets rang again. The scorpions and twelve-pounders were firing roundshot now, globes of cast steel. You could just see them traveling through the air, a whistling sound under the *tung-whack!* of heavy truck springs letting go and the throwing-arms and slides hitting their stops. Where they struck men and horses *splashed*, and the metal globes went bounding and tumbling along the ground for scores of yards, breaking legs like matchsticks.

"Pikepoints front . . . *down!*"

There was a bristling ripple all along the Bearkiller line as the call was transmitted by the drums and bugles and fifes. The front five ranks of pikes came down level, the first three held underarm at waist height, the next two chest and shoulder-height. Each block was a solid wall of staggered glittering points, with three ranks at the rear still upright and ready to step into any gaps.

"By the left . . . left *march* . . . Forward!"

Trat-rat-tat-rat-tat, and the wall of blades began to walk. There was a crashing bark from ten thousand throats:

"*Haakaa päälle!*"

That was the Bearkiller war cry. Mike Havel had been about half Finnish by ancestry, despite the Czech name an immigrant great-grandfather had been landed with by a petty clerk utterly unable to spell or pronounce the original arm-long string of Karelian consonants. For the Outfit he founded he'd adopted the old battle chant that had once had half of Europe crowding into its churches to pray:

From the terrible Finns, Lord deliver us!

"*Haakaa päälle!*"

"What's that mean?" Mark asked as they nodded to the Bearkiller leaders and turned their horses away. "Colonel Ingolf Uncle, sir."

"*Hack them down!* more or less." Ingolf grinned. "Mary filled me in on it."

A roar to make the earth shake: "*Haakaa päälle!*"

"*Hack them down!*" Rick said. "It's got a certain earthy simplicity. I like it. And over there, they don't."

Ingolf grinned wider and shook his head, the particular expression a man got at seeing an enemy suffer; there wasn't going to be *anyone* very happy over there on the other side just now. Major Jaeger reined in beside him as the First Richland and the Sioux fell into column and sat their horses behind the advancing infantry, amid the ambulances and the light supply wagons tensely ready to dash forward and bring wounded out or sling bundles and crates of crossbow bolts and artillery ammunition and spare pikes and whatnot. A lot of them were teenagers too young to fight, or other non-combatants. The Bearkillers had brought everyone who could do something useful, and from the looks they were organized right down to the boot-laces.

"Damn, they've got sand going straight in from the march like that!" Jaeger said, grinning; there was a spatter of someone else's drying blood in his brown beard, and he absently rubbed at it. "That is a pretty sight."

Rick Three Bears chuckled as he finished doing some quick work on a nick in the edge of his shete with a whetstone and slid it home in the fringed, beaded scabbard hung from his saddlebow. He preferred to rely on the two long knives strapped to his thighs if he was dismounted.

"No shit. *Atanikili!* Awesome, dudes! Glad they're on our side. Hey, we should get our quivers filled while we can, all that stuff."

It was a splendid display of arrogance, infantry advancing on horsemen. The Bearkillers handled the way the terrain rolled with nonchalant ease, keeping their alignment and flowing around obstacles like an incoming tide. Some of the artillery were firing over their heads now—which showed both skill and an unusual degree of trust. Some of the shot trailed smoke; thick glass globes of napalm, wrapped in fuel-soaked cord. The first volley of them slashed home. At this distance the impacts were little blossoms of yellow flame and black smoke. Close up it would be clinging fire spattering in all directions, horses with their manes on fire, burning gobbets taking off a man's face or running down under his armor while he rolled and screamed and beat at himself with blackened hands.

They were just close enough to see a twelve-pounder's crew pumping madly at the handles of a tripod-shaped arrangement, sending water through armored hoses to the hydraulic bottle jacks built into the mechanism of their weapon. There was a ratcheting *clackclackclack* as the springs bent and the throwing arms cocked backward and then locked. The loading squad moved with the precision of dancers to the command of the battery officer standing with binoculars to her face:

"Target cavalry front . . . Range eight hundred . . . load flame . . . ten degrees left traverse . . . fifteen elevation . . . ignite fuse . . . *shoot!*"

A massive *tung . . . tung . . . tung . . . tung . . . tung . . . tung . . .* sound as the six throwers in the battery cut loose, the recoil moving the shooting part back against the recoil cylinders that transmitted it through the trails and into the ground. They were well-made pieces; you could have balanced a coin on the top of the road wheels and not had it slide off. Then the whole began again—they were nearly as fast as crossbows, which was very good practice. He unlimbered his own binoculars.

That brought them close enough to see a signaler over there among the enemy blowing his cowhorn trumpet; the blatting *hu-hu-hu-huuu* carried well, and more than one was echoing it. He could also see some Rancher hitting an enthusiast who didn't want to pull out over the head with his bowstave. The Cutter nonformation turned and cantered away eastward with its wounded and dead draped over their saddles, leaving a scattering of bodies and crippled horses. A few Bear-killer lancers trotted forward to finish them off, an unexpected display of sentiment from a bunch he'd started to think were inhumanly businesslike. The rest halted, and the pikepoints swung upward again in a show of casual panache as they all about-faced and marched back to their starting point.

"Looks like the Cutters've had as much as they want and a bit more, sir," Jaeger said, rubbing his hands with glee.

"Yeah," Ingolf said. "This bunch, for now. They're between the devil and the deep blue sea, you betcha."

"My ass bleeds for them," Rick said, starting to make himself a cigarette one-handed. "*Šicáya ecámu!*" he swore, mumbling around the thongs as he found the pouch empty. "You got any more makings, cousin?"

Ingolf snorted and raised a fist with an elevated middle finger; he smoked a pipe occasionally, but the tobacco habit had died out here in Montival, except among some tribes who used it as a sacrament, part of their religion. What little tobacco available locally was so bad you pretty well *had* to be deeply religious to use it. The Sioux made ceremonial use of it too, but plenty of them also smoked because they liked it, since they could import good-quality weed from the Midwestern bossmandoms. His own Readstown area had produced fine leaf even before the Change, and still did—Ingolf had brought twenty pounds of it back west as they passed through his birthplace, packed in sealed foil-lined boxes. Mary hated the smell, but tolerated him as long as he only used his pipe occasionally; appeals to the example of hobbits, wizards, dwarves and Rangers in the Histories had fallen on deaf ears.

I incline to the elven side of the Force, was all she'd say on that subject, some old-time reference she'd picked up from her aunt.

"No," he said. "Not one ounce to spare."

"Brothers-in-arms!" Rick said.

"I trust a buddy with my life—" Ingolf began, an old soldier's litany.

"—but not with a girl, a bottle, or smokes," Rick finished. "Have a heart. I don't want to die with the jitters."

Ingolf laughed and tossed him his own pouch. "OK, let's get to work," he said.

Their supply train had caught up with them; that was fairly easy, for light cavalry. Mark handled off-saddling Boy and switching the tack to one of his remounts. Ingolf would have been shocked if it hadn't been done quickly and perfectly, but he gave it a swift check anyway.

The rest was a few minutes of routine; replacing lost items of gear, filling quivers, taking canteens to the carts that held tanks of clean water, putting on nose bags and giving the horses a quick hit of oats rolled with molasses for energy. He saw to handing their wounded off to the Bearkillers personally, and Jaeger did an inspection too. His mother-in-law's army had field medics as good as any he'd ever come across, their mobile clinics were beautifully equipped and almost painfully clean, and he finished the miserable chore feeling as good about it as was possible, making sure all his people were tagged so they could be identified later come what may. But—

"Well, hello, Ingolf, you handsome macho brute," Dr. Aaron Rothman said, as he ducked out from beneath the tent. "What're you doing after the battle? Presuming you're not dead or visiting me in my professional capacity."

Even if their head medico is as swish as all hell and likes to screw with your head, he thought resignedly. *Not that I've got anything against queers, and Mary always calls him "uncle," and so does every other Havel and Larsson younger than Signe and Eric. Old family friend, obviously. Juniper and her kids treat him that way too.*

He'd campaigned with some queers who were first-class, and more switch-hitters. What they did in their off-duty time was their business as long as they were polite about it, which they were no more or less likely to be than cavalry troopers of more orthodox tastes; Ingolf had a soldier's priorities, not a priest's. But Readstown was a conservative little place in the back of beyond, not a great and sophisticated metropolis like Des Moines, and your upbringing stuck at a level below conscious thought or belief. Gay people there mostly kept quiet about it and were glad to get live-and-let-live.

"You're too old for me, Doc," Ingolf said with mock sadness, thumping his fist on his chest in a display of grief. "It's a cruel fate that keeps us apart."

"I swear, straight people exist to make life dull. Where's your spirit of adventure, your get-up-and-go?"

"It got up and went a long time ago. Besides, I'm married."

"You people can even make *sex* dull," Rothman replied, grinning.

He was in his sixties and slimly elegant even in shapeless green scrubs and a surgical mask hanging down around his neck, with a neatly trimmed white beard and mockingly intelligent brown eyes, and a limp. That was because he'd lost a foot to a cannibal band not long after the Change, one that kept the meat fresh as long as possible by removing it in installments; the incipient Bearkillers had rescued him on their westward trek in Idaho, and he'd been in charge of their medical service and doctor-and-nurse training program ever since.

Apparently among Bearkillers medicine had become the occupation of choice for people like him, one of those chance-made local customs you found all over the place. A set of ambulances came up, and Rothman turned away from the banter as if a switch had been thrown, his face as intent as a watchmaker's at his workbench.

"Triage!" he snapped, and other green-clad figures came running. Then as he bent over the first bloodied figure, easing a field-bandage free as aids snapped the armor loose with bolt-cutters: "Sucking chest wound here! Plasma and drain, stat!—"

Ingolf nodded and swung back into the saddle, reaching into the saddlebag for one of the Dúnedain honey-nut-fruit-cracked-grain confections, peeling off a corner of the leaf that wrapped it and gnawing away a bite. They had most of the field rations he'd ever encountered beat all to hell, though the Mackenzie equivalent—they called it *trail mix*, for some reason—was almost as good.

And it was going to be a long, long day. For all of them.

CHAPTER TEN

THE HIGH KING'S HOST
HORSE HEAVEN HILLS
(FORMERLY SOUTH-CENTRAL WASHINGTON)
HIGH KINGDOM OF MONTIVAL
(FORMERLY WESTERN NORTH AMERICA)
NOVEMBER 1ST, CHANGE YEAR 25/2023 AD

Frederick Thurston lowered his binoculars as the last of the screening cavalry drifted back, shifting balance as the horse made the beginning of a motion under him and squinting into the rising sun.

"Extended order," he said. "Deploy them now."

"Sir—" one of the battalion commanders said.

He grinned, feeling a tautly controlled fear that came out as exhilaration.

"Matt, this is either going to work, or it isn't. If it doesn't work, we're all going to die, the officers at least. If it does work, we want to win as big as possible."

"Yessir."

"To your units, gentlemen. The God, Goddess, spirit, philosophical consolation or lucky rabbit's foot of your choice be with you. Major Woburn, with me— your battalion hasn't shown up yet."

"I expect they'll be here shortly, sir," Dave Woburn said calmly. "And ready for action."

That brought a chuckle from all of them as they dispersed, since Woburn's battalion was on the other side. The signalers set their lips to the mouthpieces of their coiled brass tubae and then brayed a complex set of commands; the battalion and company signalers took it up and relayed it, with one long sustained note at the end that meant *execute*.

Fred turned in the saddle to watch. The understrength brigade he commanded was cobbled together out of prisoners who'd come over to him, and of those who'd slipped across the lines to join on their own initiative because they couldn't stomach Martin's growing tyranny or the spreading knowledge of what he'd done.

I'm not worried about their determination.

Both options involved taking really deadly risks for yourself and your relations, potentially fatal decisions that had to be made in cold blood with full knowledge of the implications. And Rudi could weed out infiltrators, though he didn't have the time to do it all that often.

What concerns me is their organization. *They're all first-rate trained troops and they're willing, but men need to practice working together, just like anything else.*

So far they were doing it smooth. The columns opened out like a fan into a formation two deep, the rear rank staggered so that each man in it faced the gap in the line before him. Every soldier held his big oval *scutum* out in his left hand for a moment, and his *pila* by the middle in his right; there was a shuffling ripple as they moved until the spear points touched the shields.

It was an orderly formation . . . but not one that could fight a stand-up battle. This was how you arranged men for a skirmish, or a pursuit, to cover the maximum possible front. In normal battle order it would take nine battalions and a couple in reserve to cover this much with sufficient depth to give the array depth and punch and staying-power. Call it three full-strength brigades in a two-up-one-back formation . . .

That much was probably coming at him. This particular segment of the Horse Heaven Hills was close country, ripples running southeast to northwest, covered in sere bunchgrass and occasional sage, olive-green and brown. Nowhere too steep for infantry in formation, but he wouldn't want to use much cavalry here, and artillery would be cramped. Passable for infantry, and one which would give them relative advantage against any other arms.

Well, bless you, Rudi. You really caught the terrain at a glance. Dad always did say an eye for ground was an essential talent.

Another glance over his shoulder, and the nearest balloon was snapping out details of approaching enemy forces.

Three brigades coming at us, right enough. It's inconvenient, the way you can read our strength easily from the banners . . . Maybe we should rethink that, after the war. If we win, we won't need such a big standing army anyway, we can put more into irrigation and roads . . .

It was time. His father had told him that pre-battle speeches had gone out of fashion in the centuries before the Change, but they'd made a comeback since, along with much else, and now it was a skill that a commander had to master. The men needed to see that their leader was there with them and hear him—not just the words, but the confidence behind them.

He turned his horse and rode along the ranks at a slow canter, waving his hand to the cheers; then back again, stopping at intervals so that everyone could hear what he said. There wasn't much background noise, either. A distant brabble; the fighting had started closer to the Columbia, but far enough away that you just heard a rumbling burr. The wind whistled a little, and there was a thuttering, ripping sound as it made the banners and flags dance.

"All right, men," he said. "We're not here because we *want* to fight our brothers. We're here to keep them from fighting for the Prophet and the CUT. If we *have* to fight them, we will; I'm not going to ask you to commit suicide. There are reinforcements we can fall back on—they're waiting behind us. I *am* telling you to take a risk. Anyone here have a problem with that?"

The answer was a wordless growl, and then a thudding hammer as men beat the shafts of their spears on the metal bosses of their shields, the *umbo*. When three thousand men did that, it struck you in the face like a huge diffuse blow as much as a sound in your ears.

"Sound *execute special orders*," he rapped out.

The tubae sounded again. Every man in his line laid down his shield with the face to the ground and the back and its handgrip uppermost, then went down on his left knee and planted his three pilae point-down at his right side—the two heavy short-range ones with the iron ball just ahead of the handgrip, and the lighter long-range javelin as well.

Frederick nodded. *Right. That looks as peaceful as possible when you can get everything back and ready to use in a second or so.*

A scatter of skirmishers came over the nearest ridges, trotting forward in loose groups, fast agile men with coyote-skins down their backs like cloaks, the heads mounted over their steel caps. They wore only light mail vests over their uniforms, and carried crossbows or bundles of short javelins rather than the heavy six-foot throwing spears of the line infantry. They halted at the odd spectacle before them, wavered, then fell back at a shouted command; they were tasked with giving the front-line commanders last minute intelligence in nearly real time, and with fighting only as needed to do that.

A stir behind him drew his eye; two coaches, halting amid the ambulances. He cursed in sudden recognition and heeled his horse over.

"Goddammit, I gave specific orders—" he began, then recognized the woman on horseback beside the coaches. "Virginia, what the *hell* is going on here? I thought *you* were watching them!"

His wife was in her early twenties, like him; she was in a less flamboyant version of her usual Powder River Rancher's garb, jeans and boots and Stetson. There was a light mail shirt under the sheepskin jacket, though, as well as her usual saber at belt, bow and shield at her saddlebow. Her narrow face was troubled.

"Honey, I just couldn't stop her! Short of layin' hands on her or havin' the guards do it. I'll fight *for* your mom, but I ain't having a fistfight *with* her."

The door of the coach opened, and his mother stepped down. He'd wondered sometimes if there was truth to the old saw that men sought women for wives who reminded them of their mothers. Right now Cecile Thurston was looking grimly determined in a way that

Virginia would need decades to achieve, but there *was* a certain likeness in coloring and build and basic strength. She was in the sweater, jacket, jeans and riding boots that well-to-do womenfolk in Boise's territories usually wore when they traveled in the cool season; and she looked older than her forty-seven years. As she had since his father died.

Since Martin murdered him.

His young sisters Jaine and Shawonda were with her, also dressed for travel—and *not* in the Protectorate styles they'd been affecting while stashed with the High Queen as his mother traveled and repeated her story to new audiences. His gaze swiveled to the other carriage. The woman who opened *its* door had been more than beautiful and was still very good-looking, her long blond hair up in a Psyche knot under her broad-brimmed hat. She was also pregnant enough to definitely show.

"Juliet," he said flatly to his sister-in-law. "I'm glad you didn't bring . . . your son."

Then he blinked in surprise. The man with her was . . .

Rimpoche Tsewang Dorje stepped forward. He was ancient or ageless, his ruddy-brown face wrinkled and seamed like the Tibetan hills that had given him birth so many years ago. As usual except in deep freezing cold he wore only sandals and the shoulder-baring saffron robe. His body had a scrawny, stripped-down look as ageless as his face.

He met Fred's eyes and smiled; they'd become good friends while the Quest overwintered in Chenrezi Monastery on its way east, hiding and healing from wounds suffered in brushes with the CUT. The monk had arrived a while ago with twenty-five hundred horsemen from the Valley of the Sun, escorting Fred's mother and sisters and Juliet after they'd been rescued by the Dúnedain. There hadn't been much time to talk since, though he'd heard the Rimpoche had been spending a lot of time with Juliet.

Who, Freya knows, could use some spiritual guidance!

"Young man," the monk said. "You are angry that these women endanger themselves; but have you not marched out this day to wager your life?"

"I'm a soldier," he said shortly.

Uh-oh, he thought. *We spent months in Chenrezi Monastery and I never once won an argument with this guy. Never even really* had *an argument, somehow. The only way* not *to end up agreeing with him is not to have the discussion at all and even then you start arguing with yourself.*

"Have you ordered your men to kneel and ground their spears in order to prepare for the clash of arms?" Dorje asked mildly.

"No," Fred said. "I'm . . . hoping there won't be a fight. Here, at least."

"These ladies can aid your purpose, which is to prevent men from killing. Any fool can kill; it takes wisdom to prevent it, and there is never enough wisdom. As for the risk, they cannot be harmed any more than you can."

"Rimpoche, that's my *mother* you're talking about! And my sisters. And . . . well, it's my duty to protect Juliet too. I'm her children's uncle."

The abbot smiled, gentle and implacable. "This is part of your trial. If you have courage it shall certainly be tested; because in all this universe no quality lies latent forever. Do not shrink from your own test, and do not seek to deny theirs to others. Without trial, there is no growth."

Fred took a deep breath. "Major Woburn!" His new-minted follower came up. "A platoon for guard, please, to accompany the ladies. Cap their spears."

That meant putting a small wooden ball on the tip; it was more a symbol than anything else, since it could be flicked off in an instant, but symbols were important.

His mother smiled in a lopsided way. "I'm not going to let everything, Larry . . . everything your father . . . worked for be torn down, Fred."

"I should have known," he said resignedly. "All right. But only if you're mounted."

He paused to point at Virginia. "And *you* keep back here with some remounts. I'm counting on you to pull them out if things go bad."

She wasn't happy, but she nodded and gave him a smile and a thumbs-up gesture. Those arrangements would give them *some* chance to get out if it went into the pot. Eager hands brought horses forward and adjusted the girths. Heads were turned as they threaded their way forward. There wasn't any sound—he'd have been shocked if they broke discipline that way—but Cecile smiled and nodded to the men, and Janice and Shawonda waved.

Juliet's face might have been carved from bleached ivory, but the Rimpoche trotted unconcerned at her saddlebow. He had a knack of being unobtrusive in plain sight when he wanted to be, which wasn't all that easy for a Tibetan in Montival. Fred sent a glance to his mother that told her that he *was* surprised to see Juliet here, risking her own precious sleek skin. Cecile shrugged with an unreadable expression that wasn't quite a smile. Her attitude towards her daughter-in-law wasn't *quite* one of unmitigated contempt.

And I *never thought Juliet was a coward. Other things, but not that.*

His stomach was in a knot and he could taste acid at the back of his throat; but this *would* make success more likely; if Lawrence Thurston had been the stern, hard father of the nation who'd kept the dream alive through the terrible years of hunger and plague and fear in a universe come loose from its moorings, Cecile had been the mother. And Juliet had a special status. Everyone knew that she'd been a lot of the political brains behind Martin's rise.

It also raised the risks of failure. Counting Virginia, nearly everything he had of kin was riding with him right now, in sight of Odin and artillery.

He grasped the valknut that hung around his throat above his armor; he'd come to follow that path, and learned more of it in Norrheim, on the shores of the Atlantic. Heard the High One speak himself, through the seeress He possessed, and claim one Frederick Thurston as His own. The Lord of the Ravens had his own purposes in the world, and to be one of His favorites was a double-edged sword. He didn't spare Himself . . . and wouldn't spare you either.

Memory flitted through him, memories of things seen with the eye of the soul in a place very far away: upward across a bridge sparkling with color, beneath gigantic stars, towards roofs thatched with spears of glittering gold where auroras crackled. A path that could only be walked unflinching, the way a man locked shields with his oath-brothers and paced towards a line of spear points and glaring eyes.

Father of Victories, I am Your man. You gave an eye for wisdom and sacrificed Yourself unto Yourself. I am ready to fight on this battlefield, either with steel or with craft, and You are God of both. Aid me now that I may aid my folk and those who look to me and the King to whom I have plighted faith, and I will pay the price—be it what it may. I myself am the sacrifice I offer to You.

Steel stiffened him; a memory of his father, nodding as he surveyed some task everyone thought was impossible and calmly settling down to it.

"Let's go," he said, and walked his horse forward.

The Eagle standard and flag of the Republic went with him; the squad Woburn had peeled off trotted easily, keeping pace with the horses at a slow jog despite the weight of steel and wood and leather on their bodies. A thunder sounded ahead, a familiar *boom*-huff-huff-*boom* sound. His mouth tightened; he knew that all too well, and it was a lot less comforting coming at you than it was when you were part of it. Thousands of men walking in step and marking it not with drums but by slamming the inside of their curved *scutum* with the shaft of their spears at every step, each pace the long yard of Boise's army. It was as if he could smell their approach, a rank scent of oiled leather and sweat and steel.

A great deal depended on which battalion came over that hill . . .

He squinted into the sun. It seemed to ripple and

sparkle along the crest ahead of him; pila-points, the sharpened metal catching the sun behind and throwing it forward in eye-hurting blinks.

And did they hesitate just an instant when they saw who was ahead? I think so. I'm betting a whole lot that's so.

Dave Woburn was walking beside Fred's horse, shield slung and swagger stick in his hand. He missed a step, then half-skipped to make it up.

"That's the Sixteenth, sir!" he blurted. "My boys!"

There was hope in his voice, and a tightly contained hurt. Fred nodded to himself. It couldn't be easy, the thought of fighting the unit you'd sweated blood to train and lead, that was home and family to you. It would be like striking at your own flesh with your sword.

And it's just now occurred to me that I'm walking towards this man's own troops and that if he turned me over to them there's almost nothing my brother . . . the man who used to be my brother . . . wouldn't give him in reward. Well, I decided to trust him. Rudi vouched for him . . . and if I can't pick who to trust, I'm not fit to command anything anyway.

Something similar seemed to have passed through the defector's mind.

"Ah . . . thank you, sir," he said. "I just hope . . . They're good soldiers, sir. The Sixteenth isn't supposed to be a fancy elite unit, but I'd match them against any other outfit in Army in a straight-up slugging match."

"Major Woburn?"

The man looked up; he was older than Fred, but not so very much. Fred went on:

"My father once said to me that a good officer has to love his troops and love the Army. But the Army exists not for its own sake but to serve the State by winning victories, so we have to be ready to destroy the thing we love."

"That's hard, sir."

"He was a hard man, but for good reasons. And let's hope we *don't* have to do that. Because the best possible thing for those men over there and for the country would be if we can talk them 'round . . . oh, *hell*."

He felt his stomach sink. "Sir?" Woburn said.

"Fred?" his mother inquired.

"The biter is bit. I just realized what I have to do, and charging with my sword in hand would be a *hell* of a lot easier."

And a certain Person is answering me, I think. I said I'd give anything . . . and the first thing He asks is a part of my pride and a type of courage that's a lot rarer than what you need for straightforward fighting. Maybe He is trying to tell me something.

At Woburn's look he went on: "If I try to talk to them, it's political—can't help but be. Someone might well think that's dirty pool and justifies throwing a spear even under a truce flag. You, not so much. You, with Mom and the others, not so much at all."

His mother shot him a surprised glance. "You *have* learned a lot over the last few years, dear."

"It's the company I keep, Mom." He looked at his sisters. "I'll be right behind you."

"You're right, sir. I know my second-in-command . . . Jack Simmons . . . and my battalion sergeant major, Dan Lindquist. They're not going to offer violence to your ladies. And I think . . . I really think they may listen."

Shawonda was the elder sister; she moistened her lips and nodded firmly. Her face was still round and unfortunately acne-spotted, but you could see the woman through the girl more now.

"He was our dad too, Fred. And they're a lot less likely to throw spears at two mothers and some kids."

There was no answer to that except a stray thought that Shawonda was a teenager now, and not young for her age—hanging out with Matti had probably been an education, too.

"I remember Dan Lindquist," Cecile Thurston said thoughtfully. "Your father rescued him and his family on that mission to Lewiston, during the plague year. A good man, very solid. Quiet and not ambitious, he refused a commission, but nobody's fool. His wife's a doctor."

Fred motioned and the white flag of parley went up. Then he reined in; he was close enough to see details—the stiff plowboy face of a ranker under the beetling brow and cheek-guards of his helmet, a mended strap in a sword belt, the distinctive thin scarring lines in the facing of a shield that marked where blades had struck. Well within pila-cast now, and there were batteries of field artillery moving up, keeping pace with the marching battalions even if they hadn't yet been turned around to put the business-ends forward.

The Sixteenth's tubae signaled the halt. It came with a crashing unison and deep shout of *hoo-rah!* The troops were in march-to-contact order, their packs left behind, shields advanced with some of the weight taken on the leather strap around the neck but most held by the left hand on the central grip; two of the pila were held there too. The third was over the shoulder, ready to raise into the casting position at the word of command, or to snap down to present a hedge of points if cavalry approached.

Fred could see Woburn striding forward briskly, then pausing to salute the unit banner. The command party around the flag could probably see who he was by then and that the ones following him on horseback were unarmed women.

The effort of will to keep motionless made sweat break out on his face, like dew on a mask carved from teak. He could smell the rankness of it, and a sudden stab of nausea made him swallow and clench his teeth; he couldn't even spit to clear his mouth, someone might take it wrong . . .

Every eye in the Sixteenth was on the scene around the banner and the signalers. Voices were raised, and there was a ripple as the sideways crests of the officer's helmets tossed. Cecile was closer now, pointing to one man after another—

Using their names or their parents'. Their wife's name, too, and their kids', probably. Reminding them how Dad saved them, gave them a life and a chance at a home.

One of the company commanders shook his head again and again; he and his sergeant backed away, hands on the hilts of their swords, then started to turn and stalk back towards their command. Two other officers grabbed the company commander by his arms and held him despite his heaving struggles; the Sixteenth's senior noncom stepped close to the sergeant and said something. It looked like he was whispering at point-blank range. The man stopped frozen in mid-stride, cast a quick look at his officer, and then slowly, slowly unbuckled his sword belt and held it out. Woburn's second-in-command stepped over, flipped the captive officer's helmet off and coldcocked him with a single brutally efficient punch behind the ear; the two who'd been holding him laid him down with brisk speed but no unnecessary roughness.

Woburn nodded. Fred's mother and sisters and sister-in-law rode their horses down the front rank, calling out:

"Don't do it! Don't kill your neighbors and your brothers!"

Juliet's voice, a little higher and more desperate: "Martin isn't worth it, he killed his father, he tried to kill me! *Martin killed the President!*"

There was a stir down the ranks, incipient panic. Woburn looked over his shoulder, and Fred nodded. The major nodded back and snapped a command.

The tubae brayed: *attention to orders!*

Silence fell, the rattle and murmur that had preceded it suddenly conspicuous by their absence. Woburn's voice lifted:

"We're sitting this one out, boys. Battalion—"

The order echoed down the ranks: "Company—"

"Platoon—"

"*About face!*"

A unified grinding crash, as the infinitely familiar sounds played on the men's nervous systems—something *comfortingly* familiar, as well.

"Battalion, *take knee and ground arms!*"

They obeyed. Fred looked over his shoulder and raised his hand in signal. The prearranged shout started then:

"Sit it out! Sit it out! *Sit it out! SIT IT OUT!*"

The Sixteenth was startled by the crash of sound behind them, but only for an instant. Then *they* started shouting too, deafeningly loud in their denser formation. Behind them to the east the follow-up battalion was coming to a ragged halt. To either side the forward march had slowed to a crawl as well. As he watched, one unit broke ranks, a platoon turning and taking a knee, another trying to march forward through them, an officer pushing at men with his swagger stick until a spearshaft knocked it out of his hand and then decked him.

Woburn came trotting back with the Sixteenth's command party at his heels.

"It worked, sir!"

Fred grinned at him and returned his salute with a snap. "So it did, Major. Let's get this organized, but I think—"

He looked around at what would *not* become a battlefield. Not far away the crew of a field-piece were carefully extracting part of the control gearing for their weapon, and then the gunner equally carefully put it on the trail and started to hit it with a hammer.

"—I think we just took about one-quarter of the other side's pieces off the board. Let's get the sit-down strike organized."

"Ah—"

That was Lundquist, the Sixteenth's senior noncommissioned man, a tough-looking stocky man in his late thirties.

"Ah, sir, what if the high command orders in troops to put down this, ah, disorder?"

He pointed with a pila; the brigade command post

was decamping to the rear, fast and in fairly good order. Individuals and clumps were following as the formations shook and writhed, sorting themselves.

Martin had the higher levels sewn up, Fred thought, nodding. *He just didn't realize that men aren't chesspieces. What was it Rudi said? Every helmet's got a head under it, and the head can* think.

"That," he said cheerfully, "would be a very foolish thing to do, sergeant-major." Then, louder: "Courier! And major, we have work to do."

The women rode up. His mother leaned across and touched his face.

"Your father would be proud, Fred. So proud."

"Yes!" Rudi said, reading the dispatch, grinning like a wolf as he crumpled it in one armored fist. "Yes, by the Gods of my people, *yes*!"

Then he spent a second quieting his horse; the beast had sensed his tension, even through the heavy knight's saddle.

"Fred succeeded, then?" Ignatius said.

"Better than I'd hoped," Rudi replied.

He turned his head. "Courier to Knight-Brother Commander Cyril. *Rally behind the Corvallans and place yourself at Brigadier Jones' disposal.* In clear, and verbal."

Two riders dashed off westward. Rudi turned back to Ignatius and went on:

"That's less than three thousand men on our side out of the fight and upward of nine or ten thousand of theirs—a sixth of their total foot strength and over a quarter of the regular line infantry and field artillery

Boise brought onto this ground today. There's our remaining disadvantage of numbers gone at a stroke, and without a man slain! They're all taking a knee and chanting *Sit It Out!*"

His grin turned to the particular slightly smug smile a man uses at the discomfiture of an enemy, and Ignatius shared it with him in a moment of pure communion. Rudi went on:

"And probably Martin Thurston, or the portion of him that's still a soldier, doesn't know whether to shit or go blind, the spalpeen. He thought he'd punch through there, which just on the numbers he should have done, but now it's locked down—and he can't shift those men elsewhere against those they *would* have fought, either, or strike at them without risking his army falling apart altogether. Those men are as much out of the fight as if they were dead. I've his face in the midden on that spot, and a boot on his neck holding him there, may he have joy of the fresh steaming dung. Human beings aren't numbers on a list and a ruler should remember it."

"Will you go there, Your Majesty?" Ignatius asked. "To consolidate the gain?"

"By the Threefold Morrigú, no! They're not joining in to fight *for* me, not yet—though afterwards they may find they have little choice, and then I'll introduce myself to smooth things along. What they're saying this moment is that they *won't* fight their own and feel no overwhelming loyalty to Martin Thurston. The which suits me down to the buckles of my shoon, not to mention to the cockles of my heart, for now. That'll be a delicate dynamic there; I won't risk upsetting it with my alien, magical and all-too-monarchical presence."

There was a golden circlet on the helmet Sandra's artisans had made to go with this suit of armor; as well as a spray of raven feathers on either side, and the round curve of the visor was drawn down to a beak-like point at the bottom and the whole scored with niello patterns to suggest black feathers. When he had the visor down, he looked remarkably like a raven, which was appropriate enough since that was the totem of his sept and the form the Mother had taken to claim him. A raven with a crown, which didn't look as odd as one might think.

It isn't an overall effect to appeal to a bunch of wavering Boiseans raised to revere the name Republic, though. They're old-fashioned there.

Aloud: "Let Fred and his ladies handle it; they speak the language. Literally and metaphorically."

"We did better than we knew, rescuing him when his father was murdered," Ignatius said thoughtfully.

"Threefold return," Rudi said.

"Bread upon the waters."

"Same thing. And the Dúnedain likewise when they plucked his mother and sisters and Juliet out of Boise's citadel. You might call that a light blow set against the clash of armies, but it was a shrewd blow right at the fracture point, so to say. The way a granite block can be split with one tap, if you strike it exactly so."

His face went grim again. "We've enough to do with the ones here, though."

The Boise troops to the east of him were coming on with a smoothness like a sheet of oil; the rising swell of land he and his command group occupied gave him a disconcertingly good view. The contingent facing them were Corvallans, pike and crossbows much like the

Bearkiller foot—the two realms were neighbors down there in the Willamette, and despite friction had been close allies with each other and the Clan since the early years after the Change. As he watched the command rang out; *pikepoints down!* and each block turned into a bristling hedgehog. Field artillery was already firing on both sides, the blurred arcing streaks of bolts loosed at extreme range.

Where they struck men went down, usually with a rag-doll finality; the four-pound bolts made absolutely nothing of any shield or armor a man could wear, tearing off limbs or killing by shock alone or ripping out hearts and spines and lungs. The pike formations rippled slightly as rear-rank men stepped forward to take the place of the fallen and helpers dragged away bodies and the wounded. Across the shallow dry vale that separated the armies the same occurred, but on the move as the Boise battalions came on at a stolid jog-trot.

And as each right foot hit the ground, the pila went *boom* into the shield. *Boom-chuff-chuff*-boom, like a force of nature more than anything human, or some great fabled machine of the ancient world.

There was a tooth-grating *brang* as one of the four-foot bolts struck the shield of a springald in front of him, rocking the weapon and sending bits of the missile flipping up end-over-end into the air like jackstraws that soared half a hundred yards. Closer, and the roundshot began to fly, striking and skipping and bouncing along the hard earth to snap legs and smash bone to splinters. The defenders had the advantage there, but the Boisean artillerists were working hard, leapfrogging half-batteries forward to keep up so they could support their foot with half the throwers at least.

Two twelve-pound shot struck a team just as it was wheeling a scorpion to the front, and the sound the horses made ripped right across the front. Rudi bared his teeth. Down in the ranks, the stink of fear would be heavy now. And the smell of blood and smashed-open bodies; like hog-slaughtering in the autumn if someone was clumsy with the hammer and knife, except that there was no hearthmistress on hand with a bowl of oatmeal to catch the blood for puddings and sausage, and pigs didn't scream for their mothers in human speech.

Crowded in shoulder to shoulder, the forest of points and shafts out ahead, the massive presence behind your back, no room to dodge so you let your eyes blur out of focus because watching it come for you made it worse. Chanting and shouting to shut down your mind, the white noise in your head pierced only by the conditioned reflex of training and the knowledge that your brother and your cousin and the neighbor whose sister bore your babe were there with you, ready to tell others what you'd done.

So spit on your hands and brace the pike, work the lever and listen to the loading cadence, bite back the fear and the angry outrage that all these strangers are trying to kill the one precious irreplaceable you . . . think of whatever helps. Think of your friends, of what you'll do when you march home from the war, of a baby held up under a tree on a summer's day or the sweat and ache of the harvest or a wagon frame taking shape under your hands, of a beloved face smiling at you from the pillow by candlelight while cold rain falls outside. Or think of nothing at all but what you must do; and do it.

Tubae brayed across the enemy front, and the whole array coming to the attack rippled and shifted; sections sank back, others forward, until it was like the points of a portcullis rather than a walking wall, all without a pause and across a rolling hillside.

"Oh, Anwyn's Hounds take it, *I want those men on my side,*" Rudi cried involuntarily, with the reflex of a warrior born and trained.

Ignatius nodded in a similar professional appreciation. "They've learned about fighting pike-and-shot formations in the past couple of years," he said.

That the temptation of trying to rush the crossbowmen is a trap, and it's better to swallow the losses of doing it head-on against the points of the pikes instead, Rudi thought.

The monk crossed himself and spoke more gently: "Kyrie eleison. Kriste eleison. Mary pierced with sorrows, pray for us sinners, now and at the hour of our deaths."

Shouts and bugle-calls ran down the Corvallan ranks: "Set sights for two hundred yards! *Prepare for push of pike!*"

The pikemen began to stamp, running slowly in place, a thunder of hobnailed boots and rattling armor. The long honed blades at the end of the sixteen-foot weapons glimmered as they moved. Between each pike-phalanx was a triple line of crossbowmen, standing and kneeling. The formations moved, like grass swaying a little at this distance, as each set the aperture sight on their weapon by turning a knob over the locking bridge.

A little circle near your eye, the blade at the front, bring
it down onto the target . . . it's just a target, not a young
man missing his mother and wishing he were back in a
cold shed mucking out half-frozen manure instead . . .

Rudi murmured to himself what the officers and sergeants would be repeating as they paced behind the
lines with their half-pikes or stood sweating in the line:

"*Steady, steady . . . open your eyes, Sally, they won't go
away 'cause you don't look at them! Pick your man, everyone pick your man, no firing into the blue . . . pick your
man, aim low, Jesus love us, Miguel, are you trying to poke
of those fucking gliders in the ass or what? Get that thing
level . . .*"

Fire-shot was arching back and forth now, trailing
smoke. The artillery were working with desperate speed,
trying to take each other out before formations could
be broken. The screams where the flame landed were
loud enough to hear, like needles of sound through the
thunder and brabble.

"Volley fire by ranks at two hundred yards. *Don't*
forget to adjust your sights between rounds. Front rank,
make ready. Present! *Aim!* In volley . . . *fire!*"

There was a huge blurred unmusical sound of vibrat-
ing string and steel as thousands of crossbows released,
then an instant later something like bucketfuls of peb-
bles tossed hard on sheet iron and logs. Men stumbled
all along the Boise front as the short heavy bolts
punched into their big shields. Others dropped as the
bolts went through or slipped between, their pyramid-
shaped heads smashing into meat and bone.

"Reload, load in nine times! Second rank, make
ready . . . present . . . aim . . . in volley *fire!* Reload in

nine times! Third rank, make ready . . . present . . . aim . . . in volley *fire!* Reload in nine times! First rank, make ready . . . present . . . aim . . . in volley *fire!*—"

The front of the Boise formations was eroding like sand hit by steady rain, but it closed up as it advanced. The shields of the rear files went up, a big sloping roof presented to the front, and the men were shouting in cadence as they picked up the pace to a slow pounding run:

"*Hooo*-rah! *Hooo*-rah! *Hooo*-rah!—"

Rudi made his teeth unclench and his fist unknot on the reins. *Here I am, High King and commander of the host, and I'm more helpless than the least of those stretcher-bearers.*

A pair of them went by, the wet canvas dripping beneath its burden.

At least they're acting, *not sitting on a horse making an example!*

The Corvallan bugles blared, and officers shouted:

"*Pikes will advance to contact! By the left—at the double-quick—charge!*"

The pike-hedges charged at a controlled pace, stepping off in unison from their jog in place into instant motion despite the weight of the long weapons and their own armor. At the same instant, tubae snarled and men shouted in the enemy ranks, harder to hear. The order was instantly clear to see, though; every single man in the front rank of the enemy pivoted on his left heel and threw one of the heavy six-foot javelins he carried.

A cloud of them rose and fell, seeming to accelerate as they sleeted down into the pikemen. Then the second rank threw, and the first again, and the third, and the second, and the first, in a continuous stuttering ripple until all of them had launched their three spears. Whole clumps fell across the front of the Corvallans, and here and there pikes crossed as files tangled. The rest continued, stamping over the bodies of the dead and the ones who screamed and writhed with whetted iron in their flesh, or picked themselves up and staggered forward again when the heavy spears bounced or slid from the hard overlapping plates of their armor, but sheer momentum knocked them down.

Then a uniform crashing bark of:

"*U-S-A! U-S-A!*" from the Boiseans.

Hands snapped down to the short broad-bladed stabbing swords hung at their right hips and flipped them out, held angled up to thrust or hack down towards an ankle. They tucked their shoulders into their shields and charged towards the advancing bristle of pikes.

The sound of impact was muffled but enormous when that many armored forms ran into each other, and it went on for seconds before it settled down into a roaring blurr. The Boiseans took the points of the pikes on their shields, shoving with their comrades pushing at their backs or lofting more pila overhead into the mass. Men pushed, grunting and heaving, hacking at the pike-points and trying to cut them free of the shafts, the swordblades clanging and showering sparks as they struck the long lappets that protected the wood behind the heads. Here and there the Boisean line buckled where three or four pikes pushed against a single shield; more held overarm smashed forward in two-handed stabs into faces and shoulders and chests with all the wielder's weight behind them. In other spots the Boise-ans bashed and shoved and slid their way to closer quarters, swords busy.

And the crossbows shot, and shot, and shot; the rear ranks of the Boiseans threw volley after volley of pila, and Rudi could see light two-wheel wagons coming up behind them and men passing out bundled spears. The artillery on both sides was arching its loads over the heads of the locked scrimmage in front, landing in the rear ranks with splashing fire or the snapping impact of heavy iron.

He nodded grimly, measuring distances with his eyes. The two forces had simply run into each other and were locked like a pair of elk bulls in the mating season. Horns together, muscles rigid—nothing moving, but huge forces balanced in tension threatening to buckle through at any instant.

And this is the most expensive type of fight there is, he thought. *Equal forces of good soldiers head-to-head, neither willing to take a step back, hammering away and in spare moments pouring down some water and cursing the idiot who got them into this.*

As if to echo the thought, Brigadier Peter Jones rode up. He was in three-quarter armor himself, with the visor of his sallet raised like Rudi's, looking like a very large billed cap; beneath it his face was lined and grizzled, that of a tough-fibered fit man in his fifties. His command staff were behind him, and a standard-bearer with a flag that showed an orange beaver's head on brown, its vaguely anthropomorphic face locked in a scowl. Usually Corvallans took a squad of young women in sweaters and short skirts along on campaign, who performed arcane ritual acrobatics and chants before action started; it was some legacy of Oregon State University, a brotherhood of learning which had formed the seed-crystal of survival there. They'd skipped that this time—the girls were cross-trained as nurses or clerks or whatnot, of course, and would be busy anyway.

"Sir. Ah, Your Majesty," Jones said.

Rudi suppressed an impulse to say, *Ah, and it's still Rudi, Pete.*

The man was an old friend of the family; Juniper Mackenzie had met him the day after Rudi was conceived, when he'd been a very junior officer in the newly-founded military of Corvallis, and he'd been a frequent visitor at Dun Juniper all Rudi's life. But the situation required a certain formality.

Jones went on: "We're holding them for now. But if they put in further reserves, I'm going to need reinforcements myself. Most of my men are already in the line and it's too damned early in the day to be fully committed."

From the look in his tired blue eyes he wasn't expecting the help he needed; every senior commander knew how stretched they were. There was a certain brute arithmetic to war, all things being equal, and no prize at all for coming in second. Rudi nodded to him and returned his salute; Corvallis used the old American style . . . like Boise.

Nothing wrong with that. Boise is not the enemy; the CUT and its agents are.

"You'll have reinforcements," Rudi said. "I'm stationing the Queen of Angels Commonwealth contingent behind you here, and they're to be under your command. That should do to plug any holes, and you've got the Bearkillers south of you."

Jones' face split in a grin of pleasure for a moment. The Commonwealth wasn't the largest contingent in the motley alliance that made up Montival's host, but it was high-quality. And it included the Knight-Brothers of Mt. Angel, who were also not numerous but universally respected . . . or feared.

"I'm glad you can spare them, Your Majesty!" he said.

Rudi held up the crumpled dispatch. "Around ten thousand of Boise's troops have decided they don't want any part of this battle and are sittin' it out," he said.

Jones swore in amazement, and Rudi raised a cautionary hand: "So are *our* three thousand Boiseans . . . but that was by design and the advantage is heavily to us. The sit-down means I can strip that part of our line naked at acceptable risk."

The Corvallan commander swore again, delightedly and fluently, then:

"Lady Juniper's Luck! Or High King Artos', now."

"It evens the odds, no more. I'll not take more of your time. Hold them for me, Peter. Just hold them."

Jones saluted and wheeled his horse about. Rudi cast another glance at the jammed mass below, then over his shoulder at the nearest observation balloon; messages were flickering up and down the line of them. Ignatius closed in at his side as they turned their horses north, along the roadway that paralleled the Montivalan position for most of its length.

"Ah," he said, grinning. "Now it's *my* compatriots, Your Majesty."

A force was approaching from the east, out of the stop-zones where his all-too-scanty reserves were deployed, the foot marching beneath the banners of their guilds and confraternities. A column of horsemen in full armor led them, visors up but lances in rest and shields on their arms. The gear was much like that used by Association men-at-arms, but colored a plain medium brown, and all the long teardrop shields the same with a black raven and cross—the emblem of the Order of the Shield of St. Benedict. They were singing and riding at a slow walk to keep pace with the infantry and spare their chargers; Rudi recognized the tune as a Christian hymn much used around Yule—"Good King Wenceslas," he thought—but the words weren't familiar:

"Praise the Maker all ye Saints
He with glory girt you
He who skies and meadows paints
Fashioned all your virtues
Praise Him peasants, heroes, kings!
Herald of perfection
Brothers, praise Him for He brings
All to resurrection!"

"I like to see men go to a fight in good spirits," Rudi said. "We're all going to need spirit like that before the day's over."

"I think many in your host have it, Your Majesty," Ignatius said soberly. "They fight for love—of people and family, a cause close to the heart, a dear familiar place—and that is stronger than hate."

He signed the air before him with the cross, and the bearded monk leading the approaching force with the banner hanging from the crosspiece of his staff gravely returned it, then smiled like a delighted child.

"They're all going to need it," Rudi said. "It's their battle, more than mine. And they must win it for me, and for us all, down to the lowliest crofter with a pike or most junior squire at his lord's heel."

CHAPTER ELEVEN

THE HIGH KING'S HOST
HORSE HEAVEN HILLS
(FORMERLY SOUTH-CENTRAL WASHINGTON)
HIGH KINGDOM OF MONTIVAL
(FORMERLY WESTERN NORTH AMERICA)
NOVEMBER 1ST, CHANGE YEAR 25/2023 AD

The High Queen's party cantered forward, her banner of the Lidless Eye taking the breeze beside the triangle-and-delta of the Grand Constable's; another lance carried the Crowned Mountain and Sword of Montival between them.

Royal squire Huon Liu spat aside to get the harsh alkaline dust out of his mouth; tens of thousands of shod hooves and hobnailed boots had ripped the thin sere grass of late summer here on this stretch of the Horse Heaven Hills, and the few rains hadn't been enough to lay the light volcanic soil beneath. Dust blew tawny about the fetlocks of the horses, and the rays of the westering sun behind them turned it to a mist of gold all along the front where the armies had met and clashed and parted since dawn.

"Grit gets right into your teeth, doesn't it?" Lioncel de Stafford said quietly.

"Yeah," Huon said.

He gave his friend a look; the dust of a hard day made him seem older and Huon was struck again with how much he looked like the Grand Constable, which was sort of odd when you thought about the . . .

Complex, Huon decided, pleased with his own sophistication. *Complicated*.

. . . *complex* family arrangements. Though you never knew how much of the rumors were true . . . Thinking about some of them was enough to make you shift uneasily in the saddle at the sinful images. Rather intriguing sinful images, at that; he was dolefully sure that "impure thoughts" were going to figure in his next confession, which was sort of doubly embarrassing when they were sinful thoughts about your friend's *mother*, of all people.

It's easier to be brave in company, though, he thought, and went on quietly:

"This is it."

"Yup," Lioncel said. "The jugglers and tumblers and dancing dogs have done their acts, the tables have been carried out, the floor swept, all the dancers are in place for the Grand Volta and the music's about to start."

"Dust and Sweat Pavanne with Scrap-Metal Accompaniment," Huon said, and Lioncel chuckled.

Elsewhere the din of onset sounded where the great hosts came together in an embrace of desperate violence as they had all day, but in this space and moment on the northern flank the mutter was a far-off burr; Huon felt his brain stutter as he tried to take in how *big* this battle was. Half a continent was here, with edged metal in its hands and murder in its heart.

Beneath the distant surf-roar was the creak of leather

and clatter of metal from the royal party and the hard clopping thud of hooves bearing the weight of horse-barding and metal-sheathed rider, and beneath *that* the same sound from so many thousands more at a little distance, turned into an endless grumbling rumble that you felt up through your seat in the saddle as much as heard.

The High Queen looked over her shoulder and grinned, her white teeth flashing in the shadow of her raised visor, the black ostrich plumes rippling above.

"Mud's worse than dust, squire," she said lightly. "Much worse. This is a *good* day to fight, and the best of company to do it in! Even if it is thirsty work. A drink, if you please."

"Your Majesty," he said.

He grinned back as he said it and brought his courser forward, leaning across to put the canteen in her hand. She nodded at him and drank; he felt his heart lurch with a vassal's love and loyalty, dread and a furious exhilaration like nothing he'd felt before in his fifteen years. His own swig afterwards at the water cut with cleansing wine seemed like a sacrament.

Ahead of them, at right angles to their course, a long line of horsemen stretched north and south, twisting with the rippling curl of the land and far enough back that they were hidden from the enemy to the east by the crest ahead. More came up as he watched, trotting behind the ranks of the Montivalan host and falling in around the standards of Count and Baron as the heavy cavalry was withdrawn from the rest of the kingdom's battle line and concentrated here.

There was a ripple of movement as spare destriers

were led up and men-at-arms and squires and varlets switched saddles and horse-barding to the fresh mounts. Destriers were trained and bred for aggression, and most of them were entire stallions; they knew exactly what the weight of padded leather and steel being buckled onto them meant. Squeals of rage sounded, and here and there one reared. More stamped and mouthed the heavy jointed bits, foam dripping from their jaws.

A cheer went up as the High Queen's party came through the line and trotted along it, banners fluttering; Huon saw men grinning as they thumped fist to chest or bowed in the saddle. Some shouted out:

"*For the Light of the North*!"

He felt a twinge at that; Odard had been a troubadour as well as a knight, and he'd made a song in Mathilda's honor with that title. It had become very popular recently. Chaste and hopeless love by a lowly knight for a lady of impossibly exalted degree was a staple of the stories, but after recent experiences Huon suspected it was better in a *chanson* than in day-to-day life. It all seemed a lot less theoretical since that haystack.

"What news, Your Majesty?" one baron called. "Do we charge?"

Mathilda laughed back. "Do we charge? Is the Holy Father a Catholic? The High King brings you a great gift this day, chevaliers, esquires and men-at-arms of the Association. A *cadeau* beyond price. He will give you a chance to die with honor!"

That produced a laugh *and* a cheer, and more up and down the line as the words were passed from man to man beyond immediate hearing. The chevaliers were in the first rank, a linear forest of bright steel lanceheads atop the twelve-foot ashwood shafts. The plate armor of the men and the articulated steel lames that covered the head and necks, shoulders and breasts of their mounts were often burnished until they glittered as well, and through it shone the bright colors of four-foot kite-shaped shields blazoned with the arms and quarterings of Count and Baron and Knight and the shining gold of their spurs.

The lanceheads wavered a little as the men shifted and the horses stamped and tossed their heads, and the brisk wind caught the pennants and streamed them out behind. The second rank were household men-at-arms of the nobles and manor lords and those squires old enough to ride to battle armored cap-a-pie behind the knights they served; spaced along the line in back were clumps of mounted varlets and younger squires like him, ready to dash in with a spare horse or a new lance or to rescue a knight down and wounded and carry him across a saddlebow back to the field ambulances.

Men were taking a final swig of water cut with rough wine, handing the skins down the rank, tugging to settle their sword belts one last time, touching the war hammers or maces strapped to their saddlebows. Making ready to die as each felt best, some silent, others passing one more foul joke, more crossing themselves and muttering a prayer, shaking hands with a sworn comrade or looking again at a photograph of wife or leman or child tucked into the inside curve of their shields. Men who could afford destrier and full armor could pay the high price of a camera and its operator.

He'd thought he would be envious of the squires old

enough to hope for their golden spurs this day, but now he knew they envied *him* his place by the Queen's side.

Lord Chancellor Ignatius said squire to the High Queen *would be a post of honor and peril, and he was completely damned right, may Saint Benedict bless and keep him. I wouldn't trade places with anyone here, not for twenty manors and a Count's blazons. Plus I don't have to wait in ranks. I get to see everything and know what's really going on! I'll really have a story to tell Yseult . . .*

He spared a brief prayer for her, too; his older sister would be stuck helping the nuns and doctors in the field hospital well back, seeing only the wreckage of war and not feeling this driving excitement. The knowledge that destiny was at work, that you were part of the wheel of fate turning on the pivot of mighty deeds . . .

St. Michael witness, I'll have a story to tell my grand-children when I'm an old man! There's been nothing like this since the Change, nothing!

Or he might die today, of course, and House Liu with him. He knew that, but the thought seemed remote, like a line sung in a *romaunt* in a hall after dinner.

"Saints Valentin and Michael be with me," he murmured very quietly. "I will burn a candle the length of my arm from wrist to elbows for them both when the war is done and I ride back to Castle Gervais."

At the middle of the long line the banner of House Renfrew and the Counts of Odell fell in beside the Lidless Eye of House Arminger. Others trotted to meet them, beneath the blazons of Chehalis and Tillamook, Molalla, Skagit, Dawson, Walla Walla and more and more, all the great families of the Protectorate. When they drew rein, not all the glances exchanged were friendly, and there was a little jockeying for position as horses were spurred accidentally-on-purpose.

"My lords, there's no time for precedence and state," Mathilda said crisply. "Just your bannermen and signalers, please."

House Renfrew of County Odell was led by Viscount Érard, a square, hard young face under the visor, blue-eyed and rough with dusty brown beard-stubble. His helmet looked a little incongruous, obviously a brand-new spare brought up during a lull in the action worn atop a suit of plate that had more than its share of fresh dings and nicks. He was probably on his second or third shield of the day; a sword might last a lifetime, but a shield was lucky to see out a few hours of strong men and heavy blows.

"My lord your father?" High Queen Mathilda asked. "I didn't hear the details."

The heir to County Odell shrugged in a clatter of metal. "The chirurgeons say he'll be on his back for six months and limp when he walks again, Your Majesty. Pelvic cracks, hit with a war hammer, they have him in traction and on blood-thinners, but he'll live, for which God and St. Dismas be praised."

"Amen!" the High Queen said, crossing herself. "He *would* try to take on a younger man's work."

Érard grinned. "He told me that until today he'd always thought it was just a metaphor, Your Majesty, but that now he can indeed truthfully say he's *busted his ass* for the Crown."

She raised her eyes a little in fond exasperation; the Grand Constable just blinked, but there was a bark of harsh male laughter from the noblemen before the High Queen went on:

"Ride with me a moment, my lords."

They crested the rise, two-score horsemen, and rode a little down it. Ahead of them the land sloped eastward, a gentle surface with only a little roll to it for several thousand yards; then some steeper ground. The shadows of the lances lay long and thin before them. The ground was open, save for the rust-streaked mound of brush growing in drifted soil that marked the grave of some great farming-machine of the ancient world, the size of a peasant's cottage and dead with the Change long before he was born.

The rest was pasture, nothing growing more than knee-high . . . except the piled bodies of men and horses, of which there were a fair number scattered here and there. Everyone but the screen had kept below the crest as the heavy horse moved into position, but that had meant a fair bit of fighting to keep eyes away as both armies extended their flanks northward, reaching for advantage.

"That's good ground, that's very good ground, Your Majesty," Count Chaka of Molalla said admiringly, his smile splitting his broad-featured dark-brown young face. "You couldn't find any better. Not for a knight's battle."

Piotr Stavarov of Chehalis nodded silently, his pale blunt jowly face looking very like a wolf's for a moment; by what Huon suspected was no coincidence, the arms on his shield included a white wolf *passant*. Countess Anne of Tillamook wasn't here in person, of course, but her contingent was and her war-captain Baron Juhel de Netarts, the Warden of the Coast March. If the company of the greatest nobles of the PPA intimidated him, he didn't give any sign, just tapped fist into palm on either hand like a man absently settling his gauntlets as he frowned, narrow-eyed.

"The Grand Constable picked it and the High King confirmed the choice," Mathilda said. "We've spent considerable blood today getting things set up this way."

Out there, men were fighting right now, and his breath came quicker at the sight. Not the smashing impetus of a charge *à l'outrance*; this was the darting quicksilver snap-and-slash of the eastern light cavalry, the way ranchers and rovers made war.

Huon could see little knots and groups of riders tiny with distance, each trailing its plume of dust. The twinkle of arrowheads as the horse-archers swept past each other, rising in the stirrups to bend their short thick recurve bows. Now and then two groups would dart together, and the sabers and shetes came out, the blades swinging in deadly arcs. He thought he caught the faint *ting*-crang! of steel on steel and the shrill war-shouts. Or possibly of men screaming in mortal pain and fear of death. Once a melee ran over a knot of the fallen, and the black wings of the carrion birds squabbling for tidbits exploded upward like a torrent of grief.

He grimaced a little at that. He'd seen men die—you couldn't grow to his years without that happening, in the modern world—but the birds were an uncomfortable reminder that at seventh and last people were made out of meat.

With souls, remember that, Huon. So many to Heaven or Hell or Purgatory today . . . Holy Mary, Mother of God, intercede for us sinners, now and at the hour of our death.

After a moment he noticed the leaders had given the skirmishing only a glance as they turned their field glasses about. A squire was supposed to learn by example as well as precept, even a very new and very young one; and he had the luck to be a squire of the royal household, with more to see than how to hold a lance and charge when the trumpets blew. His left hand was busy steadying the two spare lances that rested with their butts in a rawhide bucket at his saddlebow, but he managed to get the small pair of binoculars cased at his waist out and up to his eyes; the light squire's sallet he wore didn't have a visor to get in the way.

The Association foot was northward to provide the base on which the chivalry would pivot, blocks of spearmen and crossbowmen and field-catapults between them; beyond that only swarms of light cavalry, screening the flank of the war-host of Montival. Some of them were from the eastern manors of the Protectorate, where the PPA bred its own cowboys; more were from south of the Columbia, refugees from the Central Oregon Rancher's Association territories occupied by the enemy. They weren't very organized beyond the level of individual ranches, but they certainly had plenty of spirit. And not much inclination to take prisoners. They wanted their homes and grazing back, and they wanted revenge.

South beyond the last Portlander banners he could just make out the positions Clan Mackenzie held, the long, jagged hedge of swine-feathers planted point-out and behind them the harrow formation of the kilted archers. They weren't engaged right now either; the thick drifts and windrows of dead out three hundred paces beyond their position showed why, and what happened when a charge tried the arrowstorm. And the goose-feathered arrows standing in the ground so thick that they made a gray haze over it where the flail had fallen, hundreds of thousands of shafts falling out of the sky like hard steel rain.

Eoghan—youths and maidens about his own age who were something like squires in a rude tribal fashion—were running about there, snatching up armfuls and rushing them back to the reserves. Far and faint he could hear the triumphant pagan war-chant of the clansfolk roared from thousands of throats:

We are the point
And we are the edge—
We are the wolves that Hecate fed!

Huon shivered a little and crossed himself as it ended with a rising banshee shriek and then silence save for the eerie wail of the pipers; so did Lioncel. Mackenzies weren't actually evil, the way the Church Universal and Triumphant was, even the most stiff-necked Catholics admitted that. But . . .

They are very, very strange and weird. I'm glad I was born among sensible and civil folk with normal customs and in the bosom of Holy Church.

Mathilda bent her wrist to look at the watch tucked under her armored gauntlet, then up and back at the nearest tethered balloon behind the Montivalan lines. A heliograph snapped a signal from the basket below, bright enough to leave after-images. Huon could read Morse; it was part of the training a youth of gentle blood received, but this was in code and gibberish to him.

The High Queen followed it; Huon could see her lips moving slightly as she decoded mentally.

"Not long now," she said. "The High King is on his way. Rudi's coming."

The Grand Constable nodded and spoke, her voice as cool and expressionless as her pale grey eyes:

"It's our turn to do something besides feint and skirmish, and start bearing our share of the heavy work. Most of the action has been down towards the Columbia, the Bearkillers and the Corvallans. And the Yakima regiments."

There were a few muttered grumbles, from the retinues of the great lords if not from the noblemen themselves, and Mathilda laughed.

"Be content, my lords, be very well content. The High King hasn't stinted our plate. Take another look at who we're facing now."

Stavarov's field glasses were a heavy Zeiss model, pre-Change heirlooms his elders had looted early in the first year. You couldn't really stand in a knight's saddle, your legs were already about straight and the armored saddlebow and curving crupper locked you in place, but he managed to come up a little as he leveled the binoculars and peered eastward.

He grunted and then spoke bleakly: "The Sword of the Prophet. They've got that lacquered armor. Just about the color of dried blood, I can make that out, now that they're closer. There are Satan's own lot of them! At least as many as we are here. They're the only real lancers the enemy have, and they're bloody madmen, too."

"The High King shows his trust for us by using our

chevaliers against the enemy's elite. That'll satisfy the most sensitive man's honor," Lord Chaka said happily.

Huon nodded to himself; he'd been a page for a while with House Jones, and he liked and admired the young Count.

"Yes," Stavarov said dryly. "Though it may be less good for his body."

Everyone chuckled at that except Tiphaine d'Ath, and she unbent enough to quirk an eyebrow. Mathilda went on:

"And our Boiseans versus theirs in the center, though that was more talking and less fighting and then the lot of them just sat down. That was . . . fortunate. They've been giving the Corvallans and the Yakima foot hard trouble, they certainly don't have any objection to fighting *them*."

Everyone but the Grand Constable *grinned* at that, though Huon noticed that the High Queen's expression was a little strained; he'd seen how tight-wound she'd been about it, before things came right.

Just then trumpets sounded; faint, but out in the fields between the main armies. The enemy light horse were withdrawing. So were the Montivalan horse-archers, forming up and heading northward around the PPA's position, some in ordered ranks while others just streamed away in a clotted sprawl that still gave the impression of coiled danger. A smaller party came cantering towards the High Queen's standard, and everyone waited.

There's a lot more waiting to war than I'd thought there would be, Huon thought. *They leave that part out of the songs.*

He leaned aside and whispered that to Lioncel, who snorted as he smothered a laugh and then said sotto voce:

"*And then Bold Sir Dagobert/He did yawn/And then he did scratch himself/With a stick up under his breastplate/And wish he could get down/From his faithful steed Papillion/And take a leak . . .*"

The three horsemen reined in, saluting; the High Queen returned the gesture gravely with a thump of fist to breastplate. Off to the side, Huon *thought* she winked. Certainly Lady Mary of the Dúnedain did, the more conspicuous for the eyepatch. She was tall and slim and elegant in her dark green-and-black Ranger war-gear, spired helmet and brigandine with polished bronze rivets holding the little steel plates between the layers of leather. Huon found himself fascinated by one of the men with her; *he* had a headdress of buffalo hair and horns, black-and-white war paint on his face, a vest of white bone tubes across his mail shirt, eagle feathers woven into his braids and several fresh scalps slung from his saddle, besides tufts of older ones sewn into the outside seams of his buckskin pants.

"Saw 'em off," he said. "The Dúnedain punched through while we tied up most of their screen and got a look. They've got some good horses, the Rangers, and they ride pretty well. For white-eyes."

The Sioux rolled a cigarette in a leaf wrapper one-handed as he spoke, flicked a lighter and ceremoniously inhaled a lungful of the smoke. Huon watched with interest. Some of the tribes in Montival used tobacco as a sacrament—the Warm Springs confederation and the Yakama among them—but he'd seldom seen it himself.

"It wasn't too much like hard work, either," the Indian said cheerfully. "I'll leave that to you guys."

Rick Mat'o Yamni, Huon reminded himself. *A war chief of the Lakota. Who are part of Montival now, and invading the Cutters from the eastward. St. Stephen's wounds,* but this is a big war!

He handed the cigarette to Lady Mary's husband, passing a hand through the smoke before he did. Ingolf Vogeler inhaled, in a way that showed he was accustomed to the peculiar habit. He had a strange accent too, at once flat and harsh and slightly singsong; he was from the fabulous lands of the far east, east of the Mississippi itself, though he looked mostly like a battered fighting-man a little past thirty with a cropped brown beard, nose slightly kinked by an old break, and dark-blue eyes; his deeds were legend, though. He'd been the one to bring the news of the Sword all the way from Nantucket to Montival, and had accompanied the High King on the Quest all the way there and back again. They called him Ingolf the Wanderer, and it was said no man since the Change had crossed from the eastern sea to the western so many times.

He spoke to the High Queen with casual friendliness; they'd been on that Quest together, after all.

"They weren't trying too hard, Matti. The light horse weren't, that is."

When some of the Counts scowled at him, he added: "Your Majesty. Just screening while the Prophet's bone-breakers got into position."

That's right, they have different ideas about rank and station off in the Midwest, Huon reminded himself. *Though Lord Vogeler is nobly born; his father was a Sheriff, which is a baron, near enough, from what I've heard. He married Lady Mary, who's the High King's half sister and daughter of Lady Signe of the Bearkillers, and so a princess twice over. And of course he was one of the High King's companions.*

For a moment he felt pure sea-green envy; Ingolf's name would live as long as honor's praise was sung, and so would Lady Mary's and the others who'd made the great journey and shared its perils. So would his elder brother Odard's name and fame go on down the ages, who'd been with them and who'd died on the cold shores of the Atlantic. Squires generations from now would hear the ballads and try to model themselves on him.

Well, I'm young yet. Odard brought great honor to our House, but I'll do my part too.

Ingolf went on as the High Queen took the smoking cylinder and joined in the ritual: "They weren't really pushing at us or even trying to keep us out of sight of their main battle line, just making us keep out of bow-range so the Sword of the Prophet could get into position and get ready without being harassed, I think."

"They're deploying by companies of around two hundred, flank to flank in a triplex formation," Lady Mary added. "Tricky, charging in a three-deep line—"

Huon nodded unconsciously; moving horses were big objects and collisions a disaster waiting to happen.

"—but from the way they moved I think they're up to it."

Ingolf nodded. "This is the big push, probably the last they can make this fight. Seems like we all had the same idea; the southern half of this . . . screwed up battle—"

"I think the phrase you're looking for is *cluster-fuck*, Lord Vogeler," Tiphaine d'Ath said crisply, which brought a chuckle.

He nodded and handed the cigarette back to Three Bears; Lady Mary made a slight moue of distaste as it passed her:

"—the southern part of this *gigantic* cluster-fuck . . . is tied up solid for now. So they're going to hit us as hard as they can here on the north. I don't think they realize how many of your lobster-backs are here. If *they* think they've got all our reserves pinned down piecemeal, they'll calculate on ramming home a charge and breaking this flank, then rolling us up because we don't have enough left to throw in and stop them."

"And we're going to do that to them," the Grand Constable said. "Any field artillery with the Prophet's men?"

"Not that I could see," Ingolf said.

Lady Mary nodded. "We Rangers got as close as we could, about half ordinary arrow range—the Sword carry bow and lance both, it wasn't easy—and didn't spot any."

"They don't like it, the Cutters," Ingolf said. "Too many gears, some crazy religious thing."

"We could bring up some batteries from the general reserve," Count Piotr said thoughtfully. "Soften them up."

"Then they'd retaliate in kind, my lord of Chehalis, and this would turn into another artillery duel," Tiphaine replied. "They may not approve of complex machines, but they've still got a lot of Boisean artillery working for them. On balance, and right here, taking

the springalds and scorpions off the table is a net advantage to us if we want to force a rapid decision. Besides
the no-fun-at-all part of having roundshot and four-foot
darts and balls of napalm shot at you."

Everyone nodded; Association nobles *used* artillery
and heliographs and field-engineers and the other ac-
coutrements of scientific modern war, but most of them
didn't really *like* the contraptions of springs and levers
much. Knightly accomplishment lay in the clash of lance
and blade. From the slight pursed expression around
the Grand Constable's mouth, she didn't agree, at least
not in principle.

Lioncel caught Huon's eye, inclined his head towards
his liege-lady and nodded, mouthing almost silently: *She
can't stand that Society bullshit.*

Huon was surprised the other boy had known what
he was thinking, and mildly scandalized; his family *had*
been Society—the Society for Creative Anachronism, a
heroic band who kept alive the arts of knightly combat,
the skills and graces of noble life and good lordship before the Change. Or at least his mother had been; his
father had been a free-lance man-at-arms who rose to
noble rank during the early days of the Association, like
many others in the terrible years. That made his mouth
thin a little. His parents were dead, his father long ago
in the Protector's War and his mother more recently,
dying by the sword for treason.

And she actually was *a traitor. She could have gotten us
all killed and the estates attainted, she nearly did, only
Odard's deeds and the High Queen's favor saved us from
the Regent's anger . . . but she was still* Mother.

Just then a new sound came from the southward,

deep and thudding, blurred by distance—and, Huon realized, because tens of thousands of voices could not call in perfect unison even if they tried. It grew and cleared as it approached, and behind the wave of sound came a band of men beneath a great banner of green and blue and silver, the Crowned Mountain and Sword of the new High Kingdom of Montival. Knights of the Protector's Guard, some Bearkiller A-Listers, and the bowmen of the High King's Archers following on their bicycles.

And the shout . . . an enormous guttural sound, like Pacific surf growling on storm-beaten cliffs:

"Arrrtos! Arrrrtos!"

The High Queen swept her own hand up. "*Artos and Montival!*" she shouted, like a bronze bell pealing!

Now the ranks of the knights and men-at-arms were taking up the call, thunder-loud and close, like a chorus of trumpets. Some of them were hammering lance-shafts against their shields as well, a drumbeat to the chorus:

"*Artos! Artos! ARTOS!*"

The man in the lead of the approaching party reined in his great black horse, its hoofs beating the air for a moment; Epona was nearly as famous as her rider, like something from a *chanson de geste*. He drew his sword, his left hand reaching for the long blade hanging at his right hip, and thrust it high. Huon felt and heard himself grunt a little, as if something impalpable had punched him in the gut like a quarterstaff. It was the Sword of the Lady—

Obviously the Virgin Mother of God, though the poor pagans don't realize it.

—forged in the world beyond the world like Curtana or Durendal or Joyeuse, and it *shone*. Not with light . . .

At least I don't think *so,* he thought, blinking and taking a shaky breath; he'd seen it before, but you never got used to it, never. *Not just like a bright light. As if it's shining* inside my head *somehow.*

In form it was a knight's longsword, thirty-six inches of tapering blade; the guard was a shallow crescent like the new Moon, the double-lobed hilt of silver-inlaid black staghorn, the pommel a shaped crystal of something like opal gripped in branching antlers. If you were close enough the swirling patterns in the not-really-steel drew your eye, falling inward and inward through infinite shapes that were always the same and never repeated, until the universe seem to be opening *outward*—

But it *glowed*, as if it lit all about it and at the same time washed it out to a faded dream, too *real* for the world of common day. For a moment Huon Liu felt as if he were a figure in a tapestry or an illuminated missal. Then like a hero himself, simply because he was here and following the Sword's bearer.

He tore his eyes away. The sound of the cheering cut off, falling to a murmur and then something like a collective intake of breath as the blade pointed high. Then the High King sheathed the sword, waving to the host and drawing rein beside the Queen with a friendly nod to Rick Three Bears and Ingolf and his kinswoman.

His suit of plate showed evidence of hard recent service, and the visor of his sallet had been torn away. Huon could see the ripped hole where one of the pivots had been, just in front of one of the two sprays of raven feathers that ornamented the helm; he blinked as he realized that Artos had probably simply gripped it with one hand and stripped it off when some foeman's blow bent it out of shape, casually rending the tough alloy steel. The face beneath was a young man's, in his midtwenties and with a straight-nosed, high-cheeked look; the strong cleft chin was only a little concealed by a short-cropped beard as bright red-gold as the locks of hair that escaped the mail coif. Blood had trickled down from a cut across his forehead and dried, with smears showing where he'd wiped it out of his eyes with a palm.

Lord Chancellor Ignatius was with him, in the plain good armor of his Order; he nodded to Huon with a smile and then made an imperious gesture behind him, and someone passed forward a fresh helmet; its surface was beautifully worked in a feather design of black niello, but obviously battle gear and not for parade.

"*Now*, Your Majesty. We are not going to lose you to a stray arrow. Not from carelessness."

"Arra, and I thought my mother behind the battlefield," the High King said, in a strong pleasant Mackenzie lilt; but he unstrapped the damaged helmet, tossed it to the attendant and accepted the fresh one.

"And the best of the day to you, my lords, my lady wife and Queen," he went on, trying the visor. "It's time, I think."

"If the other side thinks so too," the Grand Constable said, in what wasn't quite agreement. "It takes two."

Artos—who had been Rudi Mackenzie—grinned. "They will. It's breaking contact that the Prophet wants now, and for that he has to rock us back first, lest we wreck his host with our pursuit. Perhaps he still hopes to carry the day, the creature. It isn't a favorable prospect they're facing otherwise, retreating through hostile land they've already stripped bare of everything that isn't behind fortress walls or hidden in the hills, and with winter looming."

"Past *my* people, Your Majesty," Count Felipe de Aguirre said.

He was Count of Walla Walla and the Eastermark; the city and the castles of the County Palatine still mostly held out behind the enemy's lines and harried their outposts and foraging parties with slashing mounted raids and ambushes and arrows in the night. Not to mention the fact that he'd left his Countess to hold the chartered city of Walla Walla in his name when he joined the host of Montival; there was a hungry look in his dark eyes, and the squire was glad it wasn't directed at him.

He's a young man too, a Changeling like me, like the Queen and the High King, Huon thought. *This is our time. It's our world now, the Changelings' world.*

"Indeed, it's bloody and useful work they've done and will do," Artos said to the Count Palatine.

Then he went on to them all; the nobles leaned forward a little, tightly focused:

"See you, they've tried hard all day to hammer our right back and away from the Columbia to cut us off from supply and water, and it didn't work . . . didn't ever *quite* work, though they came close more than once. They tried to push at our center . . . and Fred Thurston stopped *that*, the luck and cleverness of the world. Now we're going to hammer *their* right wing back. Against the river and its gorge if we can, and put those unforgiving cliffs under their backsides, the which will be profoundly discouraging to the *omadhauns* if we can pull it off. Or we may be able to chase them all the way to the lower Yakima and catch them at the bridges. To your men, then, my lords, and the Powers strengthen the arms of your knights, for the fate of the kingdom and all our folk rest on the points of their lances and the edges of their good swords this day."

There was a thump of salutes and the noblemen turned their mounts and cantered back to their places, each taking his post at the head of his *menie*, his fighting-tail of household knights and men-at-arms and vassal barons and *their* followers.

The High King turned to Ingolf and his companions. "Ingolf, you carry the word to the CORA Sheriffs; and Mary, you to the lords of the Association light horse. If we can break the Sword of the Prophet the enemy will fall back as best they can. Don't let them rally."

He slapped a fist into a palm for emphasis, a flat smack of steel on leather.

"I want a merciless pursuit and a relentless one. It's a profound shaking of their faith in the Prophet and the Ascended Masters I intend, and for that I want the survivors running shrieking in terror until they hit the Bitterroots and not stopping overmuch along the way. Harry them. Take whatever chances are necessary. See that the remount herds are well forward so our horse-archers can keep up the pace as long as needful. And give them my solemn word I will hang any man who stops to plunder anything but food, weapons and fresh horses while the enemy are still running."

Ingolf raised an eyebrow. After a moment Huon understood; those spare horses were the main wealth left to most of the mounted bowmen who'd lost their lands and cattle to the enemy. Bringing the remounts forward would mean they could follow a beaten opponent for days if necessary. It also meant they could lose the herds entirely if *they* were the ones who had to fall back. Artos nodded acknowledgment before he went on:

"But that's only risky if we lose, and I don't intend to. Get them ready, brother-in-law; promise and threaten as necessary, but do it. And you, sister mine. Now."

Ingolf nodded and made a casual salute. Lady Mary delivered a more formal one in Ranger style. Rick Three Bears just flicked the stub of his cigarette away.

"You should have more Lakota out here, if you want a *merciless pursuit*, Strong Raven," he said. "But hey, we'll do what we can."

"I'm sure you will. Farewell, and the Lady shield you and Lugh lend his spear to strike down your foes."

They cantered off, skirting the rear of the Association lancers. Huon smiled to himself as Mathilda stretched out a gauntleted hand and Artos took it in his for a moment.

"Together, my heart," he heard the High King say softly.

"Always."

Mathilda chuckled. "How Odard would have loved this!"

"He'd have charged like William's minstrel Taillefer at Hastings, tossing his sword up and catching it and singing the *Chanson de Roland*."

Then the King's smile died, and his head swung towards the enemy. He spoke again, more softly still, as if to himself or to something or Someone invisible to common sight:

"Peace to the sky
Sky to the earth
Earth beneath sky
Strength in all."

Then: "Morrigú-Badb-Macha, hear me. Great Threefold Queen, Red Hag, Battle Crow, Dark Mother, She who is most terrible in majesty amid the shattering of spears, You claimed me long ago and ever have I walked with Your power. To Your black-wing host I pledge the harvest of the blood-watered field whose crop is the skulls of men. Grant me victory as I strike for the land I am sworn to guard, for my folk and their homes and their children yet unborn. Let that land fight for us, whose flesh and bone grew from this good earth we till. And know that if this is the day when the King must die for the people, then I go to You consenting, with open eyes, as to a joyful feast. So mote it be."

Huon shivered, as for a moment great sable wings seemed to swirl around the High King's form, caressing and enfolding. Then he shook off the pagan fancy. The King's voice was hard and firm as it snapped out:

"Sound *advance!*"

Trumpets screamed as the signalers blew, and then others took them up behind, all down the line. Huon turned and felt his eyes grow wide; Lioncel swore softly by St. Michael. The lance-points showed first, then the pennants. Then all at once miles of ridgeline bristled like the scales of some great beast, like a dragon waking on its bed of gold in terror and majesty. Glittering steel and blazoned shield, plumes and banners and destriers rising in caracole, as men roared out the war cries of their Houses and tossed their lances in the air, more and more . . .

A savage blaze, an exultant splendor like a dream of glory come to earth.

"*Face Gervais, face Death!*" he shouted, his voice lost in the roar as he called the war cry of his barony and his bloodline. "*Artos and Montival!*"

"Lance!" Mathilda Arminger snapped, holding out her right hand without looking around in a gesture unmistakable even in the tumult.

Huon juggled reins and gave a grunt of effort as he levered the ashwood shaft into a position where she could slap her palm on it. Lioncel was doing likewise for the Grand Constable; then they dropped back together as the plate-armored leaders and guardsmen drew into a blunt wedge behind the banner of the High Kingdom. The world blurred into hammering sound and steel as the main body came up on either side.

"Blow *prepare to charge!*"

The long Portlander oliphants screamed, like silver in torment. The chivalry of the Association was riding to war, eight thousand lances strong, and the earth shook beneath the hooves of the destriers.

"*À l'outrance—charge!*"

CHAPTER TWELVE

THE HIGH KING'S HOST
HORSE HEAVEN HILLS
(FORMERLY SOUTH-CENTRAL WASHINGTON)
HIGH KINGDOM OF MONTIVAL
(FORMERLY WESTERN NORTH AMERICA)
NOVEMBER 1ST, CHANGE YEAR 25/2023 AD

Rudi took a last look to his right and left and right as the canter built to a gallop, then knocked his visor down with the edge of his shield; he needed no hand for the reins, not with Epona, who had known no bit or bridle in all their time together. There was the familiar sensation as the world went dark save for the long slit of brightness that framed his vision ahead. A darkness full of thunder, the thunder of eighty thousand hooves as the two great masses of horseman swept together over the sparse bunchgrass and hard dirt of the plain. The line stayed even enough, but grew slightly jagged as the faster horses drew a little ahead, like a huge jaw full of steel shark's-teeth. Everything had shrunk to the point of the lance in his left hand where it angled over Epona's plunging head and the men ahead.

The Sword of the Prophet were shooting as they charged; arrows went by with that grating malignant whirr, and here and there in the great line of lancers one found a target in man or horse and an image of martial glory suddenly turned to a tumbling mass of hideously vulnerable flesh. Their comrades opened out about them and closed up again without checking as the long lances slanted down in a bristling wall of steel points driven by ton-weights of armored destrier and man. Where necessary, a rear-rank man lifted his steed in a leap over the fallen. Most of the shafts broke or flicked from the curving surfaces of the plate, or stood quivering in the long shields.

Arrows from powerful recurves could be a deadly threat to knights, but only if the horse-archers could dodge about and strike from beyond reach for volley after volley. Here there would be no time or space for that. Behind the visor Rudi's teeth were bared in a wolfish snarl; he could almost pity the commander of the Prophet's elite troop. He'd hoped the Montivalans had been tied down throughout the day, set up for the final smashing blow . . . and now the tables had been turned, and he had no choice but to launch the death-grapple against much worse odds than he'd expected and hope and pray to his Ascended Masters that it worked.

I almost *pity him*, Rudi thought.

Far beyond the carnivore concentration of battle some distant part of him *did* pity the Prophet, Sethaz. He'd probably been an evil man, and certainly ruthless; but nobody deserved what had almost certainly befallen him when his father died and the mantle of the Masters descended on him. Rudi hoped that the Prophet was here leading his private regiments; the Sword of the Lady could deal with him, freeing the man into clean death . . . and possibly ending the war at a stroke, or most of it.

More shafts whined by, or glanced from his armor or thudded into the shield he kept up under his chin. The enemy swelled from a shape coming out of the dust into a great vision-swallowing line of men and animals with shocking abruptness, spired helmets with spikes and red ribbons streaming from them, dull-red armor of steel and cuir-bolli, good big horses but not destriers and not barded. The stinging clouds of arrows ceased as the Prophet's men cased their bows, slid their round shields onto their arms and lifted the lances out of the scabbards behind each man's right hip with a smooth coordination that was like one man acting, or a dance. The line of shields with the rayed sun on them were like some great beast opening its manifold eyes and glaring, and a harsh barking cry rose from nine thousand throats:

"*CUT! CUT! CUT!*"

Rudi's snarl widened. The Sword of the Prophet was a weapon that had been forged for war in the far interior, in what had once been Montana. Against light cavalry with little or no armor they were supremely effective because they were far more flexible than the Association's knighthood, able to shift instantly from missile fire to shock action with disciplined precision, like Bearkiller A-Listers though not as heavily armed. They couldn't be pecked to death by a lighter opponent, and they could hit very hard at need.

All that the Associate nobles of the north-realm could do was one thing, really. Charge home with the lance and finish the matter, smashing away toe-to-toe with sword and war hammer.

But they do that one thing very, very well. And here the Prophet's men have no choice but to meet them on my chosen ground. Trying to match that one thing on its own terms.

Seconds now. He jammed his feet hard into the long stirrups, brought the lance fully down and couched the weighted butt tightly beneath his left arm, the pennant behind the point streaming and flapping and popping as he clamped his hand behind the shallow metal bowl of the guard on the shaft. The big horses were stretching their legs all-out now as the last hundred yards flashed by, fast as racing mounts when they had time to build their full shattering momentum.

Epona recognized the moment and gave it her last magnificent effort, drawing a little ahead despite the best efforts of the Protector's Guard knights around Rudi and Mathilda.

A leveled spear faced him. His lance punched past it. Into and through a breastplate, with an impact that wrenched him out of a trance of concentration as the weight of man and armor and galloping horse on both sides all struck behind the point. His torso slammed back into the high chair-like cantle of the knight's saddle, and harder still as the spear struck his own shield and glanced off it and bent him back. Epona stumbled for a single pace, and the Cutter went over his horse's crupper with a violence that snapped the tough ashwood of the lance across and left him lying with four feet of it through his torso.

Rudi Mackenzie threw the broken stub aside and swept out the Sword of the Lady. The action felt like perfection in his own mind. Diving into the crest of an ocean wave and flying landward, riding forces huge and terrible like a sea-otter tumbling fearless and utterly alive within the storm-surge. Epona turned beneath him as nimble as a colt, though her sides were heaving against the barding like a great bellows. He could see her eye rolling wild behind the wrought steel of the chamfron, and there was blood splashed across it.

"*Morrigú!*" he shrieked, and cut, and ruin fell away.

Black wings enfolded him, bore him up. He danced with them, amid clouds and lightnings . . .

Dust hid his surroundings, a cloud of it from tens of thousands of hooves. Time had passed; he knew that somehow. Knew that the chevaliers had ridden through the enemy line, and that three times out of four it had been an Easterner who went hurtling to the ground wounded or killed by the longer spear and the greater skill and the heavier armor. There were knights with him, and Matti, the Protector's Guard and some of her *menie*. And not far away a clump of men in armor the color of dried blood, the Sword of the Prophet, grouped around a great banner of the rayed Sun.

And among them a man with a shaven head and a tuft of chin-beard. A man who had been young recently and now looked as if he'd watched the world cool from molten rock.

Sethaz.

Their eyes met. *That* was like a blow from a mace felt through armor; Epona threw up her head and neighed, and beside him Ignatius grunted and flung up his own sword. Time froze, thick as amber honey on a cold morning. He could see—

*   *   *

Bjarni Ironrede, King in Norrheim, corked his canteen.
"Time, now, oath-brothers," he called. "The shield-
burg walks."

Beside the Norrheimers the greater array of the
Mackenzies were moving too. Each of them walked forward and pulled out their swine-feather. Those were
two sections of ashwood a yard long that clipped together, one tipped by a narrow-bladed shovel and the
other by a spearhead. The archers twisted them free of
the joining collars, slipped them into the loops beside
their quivers, put an arrow on the string of their bows
and went forward to the attack.

That meant hopping and scrambling over the litter of
arrow-bristling corpses, men and horses both, that lay
where the line of points had stalled them in the unmerci-
ful killing ground of the longbows' point-blank fire. Beyond that the bodies didn't lie so often atop one another,
but they nearly carpeted the ground in straggling lines
where attacks had crested and fallen back like the surge
of a retreating tide.

The scrim in front of the Norrheimers was more concentrated, where the CUT's spearmen had piled up in
front of the shield-wall and been stabbed and hacked to
ruin with point and blade and swinging ax. They clambered over it, Bjarni watching where he put his feet and
occasionally thrusting downward to put a foeman out of
their pain. They hadn't dared turn in against the Mackenzies, not while the living fortress of Norrheim had
stood.

Beyond, the dead were scattered rather than piled on
each other, and there was room for ordered lines. If

enemy horse made a dash at the archers, his men would meet them.

"Swine-array!" he called.

Shield to shield, the Norrheimers fell into a blunt wedge like the head of a boar, ready to gore and crush and utterly destroy. His own banner went up at the point, the black raven with its AA blazon seeming to flap its wings on the triangular surface with its stiffening batten at the top edge and its fringe of tassels. His mother had made that banner in the days just after the Change with her own hands, and his father had carried it north through the wreckage of a dying world to the founding of Norrheim. Bjarni had won the throne beneath it at the Six Hills fight. The sun behind them threw the shadows of men and spears long on the ground before, monstrous and troll-like amid the hard stink of death.

It's a long way to come to spill your blood on this dry ground, he thought.

A bitter longing for the pine-scented breezes of the homeland seized him for a moment, and for the faces of his wife and daughter and the son who would take his first steps without him there to see. He shook it off, shrugging his bear-like shoulders into the weight of his hauberk and the padding beneath, and working aching fingers on the grip of his shield and the hilt of his broadsword. Aloud he shouted in a bull bellow:

"The *trollkjerrings* of the CUT came to Norrheim with their army of wild-men and foreign reavers. Artos Mikesson aided us. With his might and main he fought for us, spilled his blood and that of his sworn men, when we did battle to defend our homes, our wives, our children and our land. Now we repay all our oaths!"

258 S. M. STIRLING

Another deep breath; he was a man of medium height but stocky-strong, and he could outshout the thunder like his friend Thor:

"*Forward, Norrheimer men!*"

To himself:

Without him Norrheim might not have survived, my hall would lie in ashes. And I would not be King. A man pays his debts, and only the lighter ones can be met with a golden arm-ring.

His followers were picked fighters from all the Norrheimer tribes, his own Bjornings, the Hrossings, Wulfings, Kalkings, Verdfolings, Hundings. He saw them stiffen and stride out when they heard his words, despite the long day's weariness and the wounds many bore.

"Thor with me!" he shouted. "*Ho La, Odhinn!*"

Feet pounding, the Norrheimer array trotted towards the retreating enemy.

Lioncel de Stafford cursed and hauled at the half-conscious body of Sir Rodard where it lay with one leg under the body of his dying horse. There was an arrow through the chain-mail grommet under the knight's left arm, and he shrieked feebly as the squire pulled. Blood rivuleted over the armor, but it was a risk of death against a certainty; there were still Cutters around, those willing to sell their lives for the chance to kill one last time. The dust settled a little, and he saw armored figures looming out of it; he almost sobbed with thankfulness as he saw that it was Lady d'Ath and Rigobert de Stafford and their *menies*. Less the dead and fallen, but those still in the saddle were the most of those who'd started.

"Sir Ivo, see to it," the Grand Constable snapped.

Men dismounted and completed the task Lioncel had begun, their hands impersonally gentle as they pulled off armor and applied a pressure bandage; one took a hypodermic out of a boiled-leather tube and injected the fallen knight. Lioncel staggered back and bowed, then snatched up a canteen. Drinking the tinny-tasting water heavily laced with wine was the most pleasurable thing he'd ever done; he coughed some out, drank again and began to feel like a human being. He also felt the sting of sweat in minor cuts, the ache of bruises and a sharp pain in his side that *might* be a sprung rib or just a bone bruise. The brigandine would hold it either way, and he could breathe without coughing blood. A coolness in his hair made him realize that his helmet was gone, and he caught himself looking around for it before he realized it was probably lost forever and possibly trampled into scrap.

The Baron of Forest Grove looked around himself, at the bodies of horses and men and lone figures wandering or calling for comrades, lords, followers. More and more of them trickled in to the banners of the two nobles by the minute, some with more presence of mind than most leading strings of horses they'd gathered up, and dismounted men eagerly swung into the saddles. Sometimes they had to scrabble at it; vaulting into the saddle in full armor was one of the tests of knighthood, but that was when you were fresh and the horse knew you.

"What was that favorite expression of yours, my lady d'Ath?" Lioncel's father said.

She seemed amused. "No, for once it *isn't* a cluster-fuck, Rigobert. We've broken them; they were fools or desperate to try and meet us lance to lance, but it's disorganized us as well, we're all over the place. Hear that?"

The oliphants were screaming again, and kettledrums; Lioncel let the sound penetrate his mind, and suddenly it made sense: *Rally. Rally. Rally . . .*

"Where's the rest? Where's the King?"

"Probably mostly within catapult-shot, once the dust settles, getting together catch-as-catch-can the way we are. And believe me, we'd know it if the King were down. Time to get this tidied up; the destriers can't push a pursuit anyway. Let *our* cowboys handle it, we just have to see off any remnants who feel like being heroic."

Hands linked to make a step and helped Lioncel into the saddle of a horse, from the unfamiliar feel of the saddle an animal that had belonged to an enemy until a little while ago. The stirrups were slightly long but they would do, and the height and feeling of a willing horse beneath him immediately made the world seem more controllable. Then a stir went through the knights and men-at-arms, a growl like a satiated tiger threatened while lying-up on the body of its kill. A ragged band loomed up, in dark red-brown armor. A snarl rose as they hefted heavy shetes and plainsmen's bows.

Rigobert laughed and let the steel haft of the war hammer in his right hand slope back over his shoulder. Lioncel's liege smiled, a slight and terrible expression that showed teeth white against the dust and blood on her steel-framed face. She drew her sword, a delicately precise motion like a hummingbird drinking from a flower, and raised the blade to point as her followers and Rigobert's settled their shields and knocked down visors.

"My name is Tiphaine d'Ath," she said, in a voice that started out cool as water in a mountain brook.

Then it rose to an astonishing soprano lioness roar. "And . . . *you* . . . are . . . *in* . . . *my* . . . *way!*"

"We can't hold them!" a voice bawled in Peter Jones' ear. "It's like trying to wrestle a mill-wheel with your bare hands!"

The commander of the Corvallis Field Force coughed and spat and wrestled his bent visor up. His body felt as if his blood had all been replaced with lead just on the point of melting.

Christ, fifty-five is too old for this.

He hacked up dust and spat phlegm mixed with blood from a cut where his mouth had been struck against his own teeth. With the visor out of the way, his first sight was of the butt of a glaive, coming far too close as the wielder drew it back and then slammed the heavy weapon forward. The Boise soldier just beyond couldn't get his shield up in time because two pikes were embedded in it and pushing hard, and the point of the blade crunched into his face just above the bridge of his nose with a sound that carried even over the roar of shouting and the clash of metal and trampling of thousands of feet.

More dust cut visibility to a few dozen yards, but all he could see anyway was a tangled heaving confusion; many of the first rank of pikemen had dropped their long weapons and were fighting with sword and buckler. And not doing very well at it, against men whose primary weapon was the gladius and shield. If it hadn't been for the remaining pikes and glaives slamming forward over their shoulders . . .

"*U-S-A! U-S-A!*" the Boiseans barked.

You could feel the momentum in it, and they shoved forward in a stabbing, chopping mass.

"Hold them!" Jones shouted. "Just fucking *hold* them!"

But we can't. Not for much longer.

Time began again. Sethaz smiled, and for an instant Rudi felt an almost irresistible impulse to slam his fists into his own face simply so that he wouldn't have to see that expression for another second. Sethaz' eyes blinked, and for that single moment the pupils were black and enormous, filling them from lid to lid, windows into an emptiness where matter had decayed to nothingness in a final squeal and even space itself grew tattered.

Then it passed, and they became almost human once more. The Prophet turned and spurred away with his followers behind him, their speed rocking up to a gallop.

"No!" Rudi said sharply, at the rattle of gear behind him.

Mathilda looked a question, pausing as she drew her sword.

"There's more urgent work to hand," Rudi said grimly. "Get me the Grand Constable."

She wasn't far away; the dust was subsiding, and the falling sun turned it into a mist of gold out of which she and her knights loomed. For a moment they were like figures in a tapestry in a castle solar, until the reality of blood and sweat-stink and battering showed.

"Your Majesty, we have a victory," she said, bringing her sword up to salute.

There was fresh blood on it. Rudi was spattered all along his left side, and further. He glanced at the Sword of the Lady, and blinked slightly to see it shining as if fresh from an armorer's care . . . though in fact it never needed to be polished or sharpened that he'd been able to detect, even when it had just slammed through metal armor. Nothing clung to it, either.

Unlike my hands, he thought with grim amusement, feeling the sticky salt that soaked his gauntlet and jelled against the callused skin.

The feel of the whole battle flowed through him, a balance of forces like two huge beasts grappling through a thousand tentacles and jaws.

"We have a budding disaster on our hands too," Rudi said briskly. "The Boiseans are pushing home an attack with all they have left on the Corvallans south of here and they're close to breaking through, breaking the line between the Bearkillers and the regiments from the Free Cities."

He raised the Sword a little as an answer to the question he saw in their eyes, though it was a bit more complex than that.

"That doesn't make any sense!" Mathilda said; at the madness of it, not the manner by which he'd gotten the information. "They can't win now, that'll just put them in the bag! They should be *retreating*."

Tiphaine nodded—she'd been one of the military tutors who'd taught both of them and the logic was irrefutable—but Rudi shook his head.

"It makes perfect sense from Sethaz' point of view; it

means he can get more of *his* forces out, because I cannot order a general pursuit until the Boiseans are dealt with. And the army of the United States of Boise has shown itself most unreliable today . . . from his point of view. Better to sacrifice them to preserve men he *can* count on. And to kill as many of ours as he may, to weaken us."

"It's suicide for the Boisean forces," Tiphaine observed neutrally. "If I were Martin Thurston . . ."

For all the blood and flecks of hair and brains that coated half her armor, her voice still had that cool impersonal observer's tone. She might have been discussing a battle fought centuries ago.

"Martin Thurston's mind has not been his own for some time now," Rudi said. "D'Ath, I need thirty or forty *conroi* of lancers; more if you can, but that number at least and quickly. Get them together from whatever's to hand; don't stop to match vassal with liege if they're separated. Strip the barding from the destriers, cut the buckles and let it lie. We need to move *fast*. Matti, you'll be with me. Rigobert, I'm leaving you in charge here."

He extended his left arm and swung it slowly from left to right.

"If the Prophet is leaving us a prize we can't refuse, we'll take as big a bite of it as we can. You swing in like this with the rest of the men-at-arms as soon as you can get them organized again. Probably *some* of the Boisean commanders will disregard orders and retreat as fast as they can, but we'll put those who don't into the bag. Use the men-at-arms for the outer tip, and the Association foot for the rest of it. Our light horse can press what's left of Sethaz' cavalry. More will get away than I'd hoped, but we need to deal with this."

D'Ath had been rapping out orders while he spoke to the Baron of Forest Grove, and her *menie* had already dissolved into a mass of messengers, directed at the first clumps of knights and men-at-arms to hand. The nearest were already turning and cantering towards the High King's standard.

"Now we *ride*."

Epona's breath was harsh; foam coated her forequarters and spattered on his leg-armor, the smell heavier than the blood drying on his armor. Downslope with the setting sun a huge disk of red behind him he could see the standards of seven or eight battalions of Boise infantry, but the ranks were inextricably mixed, and they were more like clumps than precise formations as they heaved against the thinning line of Corvallans.

Knots of men stumbled and hacked and stabbed, and a circular hedge of pikes held out around the wreck of two field-pieces with crossbowmen standing and shooting from the tumbled machines. The war cries were croaks and grunting now, but the hard rattling clatter of steel on wood and leather and steel still sounded, and the dull pounding of boots on soil moistened by the blood of the corpses that almost covered the ground.

"Get my people out," Peter Jones wheezed.

An aide was supporting him; one leg was a mass of red from the knee down, with bone fragments showing pink-white. A medic was trying to administer morphine, but the man waved it away, despite the sweat of pain that was washing blood and dust in rivulets down his stubbled face.

"We held them as long as we could."

"You held long enough," Rudi said.

Frederick Thurston's face was stark-grim as he watched. "He's thrown away two or three thousand men killed or crippled," he said bitterly. "That's the Sixth in the center, they were always closest to him; he served with them as a junior officer and they backed him when . . . he did it. And now he's *murdered* them. Them, *too*."

Rudi nodded, showing teeth in what was not a smile. *War is waste. This is madness and futility and waste thrice compounded.*

He turned and looked behind him. There were the better part of seven hundred lancers there; a few score less than he'd started with, less the ones who'd dropped out with foundered horses along the way. Many of them had managed to snatch up fresh lances, and they were in front. Behind were the others with their swords and war hammers ready. The shields were mostly ragged from blows, and the armor dinted and dimpled; the bright colors of heraldic devices scored and broken.

"Edain," Rudi said.

The commander of his guards was red-faced; bicycles could outrun horses in the long run, not the short, and the distance from here to the northern end of the Montivalan line was just on the cusp between the two. He was streaming with sweat, and so were his followers, but they were all there—less those wounded or killed during the day's fighting.

"I'm taking the men-at-arms in. You follow on our flanks. We've reinforcements moving here as fast as they can, but we'll have to rock that madman back first. Get the Archers in on either side and give the enemy more pinfeathers than a goose. It'll be tricky shooting but if anyone can, it's your lads and lasses."

"Aye, Chief," he said, his gray eyes steady; he knew Rudi was accepting a high risk of friendly fire as a cost of doing business in a crisis. "It'll be done."

Rudi turned and raised the Sword. Tired as they were, the men behind him growled at the sight. He could feel their anger, colder than the first flush of exultation that had carried them into the great charge that broke the Prophet's guardsmen, and all the more dangerous for that. He was one with the battlefield, and with the ones fighting on it.

"One last charge, gentlemen and chevaliers. One last charge and we carry the day. Upon the enemy—*Haro!*"

"*Haro!*" crashed back at him. "Haro, Portland! Holy Mary for Portland!"

"Will you follow me, men of the Association?"

"*Artos and Montival!* Death . . . death . . . *death!*"

He brought the Sword off his shoulder and slanted it forward. A clump of the surviving Corvallan signalers were gathered around them; they started to sound *retreat at speed*. Down the slope men tired beyond bearing still heard the familiar notes. The more so as it finally gave them permission to do what everything but sheer willpower and the stubborn pride of their disciplined valor had been screaming for hours: run. Apart from the knot around the field-pieces every Corvallan still fit to move threw down their weapons and took to their heels, most dashing to either side where formed units still held out, a few directly to the rear.

Some of those kept coming, heedless and witless at last as they let panic take them. When they saw the mass of lancers, more swerved or threw themselves down and buried their heads between their knees with their arms wrapped around their heads, trusting to their armor and luck and babbled prayers. The oliphants screamed their high silver shriek once more.

Tired horses stumbled into a trot and then a canter and then a shambling gallop. Epona's nostrils were red pits and slobber coated her neck as her lungs foamed out, but she drew ahead of the others stride by stride. The Boiseans were lumbering forward rather than pursuing, near the ultimate tipping-point of exhaustion themselves; probably only the fact that their minds were clubbed half-unconscious by fatigue kept them going. He could see one man making mechanical thrusts one after another at opponents no longer there. Pride and reflex drove them on, until they realized what was coming down the low slope at them.

Even then clumps of them came together and overlapped their shields instead of running, but their spears were gone, and there was nothing to make a hedge of points. Even destriers wouldn't impale themselves, but they were trained from colthood to run at straw figures of men with shields. The rough wedge struck, lance-points and rearing smashing hooves, a multi-ton mass ripping into the scattered footmen.

Rudi slashed. The Sword of the Lady cut through the staff of the Sixth Battalion's flag standard. A man picked up the six-foot stub of it and threw it at him as if it were a javelin; he caught it on his shield and slammed the mass away. Epona's forehooves flashed out, and something broke where they struck. A *snap* went through Rudi, clicking his teeth together. Then she leapt off her haunches once more, with something of her old strength and grace.

Rudi shouted, raising the Sword again, and men began casting down their weapons or turning to run, or simply falling to their knees with the blank beaten expressions of those pushed beyond all human endurance. One stood, wolf-snarling at him. He snatched up a fallen pila and threw. Rudi knew that pure arch even as it left the Boisean's hand; it had the cold inevitability of certainty. All he could do was drop his shield and pull his feet out of the stirrups as the sharp steel thudded into the base of Epona's neck.

The labored grace of her charge turned into a wheeling fall. Momentum threw him clear of the saddle, and he was turning through the air; then the ground hit him in the back and side, hard enough to stun through the armor. Men were running at him, the hard core who wanted revenge more than a chance to get away, or who'd adopted the Prophet's faith. The Sword was still in his hand, and it seemed to pull him up even while his lungs were straining to take the first breath as he came to one knee. A man raised a spear above him before he regained his feet, but something flicked between them; then he was falling backward with a cloth yard shaft in his throat, coughing out a gout of blood past an expression of agonized astonishment.

Men died in a sleet of arrowshafts that punched right through hoop armor and shields. An instant later only one was on his feet, a dark man in armor that had the distinctive sheen of high-strength alloys. His eyes were pools of blackness as he poised his blade.

Rudi rose, and the Sword of the Lady drove forward. There was a crisp popping sensation up the hilt, Martin Thurston jerked to a stop with Rudi's sword-hand only an inch from his breastbone and two feet of not-steel jutting out shining furnace-bright from his back.

The dying man's eyes flared open. Everything fled from them except pain and the knowledge of death. Rudi came fully upright and grabbed him under the arm, ready to ease him down and pull the Sword free and let the lifeblood out to end his suffering. That put their faces close together for an instant, and even then Rudi was conscious of his astonishment as the other man spoke in a breathy whisper that sent red bubbles swelling and popping on his lips.

"Thank . . . you . . ."

The eyes lost their focus on Rudi, and the voice went thinner:

"Juliet . . . Larry . . . I'm sorry. Dad."

Mathilda was kneeling beside him when he came to himself. Rudi was vaguely conscious of voices—Fred Thurston's, taking a surrender; Tiphaine d'Ath tongue-lashing some nobleman into granting quarter. It was all distant as he touched Epona's neck. She snorted very quietly and rolled her eye towards him, but her head only left the ground for an instant as she recognized him. There was a blind questioning in the glance, as if she asked him what kept her from rising to her feet and carrying him once more and what he meant to do about it.

"Goodbye, girl," he said. "I'm—"

She gave a final sigh and he felt the huge muscles of her neck go slack. Then he let the tears flow from beneath clenched eyelids. Matti's hand closed on his shoulder, more sensed than felt through the steel.

"Rudi, I'm so sorry," she said gently. "She was with you so long."

"She . . ."

A wail escaped him, the high Mackenzie keening for the dead. He throttled it off before it could take him into the full rhythmic surge of grief.

Instead he rose dry-eyed, though his Clan didn't account tears shameful in a man.

"I am the King," he said to Matti's glance of concern. "And there is King's work yet to do this day."

He raised his voice: "Signal to the balloons, transmit to all units: *general pursuit!*"

The flames of the funeral pyre burned hot, so hot that there was little scent save a darkness that curled in the throat with each indrawn breath; it was most of a rough barge of Douglas fir wood made for the campaign, broken up like many others this night to serve a final need and stacked in a lattice of timbers stuffed with brush for kindling. The resin-soaked wood exploded upward and the wind carried the tower of red-gold southeastward, towards the river far below, sparks like stars in the gathering dark. More pyres starred the edge of the waters, for a mile and more downstream; the contingents would bring the ashes of their fallen home to rest among their own.

"You did it all perfectly," Mathilda said softly beside him. "There's time for the man within the High King now."

Rudi nodded; the tears were running down his face,

unchecked this time and soaking into his short red-gold beard, but his voice was calm as he looked out over the night.

"They'll say this was the kingdom's foundation and a springtime of hope, someday, this great victory. They'll sing of it."

He nodded towards the funeral fires. "But this is Samhain, and there's grief enough to fill the world and Otherworld."

Her arm went around his waist, and her warm solidity leaned against him; they were both out of their armor at last.

"Men die, and horses die," she said gently. "Grief dies in the end too, or grows gentle. We go on. Until we don't."

He nodded. "Death is part of life. But it still hurts. Epona bore me to battle and across half a world, and there were things she knew of me that no one else did, not even you, my love."

The roaring crackle gave them privacy, though a surprising number of others had come to mourn as well, Mackenzies keening a little way off, but a scattering from all the host.

After a moment he stepped forward and threw back his head and gave the wail for the beloved dead, keeping the note high until his chest ached and his head throbbed. Then he raised his hands skyward in the Old Religion's gesture of prayer and called:

"Go in peace to the meadows of the Land of Summer, sister of my heart, comrade, friend. Run free and wait for us there. The threads of our lives are woven together, yours and mine and the ones we love. We shall return to meet

again in other times. Yet never more shall it be Rudi and Epona, a boy and his horse, riding free in the summer wind again."

He stood while the fire burned. At last Mathilda pulled gently at his arm.

"Come, my darling. Come and let me hold you, and sleep."

CHAPTER THIRTEEN

TIMBERLINE LODGE
CROWN FOREST DEMESNE
(FORMERLY NORTH-CENTRAL OREGON)
HIGH KINGDOM OF MONTIVAL
(FORMERLY WESTERN NORTH AMERICA)
NOVEMBER 6TH, CHANGE YEAR 25/2023 AD

Timberline Lodge was on the southern slopes of Mt. Hood, a sprawling handsome thing of native stone and huge hewn logs, steep shingle roofs and cupolas. It was high enough that the breath of humans and horses smoked in the cold air as they came up the road from the east, and the moss-grown roofs were dusted with snow. More lay on the boughs of the Douglas fir that coated the steep mountain slopes behind, upward and upward to the towering white cone of glacier and snowfield, glowing red now as the sun set behind it. The air smelled slightly of conifer woodsmoke from the tall chimneys, and more of a wild damp green scent, the tang of early highland winter, trees and earth, rock and water and ice.

The lodge and a million acres of wilderness was an ancient possession of the Lords Protector of the PPA, which was to say that Norman Arminger had grabbed it off not long after the Change.

Which meant in practice that from that moment it belonged to the other kindreds, to Brother Wolf and Sister Tiger, not to mention Cousins Doe and Elk, he thought, smiling a little to himself. *With humankind stepping lightly upon it, more so than for many a thousand years, while Earth heals Herself. So the Powers have their little jokes with us!*

Rudi Mackenzie had been a frequent guest here since the end of the War of the Eye fifteen years ago, as the peace treaty's terms meant he spent part of every year in the Association's lands, just as Mathilda spent part with the Clan. This was where Rudi had learned to ski, and he had many a happy memory of hunting these cathedral forests, or hawking and fishing, or just enjoying the beauty of the flower-starred mountain meadows and hidden lakes and waterfalls.

He'd been curious enough to look into the history of the place a little, despite the fact that the last century of the old world had never been his favorite when he had the time and inclination to glance into stories of the past. The Lodge had been built nearly a long lifetime before the Change by a high ruler of the old Americans called Franklin, to give his laborers and craftsmen work and bread in a time of drought and dearth. They had produced not only the sturdy bones of the place but a wealth of carving and tapestry, fine wrought iron and whimsical copperwork.

Which was good lordship, sparing their pride and nourishing their honor by giving them something real to do rather than just a loaf tossed as to a beggar, he thought, and went on aloud as the royal party drew rein:

"They did their work honestly here, the ancients."

"And it doesn't *look* weird and ugly and useless," Mathilda said. "The way a lot of their stuff from just before the Change does. It looks like a *real building* and fit for what it's supposed to do."

"And not like the uninhabitable bastard offspring of some mad smith's affair with a glassblower, good only for salvage and forging and hammering into something comely or at least useful."

She nodded. "Almost modern, in fact."

They dismounted a little cautiously. Both of them were still stiff and bruised and feeling the minor cuts and scrapes that even the luckiest carried out of a long hard battle and pursuit. It was the way you felt when you *could* function at ten-tenths of capacity if you had to . . . but you didn't want to unless you did have to, from inescapable necessity. He looked at her and made mock-puppy eyes, and her strong-boned face replied with a grin—cautiously, again, because one side of it was bruised where a shield had hit it with the visor up. They'd planned on a bit of a honeymoon here . . .

Sure, and we'd be rubbing wounds on wounds.

Even if you were young and hugely fit as they both were, recovery took a little time; and they'd be back in action soon enough.

A steward and helpers hastened up to hold the horses of the mounted and open the doors of the carriages; besides Rudi and Mathilda, there were delegates from all the more important communities in the High Kingdom. The attendants who greeted them were either very young, very old or very female, with none of the ranks of green-clad foresters he remembered from earlier occasions. Mathilda held out her hand and the ancient steward leaning on his white staff of authority bent to kiss it.

"Goodman Kohnstamm," she said, smiling affectionately. "Your grandsons send their greetings, and they're all well, no serious wounds."

"Thank you for the news, Your Highness . . . I mean, Your Majesty . . . It's very good to see you again, and you as well, Your Majesty. My lords, my ladies, please enter and be welcome. We've done our best, but . . ."

"But it's wartime, and it's acutely aware of the fact I am, Goodman," Rudi said. "You're a perfectionist, I fear. I'm a bit clipped and battered by the war at the moment myself, and so I don't object if the same is true of the Lodge."

That got him the ghost of a smile, though he suspected the old man wouldn't really be happy until he got his people back. Maintaining a place like this took a considerable labor force, and apart from timber, stone, wild produce and game, all the supplies had to be brought in during the short summer season. Doubtless they'd been cutting back to a minimum and all working very hard indeed with most of their strong young men and skilled artisans away at the war, though it would help that few nobles were visiting either.

There was a heliograph tower built into one corner of the Lodge, a tall framework of fir-trunks erected after the Change with a round cabin atop its pyramidal shape. It was manned by a military signaling party sent on ahead by Chancellor Ignatius, connecting them with the PPA's network in Odell, and from there throughout most of western Montival.

Looking at it, Rudi murmured: "I find myself feeling

itchy when I'm out of reach of those things the now. Yet it's also like having a piece of uncomfortably energetic machinery rammed up your arse, so it is. I grow nostalgic now and then for the Quest, when we were alone together and with our friends. Or for a quiet winter in Dun Juniper, when you had only your thoughts and neighbors for company and solitude was always a short walk away."

And is it the heliograph net I'm complaining about, or the Sword? he asked himself. Then: *Best not to think of that.*

Mathilda snorted as she took his arm; she was in an Associate noblewoman's riding dress today, a green fur-trimmed affair with a divided skirt.

"And off in the Midwest and the Wild Lands wilderness we worried about what was going on at home all the time. Not knowing drove me crazy when I thought about it. What's more, the enemy can . . . send messages, somehow. That's how they followed right at our tails all across the continent."

They both grimaced a little at that. The means the CUT used were gruesome. The word Christians used for them most often was *diabolist*; not being given to dualism, the Old Religion didn't usually think in those terms, but he could see their point with regard to the Prophet's followers.

And I don't understand the Power behind them, he thought. *I do understand it's no friend to humankind.*

"I'm not saying I'm against the network," Rudi said. "Indeed, and your mother was farsighted and wise to insist on linking so much of her domains together so, and when we have the time I'll be pushing all the realms to do likewise for Montival as a whole. Just . . . there are drawbacks."

They passed through the great doors in the stone entranceway; within was a wall panel in cast bronze, showing two men kneeling to a stag with a cross between its antlers. Mathilda signed herself and genuflected to Saints Hubert and Eustace, the patrons of hunters. Rudi clapped his palms together softly, then held them before his face as he bowed.

And if my reverence is to Cernunnos, Horned Lord of the Forest and Master of Beasts, who's the worse for it?

The huge main hearth inside was already blazing, and the great hall of the lodge was already pleasantly scented with dinner as the guests were shown to their rooms to settle in before they assembled again.

The rustic theme was continued in the common chambers, with massive stone walls giving way to man-thick timbers above, and a great hammer-vaulted roof above. Much of the wood was carved with patterns and whimsical beasts, some of it pre-Change work and more added since; House Arminger had rescued a set of good makers and turned them loose here with nothing to do but play with their craft on a vast canvas for years.

Strange man, Matti's father, Rudi thought as he handed his long fur-lined coat and gauntlets to an attendant with a nod and smile. *And a bad one, on the whole; but there's no denying he dreamed grandly and that much of his work will live.*

Sandra Arminger shed her enveloping ermine cloak into the hands of one of her ladies-in-waiting. She hadn't been listening too overtly, but her brown eyes twinkled a little under the silver and diamond-bound wimple, one of fine bleached wool for outdoor wear. She'd always been uncomfortably good at following his thoughts.

Also you, good mother-in-law, have a knack for turning dreams into shaped timber and dressed stone, money and grain-silos and men-at-arms, heliograph stations and bonds of allegiance and fear and obligation.

There wouldn't have been any prospect of winning this war if she hadn't left the PPA rich, well-governed and its armories and magazines stuffed to overflowing with every reserve such a conflict needed, from boot-grease and dried beans to crossbow bolts. But . . .

I love you dearly, foster mother—you saved my life from your bachlach of a spouse, and you helped raise me all those years—still I don't know if you're all that much better a human being than he. All these preparations weren't aimed at the CUT; we didn't know they'd be a menace to us until a few years ago. Maybe you were just being thorough and, what was the old word, paranoid . . . or not. Yet you reared Matti to be better than either of her parents, but not less in her abilities. And you taught us both much of kingcraft; as witness the way you embraced the idea of Montival—seeing that your grandchildren would rule it and being just as satisfied with that as with hammering everyone into obeying you, or more so.

The trip to Timberline Lodge had been nothing much for the moiety of the guests who were warriors and used to living rough; nor so very hard on the others, since for them it had been by rail-car to Castle Odell and then by carriage and sleigh to the Lodge. Rudi was still grateful for the tub ready in their quarters, with wisps of steam rising from water scattered with dried rose-petals. It was of a strange, smooth stone he didn't recognize offhand, salvage from some mansion or other, and more than big enough for two.

"Sure, and it was thoughtful of your mother to insist we take the royal suite," he said as the aches and chills soaked away, and sighed. "After she spent so many years getting it just as she wanted it."

Mathilda stuck out her tongue at him, then sank under the surface and scrubbed at her hair. Rudi did likewise. He wore his shorter—shoulder-length as opposed to the way hers was approaching the small of her back again—but he felt the same ghost-presence of sweat and oil from weeks in the field, even if it wasn't really there anymore; they'd soaped and rinsed under the showers like civilized people before they got into the actual bath.

You always did that, even if it meant throwing buckets of the water at each other rather than standing under a cut-bronze showerhead as they had here. Nor was this the first hot water and soap they'd dived for once they weren't sleeping on the ground and spending their days in armor anymore. But somehow you didn't feel really at ease until you'd made up for all the washing missed while bath meant a helmetful of cold water and a well-used cloth.

"Mom put us here because it makes you feel out of place and embarrasses me," she said when they had surfaced, raising her arms to wring out her hair. "I love Mom, but her sense of humor . . . sometimes . . ."

Rudi watched the play of light on glistening skin and sweet curves for a moment with enjoyment, and the more so as a deep blush ran up from breasts to neck to face.

"Rudi!"

"I have permission from your God!" he said, grinning, letting his hands drift under the surface of the water. "Father Ignatius said so at the wedding!"

They'd been the closest of friends since they were ten; they'd sworn the *anamchara* oath then, despite their parents being at war, or possibly because of it. Her father had killed his, for that matter, and vice versa. Becoming lovers had made it even better, he found, but Mathilda was still a little shy of that.

Well, he thought tolerantly, as she purred and wriggled a little. *Strange folk, Christians.*

"Ummmmm . . . no. We're due at dinner," she said reluctantly. "Plus I'm *sore*. In strategic places."

"Alas, we're *both* sore, though if we're *very careful . . .*"

"Rudi!"

He laughed and swung out of the bath, extending a hand to help her do likewise, and they made use of the fluffy heated towels on each other instead, also carefully. The royal suite didn't follow the rustic scheme of the rest of the Lodge; Sandra Arminger had had it redone to her specifications over two decades, and she regarded hunting as *wrestling in the dirt with animals* and skiing as *falling downhill at speed and on purpose.*

Her concept of healthy exercise was using a pre-Change instrument of torture known as a Steppercizer, which she subjected herself to doggedly but strictly in private and for a set number of hours every week. She tolerated and used the sports of the Protectorate's nobility as part of her system of rule without pretending to like them or take them seriously.

And for fighting, she has people like me or d'Ath, he thought ruefully.

Hence the cool beauty of glazed tile on the floor, pale mottled blue edged with flower patterns, the silvery marble sheathing on the walls and the incandescent-mantle gas lamps behind holders of silver fretwork. The windows showed a yellow glow from a few lanterns outside, and beyond that a steady drift of white flakes out of the dark sky.

"Brrr!" Rudi said. "I'm not sorry to have an honest excuse to be indoors this day, rather than trying to get a fire going in a winter bivouac."

"It's mud so far in the war-zone, not snow, mostly, but I know what you mean," Mathilda said, coming up beside him and laying an arm around his waist. "I could even pity the Cutters. They're a lot hungrier than our men and we torched a lot of their baggage train here and there. Including the tents."

"Threefold return, acushla. They stole a good deal and burned even more and now they're in want. Let's go eat, if the prospect of word-fencing with all those folk over the meal doesn't put you off your feed."

"No it doesn't," Mathilda said cheerfully, then winced a little as she smiled; she touched the left side of her face gingerly. "I was careless. He got me with the shield-boss; I should have had my visor down and my shield up. Thank St. Apollonia I didn't lose any teeth, but I even have to *chew* carefully, dammit!"

"The fellow who did it is accounting for his own carelessness to the Guardians," Rudi pointed out; she'd stabbed him up under the chin and into the brain before the blow fully landed.

He used one of the towels on her seal-brown locks, darker now with the water.

"There, that's got your hair more-or-less dry."

"The wimple will cover it," she said, winding another around her mane. "There, that'll help."

The bedchamber was equally splendid, with a ceiling of fine plaster subtly carved in willow patterns and a cheerful fire crackling on the andirons in a hearth whose surround was of marble done in Venetian-Gothic fretwork. The pale décor was broken only by the vivid colors of the Portland rugs with their patterns like wildflower gardens in spring, and the air was subtly scented with sachets of dried lavender and roses and meadowsweet.

Not even a hair remained of the Regent's cherished Persian long-haired cats, but the rooms somehow reminded him of them and made him feel a little rough-hewn and uncouth. His clothes had been laid out on the four-poster bed. He disliked attendance when he dressed, and fortunately Mackenzie formal gear could be donned without help beyond what Mathilda gave.

Linen drawers—it was a slander that clansmen went bare beneath the kilt—and long saffron-dyed linen shirt went on first; then the kilt, of course, in the green-brown-dull orange Mackenzie tartan; short, tight green Montrose jacket with a double row of silver buttons; silver-buckled shoes and green knee-hose; brooch of curling silver-and-gold knotwork and turquoise at his shoulder pinning the tartan plaid wrapped across his torso and falling almost to his heel behind; more fancywork in wrought bone and precious metal on the hilt of his dirk on its tooled-leather belt and the little *sgian dhub* tucked into the left sock; badger-fur sporran . . .

"There," she said, adjusting the flowing lace jabot at his throat and the cuffs of the same material. "You look splendid. In a barbaric, backwoods way, of course."

He grinned at her, took her head between his hands and kissed her between the eyebrows and on the tip of her nose and on her lips.

"And you will look splendid in your cotte-hardie, *mo chroi*. Though you'd look even better as you do now in nature's garb, and a deal more comfortable."

She stuck out her tongue again and donned her own underwear; then she rang a small bell. He sat in one of the spindly chairs—which took his solid somewhat-more-than-two-hundred-pounds without creaking—and crossed his arms. He wasn't a bulky-built man, but he was two inches over six feet of long-limbed height, and not slender either. Except the way a leopard was.

"Welcome, mesdames," Mathilda said to the three who came in answer. "What do you have ready, Yseult? You've got a very good eye."

The young woman—she was just about seventeen—frowned and flushed a little.

"I think the pink, Your Majesty."

"Pink?" Mathilda said dubiously.

"The deep wild-rose pink. Cotte-hardie and sideless surcotte both, the surcotte with your arms in silver and onyx. And that would go very well with the collar of plaques, the moonstones and white jade. The wimple . . . iron gray. Deep rose or maroon would do, but I would pick the gray, Your Majesty.

"Gray it is."

"Jaine, why don't you get started on Her Majesty's hair, just a Dutch braid down the back I think, I showed you that. Finish it with the coral bead snood, the bamboo coral, it's that lovely pale gold color—and tourmalines for the headpiece, the watermelon tourmalines in electrum with the niello clasps."

"That sounds lovely, Yseult. I put myself in your hands."

His position let him watch while Jaine and Shawonda helped Yseult off with her towering double-horned headdress and they went to work; you *couldn't* put on a cotte-hardie by yourself, any more than you could a suit of plate armor . . . to which it had other similarities. He was privately amused at the sight and at the rather odd Protectorate idea of rank. In most places where there were masters and servants, such would be servant's work, albeit an upper servant's. Among nobles, Associates pages and well-born girls such as these thought it an honor to serve so those of higher rank, for all that their families held estates and manors and castles themselves.

There's a deal to be said for it, if you're going to have a nobility at all, he thought.

Mackenzies had no rank of that sort unless you counted the Chief, being in the main crofters and craftsfolk living in a rough equality.

The younger generation of lords up here are the better for learning to serve before they command, the Changelings, compared to their elders. Many of whom were not much more than bandits in fancy clothes, at seventh and last.

Aloud he said: "Your brother Huon won great honor for himself in the battle, Lady Yseult. And for House Liu."

The girl blushed and curtsied without missing a beat as she arranged the complex forms of the silk wimple. Her father's father's heritage showed in the tilt of her eyes and the high cheekbones, but those eyes were a deep blue and the hair that fell beneath a maiden's open wimple was thick and fine and corn-yellow. Three small scars on the left side of her face accentuated her comeliness rather than detracting from it.

"And the white suede leather belt and scabbard, I think *under* your sideless surcotte. The sword hangs more elegantly and drapes right along with the surcotte, Your Majesty," Yseult said seriously.

Mathilda nodded soberly. It wasn't a knight's weapon; wearing one of those to a banquet would be a bit conspicuous. The eighteen-inch blade was quite functional, though, and probably just as effective at close quarters. The Church Universal and Triumphant favored assassination of enemy leaders as a tactic, and they'd tried to kill both Rudi and Mathilda at banquets before. It was violently unlikely here . . . but not altogether impossible.

Fortunately dirk and sgian dubh *are expected to be part of my formal dress*, Rudi thought. Aloud he went on:

"And you two and Fred together did still more, Jaine, Shawonda," he said to the two younger maidens; they were sisters, dark-skinned and curly-haired, one a teenager and one just on the verge of it, looking a little unaccustomed to Associate dress. "There are thousands of your people alive today, walking upon the ridge of the world, who the Red Hag would have reaped upon the bloody field, if your brother had not been. And if you had not risked your lives to aid him."

He tactfully didn't mention their *other* brother Martin, for most of this war General-President of the United States of Boise, parricide, tyrant, and until his recent death at Rudi's hands, a puppet of the Prophet Sethaz.

They nodded shyly, busy about their task but darting him glances now and then. Both had adapted to exile with the flexibility of youth; he thought they also found their stay in the PPA romantic, exotic and colorful, a welcome distraction from the civil war within their family that was rapidly spreading to their country as a whole.

They'd probably have adapted just as well in Sutterdown or Dun Juniper. Nor was he blind to the fact that he was tall, handsome, dashing and a great warrior with a charming smile . . . and for that matter, a good singing voice. Those were some of the assets that luck or the Powers had gifted to him. Schoolgirl crushes were among the results, sometimes amusing, sometimes annoying, sometimes both; and the Thurston sisters were basically too sensible to be annoying.

Though when we liberate Boise and get them back home, they'll probably be glad to shed the cotte-hardie and wear pants or a housedress again! Hmmm. Nor would it do to make them appear too much like Associates in front of their own folk before then. Castles and fiefs don't appeal, there . . . which is natural enough. They seem better from the tower looking down than the ground looking up, to most.

When they'd finished, the three young ladies-in-waiting stepped back, admiring their handiwork; Yseult took an extra moment to apply a very slight touch of a yellow-based face-cream, with rice powder over that, which disguised the color of the bruises a little. Then she looked at Mathilda and sighed with her hands clasped beneath her chin.

"Lovely, Your Majesty!"

Mathilda smiled at her, and for a moment her strong-boned, slightly irregular features were beautiful indeed.

"You're far prettier than I'll ever be, Yseult, no matter what the milliners and jewelers do, or even skilled ladies-in-waiting."

"I respectfully disagree," Rudi said, coming to his feet and waving off their curtsies as he swept back his plaid and settled it with a shrug of the shoulder.

"And now you might as well be off to visit your brother, Lady Yseult, and you two to see Fred before he's locked up in the debate disguised as a meal we face; we'll be up late, I think. Forbye I apologize that the State dinner is for principals only, but the food will be the same and the merriment better among the rest of the household."

Jaine and Shawonda helped Yseult back on with her own headdress, and she sailed ahead of them—a metaphor the more fitting for the height and trailing gauze, a daring fashion statement that would make going through some doors awkward—and opened the double slab of worked teak starred with silver rosettes and birchwood inlay that closed the royal suite. Rudi picked up the sheathed Sword in his right hand; sometimes that still felt more natural, despite all the practice he'd put in since the wound made his right just a trifle slower and weaker. That let him extend his left arm, though, which was the courtesy side in the Protectorate. Mathilda tucked her hand through it.

In the corridor outside they were back in the ruder splendor of the Lodge proper, lit by alcohol lanterns that flickered slightly in the occasional draught, casting restless shadows on the high beams of the ceiling and fluttering the hangings; the score of archers standing along the walls with their longbows grounded before them seemed entirely in place, for all that the most of them were in Mackenzie gear. There were a trio of dogs as well, the huge mastiff-wolf breed that the Clan often took to war for scouting and guard work, as silent and alert as the bowmen.

Rudi stopped for a moment before their commander. "And how's your brother?" he said.

"Young Dickie will be fine, Chief," Edain Aylward Mackenzie said.

He tapped his helmet with his bowstave. "The mace rang his bell good and proper and sprang a few ribs through his brigandine on the backstroke. For the rest, just a straight crack in the shinbone where the horse stepped on him. The healers say he'll be ready to be shipped back to Dun Fairfax in a week or two. And then he can be fussed at by the mother and Tamar while he bangs about on crutches and swears as the little ones crawl over to chew his plaster cast and he listens to the father's tales of *his* old wounds and lies right back at him. The which will be a pleasure to them both," Edain finished with a smile.

"They both *will* like that," Mathilda said with a laugh

and nod. Then, thoughtfully: "Though I never did know exactly which of old Sam's stories *were* true."

"The grim ones, I think," Edain said, and added: "Your Majesty," dutifully as he remembered.

The head of the High King's Archers was a few years younger than Rudi and a handspan shorter, around Mathilda's five-eight, but thick in the arms and shoulders, with curly light-brown hair beneath the light sallet helm and steady gray eyes. The big square hands that gripped the yellow yew-wood stave of his bow looked strong enough to crack walnuts between thumb and fingers, scarred and already a little battered by hard use.

"Good to hear Dick's in no danger!" Rudi said sincerely; he'd been in and out of the Aylward household all his life, and Edain had been his companion on the Quest as well as a boyhood friend. "They'll be the better there for the letters."

"Letters, Chief? I sent one, but Dickie's not much of a writing man, even when his few wits haven't been scattered with a mace."

"I wrote to old Sam myself," Rudi said with a grin. "Suspecting as I did that *your* letter would leave out a bit of this and that. An arrow in and out of the throat of a certain man standing over me with a spear, for instance."

Edain scowled and blushed. "Just doing the job, Chief," he said. "As the father would expect. I wish I'd been in time for Epona . . ."

Rudi rested a hand on his shoulder for a moment: "It's fully aware I am that a battlefield is a dangerous place, brother, and what can and cannot be done. Didn't your father train me to the bow as well, and to the hunt and many another useful thing? Besides the times," he added with a grin, "he gave me a smack across the backside or later a clout to the ear, as needful."

Edain grinned back. "Remember the time we were scuffling in the dairy like a pair of hound pups and got dung in each other's hair?"

Rudi laughed outright. "And he took us each by an ear to lead us on howling tiptoe and pitched us into the Dun Fairfax pond and stood with his arms crossed while we scrubbed and scrubbed and all the folk laughed! Yes, I remember it, fearful *lèse-majesté* that it was."

Then he went on in a professional tone: "All's well here?"

"Good barracks and good rations, Chief, and we've got the guard rosters set up with the Lady Regent's household men. Naught for you to worry about."

Rudi shrugged. "Best to make sure. Carry on, then."

Carrying on included detailing a half-dozen of the archers to follow the High King and Queen, but they tactfully stayed out of conversational range, if you spoke softly. All of them had a shaft on the string, and the last two took turns walking backward.

Mathilda frowned slightly. "Rudi . . . this is a pretty good place for the conference . . . isolating everyone from their hangers-on and factions can help . . . but why did you pick Timberline especially?"

She glanced at the Sword, and he shook his head. Still slightly damp, the darkened red-blond locks swirled around the shoulders of his jacket.

"Did the Sword tell me to, you mean? Possibly. Possibly not, the puzzlement of it, for it's often difficult to tell what's . . . that and what is my own soul's prompt-ings."

He frowned as well; there were times when he didn't feel like himself anymore. And other times when he did, but like a house that had had a whole new suite of rooms added. "I . . . just *felt* that it was right, somehow. There's something here that I . . . we . . . *need*."

CHAPTER FOURTEEN

TIMBERLINE LODGE
CROWN FOREST DEMESNE
(FORMERLY NORTH-CENTRAL OREGON)
HIGH KINGDOM OF MONTIVAL
(FORMERLY WESTERN NORTH AMERICA)
NOVEMBER 6TH, CHANGE YEAR 25/2023 AD

One ritual Sandra had brought over into the modern age was a cocktail hour before dinner; that was *not* a Society legacy, and the Corvallans had the same habit, so Rudi assumed it was some custom of the ancient world. He hoped it made them feel more at ease as he sipped his—it was in a conical glass on a stem.

This one was a mixture of whiskey, sweetened cream, coffee, anisette and absinthe, served ice-cold; tasty, and with a hidden punch like a war hammer you didn't see until it hit you on the neck-flare of your helmet. His mother-in-law called it a *Moloko Plus*, and claimed for some reason that it was appropriate in a time of battle and war. He could see why. A few of these would certainly prime you for violence.

There were about a score and ten of folk attending, though some were swift replacements for those killed or wounded in the Battle of the Horse Heaven Hills; not enough to account for all the communities which now made up Montival, but some of the smaller ones let the Mackenzies or Mount Angel or one of the others they trusted hold a watching brief for them. Standing in the warmth of the towering hearths and chatting as folk nibbled on crackers topped with potted shrimp or pats of spiced goose liver or slivers of smoked salmon and capers was pleasant, but he was sharp-set enough to be pleased when the gong sounded and the musicians struck up a slow march on viol and rebec and hautboy, and he gave Mathilda his arm and led her in in a flash of silk and jewels.

Though the Sword cradled in my other arm is a bit unorthodox, he thought mordantly. *Still, I will not let it far from my grasp the now; not when Cutter assassins might crawl out from under the table or drop from the ceiling. It would warn me so, now, or guard me at least. Its usefulness grows. Also its presence is a reminder to the reluctant of what and Who stands behind me, and that They are Montival's patrons.*

Long, colorful tapestries covered other sections of the walls in the great dining hall, done with scenes of the forests and mountains or the hunt, in thread that caught the firelight and lamplight with glints of silk iridescence or with the gleam of gold and silver. Or modeled on dreams from some *romaunt* where ladies rode unicorns through fields of asphodel, with miniature dragons on their wrists in place of hawks.

His mother was in an arsaid now, the long, wrapped tartan skirt and plaid that older Mackenzie women favored for formal occasions. She wore a green shift of fine embroidered linen with lace cuffs beneath it; both were of her own weaving. A headband bearing the Triple Moon was on her brow, confining her graying red hair, and she sat with some folk from Corvallis.

One was Ed Finney, an influential yeoman they knew well from long seasons of guest-friendship stretching back to the terrible years, and Juniper Mackenzie had known his father even before that. There were a few rather lost-looking Faculty types from the city itself, and she was putting them at their ease, something for which she had a gift; they were probably a bit spooked at the neo-feudal splendors all around. Corvallis kept up more of the old ways than most.

To an unhealthy degree, perhaps, he thought. *That world is gone. If you try to hold to it, what you hold changes in your hands; its time is over, save as myth and legend. The past has its power, but it must give way to the future, and our memory of the past changes with the needs of the living.*

One of the Corvallans was drawn a little apart, looking as if he was accustomed to a train of flunkies rather than a single secretary. He *did* consult the notes and files she offered rather often, not ostentatiously but as if it were a reflex born of long habit.

It was a good idea to get them all here, where there is an excuse to keep it down to the principals rather than hordes of hangers-on and minor players before whom the leaders must posture, Rudi thought. *Hard enough to get a score of folk to agree on something, and them all men and women of power and place used to having their own way. Impossible if it were a hundred, not without taking time we don't have right now, or without organization beforehand we haven't had time for yet.*

Chancellor Ignatius was keeping himself awake, but only by dint of extraordinary self-discipline. His monk's tonsure showed occasionally when his head dipped a little, and the face above the plain dark Benedictine robe was gaunt as he gave his monarch a rueful smile; the golden chain of office looked a little incongruous against it. Being Lord Chancellor of a realm only a few months old in the midst of a major war was wearing on him harder than the Quest through frozen wilderness, battle and flight had done.

The more so as it was composed of contumaciously independent groups many of which had been—literally— at each other's throats until a few years ago. Rudi suppressed a slight twinge of guilt at what he—and the man's own iron sense of duty—was doing to his friend. The pile of paper he and Matti had had to wade through themselves was only a tithe of what landed on Ignatius' head, and all of it life-and-death important to *someone*.

I've sent smiling lads and lasses to their deaths by the thousands already, or crippled them. I'll use him up if I must; yes, and myself. That I don't like it means little save to me, for I will do it nonetheless.

One of the Corvallans spoke, in a tone that hid aggression under a show of respect:

"Now that the enemy is defeated, ah, Your Majesty—"

"The enemy isn't defeated, Professor. They've lost a battle, not the war, albeit it was a whacking great battle of unusual size," Rudi said, a slight dryness to his tone. "'Tis the end of the beginning, and perhaps the beginning of the end, but not the end itself, if you take my meaning."

Professor Tom Turner was a plump and prosperous man in early middle age, dressed in an expensive but understated jacket and trousers with an apricot-colored silk cravat and diamond stickpin. Rudi frowned—

Professor Turner, he suddenly *knew*; the Sword was hanging from the back of his chair. *Chairman of the Faculty of Economics—the Guild Merchant, they'd say in most places. And a banker; in fact, he helped reinvent the trade after the Change, when things had settled down enough. One with his thumb in any number of pies. First National Bank of Corvallis, right enough. And Ignatius says we have to go through him for some of the loans we're raising, this bond-issue thing. Otherwise it'll all be done through Portland and Astoria, and that wouldn't do at all, at all. Especially since those houses are so closely linked to the Regent. Men fear the subtle webs of the Spider of the Silver Tower, and not without reason.*

"They're retreating from our lands," Turner said.

"That depends on the meaning of *our*, wouldn't you say?" Ignatius replied. "They're retreating towards the old Boise border. If we let them go, there's nothing to stop them coming back later. I suggest reading the reports on the situation in the occupied CORA territories to illustrate what *that* would mean."

"The tyrant of Boise is dead," Turner pointed out. With a trace of unction: "Slain by our heroic leader."

"He's dead. The Prophet is not, and Martin was but the Prophet's hand-puppet," Rudi said. "I freed him as much as killing him . . . and the Prophet will be using another to control his realm. We must not let him consolidate his control there."

Ignatius nodded: "It is their intentions towards us in

the long term which matter, not their immediate capacity to carry those intentions out."

Turner spread his hands. "Except that the League of Des Moines is attacking them too. We've been hearing how rich and powerful they are off in the Midwest; let them have the rest of the fight."

Ignatius shrugged and went on: "And the High Kingdom claims Boise, New Deseret, Montana, and the lands of the Seven Council Fires of the Lakota *tunwan* . . . the Sioux."

"Well, that's another matter. Defending ourselves when we're attacked is one thing. Going out to annex foreign territory is another. I thought the High Kingdom was supposed to establish peace?"

Rudi chuckled; there were more types of fencing than the sort you did with a practice sword in the salle d'armes. His voice was calmly reasonable as he went on:

"Lasting peace, my friend, is not the same as *beating off an attack*. We're no longer facing the prospect of being overrun and destroyed, but we're a very long way indeed from winning the peace and establishing the kingdom securely. Half-done is well begun, but only if you go on to finish the job. Our children will have their own problems; I will not leave them mine as well to solve all over again."

Ignatius nodded. "In fact, Professor Turner," he said dryly, "the People and Faculty Senate of Corvallis haven't formally *joined* the High Kingdom of Montival at all. Just . . . acted and talked as if they had."

Edward Finney grinned; he was a sixtyish man with a farmer's weathered face and a still-strong body the shape and texture of an oak stump. His family's knowledge and aid had helped dozens of others set up their own stead-ings in the years after the Change. They were well-to-do and often chosen to represent their rural district in the city-state's popular assembly, in which they spoke for the rural interest as a whole. In Corvallan terms that meant he was part of the Faculty of Agriculture. Though with-out the mystic power of *tenure*, which meant something like *mana* in Corvallan dialect, and marked the inner circle of power. Oddly, it was usually restricted to people who studied things rather than the ones who actually did them.

"Some people, and I won't name names, like for ex-ample Thomas Turner, keep putting off the formal dec-laration," he said. "Last time it was because so many of our citizens were away fighting . . . which is chutzpah, *I'd* say."

The guests were seated at an oval table, hollow-centered. It was quite new, and deftly avoided the too-provocative Association habit of dividing upper and lower ranks with a ceremonial salt-cellar. Rudi cast an eye down at it, and Mathilda inclined her head very slightly towards her mother, who in turn waggled her eyebrows even more infinitesimally.

Well, yes, of course I thought of that, it said, as plainly as words.

The staff brought out the first course, also without the flourish of trumpets usual at a banquet in the Pro-tectorate, something he'd always considered a prime example of what *his* mother considered folderol. It was hot beaten biscuits and butter and bowls of soup made with chicken sausage simmered with wine, broth, garlic, tomatoes, spinach and tortellini. However grand in scale

Timberline was basically a hunting lodge and didn't go in for the fantastic elaboration of court cuisine that you often got in Portland or at Castle Todenangst. Rudi was thankful for that too—in his experience, the pasties in the shape of castles and complex sauces full of spices from oversea were as much a matter of status and appearance as genuine appeal to the taste.

And all that was somewhat wasteful, which made him uneasy, particularly right now; the Mother-of-All wanted you to enjoy Her bounty, but that didn't mean she would appreciate a spendthrift treatment of the good things won with the toil and sweat of Her children. A wise man didn't court bad luck, or tiptoe around the borders of hubris.

Everyone made their own small ritual; which in a few cases was none at all, apart from a polite pause while the others finished. Rudi made the Invoking pentagram over his bowl and murmured:

"Harvest Lord who dies for the ripened grain—
Corn Mother who births the fertile field—
Blessed be those who share this bounty;
And blessed the mortals who toiled with You
Their hands helping Earth to bring forth life."

Then he picked up his spoon eagerly; the talk died away for a while. He finished the soup with relish, ate another biscuit, sipped at the glass of dry white wine, and spoke cheerfully:

"Now, we *have* won a whacking great battle. The enemy's in retreat; we have to harry them out and pursue them to their home over the mountains and there scour the CUT off the land and bring the folk into the kingdom. They aren't the enemy, just his dupes and

tools, to be rescued as much as fought. To do that, we
need different arrangements. We've been using an
emergency levy of the whole. That won't do for a long
war fought far away. We can't take that many hands
away from the land and workshops forever; we need to
trim each contingent to those willing and able to campaign for some time, staring at snowmelt, which means
preparations must start *now*."

"A standing army," someone said.

"For now. And it'll be necessary to make my position
a matter of settled law and make sure that everyone con-
tributes as they're able, now that the most desperate
part is past. The burdens must be fairly shared, and seen
to be such. Nor can a war be run by a committee. Not
well, at least. I will consult and seek advice, but decisions must be made without trying to sit in the middle
between everyone's opinions, and they must be made in
good time—by me."

"Ah . . ." Turner cleared his throat. "Ah, Your Majesty,
there *is* the problem that Corvallis has always been attached to, ah, the heritage of Republican government . . ."

"Odd that you should say that," Sandra Arminger
said, delicately patting her lips with a linen napkin,
speaking in a clear conversational voice that carried to
the whole table without seeming loud. "As I remember
it, Professor Turner, just before the Protector's War—"

What everyone else calls the War of the Eye, Rudi
thought, hiding his amusement as he broke another biscuit and spread butter to melt into its steaming interior.
*Everyone who isn't an Associate, or at least everyone who
lives outside the Protectorate.*

His mother-in-law's glee was even better concealed,

but he knew her well enough to see the sheer artist's pleasure in her bland brown gaze. She had always felt outmaneuvering a political opponent was among the rarest of life's pleasures; if you could destroy him at the same time, that was the whipped cream on the blueberry tart. Best of all if you could demolish him with his own words. Rudi didn't share the catlike joy she took in it, but there was no denying the technique was useful or that she was the mistress of it.

Juniper Mackenzie sighed slightly and rolled her eyes even more inconspicuously; she and Sandra had shared the raising of Mathilda and Rudi for more than a decade and cooperated at need as heads of State, but you couldn't really say they were friends and most certainly not soul-mates. The smooth voice continued:

"— we, that is Norman and I, had a little conference with you in Portland in the ninth Change Year, and you were *most* willing to consider accepting Chartered City status for Corvallis, within the Association, under my late husband's protection. Eager, even."

She sipped demurely at her wine. "I have the notes of the conversation in my files, as a matter of fact."

When Sandra Arminger mentioned *my files*, strong men blanched, and for good reason; perhaps the fabled mystic Internet of pre-Change times had been more thorough . . . and then again, perhaps not.

"That's a misrepresentation of my position at the time!"

She went on, with a little cat smile of amused malice:

"Including a signed letter from you to that effect. Paper and ink are so inconveniently lasting, aren't they?"

Turner wilted a little as glares shot at him from up and down the table. However much enthusiasm there was for the High Kingdom, everyone remembered the wars against the Association and the desperate fear they'd bred in the old days, not to mention those who'd lost kin and friends. Sandra had slipped the knife in at the most opportune moment, too; early enough to discredit him with many of the others, but late enough that the shock of it would be vivid for the next little while.

She could have used it to blackmail him out of opposition beforehand . . . but then again, that wouldn't have been as effective in the long run. The problem with coercing an enemy into acting like a friend was that it didn't stick longer than it took them to find wiggle room. Putting your boot on his neck did *solve* the problem for good and all, rather more often.

Of course, it's far from the most final of Sandra's solutions. She's fond of that When a man causes you a problem, remember, no man, no problem *maxim. I most surely do not altogether like this public flaying of even such a man as this; but then, I don't like putting men to the sword on the field of battle either, and something like that is the alternative. Should Sandra be powerless against her enemies just because she hasn't my reach or weight of arm? She's spent the last twenty-five years ruling men of violence, wrapping them in nets of wit and wile they can't cleave with cold steel.*

Mathilda leaned close and murmured in his ear:

"*And she's even making use of the way everyone else felt about the Association then* without *it injuring her position now. Go Mom!*"

Turner cleared his throat, ignoring the mutter of quiet conversation around him:

"Lady Sandra, I was always interested in seizing any chance of peace," he said with a creditable attempt at dignity. "Unfortunately, your *late* husband was not a man with whom any real accommodation could be reached. I found that out to my regret. But I'm not ashamed that I *tried* to find a way to a negotiated settlement."

Not bad, Rudi thought. *Or to put it another way, you thought Norman was going to win the war that was obviously coming then and wanted to be on the winning side. You're too clever to try any such thing with the CUT, though, having seen what their word's worth. It won't hurt to make everyone think you* might *do just that.*

He went on aloud: "I hope you're not suggesting we negotiate with the Prophet Sethaz, Professor."

"Well . . . no, Your Majesty," the Corvallan merchant prince said. "But we've already made great sacrifices in this war. Next year's crop will be light even if the weather's perfect."

There were concerned nods at that; it was a valid point. Far too many strong young hands and backs had been under arms when they should have been plowing and sowing the fall wheat and barley, and far too many teams of oxen and horses had been hauling supplies or catapults instead of plows or reapers. And parts of the kingdom had been fought over instead of cultivated, including many of the richest grainlands north of the Columbia, which hadn't been planted at all. The herds had suffered, too—all the politics in the world couldn't make cattle and sheep breed or grow faster.

Nobody who'd grown up since the Change took the land's yield for granted. Those who'd lived through it . . . well, he'd known some of them who couldn't help compulsively hoarding pieces of bread in odd places until they went hard and moldy. Less extreme cases of obsession with food were too common to note.

"Sure, and we'll survive without famine, or even much dearth, if we all pull together," Rudi said, smiling. His face went stark an instant. "As I've promised many who've suffered most, we will *all* help. Montival is a great and wide land, and much of it hasn't been harmed."

"Our allies . . . the strong allies who Your Majesty has so brilliantly brought to our side . . . surely they can take more of the burden now . . ." Turner said.

Eric Larsson and Signe Havel, the Bearkiller leaders, made identical grunts of derision; the near-unison wasn't surprising, considering they were fraternal twins. Eric actually coughed a little biscuit into his second bowl of soup. He rapped on the table with the steel fist that had replaced his left hand after it was smashed by a Cutter war hammer fighting east of the mountains during the Pendleton campaign, a big scar-faced blond man in his early forties, with a look of ageless strength.

There was neither liking nor respect in the glance he gave Turner. The Outfit had always resented the way the city-state used them as a buffer during the wars against the Association and then skimped on help as well. They'd been founded by Mike Havel, who was Rudi's blood-father, common knowledge though never officially acknowledged. Havel had been honest, and not a man of blood by his own choice, but iron-willed and at need a very hard man indeed. From his example the Bearkillers had inherited a ferocious straightforwardness to the way they approached the world. It was something which made them very good friends . . . as long as you were faithful in return.

"Yeah, right. Professor—" Eric made it a term of contempt "— you may have noticed our High King managed to persuade the Iowans and the others to march into Montana, fight the CUT and then to *just fucking go home.* Rather than deciding, *hey, don't we deserve some of this territory for our trouble?*"

"The CUT helped there," Rudi said mildly. "What with their killing the bossman of Iowa and encouraging a revolt in Des Moines. Matti managed the politics of it, sure and she did; *and* she made a good friend of Anthony Heasleroad's wife."

"Kate needed help and appreciated it," Mathilda said modestly. "Besides, they've got their own internal disputes in the Midwest and a lot of the Iowan nobility . . . Farmers and Sheriffs, they call them . . . don't want their central government to have the sort of power a bigger standing army would mean, so they'd just as soon keep Iowa within its borders after the war. It's not as if they're short of land—they've got far more good black earth than they can cultivate. All that was obvious once I'd investigated a little and talked to the principals. The way we worked it they could say they wanted a clean exit strategy because they were altruistic."

Her mother beamed pride at her and made a little silent delighted clapping motion. Rudi winced slightly

at the sight. He admired Mathilda's political talents—
and relied on them—but her mother . . .

There are people whose approval fills you with disquiet.

Eric nodded agreement, but went on: "We leave
them to do all the heavy lifting from now on, and remember they haven't *seen* us do any fighting at all, and
how long do you think they'll stick to that unless they
do see it? They're helping us fight this war, but it's *our*
war. We're the ones the CUT invaded. It won't stay our
war if we don't follow up with an invasion of the enemy's heartland."

"And if it isn't our war, we don't get to shape the
peace," Signe said.

Rick Three Bears was glaring too. "And the Seven
Council Fires were promised the protection of Montival
when we agreed to join the kingdom," he said. "You
know, we Lakota get sort of antsy when you white-eyes
break treaties. Leaving us with our asses swinging in the
breeze out on the *makol*—the high plains—would bring
what you might call some bad memories to mind. We
agreed to fight with the League of Des Moines and let
them base forces in our territory and fix up the railroads
because we were promised we wouldn't be left alone to
face them afterwards. We're relying on *you* to help us
against *them* after the Cutters are out of the way. To
fight with us against the Farmers from the square states,
if it's ever necessary."

"God forbid," Sandra Arminger said unctuously, and
crossed herself with ostentatious piety. "But in that
event, the Association will of course be behind the High
King to the last lance and the last rose noble coin. We
place our resources unquestioningly at His Majesty's

LORD OF MOUNTAINS   309

disposal for the remainder of this war and for the establishment of the kingdom."

There were winces up and down the table. *Nobody*
wanted the Protectorate to have a hammerlock on the
new kingdom. It had too much land, wealth and power
for anyone else's peace of mind as it was.

"So do we," Juniper Mackenzie said. "Sure, and isn't
this the fulfillment of the vision I had when I held Rudi
over the altar in my Nemed and gave him the name of
Artos? The Clan stands by the Lady's Sword, who
guards Her sacred wood and Her law."

"Us too," Eric said.

Signe nodded—not enthusiastically, as she'd never
liked him much, but with grim determination.

"And the Order of the Shield of St. Benedict," Ignatius said. "In this I speak for the Abbot-Bishop."

More winces; the Mackenzies and the Bearkillers and
the warrior-monks had been the core of the resistance
to Norman Arminger. If you threw them in *with* the
Protectorate, they completely outweighed everyone else
put together. The other Corvallans were glaring at
Turner now, for isolating them.

"No treaties will be broken," Rudi said decisively.
"Nor will any other promises I've given; to the New
Deseret men who are still fighting, for example, or to
those of the Thurston family and their followers who've
come over to us and fought by our side at great and
constant risk. I've given my word on that, *and* bound it
to the line of my blood by the Sword of the Lady."

There was a long, thoughtful pause at that; even
Turner gave the crystal pommel behind Rudi's shoulder
a considering look. The second course came, a hearty

dish of horseradish-crusted roasted venison, with seasoned grilled potatoes, late asparagus and a winter salad
of pickled vegetables, accompanied by warm breads.
Rudi took a bite of the meat, chewed with enjoyment,
and waited; you should never interrupt an enemy when
they were making a mistake.

"Keeping large armies in the field will cause a lot of
hardship," Turner went on doggedly after a moment.
"If the enemy can't defeat us, it's not so . . . so *urgent*
any more."

*He wouldn't have accomplished all he has if he wasn't
stubborn,* Rudi thought. *I can use this man to the kingdom's good; he's very able, not to mention very rich and
very influential with his equivalents elsewhere. I just have
to make it plain that it's to his advantage to help me and
very much the opposite if he sets his will against mine. I
don't have to like him, or he me; I'm a warrior and he's a
merchant and that quarrel is as old as wolf and dog.
When you have to move manure, you use a dungfork.*

The banker continued: "We've all made sacrifices—"

"Oh, *yeah*," Eric drawled.

Signe elbowed him in the ribs. "Corvallis *has* made
sacrifices," she said. "If their Sixth Regiment hadn't
held at the Horse Heaven Hills . . . we wouldn't be
here. Unless we were forting up. We *had* to win that
battle; our army would have come apart, and every contingent would have gone home to make a last stand if
we'd lost."

"That's true," Rudi agreed. "They *stood*, and died
where they stood. I couldn't give them any help for far
too long. They bought me time, the which on a battlefield is a gift more precious than rubies. Bought it with

their blood and lives. I'm going to have *We Stood* embroidered on their standard. And presented by Peter Jones, if he lives."

Edward Finney laughed again, without mirth; several of his kin had carried pikes or crossbows with that regiment. "Yeah, *Corvallis* has made sacrifices. One of my sons-in-law took an arrow through the throat there. That's three young kids without a father. But that *sacrifices* doesn't include all of us in Corvallis, if you know what I mean."

Turner flushed. "My children aren't of service age. I've financed two whole battalions' worth of equipment out of my own pocket besides paying my taxes, and taken in and employed hundreds of refugees from the Bend country!" he said.

"Putting them to work in those factories you have interests in, you mean," Finney said. "The ones you were always bitching about being short of labor for in peacetime."

"You have refugees working on your farm!"

Another grunt of sour laughter from the landsman. He began to count on his fingers:

"Yeah. I've got . . . let's see . . . *three* nursing mothers and their babies, *six* kids under twelve and their moms, *two* amputees, and a guy who's older than I am and still has screaming nightmares about the Change and isn't too tightly wrapped when he's awake either . . . wets himself sometimes . . . and the rest of their families are all away fighting. Anyone who can walk can tend one of those water-powered spinning machines you've got filling those fat government contracts, Turner; no wonder you're not anxious to get the enemy out of

Bend so they can go back to their ranches! Farming isn't like that. My refugees aren't even doing enough work to meet the cost of their food; they *can't*, even though they push themselves hard. My sons—and a daughter— are with the army and I'm back on the farm trying to make bricks without straw and Gert's milking cows again until she has to put her hands in bowls of ice water for an hour before she can sleep, which I doubt your wife is."

"My wife is chief accountant for the First National Bank," Turner said huffily. "First National is crucial to the war effort."

"Yeah, I'm *sure* that makes her wake up crying when she turns over. So I want to get this war finished. Finished as quickly as can be while doing it *right*. And we need to put it on record that we're part of the kingdom. Which, now that Rudi . . . that Artos the High King just *beat* the Cutters, is going to be pretty damn popular back home, Turner."

"I'm sure everyone will make their fair contribution," Rudi said, and added to himself: *Provided they have no choice, some of them.*

"But," he went on, "deciding such matters is for Montival as a whole; and I myself am the symbol and agent of that unity, together with the Queen. Hence we need an acknowledgment of what the High King's rights and duties are; and a ceremony of acknowledgment. Of allegiance."

That produced a lot of talking. Most of it was positive, but unfortunately positive in a dozen separate ways. Everyone had his own ideas of what a coronation ceremony entailed, which was precisely what he and his closest advisors had anticipated. He cleared his throat.

"Brothers, sisters, I obviously can't satisfy you all! And sure, satisfying one of you would offend others—if I were to have the Cardinal-Archbishop of Portland crown me as the sole ceremony . . . I don't think Corvallis would enjoy it."

"We have separation of Church and State in Corvallis," Turner said, and Finney nodded solemn agreement. "They do in Bend, too, and a couple of other places."

"Your Majesty, I'm afraid that's doubly true of the United States . . . of Boise," Fredrick Thurston said, making a concession; most of that country would have added *of America*, for all that it ruled only a chunk of old Idaho and a few bits adjacent. "The whole concept of hereditary monarchy is going to be a tough sell without getting religion into the mix. Any hint of an establishment of religion would be a gift to . . . to the present regime."

Meaning, your late elder brother's henchmen, Rudi thought compassionately. *He tried to kill you too, and then to blame you for your father's death. His closest followers cannot turn back, not when they went along with that. And they've probably discovered that their bargain with the Prophet was the sort of deal a house-cat makes with a coyote.*

The tall, dark young man spoke politely but firmly. Rudi and he were good friends—they'd gone all the way to the Atlantic together and back after his father's murder. He'd always been brave as you could wish in a fight, but the High King was glad to see that the last traces of youthful diffidence had faded. Being head of a taut little army of twenty thousand men rather than a refugee living by charity was adding powerfully to his self-confidence.

"The Clan wouldn't approve either, boyo!" Juniper Mackenzie said, grinning. "And we don't have separation of covenstead and anything whatsoever."

"You *have* to have a Catholic coronation ceremony, Rudi," Mathilda said, her brows knotted in thought. "I don't think there's any alternative there."

"Indeed, and I wouldn't deny it," Rudi said cheerfully. "I've no objection at all."

He thought Ignatius winced slightly. Applying the holy oil to the brow of a pagan King was going to stretch his faith's standards a little, though it wouldn't be the first time. His Church had a very long history and had learned the value of patience a very long time ago.

I feel some sympathy, my friend, he thought. *But only some!*

From the way the other man's shrewd dark eyes looked at him under a raised brow, he thought the cleric understood him perfectly. They'd been in each other's company for years now and in circumstances that revealed the soul. He went on more seriously:

"So since I can't choose *one,* I'll choose *all,*" Rudi said, which had everyone blinking at him, except those who'd been in on it. "After the war I'll made the rounds and go through *everyone's* chosen ceremony. Religious, secular or a mix, just as they please. For each land . . . each little homeland of the heart; and in those I will be the suppliant, the suitor courting favor from the spirits of place and their folk. Which in some places, Boise for one, may be more like making a treaty."

"Well . . . that will take a while," someone said.

"Arra, I'll need to get to know every district and they me, anyway," Rudi said. "But for the present we need one ceremony that *is* for the whole of Montival and an acknowledgment of the same when it's over. And *that* ceremony is between the High King and Queen and the realm as a whole."

Turner remained silent, which Rudi deliberately took for assent, nodding as if pleased . . . which he was, more or less. The Grand Constable of the PPA mopped her plate of the last of the juices of the rare venison, ate the heel of bread, poured herself more of the red Pinot Noir—it was from her own estates, Montinore Manor to be precise—and spoke:

"Whereupon you can get back to the real business at hand, Your Majesty. They lost three, four to our one at the Horse Heaven Hills, and it was even worse for them during the pursuit, but they can afford it better. And the League of Des Moines isn't going to get much farther out on the High Plains until snowmelt. The weather there . . ."

"Ah, you farmers are all wussies," Rick Three Bears said.

Rudi grinned at her. He liked Tiphaine d'Ath, very much as you might a tiger that you were sure was on your side; she'd been a big part of his training in the arts of war, from handling a sword to deploying a regiment. But though very able, she was also very . . .

Focused, he thought. *Tightly focused on one set of problems, which is a good thing for a specialist, but a ruler can't afford too much of it. I have the Sword of the Lady, but chopping folk up is not the universal answer to the problems of kingcraft, essential though it may be at times.*

316 S. M. STIRLING

"A King is more than a war-leader, needful though that is," Rudi Mackenzie said. "You could do that as well as I."

"No, I couldn't," d'Ath said flatly. "I'm a better than competent general, but you have a gift for it—the way both of us do for the sword-in-hand. And I can lead professionals because they respect my record and I frighten them, but you can spend five minutes with a bunch of levied peasants fresh from the plow who've just been handed their first pikes and are scared out of their wits, and they'll be ready to storm Olympus. And they'll expect to *win*, which they may very well do *because* they expect it."

"Perhaps," Rudi said, though he was uncomfortably certain she was more-or-less right.

It wasn't a power he was altogether happy with, though he used it.

"War is only part of a King's trade. And he's more than an administrator, too," he added to Chancellor Ignatius.

"That he is," Juniper Mackenzie said. "For the King is the land and—"

She found herself speaking in unison with Ignatius, her words interweaving, more like a counterpoint than an interruption as he said:

"Just so, Your Majesty. Kingship is a sacred thing, from the day when David danced before the Tabernacle of the Lord, a thing which links—"

The Witch-Queen of the Mackenzies and the priestly Knight-Brother of the Order of the Shield of St. Benedict stopped and looked at each other, and Rudi threw back his head and laughed. After a moment they both joined in, and the others more gradually, though Ignatius did shake a reproving finger at Juniper and then at her son. The pages who were serving the royal party and their guests stayed solemnly intent on their duty, but Rudi thought a few of them were mildly shocked.

Ignatius inclined his head towards Juniper. "I defer to the Mackenzie. I'm not a man of eloquence, and far too tired to try right now."

Juniper smiled abstractedly at him and then went on when the laughter had passed, frowning, her leaf-green eyes intent:

"A King is a symbol, one that unites us all when we believe in it and makes us part of the same story, part of each other's story. And by *us* I'm not speaking merely of the human beings walking about at any particular moment, for we but borrow the Earth for a little while, by permission and in trust. There's the living land itself, its memories and tales in layer upon layer around every rock and stream and trail, the ghosts that haunt it and the beasts and birds and plants and trees that share it with us, with rights of their own, and the larger meaning of the Powers, however we name Them."

"My mother is right," Rudi said decisively. "There's a part of the kingship that is between me and the land itself and those Powers that ward it. That's . . . more of a thing for me and my Lady. The folk, all our peoples, are there, but through us. One family to stand for all families bound by history and blood."

"Under God," Ignatius said, politely but firmly.

"And did I say otherwise?" Juniper said in a guileless tone.

Mathilda swallowed a little uneasily, and their hands

met and gripped beneath the tablecloth. That *did* touch a little on her faith, to which she was devoted.

But if putting it in another form of words helps her, well, I've no objection to that. We're more . . . flexible about such things, we of the Old Religion.

"What are you grinning about?" she said quietly as the table dissolved into a more general conversation.

"I was thinking of something our good Chancellor said once; that debating theology with a Mackenzie was like trying to cut fog with a sword."

Mathilda snorted and freed her hand to poke him in the ribs, though also under the cover of the cloth. The plates were cleared and the desserts brought in, pastries, glazed fruit-tarts, ice cream with hazelnuts, liqueurs and coffee.

"I'll sleep on it," he said. "Perhaps it will come to me."

Four hours later he sat up gasping. Mathilda gave a muffled protest and then wholly woke herself. She crouched, watching him in the half-darkness of the room; the windows glowed with moonlight on snow, and there was a tiny yellow glimmer from the nightlight.

"What a dream," he whispered, sinking back and making his big scarred fist relax on the sheet. "My oath, what a dream!"

Mathilda wiggled until she could lay her undamaged left cheek on his shoulder.

"What was it about?" she asked softly; he could feel the slight warmth of her breath on his skin.

"I . . . can't remember," he realized suddenly. "No! I can, a little! I know where we must go."

"Where?" she said; he could feel her stiffen.

"The lake," he said. "Lost Lake."

"There?" she said dubiously. "Well, it's not too far, even with snow . . . but why Lost Lake?"

"Because it isn't lost, but hidden," Rudi said, the knowledge filling his mind like moonlit ice. "Not Lost Lake, really."

"What is it, then?"

"E-e-kwahl-a-mat-yam-lshk," he murmured. "Lake at the Heart of Mountains. The hidden Heart of Montival to be."

CHAPTER FIFTEEN

LOST LAKE

CROWN FOREST DEMESNE

(FORMERLY NORTH-CENTRAL OREGON)

HIGH KINGDOM OF MONTIVAL

(FORMERLY WESTERN NORTH AMERICA)

NOVEMBER 8TH, CHANGE YEAR 25/2023 AD

Edain Aylward Mackenzie held up his right hand with the fist clenched.

Halt, in battle-sign.

Behind him the men and women of the High King's Archers halted and kicked their feet out of the skis, then sank down into cover with arrows on the strings of their longbows. There was more than enough shelter in this dense old-growth forest of Douglas fir, silver fir and western hemlock, where the trees stood like great rough-barked pillars all about and rose a hundred feet to the lowest branch. The more so as they all wore warcloaks, mottled white and brown for winter and with bits of fir-bough tucked into the loops sewn on their surfaces.

Just pick a tree and you were concealed by trunks ten feet or more through at chest-height, at least from the front. He went to a knee behind some leafless fool's-huckleberry brush and peered forward. It wasn't too hard to move on foot, the snow hadn't had time to reach the huge depths it did here in the Cascades by the end of winter. Light stabbed down through gaps in the canopy, yellow spears of afternoon into the cavelike green gloom.

The lake shouldn't be visible yet—it was southward and downslope—but the terrain should be clear enough through patches of mist side-lit by the afternoon sun. The damp chill of the air bit, the sort that could get into your bones, and the fresh snow packed hard under his boots, wet cold against his knee above the sock-hose.

He shivered and blinked. *Or is this the land around Lost Lake indeed? I don't recognize a fookin' thing! I look at the ground and the peaks and the map and it's all there, but it's as if I've never been here before . . . Get a grip, man!*

Asgerd ghosted up beside him, nearly as silent as her husband, and on his other side Gharb, his mastiff bitch. The dog was bristling, showing a little of her long man-killing yellow teeth. His wife was frowning too. All three of them had keen senses. And all three had been beyond the world of common day, little though they might like it.

He respected the Powers and gave them Their due of rite and offering; that didn't mean he liked having Their particular attention on him. The consequences could be drastic, for good *or* ill; whether the kettle hit the pot, or the pot hit the kettle . . . Even a house-hob could cause bad trouble if things went wrong, and something a lot bigger than cream refusing to strike to butter in the churn was happening here. There was a reason the Fair Folk were called so when you named their kind aloud, and it wasn't just the beauty of their faces.

"This feels . . . odd," she said quietly, in the low conversational tone that didn't carry. "Where have you led us?"

"To Lost Lake, Anwyn witness," Edain said as softly, baffled. "This is the old *trail*, for all love."

Asgerd *had* never been here before, of course; they'd met in Norrheim on the shores of the Atlantic, in what the old world had called northern Maine. He went on:

"Look you, I spent many a summer here in the north country with the Chief as a lad, his months with the Regent and Mathilda. I've hunted and fished and walked these woods before, swum in that lake . . . with him and now and then by myself. Yes, and spent nights with my bedroll spread not long bowshot from this very ground, with no more thought of anything of the Otherworld than to ask the land's permission to take deadfall or to make the offerings to Cernunnos and the Mother from a kill. It's a bonny place and no dispute, very fair indeed, but now it feels *different*. It's a puzzlement."

"It feels as it did on Nantucket," she said starkly.

He started to shake his head, then nodded unwillingly. "Not as strong . . . no, say not as *fearful* as that," he said.

"Nantucket would have frightened a *God*," she said. "But this is . . . fey and eerie. Not fell or dire, not threatening, surely not evil, but I've a feeling that I'm not supposed to come any closer. That I might come to grief if I did, not through ill intent, but as I would if I leapt off a cliff or ran face-first into a tree."

Edain shivered agreement. Then he turned, sure that every pair of eyes would be upon them. He held out his string-arm, bent the elbow until the fingers pointed down, rotated it in a circle around that point, waggled the hand, then tapped two fingers at his eyes.

Scout in a circle. Report.

He and Asgerd waited as the skis hissed away; you didn't split into groups smaller than two, so there was always someone watching over your back. Edain stared past hers, blinked again at the glimmer that wasn't there when he looked directly, and swore softly. He knew he was a man of strong will . . .

Inherited from Da, most likely, though the Lady knows me mother . . . but I have this feeling that if I weren't determined and if we weren't under orders, it's far away we'd be by now, without really knowing why save that it seemed like a good idea at the time.

After a while the patrols returned. He wasn't surprised that the brief reports showed no human presence and even less so that none of them had gone closer to the Lake itself. After that they dispersed and waited with the patience of scouts and hunters, until Rudi and Mathilda came up.

They were dressed for the wilderness, she in Portlander hunting garb of green wool and padded leather, he in kilt and winter jacket and ordinary wrapped and pinned plaid. They leaned their skis against a tree and joined him.

"The sleighs aren't all that far behind," Rudi said.

They exchanged a snort; the amount of gear the panjandrums had insisted on hauling along for a short trip was something of a scandal. Juniper Mackenzie could make do with very little, but some of the others . . .

"What's the matter, then?" Rudi went on.

"I'll go on down there if you say so, Chief," Edain said when the High King knelt beside him. "But I thought it would best to wait for the order until you'd, ummm, seen for yourself. Look. Really *look*."

"Good man," Rudi said, and thumped him on the shoulder. After a moment: "It does feel . . . a bit strange, the now, does it not?"

"Aye, a *bit* strange. And we went a *bit* of a long way on the Quest, and that mountain—" he jerked his thumb over his shoulder, to the peak of Mt. Hood southward "— is a *bit* of a bulk and has a *bit* of a height upon it. What's happened? This used to be a spot no different from others, or no more than having a pretty lake and a fine view of the mountains to admire as you lay and fished on a summer's day."

Rudi was silent a long while; after a moment he stroked his short-clipped beard and let his other hand fall to the moonstone pommel of the Sword. Then he spoke, his voice a little remote:

"I'm not sure myself, mind you. But I'd say that the Change was a beginning, not an end. After what . . . happened . . . on Nantucket, well, that was a change as well, if more subtle. One of the things the Change said to us of the humankind was *there are things to which you should not put your hand*. Perhaps this is one that says other things, among them: *And also, there are places where you should not ordinarily go. Not unless asked and ordered, so.*"

"And it's ready to heed hints to stay away I am, and that beyond all doubt or question!" Edain said.

Rudi nodded. Just then Edain saw Mathilda catch his eyes with hers, then flick her gaze to the branches of a

big silver fir not far away. He followed the gesture automatically himself; they'd all done a great deal of skulk-
ing and scouting together on the Quest. Two large
ravens were sitting side by side on a branch, and he
hadn't noticed them before. They launched themselves
into the air in a wide circling gyre with loud *gruk . . .
gruk . . .* cries, dodging amongst the tall trees, then
headed off down the slope towards the water along the
overgrown trail. Mathilda crossed herself twice, and her
lips moved in prayer.

"O shluagh!" Edain swore, to avert the attention of
the Fair Folk and ask their aid if they did notice him.

He made the sign of the Horns, and the Invoking
pentagram as well. Asgerd touched her valknut, and
Hammer-signed the air. To his astonishment Rudi stood
and laughed, loud and long and with genuine merriment in it, hands on hips as he shouted to the sky:

"And it's a meddler and a troublemaker you are, Old
Man, wandering about the world and sticking your
spoon in any number of stewpots!"

He pointed his index finger at the departing birds:
"As for you two . . . could it be, just, that you're giving
me a message the now? You could make it plainer, that
you could . . . pull a little written sign through the air
behind you, say, or dance a merry jig about us and too-
tle a march on the bagpipes the while!"

The laughter died, but his blue-gray-green eyes were
still lit with it. "We'll be on our way, then, Edain. There's
no danger . . . or at least none that blades and bows
could guard against. You and the rest will be safe enough,
I'm thinking. But if I were you, I'd not hunt just here
today, nor take any wood that wasn't already fallen."

"The Mother-of-All have pity, no!" Edain said sincerely.

"And I would so advise the others when they arrive. We may be a while," Rudi warned.

Edain shrugged. "We've only been on the trail two days and a bit, and at a pace a six-year-old could have bettered. We've bread and butter and cheese and cold pork and apples, and for that matter cakes and ale from the Lodge. It's a poor excuse for the High King's fighting-tail we'd be if a night or two in the woods was a hardship. The complaints of their high lordships, that'll be the hardest thing to endure."

"Then await us," he said. "When the others arrive, don't let them go more than a quarter-mile nearer; that bit of a level spot, you know it. They should be able to see . . . something . . . from there."

"I'll have no trouble with them keeping their distance," Edain said grimly. "Even the mighty mucks who think so well of themselves. I may have to boot the odd arse to get them that close."

Rudi nodded. He and Mathilda set their skis down and slipped the toes of their boots into the loops.

"Are you sure I should be here too?" Mathilda said.

"As sure as sure, as sure as the beat of my own heart, love," Rudi replied. "We will hold this land together; and our children after us. We are one, and the land with us."

Before the Change there had been log cabins here at the northern point of Lost Lake and a small store. In the first year fugitives had passed through, often to their deaths, which was where most paths had led in that time. The passing years and resurgent life had long since reclaimed their bones.

"It's the same," she said, looking around. "But . . . how long did it take us to get here? It wasn't very far and downhill most of the way but it felt like . . . a long time. Like things were *stretched*, somehow."

The men of the budding Association had come through in the high summer of the Change Year as well, hunting the bandit gangs and little pockets of refugees trying to live by the hunt; by then the Lord Protector had been short of labor. They'd wrecked or torched the buildings to keep outlaws from using them. Afterwards men came seldom, between the green-clad enforcers of the Forest Law based out of Timberline and the anti-bandit patrols from the baronies on either side, and sheer remoteness from the tilled fields that fed human-kind. Those who did were invited guests.

"I don't think that's a question with an answer, Matti. I think this is the place we know and also . . . not."

"And getting here is partly following the trail we know . . ."

". . . and also not."

Rain and snow, insects and clinging roots had re-turned ash to the soil and reduced metal to rust and glass to fragments. Mounds of berry-bushes covered foundations and were well begun in the long toil of grinding them back into the earth, the canes standing in tangles through the knee-deep snow.

Rudi and Mathilda dropped their packs, planted their skis upright, then walked to the water's edge hand-in-hand, looking about.

More snow stood on the boughs of the tall conifers that crowded to the rim of the lake, thick and clinging as a froth of whipped cream on the dark green and brown. The water was a purpling blue as the sun sank, and in the distance bands of crimson lay against the western sky. The same color flecked the clouds scattered in mare's-tails above and painted the cone of Mount Hood, and the image of mountain and clouds repeated itself in the mirror of the water, broken only for a moment when a trout leapt with a tiny audible *splash* and re-forming as the ripples died. There were shapes moving in the clouds, like the patterns in the Sword's blade. A loon cried somewhere, its haunted call echoing through the quiet.

"As sure as the beat of my own heart that you should be here, *anamchara* mine," he said. "And that this is the rightful place."

This was daunting to him, and she was less at ease with things of the Otherworld than he, but he saw the lioness courage of her soul brace her shoulders.

"Then what do we do?" she asked.

They'd cached their oiled-leather bedrolls and the little tent, an ingenious contraption from the Lodge's storerooms. With that and a fire and the provisions in their packs they'd be as comfortable as necessary. He took a deep breath of the cold, wet air and opened himself to the world. The heartbeat of it sounded in his ears with the flow of his own blood.

"I . . . know. Now I know. Here," he said, where a rock thrust through the thin duff and scattered snow, rising to waist-height.

Artos of Montival drew the Sword of the Lady. A

ripple ran through the world, felt with the inner mind rather than seen. He touched the point to his finger, and a bead of blood welled out to lie pooled on the not-steel. Wordlessly, her eyes grave, Mathilda did likewise.

"Now make your prayer, *mo chroi*," he said gently.

She went to her knees on the other side of the snag of black rock and took out her crucifix, kissed it, and held it between her hands.

"*Ave Maria, gratia plena—*"

He faced the Quarters, greeting each with the Sword raised high across his palms.

"By the North . . ." he began, calling the shapes of the Guardians and their protections, invoking their vigilance. "By the East . . . By the South . . . By the West!"

Then: "By Earth! By Sky!"

He knelt across the stone from her. She met his eyes and then put her hands around his on the hilt of the Sword as he placed the point on the hard basalt. The strength of her grip ran through him.

"We are the land's, and the land is ours," he said, and she repeated the words after him. "Its flesh has fed us, and we are its body; its water has given us life and flows in our veins. As guardians to all its kindreds we shall be, and to that we pledge ourselves and the line of our blood so long as it shall last; until the sea rise and drown us or the sky fall and crush us or the world's end."

"*Amen*," she said.

"*So mote it be*," he replied.

And *thrust* the Sword downward with all his strength. The length of it sank into the rock with a long crackling *shunk* sound.

Rudi screamed as the world split apart in whirling fragments.

Glimpses tore at his mind. He could *feel* Mathilda beside him, their beings joined in some inconceivable way, her fear and steady willingness. Feel the new life that was growing beneath her heart; feel the coiled essences that lurked in every cell of their beings, all three, and their linkage to the Sword. For a moment he could *understand* it, and his soul recoiled from the vastnesses contained within himself.

And he could see; see all the land at once.

— And a man in the dried-blood colored armor of the Sword of the Prophet knelt in a tent, screaming as he hammered his fists against his temples, and slow trickles of blood ran down from his eyes like red tears—

— and Sandra Arminger gasped and clutched at her chest and whimpered—

— and Juniper Mackenzie smiled with a transforming joy, looking around at the snowy woods as at a world glowing with numinous life—

— and on a high prairie of thin grass where a mist of ice crystals cut vision to yards, men huddled in buffalo robes looked up in surprise as an ancient figure rose from beside the fire and began to shuffle and stamp around it.

"Dance, brothers! Dance, Lakota! White Buffalo Woman dances the world awake today!"

— and a humpback whale breached in the gray Pacific waters, falling in monumental playfulness, an ocean of spray that drenched the awed fisherfolk at their oars. More and more circled them, dolphin and orca and the slow majesty of a great blue—

— and in an abbey atop a tall hill set in green rain-misted fields, a white-haired man in an embroidered robe knelt with arms outstretched before an altar that bore the Cross; the swords of his fallen Brothers were ranked on the stone floor before it. His face lit with happiness as he felt the Man of Sorrows speak within, and behind him the monks broke into a thundering chorus—

and in Mithrilwood, Allcyne Loring paused as he laid the urn which bore the ashes of the *Hiril Dúnedain* on an altar. It was in the midst of a circle of leafless oaks, but sudden golden light ran from branch to branch and bough to bough like living fire as his blue eyes went wide. The children weeping beside him looked up in wonder, their tears drying as smiles broke free. The fire blossomed in leaf and flower of gold and silver and ruby, until the trees blazed with light and life and fragments floated like sparks among the crowd of watchers. He caught one in his hand, and it shone through the flesh as if his living self were glass.

The slow mourning music of flute and viol stopped, but notes still rang through the air, faster and faster. The watchers began to circle and pace with hands linked, whirling among the floating jewels that joined in the rhythm of their movement as the children laughed and a voice whispered in his ear:

All shall be well, bar melindo, *my darling one, all shall be very well*—

— and a bear bellowed, a tiger snarled, a red mare stamped until the mountains shook, elk raced across a meadow, ravens flew about a single blue eye—

— and a man and woman danced above the High

King and his Queen, huger than the sky itself, stars glittering in Her blue robe and springing like sprays of silver where Her fingers touched the purple vault of heaven; His horns traced patterns against them as he whirled in a wild fierce joy larger than worlds, infusing all that was with meaning—

Artos screamed again, not in pain but as his being *stretched* beyond what a human soul could encompass.

CHAPTER SIXTEEN

So bright, so bright! Mathilda thought.

The chaos of images faded, lost in light. As if she stared point-blank into the sun, but there was no pain. A whirling feeling, as if she were being swept away, dissolving without losing herself, perishing and yet more conscious, more aware with each passing instant—

And she was on a hillside. She blinked and staggered a little. It was a sunny afternoon and warm beneath a sky that was a pure arch of blue. The ground beneath her was rocky but starred with small blue flowers. It was not quite a desert, but it smelled a little like the deserts she was used to, dust and spice, yet subtly different. More like . . .

Fennel, she thought. *And thyme.*

The hillside was dotted with small gnarled trees, their trunks twisted and curved and ancient, sometimes hollow. The leaves were silvery-gray and green, flickering in a slow, hot breeze and providing a thin but welcome shade. Mathilda was acutely conscious of everything, each passing instant, each scented breath of air, the distant tinkling of a bell. Downslope the land leveled out, and became small straggling fields much greener than the dusty faded color that covered the hills; she recognized growing wheat and barley. A patch of low goblet-trained vines drowsed in the sun not far away, in full leaf but before bud-set. Here and there a tree was in flower, fruit-trees but not ones she was familiar with. The shrilling of insects was a murmur in the background.

More distant was a village, dun mud-brick buildings with flat roofs huddled together, twists of acrid wood-smoke rising from beehive-shaped ovens that stood in the yards, carrying the smell of baking. Beyond that were more rocky hills shimmering in the heat and still-ness.

Mathilda bent over and touched a flower, a blade of grass, watched an insect scurry.

"Is this a dream?" she said. "I don't think so."

It was *more* real than waking life, not less. The grass blade was soft enough beneath her fingertip, but she felt that it had been carved out of something harder than diamond—something like the *idea* of diamond in the mind of Eternity. Each leaf-flutter and crawling beetle and anonymous little brown bird flitting by struck her like war hammers forged from purest *meaning*. She panted a little at the strain of it, as if taking a step here was like fighting for her life in plate armor.

But I'm not in armor, she thought, looking down at herself.

It was herself, down to the little scar on a thumb she'd gotten from a sharp stone in a brook one summer when Rudi taught her how to tickle fish. But she was wearing a long robe of coarse wool, and a headdress of wrapped linen that framed her face and a shawl. Sandals were on her feet, plain but honestly made with straps of soft leather. She began to pick her way down the hill, until the sound of rocks clicking against each other came to her.

A man worked, building a drystone wall. The work went steadily, though she could see his hands were scuffed and bleeding in a few places, and sweat rolled down his skin. He had a cloth wrapped around his head and a beard of brown hair, and his robe had been shrugged aside so that the top of it also hung down to his knees and left his sun-toughened torso bare. His face was square and strong, the eyes a yellow-brown.

"Father," she said softly, clutching at the bark of an olive-tree beside her. "Father . . . do you know me?"

Norman Arminger looked up. "Peace, maiden," he said.

I'm not speaking English, she realized; the language was unfamiliar, harsh in her mouth with glottals and rough breathings, a language for poets and prophets and warriors.

"No, I don't know you," he answered after a moment, pausing with one stone resting atop the half-built wall. "But I did. I will. Now I must work. I must serve the sheep."

"The sheep?" she said.

"Wolves or robbers may come," the man said, turning the rock and fitting it, with the weary half-grunt of a man doing hard labor and knowing that he'd do much more. "I must build the wall strong for them. I failed before because I thought it was for me. Now I must work for them. Peace be upon you."

"And upon you, peace," she whispered.

It seemed a long time that she watched him work, and she took a few steps and sat on a chunk of white limestone that heaved up like the bones of the world. The shadows lengthened, and the day grew cooler. A figure came up the track that led to the valley, a woman in the same dress as she, with a blue mantle draped across her head. She carried a bundle wrapped in coarse cloth and set it down on the half-finished wall . . . that seemed to be no nearer finished for all the long day's work.

The man faltered as the woman approached; he was exhausted now, like a convict pushed beyond what could be borne by a harsh overseer, and the smell of his sweat was rank. He gave a single tired sob and sank to his knees as she stopped, tears among the sweat on his haggard face.

"You are weary," the woman said. "I have brought you food; eat and drink and rest a little."

She unfolded the bundle and laid it on the wall. There was a clay jar within it. Mathilda knew the scent of watered wine as she unstoppered it. Two flat wheat-cakes were wrapped around some soft cheese and a handful of small blackish fruits she recognized as olives, from rare treats brought from over-sea.

"Take and eat," the woman said again, and the man did.

His hands were still bleeding, and they were callused and strong, but they moved gently on the plain food, as if it were something delicate and wonderful. As he ate he straightened, and smiled as he finished.

"Thank you," he said. "The food strengthens me. I must work until my task is finished."

"Work until you have built yourself, child of Adam," the woman said.

She turned, and Mathilda caught a glimpse of a face under the shadowing mantle; a thin middle-aged face, large dark eyes and the marks of work and grief, and a smile . . .

Suddenly she was sobbing against the woolen robe. A hand stroked her head. When she could, Mathilda spoke:

"You brought my father food?"

"My Son offers all men nourishment," she said. "Many come to it through me."

"Thank you! Then . . . then there's hope for him?"

"There is always hope, if we accept it," she said, laying her hand on Mathilda's head for a moment. "Because he loved you and your mother, your father can receive it from me. Blessings and peace upon you, daughter of Eve; and upon your children and the children of your children."

The figure in the blue robe rose and walked away, and it was like a rupture in her heart, but somehow the thought of crying out didn't occur to her. After a while she walked up the hill. It wasn't a surprise when a figure in a plain Benedictine habit fell in beside her, and she smiled at him.

"Is this real, Father Ignatius?"

The monk was as she remembered him, telling his rosary as they walked, something of a warrior's stride in the way his sandaled feet crunched on the loose rock and dirt.

"Very real, my child, though that is a complex matter. Do you remember a time I heard your confession, at the beginning of our journey together?"

"In the desert, Father? We looked up at the stars, and you said that all that glory and beauty would be finished someday, and still *I* would go on."

He nodded. "That was true. There are truths, and then there is the Truth, the One, the Wholly Real."

"That . . . *light* I saw?"

"That for which the light is simply a symbol. There is the Real, but we are like . . . as a wise man once said . . . like prisoners in a cave, seeing only shadows cast upon the wall. Until we waken, and go further up and further in, always closer."

Mathilda nodded. "And you're here to help me?" she said. "Thank you, Father."

Ignatius laughed. "We help each other; that's how we progress along the road ourselves. I'm returning a favor done to me, my daughter, and one done for me a very long time ago, if time has any meaning as I am now. Returning it the only way one really can; by passing it along to another."

They stopped on the hilltop; vision stretched all around them.

"You will see what you need to see. High Queen, daughter of Eve, mother of sons and daughters, Mathilda Arminger."

For a long moment Rudi stood in wonder with the wind ruffling his hair and the edges of his plaid; wonder, but no fear. He felt balanced and strong, motionless but implicit with swiftness in muscle and bone and nerve.

The mountain was there and the sun was at the same angle, but the very shape of Hood was different; more naked, rougher, steeper, with a plume of either cloud or smoke off eastward from its summit. The lake was a deep tarn, lost among rock and patches of rotted snow. The slopes about him were nearly bare, though from the mildness it was no longer winter, and there was a very faint tinge of sulfur in air otherwise clean as crystal.

Only a few little blue flowers starred the bare ground, and moss, and one or two tiny dwarf spruce, as if life had only just begun its conquest here.

This is the beginning, he knew. *Not long after the Ice withdrew; long enough that wind and water have changed the very bones of the mountain from this day to mine. Before our kind were woven into the story of the land. Long and long ago, before the Gods who were before the Gods.*

A stone rattled behind him. He made himself turn calmly. There were two men there, one in his late teens, another old enough to show grey in the knot of dark hair they both had tied and twisted above their right ears. Both wore leggings and loincloth and hide shoes; one had a tunic of yellow-brown leather besides, worked in patterns with shell beads.

Their faces were marked with blue and yellow tattooed stripes, and they had the broad high-cheeked look and ruddy-brown skin of the First Peoples, though not of any tribe he knew. There were hide rolls over their backs, knives and hatchets thrust through their belts, stout spears in their right hands. The spears had long lanceolate points of flint so finely worked that it had a metallic luster, of which he had an uncomfortably businesslike view since they were poised to thrust or throw.

Everything about their gear was beautifully made and often carved or colored, but it was all hide and wood and stone or what appeared to be implausible amounts of ivory, no trace of metal or cloth. He took all that in an instant, and also saw their eyes wide with the shock and fear that could turn to rage in an instant. His appearance would be outlandish beyond belief to them, and he suspected they were far less used than he to seeing outlanders or strangers. They were tall well-muscled men as well, and his instant, instinctive appraisal was that they would each be deadly quick as wolverines.

"Peace," he said, and slowly lifted his hands palm out. "Peace between us, brothers."

A woman stepped from behind them, pushing them casually apart. She wore a longer version of the tunic the older man sported, deerskin worked until it was butter-soft, hers bleached white and bearing patterns of colored feathers as well as beads and shells. Her face was framed by graying braids and had a hard strength just starting to sink into a net of wrinkles.

"*E'mi, e'mi,*" she said to the two men, putting her hands on their spear-arms and pushing them downward. "*E'mi, woam. T't'shui-Ta.*"

Rudi blinked, astonished when he thought his capacity for wonderment filled and overfilled. He understood the words, and not just the words but the meaning behind the strange forms and structures that knit them together:

"Be still, be still. Be still, my brave ones. Here is no enemy."

The men looked at each other, scowling, then stood aside. They stayed ready for instant action, but they grounded their spears. Rudi slowly brought the back of his right hand to his brow and bowed, the greeting a Mackenzie male made to any new-met hearthmistress.

Loremistress, I think, he decided, meeting her eyes. They were dark and warm and somehow reminded him of his mother in their kindly strength. *A High Priestess of the triple cords, we'd say; one who's walked with the Powers.*

She looked him over with a fearless intelligence. Then she reached into a pouch at her waist and blew a pinch of some powdered herb into his face. He suppressed a cough; the scent was green and spicy, but not unpleasant. After that she took a baton of carved ivory from her belt, looked at him through a loop in one end and started to tap him lightly with it from head to toe, chanting as she did.

When she had finished she considered him with a bird's bright curiosity, fingering a lock of his hair and looking at his eyes. She smelled of woodsmoke and tanned leather and the wilderness, and a faint scent of healthy, well-washed human. Then she spoke again in the quick-rising, slow-falling language that he now understood:

"Are you of Those Others? Is this land forbidden to us?"

Of the Fair Folk, he guessed; there was more to talking than the surface meaning of words.

He shook his head with a smile:

"No, wise woman. I am a man like these with you, a child of Earth born to die."

She pursed her lips. "We have seen no man-sign since we came south of the Great River. I walk here to make friends of the Mountains and Rivers and the Mothers of the fur and feather tribes. Is this your people's hunting range? We have heard of none like you, and the beast clans here have no fear of men."

"No," he said, suddenly sure that he spoke the truth. "This land lies empty for you. It holds no ghosts until yours come, and you will dwell in it for many lives of men, beyond counting, and the line of your blood for longer still, and always the stones and the trees will re-member you."

She stood and looked at him while the wind whistled down from the glaciers.

"You are speaking truth, man of Earth," she said at last, and then smiled like a girl. "All the kindly spirits go with you, then. We will hunt south of the river that our children may eat and grow strong; and you are always welcome on our runs, Sun Hair."

"That's remarkably authentic garb," a voice said. "Late fourteenth century, isn't it?"

Mathilda turned, a smile still on her face; the crowd was so wildly varied, like figures seen in a dream. The jugglers that had held her attention just now were quite good and in familiar motley garb like something from a court masque in Portland's City Palace or Todenangst. But there were *cars* nearby, beyond the bright pavilions and the merchant's booths of the fairground, and not the rusted wrecks that had been part of the background of her life.

Moving cars, purring along unworn roads of dark fresh asphalt as if there were great cats beneath their hoods. And the air smelled different, with an odd odor like burnt turpentine. That mixed with the more familiar scents of frying food and warm people, but there was none of the horse and ox that had always been part of her life.

"Ah . . . it's just my clothes, demoiselle," she answered the stranger politely, with a slight courtesy gesture like the beginning of a curtsy and an inclination of the head. "God give you good day."

The young woman was about her own age, dressed in a simple dagg-sleeved green kirtle and white wimple bound with a silver chain. Mathilda had found herself . . . here . . . in a court cotte-hardie; a day dress she recognized as one that rested in the cupboards in her chambers at home in Castle Todenangst. She even remembered having it taken in a little when she got back from the Quest . . .

"This stitching is lovely," the other woman said. "Is that handwork?"

"Yes," Mathilda said; then she looked up agape as something huge and roaring went by overhead.

An airplane! I'm seeing an airplane! she thought.

"Marvelous!" she whispered aloud in awe, crossing herself. "Jesu!"

Her chance-met companion laughed aloud, a warm chuckle like a hand stroking velvet. She had an ice-cream cone in one hand, and finished it with a catlike delicacy before she said:

"You *are* staying in character!"

It was the laugh that told her. The laugh and the warm brown eyes, deep with thought, and the height that was exactly the right six inches shorter than Mathilda's full-grown five-foot-eight. The strangeness was seeing those eyes look at *her* like a stranger.

"You're . . . Sandra Whittle, aren't you?" she said.

"Actually, my Society name is Eleanor," she said. "But yes . . . have we met?"

"I've heard of you," Mathilda said. "I'm . . . Mathilda."

The sharp gaze focused on her belt, which was white leather worked with silver flowers.

"Is that dagger live steel?" she said. "Those are the best costume jewels I've ever seen, too."

Mathilda blinked in puzzlement; it was certainly *good* steel, but it was one of her everyday ones, the type she'd worn since she was twelve and which marked her as an Associate. The blade was ten inches of watermarked Damascus steel, severely plain except for the rippling patterns in the metal, but the hilt was gold and silver wire braided together, and the pommel held a ruby the size of her thumbnail. She drew it from the tooled leather of the sheath and flipped it to reverse it and present it with the point towards herself and the flat of the blade along her forearm, as was courteous.

Sandra's eyes widened as she took it and weighed the solidity of it in her small hand.

"That *is* live steel, and not peacebonded!" she said. "Naughty! Though I won't tell the marshals."

"Be careful, it's—" Mathilda began, surprised that her mother was acting as if she'd scarcely ever held a dagger before and knew no better than to put her thumb to it like a kitchen knife.

"—sharp," she finished, taking it back as Sandra sucked at the slim little cut on the ball of her thumb.

"Sorry," Mathilda added.

The deep eyes were already looking over her shoulder, though. "Oh, now *that's* nice," she said cheerfully.

Mathilda realized what she'd see even as she turned her head. A man in armor was walking down the laneway towards them. Simple, old-fashioned armor, a chain-mail hauberk to the knees, split up the front and rear in horseman's fashion, a sword belt with a rather broad-bladed sword, an acorn-shaped helmet with a flared nose-guard concealing most of his face and a teardrop-shaped shield four feet long slung point-down over his back; it was black, with the Lidless Eye blazoned on it. And he moved easily under the weight; a lot of the men about were as out of condition as merchants or the worst sort of cleric, even if they went armed, but he looked like a fighting-man to be wary of. Broad-shouldered and long-legged and with a thick wrist in the hand casually on the bevel pommel of the broadsword and an arrogant assurance in the way he strode along. The crowd parted for him, sometimes with a resentful murmur.

"That's . . . Norman," Mathilda said.

"It certainly is, and authentic—notice the cross-gartering and the loose trews? Not my favorite period; I'm more a thirteenth, fourteenth century sort of girl. Nothing like a good pair of legs in tight hose, I say."

"No, I mean it's Norman Arminger."

A gurgling chuckle. "That's his actual *name*? He must have a sense of humor, then, and not be a complete Period Nazi. Well, look at the shield!"

"He's a, uh, going to be a professor of history. Eleventh-century specialist."

"*Definitely* interesting!"

She left Mathilda's side without a backward glance, sinking down in a perfectly executed curtsy before the knight of the Lidless Eye. He halted, sweeping off his helmet by the nasal and bowing; his hair was bowl-cut, but close behind the ears in a fashion Mathilda remembered vaguely from her youth.

Oh, God!

She turned and . . .

The forest was about him, the one he knew.

No, he thought. *Not quite.*

It was towards the end of the day, and summer, but late—late August, in these cool uplands, when the aspens and vine-maple started to turn and there was frost in the small hours of the night. The trees were thicker, he thought; perhaps taller. Birds were thick too on the water of the lake, and when a flock took fright at a jumping trout and cataracted skyward it was like a turning skein of smoke. Four horses grazed by the water, and as he stepped around a tree he could see a campfire burned there—an expert's small hot fire, little fume and much heat. He could smell the savory scent of roasting duck, and a man rose as he approached.

"*Bonjour*," the man said, then went on in thickly accented English. "You come share our fire, eh?"

He was shorter than Rudi by a foot, but barrel-chested and strong, with a full dark beard flowing down his chest and long hair of the same almost-black, his skin weathered and tanned oak-brown; there were deep wrinkles beside his hazel-green eyes, and he was missing the little finger of his left hand. A rifle was held casually in his right, the type with an external flint-tipped hammer at the side, and a steel-headed tomahawk and long knife in a beaded sheath thrust through his belt. He wore leather trousers and moccasins strapped about the ankle, a red wool shirt and a knit cap with a tassel. A briar pipe between his yellow teeth gave off a foul-smelling smoke.

"That I will, friend. My name is Rudi Mackenzie."

"Étienne Bélanger, me. This my woman, *Pe Ku Nen Mu*."

She was a tribeswoman, younger than the man and pretty, wearing a deerhide dress and about five months along, he judged. She handed her man a bottle and sat down easily on her hams across the low fire, watching the newcomer with a candid stare of wonder.

"You got friends close?" the man asked casually as he pulled the cork with his teeth and offered the bottle.

He didn't let the rifle go far from his hand, despite his friendly manner. Rudi wouldn't have expected otherwise, for a man with horses and gear and a good-looking woman alone in lands beyond settled law.

"I do; I've not the gear to travel else. *Sláinte mhaith*," Rudi added courteously as he raised the square bottle to his lips and took a swig, then fought not to cough as he handed it back. "To your good health!"

The which you will not keep if you drink that every day! he thought as he squatted also.

"*Salud!*" the *coureur de bois* said and drank deep, his Adam's-apple fluttering blissfully under his beard. The word meant more or less the same thing. "I hear that one before, plenty Company men are . . . *Gael*, you say, no?"

He indicated Rudi's kilt.

"You're a hunter, then?" Rudi said.

"Trapper, me!" the man said, jerking a thumb at a bundle of pelts among the gear stacked nearby. He sighed. "But maybe not no more. The beaver, she gets thin unless you go far, far east. Not like the old days. I miss them, me, miss the sound their tails make when they whack the water, but a man he must make a living . . ."

The woman handed them each a bark plate, heaped with duck and flour bannock and with a peck of berries in a twisted cup of leaves. Rudi signed his food and put a morsel aside for the spirits of place, then ate. He didn't think the man noticed, but the woman did, and gave him a sharp look. She had a small gold crucifix around her neck, which might mean anything or not much, depending.

"Indeed, the beaver are few the now," Rudi said, eating the plain good food with relish. "And . . ."

If that history book is to be believed . . .

". . . they've taken to wearing hats of silk instead, in the lands across the great water."

"*Oui*, I hear that. Mebbe this my last trip; not a young man no more, me, to travel and trap and fight. I go to the *prairie de les Française,* west of here in the valley, be *habitant* and grow wheat like my father does back around *Trois-Rivières*. Better for *les enfants*, eh?"

"Indeed it will be," Rudi said softly. "I'd say it will be a good place for them, and that they'd do well indeed."

He nodded to the woman and rose. "My thanks for the drink and the food and your company, my friends," he said. "But I'd better be getting along."

*   *   *

Portland, Mathilda thought.

But that was only from the river before her and a turn that showed her the wooded heights westward that she knew as the New Forest. There was no city wall, no ruined towers of the ancient world, no great bridges across the Willamette. The street around her was deep in mud, though she stood on a wooden sidewalk out of the worst of it. The city-smell was heavier than in the Crown City of her own day, ranker, but with the horse-dung and woodsmoke she had grown up with. The river swarmed with boats from canoes to great three-masted full-rigged ships, and also with curious things like rafts with metal chimneys and mill-wheels to either side or at the stern that she recognized as steamboats after a moment.

Fascinated, she walked closer. Nearer to the water the crowds were even thicker and rougher: fewer of the men wore the dark garb with stovepipe hats she'd noticed earlier, and there were fewer women as well. That wasn't a complete surprise; something like that would have been true of *her* Portland. She got more odd glances here too. Her cotte-hardie wasn't impossibly different from what the women wore here, but it wasn't identical either . . . and the rich fabrics and jewels attracted attention in this part of the town.

The edge of the water itself was a chaos of noise and loads going overhead on nets, of bowsprits overhanging the roadway and piles of boxes and bales, of sweating men in floppy trousers held up by suspenders over collarless shirts shifting loads heavier than they were. A stink of sweat and tobacco and now and then cheap whiskey from a staggering drunkard came through a slight cold drizzle and the more wholesome smells of cut timber, flour and barreled produce; it was evidently well into the Black Months here. She edged back and back to avoid the traffic and then dodged a wagon piled with bundles of bar iron stock beneath a tarpaulin and drawn by eight straining platter-hooved horses.

Suddenly a voice from one of the narrow alleys between tall warehouses painted with the names of their owners or gaudy advertisements for goods and patent medicines:

"Aidez-moi, pour l'amour de le bon dieu!"

Then a woman's scream. Mathilda turned and plunged in without an instant's hesitation, her left hand pulling up her skirts and her right drawing her dagger. The alley was dark, but she could see three men surrounding a slighter figure, and cloth ripped.

"Unhand her!" she snapped; it was the Crown Princess' voice that discounted the very possibility of disobedience. "Unhand that maiden, you stinking curs!"

Bristly faces turned on her, topped by shapeless caps or in one case an odd domed hat with a narrow brim over rat-tails of greasy red hair. They hesitated for a long instant. Then:

"Get out of it, ye hoor—watch, she's got a knife, Jim!"

She cut; you didn't stab, not fighting with a knife against someone with shoulders the breadth of the one reaching for her. He shrieked himself as the steel laid open his forearm and turned and ran, clutching it with one hand, bright blood red in the gray light and heavy boots squelching in the mud. The other two spread out, and one flicked his hand. There was something in it, a straight-razor held with the blade in his palm. He started to move, swift as a snake, then halted as he took in the way Mathilda held her dagger and stood poised. His eyes went wide in surprise, then narrowed as rat-thin lips lifted to show yellow teeth.

"Is that the way of it, then, fancy miss? I'll have that sticker for payment, and more besides."

One hand shot out to restrain his larger companion, and when he came forward again it was in a shuffling flat-footed crouch, eyes on her face rather than the blade.

The woman they'd been holding was beside Mathilda, panting and gabbling in French—a slurred, quacking nasal dialect nothing like the courtly version Mathilda had a little of—and holding the blouse of a cotton dress closed where it had been torn from her neck. The men edged forward—

And a hand grabbed one by the shoulder, the slim, quick one with the razor. It whipped him around right into the path of a fist like an oak maul, and there was a sickening *crack* sound; he dropped like an empty grain-sack tossed aside at a mill. The bigger man wheeled and grappled with the newcomer and then they were staggering back and forth. There was no science and little art in the way they fought, but plenty of strength and a vicious determination to do harm. Mathilda exchanged a glance with the woman . . .

Girl, she thought. *In her teens.*

Short and dark, pretty and olive-skinned and with snapping black eyes, part tribeswoman despite the cotton dress and ruched sunbonnet that contained much of her long black hair. Her full lips firmed and she nodded at Mathilda, then bent to take up a length of sawn timber buried in the mud of the alley and lifted it overhead like the handle of a threshing-flail. They poised together, Mathilda's knife ready as well, waiting for the right back to come towards them.

It wasn't necessary; the other attacker was down on his hands and knees an instant later, and the newcomer gave him a boot to the ribs that made bone crack audibly. He rolled away, then dragged himself upright and fled clutching his ribs.

The victor was panting and grinning; he picked up a knit cap and bowed, moving aside to make it clear he wasn't blocking the exit of the alleyway and glancing back to see if anyone had paid attention. Yellow lights were coming on, gaslights in cast-iron standards, gleaming on the puddles.

"Josiah Whittle, at yur service, ladies," he said. "And that was more lively and better fun than anything since the *Dreadnought* sailed from Portsmouth town."

The accent reminded her of Sam Aylward, a little, or John Hordle, though a bit crisper. He was a young man in bell-bottomed canvas trousers and a shapeless sweater beneath a blue cloth jacket with brass buttons, with a kerchief around his neck held by a ring of carved bone. Stocky-strong in build and about Mathilda's height— she'd noticed walking down to the river that she was a couple of inches taller relative to the average than she had been where she was raised. A shock of corn-colored hair was plastered to his forehead with sweat and rain, and his face was broad and freckled and gap-toothed.

She sheathed her dagger and extended a hand. "Mrs. Mathilda Mackenzie, sir," she said.

His grip was careful and extremely strong, and even more callused than her own, the hand of a man who'd spent years heaving on tarred hemp rope.

"E . . . Elaine Bélanger," the dark young woman said. "Thenk you very much, sair."

"You know these longshore rats, ma'am?" the sailor said, looking at her in a puzzled way—evidently the dress didn't match the hand.

"No," Mathilda said. "I'm not familiar with this part of the city; I was here to meet my husband, and heard this young lady cry out."

"Brave of you to come running in!" the man said admiringly, and then noticed the improvised cudgel in the younger woman's hands. "And of you, miss! I thank'ee, though it warn't needed."

"I . . ." Elaine dropped the wooden batten and gave him a look of admiration. "I am here wit' my father from the farm . . . I wander off, not used to cities, me . . . those men . . ."

"Perhaps you could escort the young lady to her parents," Mathilda said. "My husband will be anxious . . ."

This time Rudi heard the men coming down towards the lake. It was later in the season, and the ground had the cold, damp smell of hard rain; the snowline came low on Hood to the south, seen across the rising green carpet of the forest.

There were four of them and twice that many horses. All the animals had game slung across their backs; roughly gralloched black-tail deer and one big brown-black hide that must contain the quarters of a butchered bear. There was only a slight smell of blood and few flies at this season. The horses looked worn-down and so did the men; they also looked tough as rawhide, dressed in a mixture of coarse cloth and leather, both much patched. They all had rifles in the crooks of their left arms, the type with hammers but no flints. They stopped when they saw Rudi. Though they didn't level the weapons, their eyes did flicker about, and one bean-pole with a mop of shaggy fair hair under a tattered felt hat faced about to scan the trail behind them for a moment.

"How do, stranger," one said after a moment; his voice had a harsh, twanging rasp. "You from these here parts?"

"That I am," Rudi said with a smile. "Rudi Macken-zie is my name."

The lead man's face split in a smile; he was about Rudi's own age and only an inch or so shorter, though lean; his hair was a familiar shade of copper-red, and his eyes were the green of willow leaves.

"Why, dang if I ain't a Mackenzie myself!" he said. "Jeb Mackenzie. Pleased t' meet you. You'd be Scottish? My folks wuz, back a ways."

I know, Rudi thought. *Mother told me about you, I think . . .*

"Scots, Irish, this and that," he replied aloud, giving the man's hand a firm shake and then exchanging hand-shakes and names with the others. "You're new to the Oregon country, then?"

That's what they'd call it.

"Just in over the Trail. Doin' us some huntin' whiles our party gets the wagons ready to cross the pass and the workin' stock rests," the man said. "Come out to

claim us some growin' land. Just wish I'd done it earlier!"

"Hain't sittin' on th' stoop sucking on a jug more
your way, Jeb?" one of his friends said; the sharp twanging accent made him almost as hard to understand as
the Quebecois trapper had been. "Your pa was late to
Tennessee too."

"Hell-*fire*, if stoop-sittin' and jug-suckin' were all I
could do, I'd'a gone to Texas instead, Billy," Jeb said.
He turned back to Rudi: "We'd admire to have you
come t' camp and share our meat, Mr. Mackenzie, and
tell us 'bout the Territory."

"Alas, I've places I must be," Rudi said; the regret
was sincere, for a fascination was growing on him.
"You're heading for Lolo Pass, then?"

Jeb nodded. "We had a guide, 'n he said it was th'
best if you wuz drivin' stock. But he up 'n died back
around Grande Ronde."

"Got hisself likkered up 'n drowned in six inches of
water," another said mordantly. "It wuz alkali water,
too."

Rudi looked up at the sky. "I'd not waste time, then.
Not a day, not an hour; break camp at dawn tomorrow,
ready or no. Lolo is high enough that the snow can
come any time now. And you've never seen snow like
ours, friend."

The men chuckled. "We'ze from East Tennessee, Mr.
Mackenzie, not Louisiana!" one said. "Mountain men.
Winter we knows about."

Rudi shook his head and met their eyes grimly. "Even
so. When the wind from the sea hits *these* mountains, it
can bury a horse or a man in an hour. Wagons in a single

day or night, or houses for that matter. Lolo can get drifts thirty feet deep by January. Believe me, for I'm not drawing the long bow. I've seen it myself, yes, and near died of it, and that with only a small party of men who knew the woods and had good gear. Much less mothers and infants and livestock."

That sobered them. "Is the Willamette country's good as they say?" Jeb asked.

"Better," Rudi said, with a smile of his own. It grew fond as he remembered. "Gold to the harvest in summertime, and the pastures green near all the year and the orchards like froth of pink and white in the spring. Land soft beneath the plow, brown as chocolate, rich as cream and sweet as the first kiss of a maiden's love."

"Dang," Jeb said, reverently this time.

One of his friends even removed his hat. Rudi could see the hunger in all their eyes, that special desire of men of the land.

"In fact, if it's advice you want—the which is worth its weight in gold, mind you—"

Jeb Mackenzie blinked and then laughed. A moment later the others did as well.

"—I'd say you should go south down the Willamette. Around Sutterdown, say; that's a town there on the Sutter River, with a gristmill and a sawmill and good hunting in the hills just west, if that pleases you."

"It surely does, seein' as I come from Sullivan County, with the purtiest hills an' best hunting in the east. Land to break a farmer's heart, though. Well, the wife is expectin' something to cook up. Good luck to you, friend, and maybe we'll meet again."

*   *   *

Early spring, this time, Rudi thought. *And this is my time, or close to it. I recognize the lightning scar on that tree, and the old path's there under the new growth.*

His breath smoked, but the sky was clear, save for a band where the setting sun made crimson streaks. He turned into the woods northward, letting his feet lead him uphill towards the sound of voices and the hollow clop of hooves. After a few minutes he came to a little clearing, about where he'd expected the sleigh-born party from Timberline to halt, and stopped to watch. None of those who crowded it seemed to notice him this time, ignoring him as if he were a ghost indeed, though he was in plain sight and they armed and wary. He shivered a little and drew the plaid closer; he felt he could walk among them unseen at arm's length . . . but also as if this was as far from the Lake as it was wise to go.

There were more than a few of them, with pavilions and a banner and grooms leading away horses and men working to start fires. The flag on the big central tent's peak was the Crowned Mountain and Sword of Montival, and from their dress the folk came from half of the High Kingdom or more. His eyes went wider as he sought faces in the crowd.

Sam Aylward? But—

At first he thought it was the old bowman, but he looked as Rudi remembered him from his own childhood, middle-aged and strong as a weather-scarred boulder.

No, he thought with wonder. *It's Edain, the hair's lighter than old Sam's and he's an inch or so taller. Different scars, too. But not the Edain I saw a few hours past. My friend as he might be in a generation's time.*

Others were wholly strange. Who could the striking young woman in exotic lamellar armor be, the one with the Asian features and the twin curved swords, gripping a naginata? The sound of their voices was a murmur through a hundred yards, under the sough of the evening breeze through the boughs of the tall conifers. Two broke away after embraces and salutes, walking towards him.

A man and a woman, with the look of close kin, and both young, the male around twenty and the other a few years older. Both tall, walking with a quick, springy stride he recognized, warriors and hunters both. The man had dark-brown hair to his shoulders beneath a Montero cap that sported a peacock's tail-feather and green hunter's garb, with a short, heavy falchion at his belt and a bow and quiver over his back. His eyes were the changeable color that can be light honey-brown or green depending on the light, and very keen; his heels had the small golden spurs that marked a knight.

The woman was in a Mackenzie kilt and plaid and boots and jacket, long hair the color of ripe wheat in bright sunlight flowing down over her shoulders. Closer, and he could see her eyes were the blue of the lake behind him, and her features sharp-cut and regular, somewhere between handsome and beautiful, but worn with some great strain and marked by recent grief despite youth and strength. After a moment they slowed and the pair stopped, the man blinking a little and looking aside.

"This is as far as I think I should go, Orrey," he said, turning his back on the lake.

"You may have to go further someday, Johnnie," she replied soberly.

"God forbid!" he said, and crossed himself. "That's for *your* kids."

"Which I haven't had yet. Until then you're the heir."

"God and all the *saints* forbid," he said sincerely. "I've seen what the job did to Dad and what it's doing to you. I'll be the High Queen's right hand and wailing wall when you need it, and that's all I want, believe me."

They hugged for a long moment—a sibling's gesture, he decided, not a lover's, from their manner and speech.

"Reiko will be nervous for me," the woman said.

"Osian will help. I'll keep them all laughing, don't worry."

She walked past him. At her belt . . .

The Sword of the Lady itself, he thought, numb with awe as he fell into step beside her, unseen . . . though from the way she moved and held her eyes she missed very little.

Just where the woods gave on the lake she hesitated, muttered: "Well, as Dad always said, the job doesn't get easier if you wait," and stepped out into the dying sunlight.

Rudi did as well, and faced her. "Órlaith?" he said softly.

Her eyes went wide and her face milk-pale. She staggered, and for an instant he thought she would buckle; he caught her by the forearms and felt her hands clench on his with hard force. Then she was intent, her eyes probing him.

"Dad?" she said. "Is that . . . you?" Then: "No. You're too young!"

"It's Rudi Mackenzie, I am, darling girl," he said. "Just . . . let's say I'm here on the same mission as I suspect brings you. The Kingmaking."

"But I saw you—" she began, then rammed to a halt.

Rudi grinned, wonder and joy warring in him. "Die?" he laughed. "My delight, I never thought myself immortal. Except in the sense that we all are, and I've had abundant proof of *that*."

"How?" she breathed. "How is this *happening*?"

"I haven't the faintest idea; and I have it on the best of authority that Those responsible don't explain it to us because they *can't*. How can a man explain all his mind to a little child, or a God to a man? But I suspect that here, from the time the Sword plunged into the earth with Matti your mother and myself your father holding it, all times are one. And the dead and the living and those yet unborn are none so different."

She cast herself against him and they embraced; her arms were like slender steel, and the sun-colored hair smelled of the woods and some flowery herb.

"I've missed you so much, Dad. And Mother has been so—"

He made a shushing sound and laid a finger over her lips. "Arra, there are things *I* should not know. Let me find my own joys and griefs, child! It's a comfort to hear you, though. I've a fair confidence I will be a good King, but it seems I'm none so bad a father, too."

She nodded vigorously and stood back, wiping at tears with the back of her hand.

"Come, walk with me," he said.

They linked hands; hers were callused like his, the distinctive patterns left by blade-hilt and shield-grips. After a moment they came to the rock by the water; the Sword stood in it, as if it had been planted there since the land first rose from the sea.

The blue eyes looked at it and then up at him as her own blade-hand touched the moonstone pommel at her side.

"I'm not going to say *how* again," she said, a hint of the wasp in her voice. "You're as bad as Grandmother Juniper about answering questions with questions!"

"Sure, and I came by it honestly," Rudi said. Seriously: "I think that the Sword is now here forever. More, I think that it always *was* here . . . now, if that makes any sense at all; we drove it not just through rock, but through Time itself. And that this has become a place of awe and sacredness, the pivot about which Montival turns."

She nodded vigorously. "Nobody comes here except the High King or Queen and their handfasted," she said. "But you never told me much about . . . this."

"Because there are things that mean nothing until you live them," Rudi said. He grinned. "Let me guess. You're facing a great challenge, the realm is in peril, and—"

She laughed, but there were tears in it. "Lord and *Lady*, Dad, but I've missed you! Johnnie and Vuissance and Faolan have too, but . . . I . . ."

And I have your babyhood and girlhood and young womanhood to look forward to, darling girl, he thought. *While you have the grief of loss.*

Rudi faced her and laid his hands on her shoulders. "Now, this is what *I've* seen and done here—"

She frowned as he told her. "That's . . . strange. Those were ancestors, weren't they? *Our* ancestors."

"Yes. Some of our ancestors, here in this land of ours. And I was led to see and do and know what a King must. What *you* will see . . . will be particularly tailored to yourself, I would say."

"Will I see Grandmother . . . I mean Grandmother Sandra?"

"And how would I know?" Rudi said. "That's *your* story, though I suspect you will. And perhaps your own children, or your heir at least. Come. Draw the Sword."

She did, and gasped a little as he reached and pulled the other from the rock; it came free as easily as if that were the sheath. Light seemed to well about them as he reversed the blade and offered it to her. She took it reverently and he the hilt of hers.

"Quickly!" he said, and she sheathed the Sword he'd handed her.

They knelt on either side of the rock, and each touched a finger to the point, the red drops mingling.

"By the bond of blood," he said, and laid the point against the rock.

"By the bond of blood," she answered, and wrapped her hands around his.

Together, they thrust the blade forged beyond the world into the Heart of Montival.

"Rudi!" Mathilda gasped. "I've seen . . . I've seen . . ."

They fell together, shivering. She went on: "Oh God, I've seen such wonders!"

"Myself also, *anamchara* mine," he said, stroking her hair.

"And I talked with Dad," she went on, longing and sadness in her voice. "He's . . . he's in Purgatory, I think. And he said he was sorry . . ."

She shook her head slightly and fell silent. He nodded.

"Yes, that's between the three of you," he said. "And now—"

They stood, and he drew the Sword from its stone sheath. Mathilda blinked, looking at the place it had stood.

"It's still there, isn't it?" she asked. "Even if we can't see it."

"It's perceptive you are, darling. It always was and always will be there now."

She looked around at the snowy trees and the dark-purple surface of the lake. "And I can *feel* it. Feel . . . everything, a little. Feel how I'm *part* of everything."

"Myself also. It wasn't a form of words. We *are* the land. Though I suspect it'll become a bit less obtrusive as time goes on and we grow accustomed."

"It feels strange," she said. And after a moment: "But . . . you know, it feels pretty *good*, actually. Like being at home, with friends."

Rudi nodded. They packed up the gear again; a sudden thought made him glance at a shadow, the usual way of judging time even if you could afford the luxury of a watch. His lips pursed a little in surprise.

"Hardly any time at all!" he said. "And it felt like an hour or more."

"Rudi . . ." Mathilda said.

Wordlessly she pointed to their own footprints in the soft damp earth, where they'd walked to the edge of the water just after they arrived. The outlines were blurred, indistinct, and the water had seeped in to make each a miniature puddle.

"*Carson a chiall!*" he said mildly. "What on earth . . . well, we've skipped about . . . a day, would you say?"

"Just about."

He felt tired, too, as if he'd been up a day; tired and hungry, but not *bad*. More the way you felt after you'd spent a day cutting timber or pitching sheaves onto a wagon. Mathilda suddenly put her hand to her stomach.

"I'm pregnant!" she said, wonderingly. Then: "I wasn't sure . . . I've been working hard, sometimes that delays things . . . but now I know. Our daughter, our first child."

"Sure, and it's a wonderment," Rudi said, warmth in his voice. "And I'm afraid this just past will be your last campaign for a while, *a ghaoil!*"

She nodded. "That's OK. It's not as if I won't have enough to do, behind the lines, and essential work. It's just . . . seeing what will come of things."

They linked hands and walked up the trail. The Lake vanished behind them in a score of yards, and soon the musty-chill and resin smell of the woods was leavened by woodsmoke and cooking odors. It felt as if they were walking . . .

Back into the world, Rudi thought, and his stomach growled.

"And how the most exalted things give way to the fact that we must eat daily or regret it!" he said quietly.

Mathilda chuckled. "Just as it should be, dear," she said. "When God's own Son established the most holy rite of the Faith, He did it with bread and wine at a supper."

The camp of the emissaries wasn't anything fancy, but it did have some tents of considerable size. Juniper Mackenzie was the first to see the pair, and hurried towards them. Her pace slowed, and it was stately when she reached them rather than the dash and leap to an embrace he'd half-expected.

"Oh, my son," she said quietly; there was a glitter as of tears in her voice, and her eyes shone. "Oh, my darling foster girl. What have the Powers done with you?"

Then, as the others came up, she gathered the skirts of her arsaid a little and sank to her knees.

"Hail, Artos, *Ard Rí!* Hail, Artos, High King in Montival!" she cried, the steady tones of her trained soprano ringing through the camp like a bell. "Hail, Mathilda, *Bana-Ard-rí*, High Queen in Montival! All hail!"

Rudi stood, waiting, meeting the eyes of the others. They knelt in a ripple and cried the pair hail. He suspected—

No, he thought. *I know that there are few in Montival who didn't feel something, however faint, when Mathilda and I thrust the Sword into the stone. Those with the Inner Sight would have felt a great deal; and these were very close indeed to the Heart.*

When a ringing silence fell, he spoke aloud:

"I am High King."

"I am High Queen," Mathilda said, matching him.

"The land has accepted us, the ancestors and the Powers," he said. "Our blood has been bound to the land and the folk, and so it shall remain so long as our line does—unless the sea rise and drown us, or the sky fall and crush us, or the world end."

"This has been accomplished according to the will of God the Father, Son and Holy Ghost, and by the grace of the Holy Virgin Mary, Mother of God and my patron," Mathilda added.

"Is there any here who denies our right?" Rudi asked, his voice firm but not menacing. "If so, let him speak now or hold his peace hereafter."

Silence again; Professor Turner met his eyes and nodded once, slowly, before glancing down again. Yes, everyone had felt something. Rudi smiled and gestured with his palms up.

"Then rise, my friends, and let us speak together." He laughed. "And by all the Powers, let's eat as well!"

They rose and pressed closer; he hugged his mother to him and whispered in her ear:

"It was a big bit of a shout, eh?"

"Like the ringing of a bell the size of the Moon," she murmured back.

"And you're to be a grandmother again."

She pushed back a little and tweaked his earlobe. "And you think I didn't *know*?"

Sandra Arminger was looking a little staggered as Mathilda spoke to *her*, holding both hands in hers and whispering quickly and softly. Edain pushed forward and thrust something into Rudi's hand. It was a bun, split length-wise and full of a grilled sausage.

"That'll hold you, Chief," he said, giving another to Mathilda.

"Ah, and with men like you at my back, what can't we do?" Rudi laughed, and took a bite.

He inhaled the cold upland air, full of the scent of the firs, and chewed and swallowed with relish.

"Which is good," Mathilda said. "Because there's a *lot* to get done."

"A lot for everyone to do," Rudi said. "Every soul in Montival, to make it the kingdom of all our dreams."

CHAPTER SEVENTEEN

NEAR BEND
CAPITAL, CENTRAL OREGON RANCHERS ASSOCIATION
TERRITORY
(FORMERLY CENTRAL OREGON)
HIGH KINGDOM OF MONTIVAL
(FORMERLY WESTERN NORTH AMERICA)
NOVEMBER 30TH, CHANGE YEAR 25/2023 AD

The Montivalan army—or to be more precise, a detachment of several thousand including Bearkiller lancers and pikemen and crossbowmen, field artillery, CORA refugee horse-archers, and Mackenzie longbowmen—came marching southward to Bend, under the command of Eric Larsson.

It was a cold winter day in the high desert, with little flecks of hard, grainy snow falling out of a sky milky gray from horizon to horizon and darkening as the short day drew to an end. Clouds hid the peaks of the Cascades westward; in that direction there was only a hint of forest and rising rock-ridges, and the dull glow of the setting sun. The passes there were closed to anyone who wasn't on skis and traveling light and fast at this time of year, but the Columbia Gorge was always open, and they had come south from Hood River. That had taken them through County Odell, and the lands of the Three

Tribes of the Warm Springs Confederation, with supply dumps and warm welcomes.

That was long behind them now, into land where the enemy's hand had lain heavy for most of the war. The sights around them left spirits bleak as the weather. Hooves and hobnailed boots rang on the patched pavement, pikes swayed rhythmically, but there was no singing, and the commands of voice and trumpet and drum echoed with a flat dullness.

"Hurrah, we win a great big fucking victory, and this is the prize we get," someone said.

Mike Havel the younger hid his shock as best he could, but he understood the grumbler perfectly.

"Hard winter hereabouts," he said quietly instead.

His cousin Will Larsson snorted. "Bloody devastation hereabouts," he replied. "If it weren't for the shape of the river I wouldn't recognize it at all. It looks like even the buzzards have given up and moved on."

"Larsson and Havel, attend!" the commander called.

They moved their horses up with a shift of balance, reins in left hand and right hand on hip as the scabbards of their backswords clattered against the stirrup-irons. Mike's uncle Eric pointed to a breast-shaped hill that dominated the eastern approaches to the city, its base showing the stumps of ponderosa pine and aspen that must have previously relieved its bleakness.

"See that hill outside the city wall? What are the salient features, Havel?"

"Yessir," Mike replied. "Pilot Butte. Elevation around forty-one hundred absolute, just under five hundred above the general level."

"Why wasn't it fortified? Looks like it could dominate the town."

"No water, sir."

"Good," Eric said. "Larsson?"

His son nodded. "No water because the soil's very porous, sir. Lots of caves around here, volcanic tubes, and the water table is low because it drains so freely. Wells tend to collapse, too, you have to line them. You'd need very deep tube wells to supply a fort on top of the hill and it would require heavy pumping all the time and concrete reservoirs. Expensive, sir."

Since he *was* an A-Lister now, Mike dared to put in: "And the light soil would make the footings for a curtain wall and towers difficult too, sir. Relatively easy for mining and sapping operations in a siege, too."

"Good. Carry on."

Mike mimed wiping his brow as they fell back to near the tail end of the command party; their official tasking was as couriers, and unofficially they were supposed to be learning by example. Will grinned back at him.

They were both very young for the Outfit's A-List, jumped through the usual long candidacy for good service in the field; not far from here, and over a year ago, during the initial invasion. In the regular way of things, in the peacetime he was starting to think of as a children's story like trolls or rockets, they'd just be thinking of putting down their names for the testing and probably be a year or two of failure away from ultimate success.

Those two years seemed like forever to the cousins; they were both within a few months of eighteen, both around six feet, and both long-limbed with the hard whipcord looks of those trained to ten-tenths of capacity but not beyond. Otherwise they were not much alike for looks. Will was Afro-Anglo-Hispano-Indio on his mother's side, which mixed with Eric Larsson's Nordic heritage had given him exotic good looks, bluntly regular full-lipped features, skin the smooth, pale light-brown of a perfect soda-biscuit, eyes midnight blue and hair curling from under the edge of his helmet in locks of darkest yellow. Mike Havel's pale, chiseled handsomeness might have steered a dragon-ship across the Kattegat a millenia ago, with only a trace of his Anishinabe great-grandmother in the set of cheekbone and eye.

Their kinship showed in the underlying structure of bone and the gangling height they shared. More still in the way they stood and moved and rode.

"Jesus," Will said quietly as they looked around, and crossed himself.

"Loki on a stick," Mike concurred, and made the sign of the Hammer, as was customary in his branch of the family.

The strip along the Deschutes River where it ringed the city of Bend on three sides, and upstream and down, had been under the furrow since before the Change, irrigated land in the middle of the dry plains of ancient lava and volcanic ash and sagebrush desert. If anything it had become more densely settled in the past generation, producing for its tillers and the shrunken city rather than markets far away, a little green world of small, densely-cultivated farms in a land mostly sparse grazing and great estates where the Rancher was lord.

Small poplar-bordered fields of fruit-trees and vegetables and grain and fodder marked it, and the rammed-earth, shake-roofed cottages of the cultivators, or the odd clutch of church and smithy and tavern at a crossroads. Even in the cold season it had always seemed reasonably prosperous to Mike, even by the standards of the Willamette, and you were never far from the smell of woodsmoke or the sound of voices and the sight of cattle or sheep.

The smell of smoke was still there, the harsh and bitter stink of things not meant to burn. Nothing moved except the odd crow or raven. The only animals larger than a jackrabbit he'd seen in hours were dead, picked-over bones. And once a litter of skulls by the side of the road, some of them with bits of hair still fluttering ragged in the cold wind.

The contrast was more stark because he'd seen the district many a time, on visits stretching back to his childhood; the nascent Bearkillers had come this way a decade before he was born on their trek from Idaho. The memories were vivid. In spring the land smelled sweet, with blossom shed in drifts across the narrow rutted roads and often with roses trained up the walls of the houses. Now only the trampled remnants of the irrigation ditches and the stumps of trees showed where the land had lain under the hand of man; fruit tree and windbreak alike had been burned where they fell. The rafters of the houses had burned hotter, and even the tough *pisé de terre* walls had mostly collapsed inward. Pre-Change frame buildings were just scorch-marks and charcoal collapsed into the foundations.

"Worse than we expected," he heard Lord Chancellor Ignatius say ahead of him. "So much for the possibility of basing forces here against Boise. Or even Pendleton."

"A lot of this is recent," another man said bitterly; it

was Rancher Bob Brown, one of the CORA magnates. "They knew they couldn't hold it, not after the Horse Heaven Hills, and they spent the time they had left to wreck it. Goddamn it, it'll take generations to rebuild this! A lot of it was from before the Change and we'll have to redo it with hand shovels and horses!"

Ignatius made a soothing gesture. "The biggest assets were the dams in the Cascades and the reservoirs. Those are intact. This land will blossom again, Rancher. No, I misspoke. The biggest assets were the people and their skills, and of *those* we saved most."

"They need something to work with, or who in their right mind will come *back*? It's no better further out," Brown said. "My son took a patrol into Seffridge Ranch's home-place last week to see about resettling my family and our people. Nothing. Everything my father spent twenty years building up burned and wrecked, houses and workshops and barns, fences gone, our little dam broken down and the irrigation channels filled, the fruit trees killed . . . They *wrecked the wells* out in the grazing lands. And the wind-pumps. The water's mostly *deep* around there."

The leathery man in his thirties nearly spat that; to dwellers in these dry lands that particular form of destruction was nearly blasphemy. Without water, cattle and sheep couldn't use the natural growth; water and winter fodder were the secrets to successful ranching.

"We'll be the next thing to Rovers," he finished bitterly.

That was the settled Ranchers' term for those who wandered seasonally with their flocks and herds farther east, living in tents and dwelling in the driest sections.

374 S. M. STIRLING

It wasn't intended as a compliment; *filthy savages* was a good translation from the local dialect.

"The grass will grow next year, and that's about it," Brown finished. "And the only good thing is that we've lost so much stock we won't be overgrazing, even after we've lost all the hay and fodder land. We've got the breeding stock, but we won't *dare* restock to anything like the levels we had before the war."

"Everyone will help," Ignatius said. "That is the point of the kingdom."

"We will," Eric said promptly. "We're behind Rudi . . . High King Artos . . . on that. And we'll lean on the Corvallans, and the Clan will kick in."

"God knows they've helped us already," Brown said. "I don't like depending on charity."

"It isn't charity, it's *caritas*," Ignatius said forcefully. "Rancher Brown, the blow of the enemy fell earliest and hardest here. You have a *right* to expect the kingdom's help, just as you shielded the lands to the west. We all contribute as we can and must."

"But that's long-term stuff," Eric said a little impatiently.

Ignatius nodded. "A major capital investment project. Nor is this the only area to have suffered so."

"Yeah, and until then our logistics stink like an outhouse in August," Eric said. "A *crow* flying over this territory would have to carry its own food wrapped up in a sack. We can't move anything more than a few strong patrols for more than a day's journey from the Columbia, with the way they wrecked the railroads."

"Which means our movements become predictable, my son," Ignatius said. "That is . . . unfortunate."

"Arrow right in the ring and you collect the prize goose, Father," Eric said. "We'll have to ram straight down their throats. After breaking their teeth and paying the butcher's bill for that. The roads are in better condition but—"

"— draught animals would eat everything they could haul," Ignatius said. "And repairing the rails? Not practical for some time."

Mike Havel found himself nodding. Bearkiller education emphasized engineering at the higher levels—it was useful in both war and peace, and his mother's father had been an engineer in any case, and had helped set the system up.

"St. Michael's sappers might know a quick way to do it, but mine don't," Eric agreed. "It'll have to be done a mile at a time, starting with the railheads in the inhabited zones. Let's see what's left of the city. Enough to shelter a garrison, hopefully. Armies will have to stick to the Columbia, but unless we plug the gap the enemy could send raiding parties behind our lines. Their horse-archers are too damned mobile for comfort and they can live off even this wilderness for a while."

Bend's city wall had been fairly thick but low, the usual thing towns still inhabited after the collapse had run up out of concrete and rubble and salvaged I-beams in the years after the Change. The mass of it had been left in place, removing that would have taken years and thousands of laborers, but more effort had gone into slighting the gates and they were down to chest-level on a horse.

The main force spread out on the empty ground outside, pitching tents and starting campfires; Bearkillers had a set plan for overnight encampments, with ditch and dirt wall and temporary palisade and they enforced it on anyone they were operating with. Eric Larsson dumped his Spartan personal gear where the command pavilion would go up, and heard out the scout commander's reports.

"Short form, fuck all, sir. They're gone, that's the best that can be said," the man said at the end, tapping the city map, one compiled three years ago with hand-drawn notes on developments since. "This thing's a work of . . . what did my old man call it . . . *historical fiction* now. Most of the outer wall's still standing, but I think that's only because the sons of bitches couldn't tear it down. They certainly hit everything else—even dug up and trashed a lot of the water system. And . . ."

The man swallowed; he was a scar-faced cavalryman in his thirties, looking as tough as the leather of his boots. Mike felt a creeping unease at the expression on his face.

"Spit it out," Eric said.

"They chopped up bodies and threw them into the waterworks wherever they could, sir. Animals, people . . . kids, too. They seemed to have a couple of hundred kids—"

"The Church Universal and Triumphant levies children for their training and breeding camps from all their subject peoples," Ignatius said, stone-faced. "If they had already gathered them before the news of the battle arrived and thought they couldn't remove them east in the winter season . . ."

"Well . . . Sir, Lord Chancellor, it's pretty bad in there," the scout finished. "Ah . . . permission to go get stinking drunk, sir."

"I need to take a look myself," Eric said, studying the man narrowly. "HQ staff, get us set up here for now, standard procedure. Lord Chancellor, Rancher Brown, you come with me. Eyes-on is always best if you've got the chance. Oh, and Murchison, if you feel the need that badly, permission granted."

He took a bottle from his own modest wicker-and-leather chest of baggage and tossed it to the scout before they mounted again.

"That's Larsdalen brandy. The hangover won't hurt quite as much when you arrive and you feel better on the way."

Mike Havel removed his helmet and wrinkled his nose slightly as they came through the city gate and into the pool of still air held by the walls. He was accustomed to the smell of death, or he'd thought so. There was more of it in the ruins of Bend than he'd ever scented before, and it had everything from the lingering stink of ancient corruption to bodies burned in the fires that had swept the town when the Cutter garrison withdrew a day and night ago.

Their horses skirted another pile of smoldering rubble that had slumped into the street when a building collapsed, bricks and bits of charred two-by-four and miscellaneous fragments. The setting sun behind the clouds threw gray-on-gray shadows around them, and the wind was growing colder as it flicked wet ash and snow from the patches of colder ground around them.

Ahead of him his uncle turned to Rancher Brown.

"Your own patrols find any survivors yet?" Eric asked. "I know we got most of the people out before the city fell, but there must have been *someone* here or in the area besides enemy troops and camp-followers. Nobody ever makes a completely clean sweep."

"A few thousand prisoners were kept for labor," Chancellor Ignatius said from Eric's other side. "Scouts didn't report a column on foot when they withdrew. I fear . . ."

Messengers had been coming and going since the Montivalans forced the unguarded gates. Most of them were local men, refugees picked because they knew the city. All of them looked even more stunned and lost than Mike felt, and some were weeping openly. Bearkillers and cityfolk and ranchers' men alike walked or rode with weapons poised, but Mike thought that the sense of threat that hung over the ruins was not something cold steel or arrowheads could assuage.

"Survivors? A few. All raving mad, except for some kids who hid out in attics and sewers and such," the rancher replied. Suddenly his face woke from the calm of shock. "What's the *point* of all this?"

Chancellor Ignatius spoke with a calm grimness.

"To deny us a base for operations and to make reconstruction harder in the long term, Rancher Brown," he said. "And from pure malignance, the desire to inflict pain for its own sake."

Brown shook his head. "Our intelligence from before . . . before this said the Cutter garrison had their HQ up ahead, in . . ."

"A church dedicated to St. Francis," Ignatius said, nodding at the brick structure ahead of them.

It was on a slight rise, with stone steps leading up to the front doors and a big rose window over them.

"They didn't burn that, looks like," Brown observed. "Not like them to be respectful."

"They were not," Ignatius snapped, his eyes questing. "They took it for their own uses."

"I'll take a look, then," Eric said, swinging down from the saddle.

Ignatius sighed and said: "Is that wise, Lord Eric?"

Eric shrugged. "It's quick . . . don't worry, I'm not going alone."

His guards formed around him; Ignatius did too, and put his shield on his arm and drew his sword. Even then, Mike smiled a little to himself. If his uncle had a fault as a war-leader, it was the same headlong courage that made him so formidable and feared. He exchanged a grin with Will Larsson. He and Eric's eldest son stayed mounted and ready behind.

Asking permission just gives someone the chance to say no, he reflected. *One of the unofficial lessons.*

The Bearkillers—and one Knight-Brother of the Order of the Shield of St. Benedict—formed up and walked up the stairs into the church. The tall windows would provide enough light, even at this time of day. There was a pause, and then . . .

Eric Larsson, called Steel-Fist, stumbled out. The battle-hardened guard detail followed, backing frantically, their shields raised but the swords slack in their hands. Ignatius followed them; *he* had sheathed his blade and slung his long shield over his back, and he had his rosary and crucifix in his hands instead.

Appalled, several of the Bearkiller A-Listers started towards Eric. He waved them back. They could hear the clank of armor as the big man staggered around a snag of ruin and fell to his knees, retching noisily. Men and women were looking at each other. The war chief of the Bearkillers was a notoriously hard man; not cruel, but sometimes short on mercy, and the product of a generation's fights.

"What was in there?" Will Larsson asked, and Mike nodded.

That is *the question.*

"What was in there that did that to *Uncle Eric?*" he added thoughtfully.

Eric Larsson returned, accepted a canteen from one of his followers, rinsed and spat and then drank.

"No," he barked when heads turned towards the entrance to the church. "Stay out. Christ have mercy . . . right after the Change, Mike and I—"

Even then, Mike Havel had the usual moment's twinge at his father's name. There were drawbacks to being the son of a legend, especially to one who'd died too early for you to remember him.

"—smoked out a nest of Eaters. That was almost as . . . but they were just *crazy*. This—"

The rayed sun had been painted across the doors there, and the cross that had stood above lay smashed some distance from it.

"No indeed, my sons," Ignatius said slowly in agreement, walking over to push the doors closed. "There are things no man should have to see."

"Yes," Eric agreed. Very softly: "They're too hard to forget. Twenty-five years won't do it. Don't anyone ask me. Ever. And burn this. Get some combat engineers in here and burn it *now*."

He was silent as they rode back to the Bearkiller encampment. Ignatius excused himself with a simple: *I must pray.* Eric brooded until the camp cooks handed around their plates of salt pork stewed with beans and rolled wheat tortillas. Then he pushed his food around the plate for a moment before he looked up at his son and nephew.

"There's one good thing about this," he said quietly; the camp-fire underlit his face, showing how grooves had begun to seam it.

"Yes, sir?" Mike asked.

"It's a good thing to know why you're fighting," Eric said. "And that it isn't just because the other guy's as big a son of a bitch as you are."

COUNTY OF THE EASTERMARK
BARONY OF TUCANNON
(FORMERLY SOUTHEASTERN WASHINGTON STATE)
PORTLAND PROTECTIVE ASSOCIATION
HIGH KINGDOM OF MONTIVAL
(FORMERLY WESTERN NORTH AMERICA)
DECEMBER 12TH, CHANGE YEAR 25/2023 AD

"I am sorry, my lord Tucannon," Rudi Mackenzie said gently.

Castle Tucannon stood on its hilltop, a spur of land reaching out from the foothills of the Blue Mountains. There were scorch-marks on the dark walls, but looking at the slope—and the way the spur had been severed off into an island by a deep cut across the neck that connected it to the higher lands—Rudi wondered that anyone had been foolish enough to try. Only someone truly desperate, or utterly mad or both would have sent men against those frowning battlements. It was a fairly big castle, a doubled mirror-keep, and high enough that the catapults on its crenellated walls would have commanded every inch of the approach. A ponderosa-pine signal spire on the tallest tower had kept it connected to the heliograph net centered on Walla Walla all through the siege.

The manor of Grimmond-on-the-Wold below had suffered much more. Few roofs were left and the barns and winery and gristmill, sawmill and stables at the end of the long village street were wrecked. The Baron's house in particular had been utterly demolished, its thick pise walls pushed in to make an irregular mound that the winter rains were turning into mud; the High King was surprised to see his sister Mary wiping at her one eye as she came out of the empty gates.

"The gardens were so beautiful," she said. "When Ingolf and I were here in the tail-end of summer. Like something out of the Histories, gardens in Lothlorien or Dol Amroth."

The Baron's mother, Lady Roehis de Grimmond— who'd been born Jenny Fassbinder, more than sixty years before—smiled distantly and patted her shoulder. She was in a plain kirtle and wimple of brown and gray, her face gentle and thin.

"I started them, dear," she said. "My lord Amauri and I, two years after the Change. I can do it again. The damage isn't really as bad as it looks; remember, this is winter. Most of the roots and bulbs will have survived. The house was timber and soil and we have lots of both."

"It can wait, Your Majesty," Baron Maugis said, looking at the thick stumps of the oaks and maples that had lined the town square here in front of his dwelling. "We can live in the castle for a few years. My father did before he built the manor. He planted these trees for me; I can plant more, for my son's sake. The war's not over, for that matter, even if we've kicked them out of this district."

He was a young man in his twenties, of medium height and gaunt now, but strong-looking, with a pleasantly ugly face, bowl-cut reddish hair and prominent ears. He and the fighting captains behind him were worn as the patched leather and wool of their gear, but they'd held out in the mountains for months, and their raids had made their occupier's lives less than pleasant and the supply situation a nightmare. More folk crowded behind, retainers and ordinary craftsfolk and peasants down from the mountain refuges where they'd lived in tents and caves and old forest-ranger cabins in the heights that lay blue and jagged eastward. This was a fine spot for a town, though none had lain here before the Change; good water, shelter from the worst winter winds, and plowland and pasture and timber all available close at hand.

Not to mention a very bonny view, of the mountains . . . the dawn sun will be a fine sight there . . . and of the plains away to the east. I think this man's father chose wisely, and his son seems of no less wit and of great heart besides. I'm usually easier with lords in the Protectorate who are Changelings. Though from what Mary said, this one's father came here to get away *from Matti's sire, the which is a strong argument in his favor.*

A wagon train was also curled up the main street; the drovers and the escort and the local folk were unloading crated hardtack, barrels of salt meat and dried fruit and sacks of beans and flour, bales of blankets and tools and sausages of tent-canvas. Some of the locals were wrapping themselves in blankets, or their children; it was a dry cold day, with the wind carrying particles of grit that made you blink if you faced into it.

"What really worries me is that we didn't get the winter crop planted this fall," the Baron said, nodding to the rolling fields to the north and east. "We stripped out most of our gear before we took to the hills, but nothing can roll the seasons back, here or at my vassals' manors."

You could see the layout of the Five Great Fields where the strips of the peasant holdings had lain, and the demesne fields of the manor-holder's home farm; there was a biggish vineyard on a south-facing slope that looked to have survived, and most of the trees in the orchards hadn't been harmed. The sweet clover and alfalfa planted in the Great Fields as rotation and fodder crops were there yet, though heavily grazed by the occupiers; but the potatoes had been dug and stolen, and the fields that should have been green with the young winter wheat were under nothing but a scurf of weeds and incipient bush. That was enough to worry anyone.

Mathilda pulled up and dismounted, passing her reins to a squire with a word of thanks as her guardian men-at-arms and mounted crossbowmen backed out of the crush. She was in civilian riding garb, a divided skirt and jacket of russet brown, with a plumed Montero cap pulled over her brown braids.

"Lord Maugis, you'll have seed corn and working stock enough by spring," she said, as the commons touched a knee to the ground and the nobleman bowed and kissed her extended hand in fealty. "As Lady Protector—"

That's right, Rudi thought with a blink of surprise. *Matti's twenty-six this coming year, and inherits. Not that Sandra will be going to a nunnery or dower-house; we need her too much, and sure, she'd die of boredom without administration and intrigues and secrets.*

"—I'm going to order a capital levy on every intact manor and Chartered town in the Protectorate to help rebuild the County Palatine. The Association takes care of its own."

There was a murmur of delight from the commons crowding behind the knights and their retainers; they had crossbows and shields and spears in their hands, swords at their belts, but their eyes lit at the thought of more plow-oxen and earth curling away from the harrows and seed-drills. A cheer went up from them all, for Mathilda and the prospect of sacks of grain and beans resting secure in their barns come next August.

"And you have the High Kingdom behind you," Rudi said when it died down.

He laid a hand on the Baron's shoulder; some things should be said and done publicly.

"I give you my thanks as well, and all Montival's," he said firmly. "The enemy troops you and your fellow lords of the Palatinate tied down may well have made the difference between victory and defeat at the battle in the Horse Heaven Hills. It was a close-run thing, there at the end, and there were all too many of them as

it was. I say to you and your vassals and all your followers *well-done, and very well-done.* You sacrificed much
for the Kingdom, and the King will not forget it."

Maugis flushed out to his prominent ears and went
to his knees; Rudi took the man's hands between his.
Behind them there was a pleased buzz at the honor
done to all through their lord.

"I am your man, of life and limb and all earthly wor-
ship, my King," he said. "God the Father, Son and Holy
Ghost and the Holy Virgin witness it!"

That was an abbreviated version of the usual ceremony of homage, but nobody could doubt the sincerity.
The Count of the Eastermark was in Rudi's train at the
moment, and he was the Baron's immediate feudal su-
perior, but he smiled and nodded as Rudi replied, also
shortening it:

"I accept your homage, Maugis de Grimmond; your
enemies shall be mine and none shall do you wrong save
at their peril; my sword shall be yours to call upon; I will
hold your honor dear as my own and give you fair justice and good lordship."

Maugis was smiling as he rose and stepped back,
though there was a very odd expression on his mother's
face, happiness mixed with some strange detachment or
incredulity. Rudi looked at her and shrugged mentally;
he would never really or wholly understand the generation that had been adults before the Change, even the
ones he'd grown up with. The lord of Tucannon was
smiling even more broadly as he brought his lady forward by the hand. She was in a riding habit much like
Mathilda's, a slim young woman with tilted eyes of a
very pale blue and raven-black hair falling in a silk tor-

rent down her back from beneath a light headdress, her face lovely but tired with an exhaustion that had little to do with sleep. An infant and a toddler were in the care of a nurse behind her, but she led a six-year-old boy by the hand herself.

"My lady wife, Helissent de Grimmond, your Majesties," Maugis said proudly. "And the war-captain who held Castle Tucannon for me . . . and your Majesties . . . all through the siege, while we harried the enemy."

She sank down gracefully, hands spreading her habit slightly as she knelt and bowed her head; the boy did a creditable imitation of his father's reverence.

"Rise, my lady Helissent," Rudi said, and Mathilda gave the other woman the kiss on both cheeks that was also a mark of favor. "I am in your debt as well, then."

The boy beamed. "I fired a catapult! Lots of times. I turned the wheel and pulled the lanyard when Captain Grifflet said to and everything! Squished 'em like bugs!" he said with an innocently murderous glee. Then hastily: "Your Majesty."

"Did you indeed, young sir?" Rudi said, grinning.

"He did," Helissent said. "As often as we'd let him! My son Aleaume, Your Majesty."

The young heir of Tucannon had his mother's eyes. That prompted something as the High King rested his hand on the moonstone pommel of the Sword . . .

"Lady Helissent, you'd be from Skagit, originally? Your brother Adhémar de Sego holds as a vassal of the Barons of Skagit?"

"Yes, Your Majesty, he holds Sego Manor by knight-service to the Delbys," she said, obviously pleased. "As my father did while he lived."

"Sir Adhémar gained much honor at the Horse Heaven battle with the *menie* of House Delby, Lady Helissent. He was wounded capturing an enemy banner, but he's healing well and expected to be on his feet in a few weeks. And your younger brother Sir Raymbaud—"

"Raymbaud's been knighted?" she said, startled into a broad grin.

"By the High Queen's own hand, for his valor in the charge against the Prophet's guardsmen. They're both at Walla Walla now with the main body. They should be able to visit you soon, perhaps over Christmas."

"My thanks, your Majesties!" she said. "You honor us."

"Not beyond your worth," Mathilda said.

Young Aleaume decided that there had been enough conversation about people he didn't know.

"Is that the Sword of the Lady, Your Majesty?" he asked. "The one from Heaven, like Excalibur in the stories?"

"Indeed it is, young lord," Rudi said, making a slight motion of his hand to halt the shushing his mother hadn't quite started. "Here."

He went down on one knee himself and pulled the sheathed Sword free of the frow on his belt, resting it across his palms at about the boy's height. The young face went serious as the boy tentatively extended a hand and rested it on the glowing stone for a moment. Then he snatched it back, but his face lit up as he met Rudi's gray-green-blue gaze.

"Did a lady give it to you in a lake? Or did you pull it from a stone?" The boy frowned. "Arthur did *both*, didn't he?"

Rudi nodded. "Accounts differ. Now, this *was* given

to me by three holy ladies, and that on a forbidden island in a distant sea guarded by pirates and awful magic.
And it has lain in a sheath of stone *beside* a lake here in
our land of Montival, and worked wonders."

Aleaume nodded in satisfaction. "And you won the
great battle with it!"

"I did indeed," Rudi said gravely. "With this and the
aid of many brave men like your father."

Cocking an eye at Mathilda and then his sister Mary:
"And many a brave woman as well."

"When I'm big I shall fight for you too, Your Majesty!" Aleaume said. "I'll be your man, and slay dozens
and dozens . . . and, and *hundreds* of cruel and wicked
enemies for you!"

"You may indeed fight by my side someday," Rudi
answered him, putting a hand on the boy's head for an
instant before he rose and reseated the Sword. "Or by
the side of my heir, who's expected along in spring, and
we'll be well served if you prove as brave a knight and
as good a lord as your father."

The Baron of Tucannon and his lady offered congratulations. Rudi grinned at Mathilda, the wonder still
on him.

"I thank you, my lord, my lady, though sincere as it
is, you're not half so happy as we! Now—"

There was a clatter of hooves, a challenge and response, and Ingolf swung down from his horse and
came towards them with a look of intense predatory
satisfaction on his battered face, slapping mud off his
breeches with the gloves in his left hand.

"Good news?" Rudi asked, as Mary came over to lay
an arm around the big man's waist.

390 S. M. STIRLING

"Damned good! The Boise commander in Castle Campscapell just turned on the Prophet's men there. Did it real neat and tidy in the middle of the night, too. A few of them are still holding out in the central keep, but they're bottled up tight, and Hauken, that's his name, he's declared for Fred and opened the main gates and our men are inside."

The news ran through the crowd and there was a rolling cheer; Aleaume was jumping up and down, certain that the foe's doom was upon them.

The which is not so far from at least a local truth, Rudi thought, smiling with a slight show of teeth and tapping his right fist into his left palm in three slow strokes. His mind went on, weighing factors:

Campscapell is a great keep and in a notable bottleneck. Now the cork is in our hands and we can keep it closed or go east through there just as we choose. Losing the castle was a bad blow, and regaining it a wind at our back. I must . . . no, let Fred reward this Hauken. He'll know how to do it properly.

Rudi raised a hand for silence after the cheers started to fade.

"Well, my friends, I'd been planning a feast of celebration here—for which we brought slaughter stock, cattle and sheep, doubly sweet for being doubly stolen as the saying goes—"

Another cheer rose on a different note, less carnivore glee and more straightforward hungry happiness; the local folk hadn't actually starved, but they'd gone short and nobody either noble or commons had been eating their fill of roasted fresh meat lately.

"—and some most promising barrels. We'll feast this

night and drink to your homes reclaimed and to this news of a victory won without blood—"

None of ours, at least

"—as an omen of things to come."

Maugis de Grimmond stepped back and drew his sword. "Artos and Montival!" he shouted, holding it high.

"*Artos and Montival!*"

LARSDALEN, BEARKILLER HQ
HALL OF REMEMBRANCE
(FORMERLY WEST-CENTRAL WILLAMETTE, OREGON)
HIGH KINGDOM OF MONTIVAL
(FORMERLY WESTERN NORTH AMERICA)
DECEMBER 19TH, CHANGE YEAR 25/2023 AD

The Bearkillers held feast for their dead in the great hall of Larsdalen.

The long rectangular room fell silent, the buzz of conversation and laughter that had filled it during the feast dying as the ceremonial drinking-horns were set out in their wrought stands, rimmed and tipped with gold or silver and carved with running interlaced animal-patterns. The central hearth flickered and boomed beneath a hood of burnished copper that led the smoke upward; snow fell against the tall windows, whispers of cold white in the darkness, but within all was warmth and light—an image ancient in the poetry of their peoples.

A fair place, this Larsdalen, Bjarni Eriksson thought. *No fairer than my mead-hall, but larger and richer . . . and strange, like its dwellers, full of things alien and familiar and mixtures of the two, like stories seen in dreams.*

Firelight and lantern-light shone on the oak wainscoting between the tall windows, wrought in sinuous forms from tales he remembered and some he'd never known; he recognized Sigurd and Fafnir, Burnt Njal, Orm the Strong, Odhinn's quest for wisdom and his old friend Thor wrestling with the World Snake. It was hung with weapons and shields as well—round concave ones marked with the Bear, backswords and lances and recurve bows, stands of plate armor and captured trophies and banners.

The fire scented the air with the subtly alien smell of burning Douglas fir, not quite like the pinewood blazes he knew, and the fine beeswax of candles from the wrought-iron chandeliers overhead; his folk used tallow mainly. Rather than young maidens, it was military apprentices who brought round the jugs, and they were full of wine from the local vineyards rather than the honey-mead that was the drink of ceremony back home, for those who could afford it.

Now wine, there's a thing of which I approve, he thought, grinning to himself and smacking his lips a little. *The vineyards are full of gnarled and ugly plants, but what they make . . . ah, that's a different matter!*

Back in Norrheim, wine was something they knew only from bottles Vikings salvaged from the dead cities—hardly familiar enough to really tell what was still good from what had spoiled in the long years since the Change. They *called* the tipples made from berries and herbs wines, but here in Montival he'd come to know the difference. The feast had been fine too, smoking platters of beef ribs, roast pork, made dishes more complex than they used in Norrheim and fantastical desserts of pastry and ice cream and fruits like cherries and apricots that were only names in the cold land that he ruled.

One thing that was the same was the roistering, roaring defiance in the face of death and grief. Even if some of these folk followed the White Christ, they knew the Nine Virtues, of which courage was the first.

He stayed quiet as the Bearkillers remembered their fallen, as was respectful, and kept an eye on young Halldor Syfridsson beside him to make sure he did as well.

"Easy, easy," he said to him quietly, while Eric Larsson invoked the White Christ for those of the fallen who had followed Him. "This isn't mead. It's stronger. Drink it more like whiskey, not for thirst like beer."

The young man's grin was a little foolish. A woman at the table across the open space from theirs was giving him cool considering stares; she was a little older, which still made her young enough—Halldor was in his late teens yet, and had come at his father's side on the great journey west. His father, Syfrid Jerrisson, had laid his bones fighting the CUT in Drumheller, and now the youngster was *godhi* of the Hrossings, though they didn't know it yet.

If they hail him when he stands on their Thingstone, Bjarni thought. *But they will; he's his father's son, and shrewd, and already a fell fighter. I'll be glad of it, and of a strong ally as chieftain of another tribe, a man who's seen the wider world and understands my thoughts. Syfrid and I were rivals more than friends; he never forgot seeing me as a child in my father's hall when he was a man grown, and thought he should be king in Norrheim. Halldor will be no man's puppet, but we'll deal more easily, I think. Hmmm. Perhaps when my sister Gudrun is old*

enough to wed . . . better to wait on that, perhaps throw
them in each other's way and see how they suit. Still, a good
thought. I'll talk it over with Hallberga when I get back.

"I drink to our glorious dead," Signe Havel called
from the high table where she and the Bearkiller leaders
and Bjarni sat.

She raised a horn carved and wrought with silver
runes at mouth and tip, her voice as fiercely comely as
her face as she looked down the long chamber, mourning and pride as naked as a she-wolf's.

"May they feast with the High One this night. May
His daughters bear them the mead of heroes, and greet
the new-come *einherjar* thus at the gates of Vallhöl:

Hail to thee Day, hail, ye Day's sons;
Hail Night and daughter of Night,
With blithe eyes look on all of us,
And grant to those sitting here victory!
Hail, Aesir, hail Ásynjur!
Hail Earth, that gives to all!
Goodly spells and speech bespeak we from you,
And healing hands in this life!

"Drink hail!" she finished.

"*Wassail!*" ran down the tables in a roaring shout.

When the toast and ceremony was finished, Bjarni
Eriksson stood and raised his own horn of wine.

"To our alliance," he called. "True folk, shoulder to
shoulder and shield to shield against our foes—from
here to the eastern sea. Drink hail!"

"*Wassail!*"

Eric's beard and mane were bright against his dark
clothing as he went on after Bjarni sat:

"Brothers and sisters of the A-List; Bearkillers of the

Outfit; friends and allies from far away," he said. "The last time we feasted our dead, we celebrated a fighting retreat."

He grinned and held up his steel fist; the burnished metal caught the flame-light and sent it back.

"And I left this hand on that battlefield. Now we celebrate a great victory. To victory—*drink hail!*"

"Wassail!"

This time the cheer made the roof shake. Not long after the first of the feasters left; Bjarni noticed that Eric and Signe, and their young sons, were drinking lightly however many times their horns were raised. A few minutes later Halldor was gone, and the one he'd been trading glances with like whetted swords. It was not long until the leaders were nearly alone at the high seat and could talk privately; this was a feast, but held after far faring and hard fighting and wounds for many. That bred a weariness that didn't go away with a few nights' rest. Shadows gathered as lamps burned down, as if to keep the talk cloaked, and the banners stirred overhead with a whisper of thick cloth.

"So," Bjarni said, putting down his horn in the wrought silver rest; the wine buzzed a little in his ears, but only enough to speed wits. "How long do you think this war will go on?"

Eric and Signe exchanged a look. Signe inclined her head to her brother and he answered:

"There will be little bands of horse-bandits raiding stock and calling on the Prophet and the Ascended Masters for a generation in the far interior," he said, looking down into his wine. "But how long until we take Corwin and burn it to the ground and gut or hang the last of the High Seekers? No more than two years at most."

Signe signed the Hammer for luck, and Bjarni touched the silver one around his neck; Eric nodded to acknowledge that he was tempting fate a little, but went on:

"One year, if Boise goes as well as looks likely; possibly before the snow falls next year, if the League of Des Moines pushes hard."

"Good," Bjarni said. "Then my revenge for the attack on my people will be taken and my oath to Artos Mikesson will be fulfilled, and I have my own kingdom to see to."

"After the Horse Heaven Hills, no one in the Nine Worlds could deny you've done what you swore," Signe said. "The enemy dead were piled before your men's shields; I saw it when we were riding next day all along where the battle line had stood. The ravens and coyotes and lobos feasted well. For its size, your force did as well as anyone on that field."

"Or better!" Bjarni said with a fierce grin. More slowly: "I've done more than fight and feast here. I've seen that you in Montival . . . and the Midwesterners . . . have arts that we in Norrheim lack. Machines, tools, knowledge. I want them for my folk. A king's might is the wealth and strength of his people."

The two Bearkillers looked at each other, then back at him.

"Good fortune to you, Bjarni Ironrede," Signe said. "That shows a proper spirit in a ruler. But hasn't the High King promised you aid?"

"Yes, and he'll fulfill that," Bjarni said. "He and I swore blood-brotherhood in my own hall, and he's a man who keeps his oaths. But I would not have Norrheim dependent on one man's bounty, even a blood-brother who is a mighty king. A king so mighty that he doesn't need anything I have."

"Or you could seek more traffic with the Midwesterners, they're closer," Signe said.

Bjarni grinned in his red beard. "Too close for comfort and entirely too numerous. I want them to think as little of me and mine as they may. Let them look west, or north, or south, anywhere but towards me and mine. You, on the other hand, are not only friends . . . you're distant friends."

"Easier to *stay* friends when there's nothing to quarrel over," Signe observed.

"What do you want of us, then?" Eric added bluntly. "We're friends, I hope, and battle comrades. But we have our own problems here, our duty is to the Outfit and Montival, and Norrheim is very far away. Until Rudi got back, we hadn't even heard you existed or that there was anything but bones and Eaters left in Maine."

Bjarni stroked his beard. "Good! No weasel words between us, then. Norrheim *is* far away, but we have treasure. Our Vikings scour the dead cities, and those of the east are greater than those of the West, and fewer have plundered them. Artos and I showed that men could cross the continent, and in some numbers and without taking many years about it. After the war, things will travel that way again, things and men."

"I can't see much trade. Not for a very long time, centuries, if ever. Too much wilderness and wild-men in the way, too few people at either end," Signe said.

Bjarni nodded. "Not many merchants, not heavy

goods, and not often. But a few things of great price, now and then, yes. We used the rail-lines coming back with Artos; and there are the inland seas, that come almost as far west as the Dominions. We have skillful sailors in Norrheim and light boats that can be portaged. You'd have to trust my promises, of course, and we'd have to settle things in detail before we put our hands to the oath-ring."

"You're a hard man, but one to trust when he pledges an oath," Eric said, and his sister nodded. "Take it as given that we'll accept your word if we reach an agreement."

"So what do you want in return for this treasure?" Signe added, sipping from her horn.

"Men," Bjarni said. "And women, for that matter. Those with knowledge of your arts; metalworking with machines, fighting from horseback, catapults, balloons, spinning-mills, railroads, all of it. Books are good, but not enough. Tools, samples, and . . . what do you call them, *diagrams*, yes. But above all, folk with the skills to use them and teach others. Perhaps apprenticeships here for Norrheimers."

Eric smiled. "No insult, friend, but I've listened to your tales of Norrheim. Why would anyone leave the Willamette for a place where the growing season is two months shorter? And where there aren't even any hops for the beer? We're not crowded. There's good land untilled not five miles from Larsdalen. It'll take a long while to fill the Willamette alone. And later, there's the whole of California and much else besides."

Bjarni made a gesture of acknowledgment with one spade-shaped, red-furred hand.

"Norrheim is cold and poor compared to your land here; but on my journey with Artos Mikesson I saw much land that wasn't. Rich land around the inland seas; what they called Quebec and Ontario in the old world, and the south shore is good too. Rich land thinly peopled, and the dwellers ignorant savages who lost all arts in the Change, who live on rabbits and freeze in the winters. Fine farmland, timber, plenty of ruins for salvage and the lakes for fishing and trade."

"The savages are Eaters," Eric said, and Signe made a slight moue of disgust.

"Not all of them; some are just poor and backward, like the South Side Freedom Fighters that Artos befriended, Jake Jakesson and the others, who've settled in the Mackenzie lands now. And my own folk grow in numbers. We live wide-scattered, but that's from choice and because good plowland is scattered too, and our farms raise many strong sons and daughters along with the barley and rye. It's in my mind that Norrheim could take much of that land around the Great Lakes. Settle some of our people there, and by their might and their craft bring the dwellers . . . or their children . . . back to the life of real men, with fields and farms and homes. They're of blood kindred to our own. And we could bring them seemly ways and knowledge of the true Gods, not just the edge of an ax. And I could make those I favored lords and chiefs there, who have no such prospects here, with broad lands and followers. In time . . . in time, a realm as great as Montival, or nearly. For my descendants, if I lay the foundations."

"You're not afraid to dream grandly," Signe said, giving him a long look.

Eric laughed. "You and I might disagree on the true Gods," he said, touching the cross around his neck. "But otherwise, yes, I see what you mean. There might be some here who would find your offer attractive; some Bearkillers, though I warn you any willing to take such a leap would likely have big eyes and be troublesome. Broken men elsewhere who've lost everything in the war and need a fresh start anyway. You wouldn't have the time or knowledge to find them, or not many of them and not the right ones, but . . ."

"But we Bearkillers would, since we have the contacts," Signe said thoughtfully. "And *I* wouldn't mind seeing those true to the Aesir spread their rule, if it didn't cost my own folk much and we had recompense from that treasure you mention. We've won much glory in this war, and we'll get much more, but not much plunder. More, we—the Outfit, not the High Kingdom—don't stand to acquire more land, either."

"All we're likely to get in Corwin is hard knocks and some scrawny cattle," Eric said as he stretched his thick-muscled arms. "It needs doing but that's all you can say."

Signe nodded. "Revenge is good, but you can't eat it or make shoes for your children out of it. Yes, Bjarni King, we should talk further about this. There will be time, over the year to come."

Eric abandoned his restraint and drained his horn, then turned it over to show that there was nothing left inside.

"It's wonderful how victory opens possibilities," he said. "It enlarges men's minds, like good wine. And sometimes makes them drunk, too."

"The end of one saga is the beginning of the next."

Bjarni nodded. "And the hanger-on of one can be the hero of another."

"And now, if you'll excuse me, I have a wife waiting," the big man said.

"So do I," Bjarni mused when he'd left. "But unfortunately, she's a continent away. She has our children and our household to occupy her, too; only memories and hopes for me."

"Your wife will have you back, and you'll dwell with her all your days," Signe said thoughtfully, and raised her horn. "I toast her luck."

Then she raised it again to the vacant chair at the center of the high table, with the Bear Helm laid on it and a great sword across the rests.

"I'm a lonely widow, and my man is dead these fifteen years. There will be no homecoming for me, not in this life."

Bjarni toasted it as well. "But life goes on, and we make the best of it."

CHAPTER EIGHTEEN

Dun Fairfax
Dùthchas of the Clan Mackenzie
(Formerly the east-central Willamette Valley,
Oregon)
High Kingdom of Montival
(Formerly western North America)
December 18th, Change Year 25/2023 AD

"Well, 'ave it out heare, then, son," Sam Aylward said, in his slow drawl. "Bit on the cold soid tu go fur a walk."

It was cozy enough in the workroom, by the standards of Edain's generation; the little airtight stove made it so, and the inner walls of thick boards and battens that had been added in the years after the Change. He wore only his kilt and a light green-dyed linen shirt with wide sleeves, fastened at the neck and wrists with drawstrings. His father had on a wool shirt and a baggy knit sweater in its natural off-white as well, and his sockhose and brogans.

"Don't rightly know what I want to say, you might say," his son said.

Edain sat on a stool and braced one foot against the wall. The space had been what the old world called a *two-car garage* attached to the farmhouse that had formed the original core of Dun Fairfax. That meant it was large enough to hold his mother's big loom and his father's woodworking bench and tools. The windows at the south end overlooking the herb garden had been added later, to give her more light for the delicate task, and the original sliding doors at the front had been replaced by a more conventional arrangement. The big chamber had a clean smell of glue and shavings and varnish and linseed oil, as well as the skeins of wool and linen yarn that shared the rafters above with billets of yew and cedarwood, plus hunks of rock-hard rootwood from curly maple or black walnut.

"'appen you 'aven't settled since you came home from the fight," Sam said. "The war isn't over yet either, of course."

His voice didn't have the usual Mackenzie burble and lilt; he'd been past forty at the Change and had never lost the deep, slow burr he'd grown up with in rural Hampshire.

"All well with you and Asgerd?" he continued.

Garbh heaved her massive gray form up from beside Edain and padded over to his father's side, politely nosing at one of his hands and thumping her tail. The two younger hounds stayed by Edain's feet, great shaggy barrel-shaped heads questing after burrs and tangles in their fur. They were a mongrel breed but mainly mastiff and Great Dane with a tinge of wolf, a new strain coming together since the Change. One that Mackenzies took on the hunt for dangerous game—bear, say, or tiger—and sometimes to war as scouts and guards.

"Never a problem, save that we've less privacy than is convenient," Edain said with a quick grin. "Less here than in the field with the host, to tell the absolute and unpleasant truth."

The old man grinned himself, his teeth still strong but slightly yellowed.

"And it's not the season for hay-lofts and swimming in ponds and ducking into the woods," he said. "You and she being wed only a year, Oi call that an 'ardship."

"Well, I'm just back for the Yule feast," Edain said awkwardly; he'd never been a fluent man. "Fair crowded it is!"

"Yus, we've still the folk from the Bend country," Sam said; every Mackenzie Dun and most households within each had taken in some of the refugees. "Champing to get their own back, they are. And a lot of their so'jers 'ave come to see the families settled here, what with things slowing down fur now."

"I don't blame them! And they fought well at the Horse Heaven Hills. Fine riders and good shots in their way with those short bows from horseback."

"There's something to be said fur recurves," his father's slow, sonorous voice said. "They're 'andy in tight places. Though a longbow is the best at the last, in moi opinion."

He jerked his head back a little at the racked bows and bundles of staves behind him; he still had his hair, but kept it closer-cropped than most Mackenzie males, and the oak-brown had all faded to steel-gray or white now. Edain was painfully conscious of how he'd aged in the years his son had been away on the Quest, the gauntness of the flesh on the heavy bones and the way his work-worn hands had begun to twist. The resemblance was strong in them otherwise, gray eyes and square faces, medium height and barrel-chested, thick-armed builds. Edain was perhaps a thumb's-width taller and the merest touch slimmer than Sam Aylward had been in his prime, with a shade more yellow in his brown hair, his mother's legacy.

"We did some good shooting with them at the battle," Edain said proudly. "And it was an Aylward who taught the Clan to shoot and how to make them, sure, eh?"

Sam grinned and slapped the table beside him with a clunk of callus on oak. The workspace behind was set up to do any type of fine cabinetry, but mostly as a bow-yer's bench and table, with a tillering rack and the gouges, chisel and tools of the trade. That and farming had always been his crafts, when he wasn't busy as First Armsman of the Clan Mackenzie.

Though it's been years since he was that, Edain thought with a little shock; somewhere in his mind his father was still the figure of stocky ageless strength he'd been in his middle years.

"Lucky thing it were, my 'aving an hobby that turned out useful-loik," Sam said. "Lucky it ran in the fam'ly."

Edain had learned the bowyer's craft from him through the pores of his skin, as he'd learned shooting; one of his earliest memories was sitting on his heels in this room, watching his father taking tiny curls from a bowstave with a curved spoke-shave blade, working with infinite patience and by eye alone.

Edain's own favorite war-bow was in the clamps right now. Mackenzie longbows were made of two D-profiled lengths of yew, bent into a shallow reflex-deflex curve that went out and in and then curled out again at the nocks, both pegged and glued into a central riser—a grip—of hardwood shaped to fit a hand and with a cut-out that let the arrow shoot through the centerline of the weapon. Yew was a natural composite and didn't need horn or sinew to give it strength, but Edain did glue a strip of deerhide to the back to keep splinters from starting—that was how failure began with a wooden stave, and you did *not* want a hundred-and-twenty pound bow suddenly snapping at full draw. Despite the coat of varnish over all, the hide had come loose in spots during hard use, and he'd been laying a new one on while the bow would have time to dry.

"Lucky we had the right wood for it," Edain said; yew grew abundantly as an understory tree in the Cascades and the Coast Range both. "Or that's the favor of the Powers."

"Lady Juniper's Luck."

A reminiscent look came into his father's eyes. "There Oi was, lying laid up in Lady Juniper's house after she rescued me from that bloody ravine where Oi'd been watching the coyotes watching *me* and waiting for me to come ripe, and she were puttin' fine seasoned yew on the sodding fire! Fair shrieked, Oi did. And again, when Oi saw she 'ad a ton or two stacked out back."

"Asgerd and the mother seem to be getting on better," Edain observed; he'd heard *that* story repeated all his life, though it was a good one. "It would be better still if she had her own hearth. Her folk out east in Norrheim don't live so tight-packed as we, and forbye we're tighter-packed than we like ourselves. It's fortunate indeed she can follow me to battle."

Sam chuckled slightly to himself. "She's a good 'un, your Asgerd," he said. "And not just for her looks—

though at your age, Oi put more on that than Oi should 'ave. Or that she's better than fair as an archer. Funny to think of Vikings and all that out there. But then Blighty's a right odd old place too now, from all accounts."

"Viking's more in the nature of a job," Edain said. "It's what they call dangerous work, like going to the ruined cities for salvage work. Mostly they're farmers in Norrheim, like us, and no more quarrelsome. Slower to anger, sure; but also slower to let it go, I'd say."

He sighed and ran a hand through his hair. "It's . . . Da, I didn't think I'd be so restless, so to say, when I got a chance to stop at home. Asgerd's happy as a horse in clover here compared to me."

"Oi did notice you spending a lot of time out hunting, or watching the sheep, which is youngster's work."

Edain nodded: "All that time away on the Quest— and then the battle—and it was thinking of this place I was, seeing meself stepping in and taking up a hay-fork as if I'd just left, so to speak. Now I've a bit of peace before the next campaign and I can't seem to . . . just take my rest. And I'm a peaceable man, but I've been getting these flashes of temper the which is not my nature when I'm not provoked. Everything's fine, and then the least little thing . . . not been sleeping well, either. Asgerd's a bit worried."

"Ah," his father said, and took Garbh's great man-killing head between his hands, rubbing her jowls until the dog whimpered and slitted her eyes in ecstasy and beat a rear foot on the floor in time to her tail. "Come on you lately?"

"Since the Horse Heaven Hills. Comes and goes,

and the less I have to do, the more it bothers me. Can't rest when I'm resting, only when I'm busy, if you take my meaning."

The faded gray eyes of his father looked through him. "Ah," he repeated. "Oi've seen the loik. Felt it moiself, after Mt. Tumbledown. And toims since, here. Stepping back 'ome's not so simple, often. Battle takes you loik that. They have . . . used to have . . . fancy names for it, but Oi think it's loik getting hit, only inside the head. You keep on going because that's what you 'ave to do. But you pay for it later. Like a poison working its way out, or the ache where a bone healed."

"I've been in fights before, Da!"

Sam Aylward nodded. "They add up, though, son. Big 'uns, especial, and that one you just finished was bloody big and just plain bloody, too, from all reports."

"That it was," Edain said softly, blinking.

"Seen that look, before, boy. Seen it in the mirror. And you've had a long time with nothing but hard graft, never knowing at sunrise if you'd be alive by sunset."

Edain ran a hand through his hair. "What's to be done, then? I know enough not to look for the answer at the bottom of a mug of hard cider; that doesn't seem to help at all, at all."

"No, it don't, not past next day's headache. Toim, that's the answer, toim and lots and lots of it. They used to have folk who attended to it special."

"Heart-healers, we'd say today."

"We're great ones for fancy names around here, aren't we? Mostly it was talking about it, s'far as Oi could see. Talk it over with Asgerd, too, then . . . or Lady Juniper, p'raps."

"I'd not bother the Chief." Edain grinned wearily. "If we ever get a room all to ourselves for more than an hour at a time, sure and I will talk to Asgerd, though!"

Shrill voices sounded through the doorway to the rest of the house, and two children came running through. They were a boy and a girl each about two years, clad in kilts and nothing else besides blue luck-beads engraved with a pentagram around their necks on thongs . . . except that the girl was clutching a honey-glazed pastry with a bite taken out of it. There was a look of wary determination on her face as well as a good deal of stickiness, and she turned and backed away from her brother. They were the same age to a day, with white-silk mops of hair cut bowl-fashion and blue eyes; their skins were still slightly golden with summer's tan. Children their age among the Clan didn't usually wear either shirt or shoes unless weather or ceremony demanded.

Edain's grin turned genuine. He'd been surprised to find he had two new siblings when he came home, apparently conceived not long after he left with Rudi and the others, and it had probably startled his parents too, being fifteen years after their next youngest. The pregnancy had been hard on his mother, who hadn't been expecting it in her fiftieth year, but though the marks were still visible he thought she considered it worthwhile. It was enough to make him wistful for some of his own, too, though that would have to wait a while yet.

"Nola," Sam Aylward said, warning in his tone. "Are you going to share that with your brother?"

"No, Da!" she said, backing away a little further. "No!"

Edain had noticed she was already well familiar with that one word, and used it often. Her brother Nigel didn't say a thing, but there was a dangerous gleam in his wide blue eyes as he advanced on her.

She also cast a wary look on Edain, holding the jam-filled pastry behind her lest he treacherously steal some of it; they hadn't had time to really get used to him yet.

"The roit answer, moi gurl, is *yes, Oi will share it with 'im, Dad*," his father said.

The gnarled hand moved with surprising deftness and twitched it out of her chubby paw. Before her lip had time to pout, he'd ripped it neatly in half, popped the piece with the bite in it back into the mouth she'd opened to give a wail of protest and then handed half to her brother.

"'ere you go, Nigel-moi-lad," he said.

The dogs all rose and padded over to the children, taller at the shoulder than their tow heads, and carefully sniffed them head-to-foot with their gruesome muzzles, provoking squeals of laughter as the cold wet noses touched skin. One of the younger dogs showed an interest in the disappearing remnants of pastry, and Garbh nipped the offender on the ear to remind him of his manners. Then faces were licked, and children and dogs collapsed into a mingled sprawl not far from the stove.

"Garbh, stay," Edain said. Her head came up. "Guard."

She laid it down again on her paws but cocked an eye at him in response as if to say: *They're the pack's puppies, of* course *I'll guard them!*

Then they sat in companionable silence for a fair time as the light faded, listening to the feather-tick of wet snowflakes against the windows and the occasional deep sigh from one of the dogs; the children had fallen asleep with the abrupt suddenness of their age, eyes shut and mouths open. It was full dark outside now, and nothing showed but the occasional yellow glimmer from someone else's lanterns and candles and once the clop of someone leading a horse pulling a light cart down the village street. The smell of cooking came stronger.

"Time to go in, Da," Edain said, feeling obscurely better.

The elder Aylward levered himself up with a grunt and they walked down a hallway past rooms currently full of knocked-together bunk beds into a big open space that held a score of people of all ages and wasn't impossibly crowded.

Mackenzies didn't make as much of rank as many other peoples; a few specialists in Dun Juniper and Sutterdown aside, everyone worked on the land and at their crafts, and even the Chief had a loom in her bedroom over the Hall and took her turn doing dishes in the kitchens there. At need everyone who could fought, and nobody went hungry in a Dun unless everyone did, which was rare.

Such rank as there was, though, the Aylwards had. This was a big farmhouse, a two-story frame structure that had been old but well-kept before the Change and had served as the initial nucleus for Dun Fairfax—the name came from the former owners. They had been elderly and very diabetic, but their supplies and stock and tools had helped the nascent Clan survive, and the folk of the Dun and passersby still made small offerings on their grave out by the gate.

One of the changes made over the years since had been to open out most of the first floor, joining the kitchen and the dining and living rooms into one space big enough for the cooking, preserving, pickling and other endless indoor work that kept the household provided for. There was a long table and chairs and trestle-benches that could be moved around to suit, and walls hung with everything from polished pots and pans near the stoves to sickles, scythes and shearing-shears. Just now several sets of bedding and futons were rolled up and strapped to tie-pegs as well, for their share of the folk from enemy-occupied lands they were sheltering.

A stairway and a trap door led down to the cellars, with their bins and barrels and racks of glass jars. Net sacks of onions, strings of garlic, bags of drying herbs and burlap-wrapped hams and flitches of bacon hung in convenient spots from the ceiling beams up here; there was a big icebox for fresh produce. Sinks and counters showed that Dun Fairfax had running water from an internal spring, and two big iron stoves with copper boilers attached for hot water shed heat as his mother and several of the refugee women worked on dinner. Rag rugs covered much of the plank floor, and a wooden border colored and carved with the symbols of the Quarters ran around beneath the eaves. Stained and painted knotwork and twining vines covered the rest of the broad band, and whimsical faces from story and legend peeked out from carved leaves.

Edain made a reverence to the images of the Lord and Lady standing on either side of the hearth's crackling fire—blue-mantled Brigit with her flame and wheat-sheaf, and stag-antlered Cernunnos. His father did the same, and then lowered himself into his special chair by the fire with a sigh.

"Pull me one too," he called to Edain. "A point o' the Special from the Boar's 'ead barrel, in 'onor of you comin' 'ome safe."

The room was brightly lit by alcohol lanterns behind glass mantles, and they gave off a slightly fruity scent that mixed with the smells of burning fir, cooking and—rather faintly—dog. Edain ambled over to a small barrel that rested in an X of plank frame on one counter near the door to the outside vestibule; that kept the draughts at bay and left a place for boots and overshoes and outer gear to hang and drip in the wet weather with which the *dùthchas* was abundantly supplied in the Black Months. The household's weapons were racked on the wall next to it, brigandines and helms, sword belts and bucklers, war-bows and hunting bows and quivers and a brace of seven-foot long-bladed battle spears, all high enough to keep them out of easy reach of children too young to know better.

His mother, Melissa, came in through the vestibule with a draft of cold, wet air and a jug in her hand; she'd just poured the evening dish of milk for the house-hob, one of a householder's duties. She gave him a kiss on the cheek.

"And one for me, too, love. Since you're by the barrel," she said.

His elder half sister Tamar was sitting at the table nursing her latest, while instructing her other boy and girl as they plaited mats out of barley straw; her man Eochu was beside them, his hands busy with awl and waxed thread on a piece of harness whose seam had come loose, and Edain's younger brother Dick was helping him when he wasn't trying to use a stick to scratch inside the plaster cast that marked where a war-horse had trod on his right shin. Symbols stood on it, from healing spells to a bawdy promise from his latest girlfriend as to what they'd do when it came off.

Their sister Fand was sitting cross-legged on the rug before the fire, cracking walnuts from a big plastic bowl with the pommel of a dirk and using the stone of the hearth as an anvil. She dropped the nut-meats into a glass jar, the ones she didn't absently eat, and ignored the younger children nearby reading aloud from a big modern leather-bound and lavishly illustrated version of the *Táin Bó Cúailnge*. That from the lofty height of her fifteen years and experience as an *Eoghan*-helper on the latest campaign, which was, Edain thought, doubtless why she was wearing her rust-red hair warrior-style in a queue down her back bound with a bowstring. Though strictly speaking she shouldn't, not until and unless she *took valor* and could stand in the First Levy's bowline.

As he watched she stood, carefully holding up the front of her kilt to contain the empty shells, then tossed them into the hearth before taking the full jar to their mother.

"Good work," Melissa said to Fand. "Now whip this. Get it stiff but not churned, mind, we want whipped cream and not butter."

The teenager uttered a silent sigh and took the bowl of thick cream skimmed from the day's milk. A machine carefully carved and turned from hard cherry-wood by Sam Aylward stood on one part of the counter, strongly clamped. She inserted the bowl and turned a crank, and beaters whirred within the thick liquid; she dropped in a little heated honey as they did.

The barrel Edain headed for held his da's prized Special Ale, and he tapped three pints into mugs turned from maple wood. The clear, coppery-colored liquid flowed from the tap, a thin head forming on top.

"My first taste of *grown man's beer* was this," he said.

He handed one to his father, set the second by the stove near his mother's hand to her absent *cheers, love* and took a first swallow from his own. He sighed at the subtle overtones of fruit and caramel, with a bittersweet aftertaste like whiskey. Stronger than it tasted too—a beer to treat with respect.

"Now, that is beer, by the blessin'," he said with a contented sigh. "Even better than I remember and sure, I remembered it as very good indeed."

"It is better!" his father said. "Oi've been workin' with young Timmy Martins—"

"Who's been a man grown and a master-brewer with children of his own a good many years now," Melissa pointed out, taking a mouthful of her own. "And if by *working* you mean *drinking*."

Sam nodded. "When Oi came 'ere I knew bowyerin' well enough, but me brewin' was from the point o'view of the consumer rather than the producer, as yer moight say. It took years but now Oi reckon as Oi've got as good a drop of Old Thumper as ever came out o'Ringwood in 'ampshoire. As best Oi can with these Willamette 'ops anyway. Which Oi reckon weren't the same as they 'opped with back 'ome, but bitter it up noicely all the same."

As Edain turned away he nodded to the boar's head carved above the tap to mark the Special Ale barrel. A boar's head clearly not on a plate, but very much attached to the rest of the beast and a very much alive and bellicose beast at that.

"The insignia o'Ringwood Brewery used ter be on the Old Thumper beer taps," his da said, "and if I ever got a letter from the Brewery in 'ampshoire tellin' me ter stop infringin' their trademark, Oi'd be deloighted!"

"Sure, we had some fine beer on the Quest, if not up to this or Brannigan's Special," Edain said. "I mind in Readstown . . . what did Ingolf's sister-in-law the brew-mistress call it . . . *hefeweizen* . . ."

"Bavarian style, then," Sam said. "Wheat beer, top-fermented. They could do good brew, if a bit chewy. And a bit loit on the 'ops for my taste."

Just then Edain's wife, Asgerd, came up the stairs from the cellar with a basket of apples in her hands.

"My, and aren't you fine, darlin'," he said admiringly.

She pirouetted, grinning with an uncharacteristic openness. Edain had seen Norrheimer women's garb before in her homeland, but he hadn't seen her wearing it much. When they met she'd been about to swear vengeance on the killers of her intended husband and pledge her God ten lives for his, which to her folk's way of thinking required breeks and jerkin. And she'd been a maiden then, while this was the married woman's version. The basis was a long sleeveless hanging dress of blue wool over a sleeved shift of saffron-yellow linen, with her hair done up in braids and mostly covered by an embroidered kerchief, and a long white apron in front held by two silver brooches at the shoulders. It wasn't fancy exactly, but the cloth was finely made, tight-woven of excellent yarn and colored with good fast dyes, and there were touches of embroidery here and there in patterns of gripping beasts with interlaced tails. It showed off her sweetly-curved athletic height well.

Though she looks even better in nothing at all but the Goddess' sweet skin, he thought with satisfaction.

Melissa smiled from near the stove, a tasting spoon in one hand and her mug in the other; there was more gray than dark-blond in her hair now, but the light eyes in her tired, lined face were kindly on Asgerd's pleasure. And proud, since it was her work.

"I was going to give it as a Yule gift, but sure, then I thought *why not let my daughter-in-law enjoy it for the whole of the season?* It'll be back to the war-trail for you two soon enough, and folded up and back in the chest that dress will go, where it does little good."

"It's lovely," Asgerd said, extending a foot and looking admiringly at the embroidered hem. "Fine weaving and fine sewing too—better than mine; my seams are always just a little crooked *somewhere*. It lacks nothing but my own set of keys at the belt."

"I helped sew!" Fand called from over by the fire. "And I went up to Dun Juniper and looked through the books for the patterns and drew them!"

"And I thank you for it," Asgerd said to her solemnly. "They are a touch of home."

Asgerd and Melissa exchanged a glance and the older woman half-winked. Edain nodded and raised a silent mug to his mother. They hadn't gotten on all that well when he first brought Asgerd home that summer, and he was glad to see the final peace-offering made and accepted.

It wasn't a small gift, either; there was a reason most common folk, even prosperous ones like his Clan, had only three sets of clothing—one to wear, one to wash, and one for festival days. Turning out a bolt of cloth needed a good loom, a skilled worker, and many long days of labor, besides the raw materials. His mother was a weaver of note, too, who didn't waste her time on ordinary rough homespun or blankets, which was all a young girl like Fand could aspire to as yet. The household sold or swapped most of his mother's cloth and used that to get plainer stuff for everyday.

Softly Asgerd went on: "I only wish my mother could see me so, to know I was settled, and the rest of my family."

"Tell you what, acushla," Edain said, drawing another mug and setting it by her. "We'll have one of the limners up to Dun Juniper *draw* you so and send it back with King Bjarni. He can hand it on to your family with your letters when he returns. Things will travel more easily after the war, and it's not at all unlikely or beyond hope that they'll be able to reply someday. The more so as the High King and your folk's Bjarni are guest-friends and blood-brothers, and sure, neither will deny you a letter or two among any bundle he sends."

Asgerd nodded silently as she set down her apples and peeled and cored them with swift dexterity, dumping the refuse in the bin that would go to the pigs. Then she arranged them in a pan with their centers full of butter and honey, broke in some of the walnuts, and added a coating of spiced crumbs over all.

"That's a wonderful idea," she said a little wistfully after the task was begun. "And maybe . . . drawings of your family and the house and the farm? That would be a comfort to them."

Edain nodded. His mother tasted the stew again, picked up another thumb-and-two-fingers' pinch of salt mixed with dried herbs from the bowl beside the stove, dropped it in, stirred, and nodded.

"This is ready; that it is. Where are the twins?"

"Bedded down with Garbh and Drudwyn and Cochnibar in the workshed by the stove there," Edain said. "Garbh won't let them wander."

Melissa snorted. "And she won't wash or dress them either," she said. "A grandmother I may be, as well as a mother again unexpected, but I remember how to do *that* well enough. *And* that men are like bears with houses for dens, when it comes to remembering such details. Rather than like human beings."

"Oh, but she did wash them, and that thoroughly and well." Edain grinned, and his father snorted a laugh as well. "Holding them down with a paw the while."

"I'll attend to it," Asgerd said, as she took a fold of her apron around her hand to swing open the cast-iron door of the stove and slide the tray of baking apples inside. "They are not puppies, nor kittens nor colts nor yet bear-cubs, to be licked clean."

"But sometimes I'm thinking they're part all of those," Melissa said. "And if there were an *Óenach Mór* of dogs, Garbh's vote would be for *puppy*, for sometimes she forgets she didn't bear them herself, and that's a fact. Now shout out the others, someone, and we'll eat."

Asgerd brought Nola and Nigel in looking even

cleaner than Garbh had left them, and wearing their shifts as well as their kilts; the dogs followed and flopped down in a corner each on their favorite bit of rug, and several of the household moggies picked higher spots to watch the intensely interesting sport of humans eating, with an especially keen eye on the bowl of whipped cream. None of the two-footed dwellers had to be called twice. His mother did the blessing, as hearthmistress—

"Harvest Lord who dies for the ripened grain—
Corn Mother who births the fertile field—
Blesséd be those who share this bounty;
And blessed the mortals who toiled with You
Their hands helping Earth to bring forth life."

Edain joined in, signing his plate and in setting aside a crumb and a drop; he noted that their guests from the CORA lands mostly did too, though a few murmured Christian graces instead or just waited respectfully. He suspected that there would be a fair number of new covensteads founded east of the mountains when the war was over and the folk who'd taken refuge with the Clan went back to rebuild their homes. Asgerd hammer-signed her plate and added:

"Hail, all-giving Earth, and hail and thanks to Frey of the rain and Freya of the harvest."

Nobody objected. The Old Religion didn't have a problem with anyone's names for the Powers, and he knew a few Mackenzies over towards Sutterdown who preferred to thank Demeter and Adonis.

There was a clatter as plates were passed and serving-spoons wielded with a will, while loaves were torn open. The food was plain enough; the stew was notionally venison, and had enough of it to give more than a mere taste, but it was mainly winter vegetables like carrots and parsnips and kale by weight, though the thick gravy was savory with onion and sage and thyme and paprika. The other main dishes were crocks of potatoes sliced and simmered with layers of onions and pats of butter and bits of bacon and topped with grated cheese and bowls of steamed cabbage. Harvest had been good enough the year that had ended this Samhain, but the Mackenzie *dùthchas* was feeding more mouths than there had been hands to work lately. The war had gone on for years, with levies at all seasons, and it wore things down and used them up.

Still, there's enough, Edain thought. *And enough bread and butter, come to that; for there's strength and life in good bread, and nothing tastes better than a hunk of it still steaming.*

There was a special satisfaction in eating the loaf baked from grain you'd reaped yourself and putting your own feet under your own table on your own kindred's land to eat it; it was something he'd missed on the Quest. For that matter, he'd taken the buck whose meat and marrow-bones had gone into the stew with one sweet painless angled shot that drove a broadhead through lungs and heart.

"How do you get the crust so firm on this bread while the crumb is so soft, good mother?" Asgerd asked Melissa. "We don't make much bread all from wheat flour in Norrheim. More barley and rye, and oatcakes, and mixed grain, save at the great feasts."

"Ah, the secret's to brush a little water on the skin of the dough when you set the loaves to start the second rising, and then a little egg-white across the top just before you bake. Then a dish of water set in the oven with it," his mother replied. "Sealing the top makes it strike high in the oven's heat, and the water keeps the crust firm."

Edain mopped at his plate with a heel of it and crunched it down, remembering innumerable tasteless flat-cakes cooked on griddles by countless camp-fires. The youngsters stared eagerly and clutched their spoons as the plates were cleared and the baked apples were brought out and topped with dollops of the sweet cream. Tamar's man Eochu was laughing at a joke of hers, and brushing a little of the cream across the babe's lips with the tip of a finger; she licked her lips and looked dubious, then brightened. Edain laughed himself as he looked down the table at his kin and his father yawning and nodding a little over his second mug of beer.

"What's funny?" Asgerd asked, leaning close to speak beneath the hum of conversation.

"That all of it . . . the fighting and the faring, the stark dealings with the Powers and the fearsome magic swords and all the rest of it . . . was for this. Just this."

DUN JUNIPER
DÙTHCHAS OF THE CLAN MACKENZIE
(FORMERLY THE EAST-CENTRAL WILLAMETTE VALLEY,
OREGON)
HIGH KINGDOM OF MONTIVAL
(FORMERLY WESTERN NORTH AMERICA)
DECEMBER 18TH, CHANGE YEAR 25/2023 AD

The High King had given out that he would spend the Yule season with his Mackenzie kindred. There had been grumbling from the great lords of the Association, all of which he'd politely ignored.

"Let them complain," Rudi said, looking up towards the lantern-glow at the gates of Dun Juniper and laughing. "If I have to dance another pavane or eat another pastry shaped like a ship or filbert ice cream carved like a knight or listen to another troubadour dead-set on seeing how many obscure kennings and references he can boot-heel into a single song, it's gibbering mad I'd go."

"I hope Mom won't be too lonely," Mathilda said as they drew rein. "Christmas by herself."

"Your mother would rather intrigue than eat her dinner," Juniper Mackenzie said dryly. "And since when did Todenangst or Portland lack for that? Throngs of people, and when she wants sympathy she has her cats, and Lady Jehane to tutor."

"She can always visit Castle Odell and sit by Conrad's bedside and talk about old times," Mathilda acknowledged. "Valentine and her girls are back from Montinore."

"With hearty thanks and strong hints from d'Ath." Rudi grinned.

He was fairly certain the Grand Constable wanted some privacy for herself and her Châtelaine for reasons not entirely unlike his own desire to get Matti to himself, or as close an approximation as was possible for a ruler. More seriously, he went on:

"And likely she'll have you to herself when Órlaith is born. If I'm to be over the mountains then, hammering at the gates of Boise or Corwin, I'll not stint myself of your company the now, love. And if any don't like it, they can do the other thing, that they can."

"All to herself? As if I wouldn't be there too!" Juniper said. "Grandchildren give most of the joys of parenthood and only a tenth the labor and pain."

"I'm sure *we* will all bear up bravely through the birth, speaking of *labor* and *pain*," Mathilda said, with a raised eyebrow under the white ermine fur of her hat.

He reached over and squeezed her hand. He was relatively certain she and the child would both come through healthy; visions aside, she was fit and well-built for the business, and would have the best midwives and healers half a continent could provide on hand. It still wasn't an easy thing, any more than heeling your horse into a gallop towards a line of points and battle-cries. And unlike that, it was one sort of fight they couldn't really share, though he would have given much to be there to hold her.

It was only a few hours past noon, but it was already gray fading to dark; there was a reason this time of year was called the *Black Months*. Snow was falling, steady and wet, on the long lens-shaped piece of sloping hillside benchland that Jeb Mackenzie had homesteaded more than a century and a half ago. The clouds had come rolling down from the Middle Cascades before they left Sutterdown, and by now the grass and hedges and bare-limbed oaks and walnuts all bore a thick covering; more still turned the tall Douglas fir and hemlocks upslope into a vision of green and brown crowned in white, with a strong mealy-damp smell that brought memory strong as thick honey back to him.

It had never been more than a middling-prosperous stock farm, despite being well over a square mile. Mackenzie family legend said the man had chosen it because it reminded him of Tennessee, though Rudi suspected it was also because the best bottom-land had either been taken up already or was swampy and required draining—certainly there was enough renascent wetland in the *dùthchas* farther west towards the river.

Later the family had moved to town—Eugene and Salem, mostly—and the land had fallen out of use save for timber; later still his mother's great-uncle had grown wealthy and bought it back and much more of the forest beside, as a hunting-ground. The childless man had doted on the young Juniper, and when he died had left it to her, though she'd been an aspiring bard (and some-time High Priestess of the Singing Moon coven) with no handfasted man, a young daughter, and a burning determination to make her way with her music.

"It still seems a little unreal, sometimes," he heard her murmur, her voice falling into old patterns. "It all changed so fast, after the Change . . ."

"Ah, well, it's just the place I grew to me," Rudi replied gently. "And very dear it is. You'd done it proud."

They clattered up the sloping road that turned right to the gates. Dun Juniper wasn't exactly a town, but nor yet was it an ordinary farming Dun with a palisade of logs if that; the wall was thrice man-height and solid, crenel-lated, the outer stucco white. Beneath the ramparts was a band of painting, god-faces and sprites and eerily man-like beasts or beastlike men. Towers flanked the gates, and from them bagpipes keened, Lambeg drums rattled thunder, and flared trumpets whose mouths were shaped like howling wolves boomed beneath.

"And not altogether unlike *radongs* in sound," an-other member of their party said.

Rimpoche Tsewang Dorje had made some concessions to the weather, including a sheepskin coat and hat. He looked up at the images, then pressed his palms together and bowed.

"You have done well indeed," he said to Juniper. Then an impish grin that turned his face into a mass of wrinkles. "Even if some of the tools were . . . borrowed."

"Stolen," she replied cheerfully. "Rampantly stolen by Gardner not least, myself among the others."

"Only something we *owned* could be stolen!" he answered, and the Buddhist monk and the Witch-Queen of the Old Faith laughed together.

The gates were double leaves of solid yard-thick timber baulks fastened together with bolts and sandwiched between two sheets of quarter-inch steel painted deep brown. On those were outlined images made of thousands of copper rivets, suggested more than seen until you let the focus of your eyes blur a bit and then vanishing again if you stared too hard. Above was the Triple Moon, waxing and full and waning; below was the wild bearded face of a man with curling ram's-horns on his head. To either side of the gates were tall forms colored and carved; Lugh of the Long Spear, the Many-Skilled, and Brigit of the flame and sheaf and harp, She whose music bound the hearts of men like golden chains.

The music ceased and a voice called down ceremoniously; solemn, but with laughter in it. Rudi recognized Oak Barstow Mackenzie, the First Armsman. This was his home as well, of course.

"Who comes to Dun Juniper near the holy season?"

he said. "Do you claim entry by blood-kinship as Mackenzies yourselves, or by guest-right, or do you offer tale
or goods or skill?"

"The chief of the Clan comes, the Mackenzie Herself," Rudi replied.

His mother took it up: "And the *Ard Rí*, the High
King himself, the Lady's Sword, comes to guest his kin-
folk."

There was a story of how Lugh had come visiting in
disguise in ancient times, and had proven His worth by
listing the skills He commanded. Mackenzie ritual always paid some slight homage to that.

The weight of the gates would have dragged if only
the hinges had supported them, massive though those
were. He could hear the *clunk* and *chung* as the locking
bars were winched out of the way, and then teams
pushed the gates open. The inner corners rested on salvaged railway wheels, and those ran on sections of track
set into the entryway. Rudi dismounted and lifted his
wife down; the others joined him, and the formality dissolved in a shouting mob as the dwellers in the home of
his childhood surged around him.

That ended with Mathilda and himself and Juniper
and his foster father Nigel Loring being carried
shoulder-high behind a pair of strutting pipers playing
"Rudi's Tain," through the streets of the settlement. It
was a welcome relief from the elaborate deference of the
north-realm, and they were suitably careful of Mathilda
while he and the others were tossed about like chips of
driftwood in a Pacific storm.

Most of the homes in Dun Juniper were built against

the inside of the wall, knee-high fieldstone foundations and close-fitting squared logs above to the shingled roofs. The woodwork was colorfully carved in sinuous running designs, but none so much so as the Hall that had started as a rich man's hunting lodge built over the old foundations of Jeb's farmhouse, and it blazed with lamp-light and firelight through the big windows, a blur of gold and glittering color through the white fog of the snow.

It had been a long, low building to start with; the early Mackenzies had doubled its size by lifting the roof and putting on another layer of huge squared logs. That roof loomed above them through the snow now, the end-rafters at east and west extending upward to spirals that faced each other deosil and tuathal, sunwise and its opposite, to balance the energies. Pillars ringed it on three sides, with the beam-ends of the second story gallery extended out over the court that surrounded it; they were carved into the heads of the Mackenzie totems, Tiger and Bear and Elk, Coyote and Fox and Wolf and more, with great wrought lanterns of iron and glass hanging from their jaws.

Somehow nobody had thought of lifting the Rimpoche; he looked about with keen interest as the others were set on their feet.

"Not altogether unlike some things in Tibet," he said. "We share a liking for bright colors and symbolic carving, at least."

"We had a lot of time in the winter and needed to practice woodworking, at any rate," Juniper said.

Nigel Loring chuckled. "It was already mostly like this when I arrived, and I thought everyone here must be either barking mad, or fallen into a book," he said.

"Or that it was the biggest, gaudiest Celtic-Chinese restaurant in the world," Juniper said, leaning aside to give him a quick kiss. "Sweet-and-sour corned beef and deep-fried cabbage, perhaps."

The oldsters do love their jargon, Rudi thought tolerantly as all three of them laughed.

The crowd went solemn again as they were set down; Rudi straightened his bonnet and plaid. The pipers put aside their drones; harp-music came as the doors of the Hall with their silver cat-head bosses swung wide. He recognized his younger half sister Fiorbhinn's touch on the strings, and voices were raised—the pure sweet ones of preadolescents, mostly her gang of musical mischief-makers. For once they were solemn, and there was an ethereal loveliness as they sang:

"*Who will go down to the holy groves*
To summon the Shadows there
And tie a garland on the sheltering leaves—"

Maud Mackenzie brought the guest-cup, a horn of hot cider with spices; now that she was Tanist and acknowledged successor to their mother as Chief of the Clan that duty fell to her. Rudi felt a pang as he took it; this *wasn't* his home anymore, not really. That feeling was redoubled when Juniper guided him to the High Seat with its carved ravens. He smiled at her grin and wink and took it, hanging the Sword from one of the carved bosses.

Aunt Judy—Oak's mother, and his mother's oldest friend—plunked a piece of her carrot cake down on the arm of his chair; she was an herbalist and healer of note, the founder and manager of the Clan's medical tradition, and also a very fine cook.

"What's a king for, if not to enjoy a piece of cake?" she said.

Rudi leaned back with a sigh and took a forkful. The Hall smelled of the dinner cooking, and of the great fir-tree in one corner—the decoration had just started. There would be music and dancing beforehand; it was a very grave situation indeed that Mackenzies didn't consider improvable by some song and dance. And storytelling, and riddles, and . . .

"What's a king for indeed?"

New York Times **bestselling author**

S. M. STIRLING

"FIRST-RATE ADVENTURE ALL THE WAY."
—HARRY TURTLEDOVE

Available wherever books are sold or at
penguin.com

s922